BRUTAL CAPO

by Lucy Monroe

1st Printing March 2024

BRUTAL CAPO

LUCY MONROE

LUCY MONROE LLC

For all my angst loving girlies who appreciate a good grovel.
This one is for you.
With a special mention for Kathleen B.
who gave her name to Bianca's bestie,
a pole dancer known on stage as Candi.
(And who will eventually get her own
story with the SAF, super intense Angelo.)

Cosa Nostra Territories & Hierarchy:
New York: Five Families
Bonanno (Queens), Colombo (Bronx), Gambino (Staten Island), Genovese (Manhattan), and Lucchese (Brooklyn): each founding mafia is led by a don who could be from any of the families loyal to them.

New York Genovese family
Don/Boss: Severu De Luca
(Also known as The Genovese and King of New York)
Underboss: Miceli De Luca
(Severu's brother)
Consigliere: Big Sal De Luca
(Severu's uncle)
Capos: Domenico Bianchi, Salvatore De Luca (Severu's cousin), Tomasso Marino, Niccolo Costa, Lorenzo Ricci, Stefano Bianchi
Head Enforcer: Angelo Caruso
(Also known as Angel of Death)
Soldiers: Luigi, Carlo, Aldo (Severu's men)
Fausto, Marco (Big Sal's men)
Las Vegas
Don/Boss: Patrizio Mancini
Underboss: Raffaele Mancini
Detroit (Don: Pietro Russo)
New England
Boston (Don: Lombard)
Known as the Lombardi Family, despite
the Americanized name for the don's family.
Chicago aka The Outfit

* All names and positions are fictional or used in a fictional capacity, a product of the author's imagination, loosely based on La Cosa Nostra structure in America.

PROLOGUE

SALVATORE

Age 20

New York, New York

Monica's eyes plead with me, her shiny blonde hair, the only genuine thing about her, hanging in messy clumps around her head.

Have mercy.

Don't kill me.

Don't kill my lover.

Her mouth is gagged so she can't beg for their lives out loud, but I hear the words echo in the silence around us.

Until this morning, I thought I was her lover and the only man she had in her life. I told her I loved her.

I fucking loved her.

I told her everything about my family, except that we are part of the New York Cosa Nostra.

I have to get my don's permission to do that and Uncle Enzo insisted on a background check on Monica before giving it.

Since my dad is my uncle's top capo, Big Sal got the job of investigating the woman I wanted to marry.

Criminals are excellent at finding the dirt on other criminals. But I was so sure Monica was clean, I gave every piece of information I had on her to my dad's guy. Only to find out that Monica is five years older than she told me, and she's not a botany student either.

She never even went to community college.

She's been living with the same man since they were teenagers. They move around the country scamming unwary schmucks.

I'm just her latest mark. A *scemo* like every other person they've bilked.

A $250,000 orchid plant is sitting in my apartment right now as irrefutable proof of what a *scemo* I am. Finding it was the hardest part, but I belong to the most powerful Family in New York. We have connections. I bought the rare orchid believing the plant would protect Monica from getting kicked out of school, or being prosecuted.

She spun a fucking good story.

Oh, Salvatore, I don't know what happened, but I killed it. If the professor finds out, he's going to press charges. I wasn't supposed to touch it, but it was so perfect. So beautiful. Blue eyes shimmer with unshed tears. *I don't know what to do.*

Not once did she ask for my help. When I offered, she adamantly refused it. This only made me more determined to save the woman I loved.

I'm a De Luca, at the top of the mafia food chain. My father might not have as much money as his brother, our don, but his net worth would put him on the Forbes Real Time Billionaires list if so many of his assets weren't hidden from the government.

"You thought you could steal from the Cosa Nostra?" I ask her, looking at Monica and her guy with disgust.

Her eyes widen with fear.

"Are you just now realizing I'm connected?" I shake my head. "What did you think? A regular student would drug you and your boyfriend and hang you up like a couple of punching bags from the ceiling?"

Like she thinks I'm going to start beating on her like the punching bag I compared her to, she starts screaming behind the gag and twisting her body. Her fear is a balm to my ego, but nothing can undo what a fool she made out of me.

"I'm not going to hit you." Her lover on the other hand?

Him I punch in the nuts. Fucker touched what was mine. That can't go unanswered.

He goes green and retches behind the gag.

"You'd better get a move on, Salvatore," one of my father's men says. "Or he's going to choke on his own vomit before you get a chance to kill him."

We aren't here alone because this isn't just between me and the couple that tried to scam me. It's Cosa Nostra business when an outsider comes for one of us. We can't let it stand.

Reputation is everything in the mafia.

My father hands me a gun. "You know what needs to happen."

I nod. My arm doesn't want to lift though. Bile rises in *my* throat at the thought of pointing the gun at Monica. Less than twenty-four hours ago, I was buried balls deep in her cunt believing I had found my home.

Like a woman could be that. Especially an outsider.

Swallowing back my urge to vomit, I ruthlessly cut my feelings off, just like papà taught me. There's no place for sentiment in a made man's life and tonight I get made. With this act of judgment.

As I lift my gun, the front of the guy's jeans turns dark from his piss. Monica is still screaming behind the gag, her legs kicking like she's going somewhere.

I pull the trigger and the boyfriend's head jerks back. His body goes limp in death.

"At least you'll be together in hell." I pull the trigger again and red blooms on the left side of Monica's chest.

Her faithless heart destroyed by my bullet.

My father claps his hand on my shoulder. "Well done, my son. You'll make a hell of a second for me."

I stare at him. Is he saying what I think he is?

"You still have to finish school, but from tonight, you're my second in command. I told Enzo you would do it." Papà sounds proud.

He should be. I'm exactly the man he raised me to be. Loyal to the mafia. Ruthless to our enemies. Willing and able to kill when necessary.

Everything his son has to be.

And all I had to do was shoot the woman I loved and kill her boyfriend.

CHAPTER 1

BIANCA

I swipe my sweaty palms down the sides of my skirt and wish I'd opted for the black one with the zipper instead of the pleather designer knock off.

It's three in the afternoon and the sidewalk outside Amuni is quiet, no long line waiting to get into one of the hottest nightclubs in New York.

After overhearing one of my roommates tell another that Amuni is hiring cocktail waitresses, I'm here to apply for a job. A job I need.

Even if my roommate hadn't gotten the part in the off Broadway show she auditioned for last week, I'd still be here. Trying to get this job instead of her. We share an apartment in Queens with another girl and the couple on the lease. They aren't my friends, but roommates by financial necessity.

The same necessity that has me here, looking for a job. I can't pay even the rent on half a sofa sleeper in the living room if I don't have a job. And I can't work at Pitiful Princess anymore.

Despite the generous curves I inherited from my nonna, I got hired to dance on the pole. I'm good at it and a favorite with the patrons because of the way my tits and ass bounce when I move.

I don't make what the girls who strip, and then come down off the stage to work the patrons, do. I'm okay with that. My boss is not.

Gino is trying to force me to work the floor too. I know what that means. Lap dances and *more* in the private rooms in the back of the club. I don't like being touched. And I sure as hell am not selling my mouth and ass so Gino can get his cut of the increased revenue.

Amuni is a nightclub, not a strip club and it has a strict policy against servers turning tricks on the side. A server can make bank on her tips without offering *extras* to patrons too.

I really, really want this job.

Now it's time to convince them that they want me.

"I'm Bianca Gemelli," I say to the security man at the door. "I'm here to interview for the server position."

He looks down at his clipboard and then waves me inside.

My name isn't Gemelli. It's Russo. Or at least it was when I was born. But when I turned eighteen, my mom offered me $5,000 to change it so there was less chance I would ever be connected back to her and my twin sister, Beatrice.

Having my own reasons for wanting to change it, I agreed. I picked Gemelli for my new last name because it means Gemini in Italian, the twins. A reminder that even if Bea never wants to see me again, she's still my twin. I am not alone in the universe. There are two of us. No matter what her and my mom want to pretend.

"I'm sorry for wasting your time, Bianca, but we aren't a strip club." Sierra, the waitstaff manager says mere minutes after my arrival, sounding anything but sorry.

More like bored.

I can't let that get to me. Getting this job is more important than clinging to pride that won't pay the bills.

"Believe me, I know."

Sierra continues as if I hadn't spoken. "We don't use dancers. If you're looking for a move up from the Pitiful Princess, try the club on 48th, Alladin's Cave."

I knew I shouldn't have listed my current employment. "If you look at the job I held before that, I was a server at a bar. I have an excellent memory and lots of experience handling a packed house."

"Yet you left to become a pole dancer at the Pitiful Princess." The older woman isn't quite sneering, but it is close.

"They offered more money and as I'm sure you are aware, living in the city is expensive."

"Tips here are decent, but I doubt you'll make more a night than you do stripping."

I don't strip. I dance the pole, wearing a sexy lace mask and practically naked. I don't take what clothes I do wear off for the patrons and I never remove my mask.

Not that Sierra is going to make the distinction between dancing and stripping.

"No one will expect me to work anything else here, though," I tell her with honesty born of desperation.

The waitstaff manager's eyes narrow. "Providing sexual services to patrons is grounds for immediate dismissal at Amuni."

"Did you miss the part that I don't *want* to provide anything more?" I ask, my temper getting the better of me.

This uptight bitch isn't going to hire me anyway, so I might as well stand up for myself.

"It's common practice at clubs like Pitiful Princess and I'm not judging that," Sierra says. "But it isn't allowed here. This club is entirely legitimate."

Someone else might not realize what she's alluding to, but I grew up mafia, even if no one knows that about me anymore. Amuni is owned by the Cosa Nostra as one of their legitimate business fronts.

Making it the ideal place to work. It's under syndicate protection, but dirty business doesn't get done here.

"Good!" I emphasize. "I'm looking for a legitimate job as a server without a boss that will pressure me to start offering my body to patrons."

Sierra sucks in a shocked breath. "Oh, I...that definitely would not happen here."

"Please, Sierra, call my references. I'm a good server. You won't regret hiring me." And I need this job.

Like yesterday.

Her phone buzzes and she picks it up to look at the screen. Not a great sign when she's willing to take a call in the middle of the interview.

She answers and steps away so I can't overhear the phone call. As she's talking, two bright color spots form on her cheeks. Then she looks up and around the club like she's trying to spot someone.

The call only lasts a couple of minutes and Sierra turns to come back to me and sets the phone face down on the small round table we are sitting at.

"Excuse the interruption," she says perfunctorily.

Kindness costs nothing. That's something my mom used to say. She's not so great at giving away that free commodity, but it is something I try to do. To prove to myself that I am not either of my parents.

"No problem," I say.

Sierra's phone buzzes again and she appears reluctant to answer. Picking it up gingerly she looks at the screen with furrowed brows. It must be a text this time.

Her shoulders stiff, she forces a smile that looks as plastic as one of my roommate's tits. It looks like someone is using a hook on either side of Sierra's mouth to draw her lips up.

She taps on her phone screen a few times and then looks up at me with that sick smile still in place. "Yes, well, I'll check your references. Is this number good to reach you at?"

She rattles off my pay-as-you-go number.

"Uh huh, I mean yes."

Sierra visibly swallows without meeting my eyes or looking around the club again. "Good. We...I'll be in touch later today."

That's a lot more positive than I expect. I jump to my feet and offer my hand to shake. "Great. I'll look forward to hearing from you."

If she really does call my references, she will only hear good things. Even Gino won't risk bad mouthing me, not after the last girl he did that to called the cops and dropped a tip about what goes on in the back rooms.

Sure, the cops are paid off, but they had to pretend to investigate and having them around made the clientele nervous. Several regulars disappeared and didn't come back to the club for nearly a week.

My temper is worse, and my boss knows it. That's the only reason he hasn't yanked me off the stage and onto some guy's lap for a dance.

Gino doesn't know what I'll do to retaliate.

SALVATORE

I'm not supposed to be at Amuni today, but Franco needs to take his pregnant wife to her appointment with the obstetrician. That leaves me here, accepting a delivery of flavored tequilas for this week's specialty drinks.

When the gorgeous redhead walks in looking nervous. I can't see what color her eyes are from across the club, but there's no missing the burnished copper of her hair pulled back in a ponytail. I bet it reaches the middle of her back when it is down.

Little tendrils stick to her temples with sweat and the fake leather skirt that should hit her mid-thigh is riding higher, teasing at what I will see if it rises just a couple more inches.

A pretty little panty clad pussy? Or is she going commando? Looking that nervous, I doubt it, but a man can fantasize.

It doesn't take superhuman vision to see that Sierra, the waitstaff manager, is giving the curvy job applicant a hard time. The beautiful woman's face shows every emotion she's feeling. Frustration. Hope. Anger.

I don't know what Sierra's problem with the woman is, but I'm lifting my phone to call her before I think about it.

"Hello. Mr. De Luca?"

"Yes. What is your problem with the woman you are interviewing?" She's young, attractive and doesn't have any of the physical tells that indicate regular hard drug use.

"Um..." Sierra looks around the club, but she won't see me.

My vantage point allows me to see her and the beauty she is talking to without revealing my own presence.

"Does she have experience?" I demand.

"Uh...yes."

"References?"

"I haven't checked them yet."

"Call them. If they recommend her for the job, hire her." I don't plan for her to keep the job long, but I want her accessible.

She makes my cock hard and she's not naked.

"Sir, that's not—"

"Did I ask for your opinion?" My employees don't talk back to me. Ever.

"No, of course not. I'll call her references."

"Tonight. I want her on the schedule by the weekend." Saturday night is the next time I plan to be in Amuni.

I'm a busy man. I don't have time to chase my prey, no matter how fun that might be. I have an itch and the beauty interviewing with my waitstaff manager is going to scratch it.

"I'll talk to Mr. Colombo about it."

"Sierra, do you like working at Amuni?"

"Yes, sir, very much."

"And you like being the waitstaff manager?"

"Oh, yes."

"Franco says good things about you."

"That's nice to know." She sounds a little more confident now.

I nod to myself. "I'll still fire your ass if you ever hesitate to follow my orders again."

She gasps.

"Are we clear?"

"Yes, Mr. De Luca. We're clear. I'm sorry, I didn't intend to—"

"Save the fucking apology. Don't do it again." I can be polite, but manners are a tool like everything else.

Right now they aren't the tool I want to use. Intimidation works.

"What's her name?" I ask.

"Bianca Gemelli."

"Send me her application." I want to know what there is to know about the woman I'm going to spend Saturday night balls deep in.

I hang up before Sierra can say anything else.

Gemelli? Huh. It's an Italian name, but not New York Cosa Nostra. If she was, I'd know. No way would I forget those mouthwatering curves and that beautiful face. Mamma would say she has the face of an angel.

I'm too much of a devil to be interested in angels. Though she's as beautiful as a painting of the Madonna, Bianca's tight skirt and the sensual way she moves says she's no innocent.

Good. Because I have zero interest in virgins.

I want to know more about the sexy beauty, but Sierra hasn't forwarded the application to me. I text her.

Salvatore: *Send the application. Now.*

Less than a minute later, my phone dings indicating a message. It's the link to Bianca's application.

Reading her previous work history, my already hard cock twitches in my suit pants. She's a pole dancer at the Pitiful Princess. I own that club too, but my second-in-command oversees the strip clubs, while I oversee our night clubs.

The rules for employee behavior at the Pitiful Princess are very different than at Amuni. No wonder Sierra is hesitant to hire Bianca.

The strippers and dancers there can offer extra curriculars to the customers and have a safe space to conduct their business. If they want extra income, and they all do, they offer hand jobs, blowjobs and fucking. We provide rooms at the back of the club for their use, and in exchange they give us half their take.

Considering they get access to clients without the risk of being picked up for solicitation, it's a fair trade.

We pay to keep vice out and they pay us to stay safe.

Bianca Gemelli was already a sure thing, but now I know I don't even have to seduce her. It doesn't bother me to pay for sex.

There are less complications that way.

CHAPTER 2

BIANCA

The strong techno beat thrums through me. It's my third night on the floor at Amuni.

I had to leave the Pitiful Princess without giving notice. Tough on Gino. Too bad. So sad. Not.

He's a greedy creep. Once he got promoted to assistant manager and put in charge of the dancers, he started pushing all of us to offer extra curriculars. Since only me and Candi *with an i* (real name Kathleen B) are holding out, he's upped the pressure on both of us.

I don't like leaving her to face him alone, but I have to get out of there to keep myself safe. No one else is going to do it.

My family taught me that lesson long before our capo tossed me on the street after executing my dad when I was sixteen.

Hoping I can protect my friend too, I'm keeping an ear out for any other job opportunities for Candi. She likes stripping, so moving to another club will be easier for her. I only danced the pole.

I don't care about being mostly naked and dancing with the pole like it's my only lover, but peeling my clothes off for an audience, bit by bit? That feels more vulnerable, and I can't do it.

Finding another club that has pole dancers who don't strip and that doesn't require lap dancing is like looking for a unicorn. And I stopped believing in fairytales when I was thirteen and had to kill a man to protect my sister.

"The big boss is coming in tonight. Look lively." Armando, the head server tonight, swats my ass.

I jump and glare at him. "Knock it off."

"I'm desensitizing you. You jump like a startled giraffe any time someone touches you. That doesn't make for good server-patron relations."

"The patrons aren't supposed to touch the waitstaff." Sierra was very clear on that.

"In theory, that's true. In practice, a harmless pat on the ass is not going to kill you."

"I'm not letting anyone smack my ass and that includes you, Armando. Next time you do it, I'll put ground glass in your shoes."

Armando's eyes widen almost comically. "What are you? Some kind of female assassin? Who even says stuff like that?"

"It wouldn't kill you, but it would hurt like hell and make you lose a few days of work for sure. Don't test me."

"How do you know I won't tell Sierra about your threat?" Armando asks, sounding more curious than threatening.

"Because then I would tell her about you touching me inappropriately." I stress the word inappropriately and give him my best look of vulnerable innocence.

I haven't been innocent in a long time, but I know how to project what I need to in order to protect myself.

"Wow. That's good. Okay, I'll leave your ass alone, but don't come crying to me when the boss finds a reason to fire you that isn't about the customer patting your ass."

Disgruntled, I glare. Armando is not wrong. If I piss the customers off, Sierra will find a way to let me go. Even if she gives lip service to the club's official policy of hands off.

"Whatever you do, be on your best behavior tonight. The big boss is coming in."

"Isn't he here every night?"

Franco manages the club and I've never actually spoken to him, only seen him from afar, but he's always here.

"Franco's the GM, but Salvatore De Luca owns the club. He comes in once a week to meet with Franco, but he does a walk through on the floor first. Whatever you do, don't threaten a customer with ground glass when he's around."

"I reserve threats like that for my coworkers," I deadpan, my mind spinning.

Salvatore De Luca. As in the don's cousin? His dad, Big Sal, is the new consigliere.

I may not be part of the life anymore, but I keep my ear to the ground for any news about the Cosa Nostra in New York.

Salvatore De Luca is a capo now. I shiver when I think of the only other capo I've met. It's not a good memory.

My dad on his knees, his expression resigned. Lorenzo Ricci, his capo, behind him, holding a gun with a silencer against his head. The muffled snick of the shot, my father's face exploding, blood and brain matter going everywhere.

Lorenzo turning the gun on me, the threat in his soulless eyes. "You a rat too?"

Me shaking my head vehemently, tears streaking down my cheeks.

"Get the hell out of here. Don't say anything to anyone. If I see you again..."
He points the gun at me.

He doesn't have to say the words. I know.

I spin around to run out the door and he barks at one of his guys to stop me. Terrified he changed his mind about killing me, I try to rip out of the man's hold.

"You're covered in your dad's blood. Go. Shower it off. Pack a bag. What do you think I am? A monster?"

I don't answer because the truth might just get me killed.

"You have thirty minutes," he says, like he's being magnanimous.

I take the fastest shower of my life, everything inside me numb as I scrub my dad's blood off my skin.

And then I pack what I can just as fast and rush down the stairs.

I'm not giving Lorenzo a reason to change his mind and I never question that if I don't do what he says, Lorenzo will kill me, or order one of his men to do it.

Capos have a lot of power. They answer to the don, but that's it. Each capo has his own second-in-command and crew of soldiers.

Salvatore must run the clubs for the Genovese, like Lorenzo runs the drug trade.

I don't know what Salvatore looks like, but that doesn't stop me watching all the men in suits who enter the club. None of them have the level of arrogant entitlement in their stance that I remember Lorenzo Ricci having.

Before the owner arrives, Sierra sends me up to the VIP area to serve. I get a sulfuric glare from the server trading places with me on the main floor of the club. I shrug mentally. I don't know why Sierra wants me in the VIP area on my third night as a cocktail server, but I'm not about to tell her how to do her job either.

I'm sure that as soon as I learn what I need to serving in the VIP area, I'll be back on the main floor and the other server, or someone else, will be back working the VIP floor.

My ears, almost numb from the volume downstairs, adjust to the lower level of sound up here and I look around.

There are four different white leather sectionals with low tables to place drinks on up here. All are occupied.

One by a group of rich frat boys if I had to guess. Another has a mixture of businessmen and women dressed to impress in club clothes. They're drinking from two opened bottles of champagne.

Yeah. No one is getting up here without at least a seven-figure annual income. And they're probably considered the poor relations to most of the patrons drinking the top shelf whiskey and real French champagne.

My gaze snags on a man in the center of a group on one of the sectionals. And I can't look away.

He's lava level hot.

Even sitting, he's a few inches taller than the other three men at the table. And they aren't shrimps. Neither is the woman I can see out of my periphery sitting to his left.

My eyes are stuck on the gorgeous guy with raven dark hair and close-cropped beard framing his chiseled features.

I need to look away before I get caught staring, but my eye muscles forgot how to shift. Until the woman lays her light brown hand possessively on his arm, saying something into his ear.

Released from its imprisonment, my gaze flicks to a beautiful face framed by short black curls, trimmed close to her scalp. She's talking to the man, but her eyes are on me. And they aren't friendly.

Does she recognize me? Because I recognize her. Nerissa James, the woman Gino's boss calls boss at Pitiful Princess. She doesn't talk to the dancers, doesn't even acknowledge our existence. But I know who she is.

Is she pissed at me for leaving without notice?

Menaggia! I need this job.

I might as well say damn. No one can hear my thoughts and I can't get fired for what they can't hear. But I'm so used to cursing in Italian, I even do it inside my brain.

Bea and I learned to swear in Italian young. Mom doesn't speak it and she never wanted to learn, so we got away with saying stuff she would have washed our mouths out with soap for otherwise.

And this little walk down memory lane is an unproductive attempt at avoidance. The boss of my former boss isn't going to disappear with any amount of wishing.

Be real. Why would boss lady know who you are, much less that you quit her club without notice?

I wish I could be as confident of that as my inner voice. Forcing myself to look away, my gaze skims past the center of the VIP space where there are more low tables, each surrounded by four armchairs.

For smaller groups? Or just the ten percenters instead of the one percenters?

One of the bartenders waives me over and I go.

He tells me how the tables are numbered and expects me to remember. There are no convenient little maps tucked away where the customers can't see like in the last bar I worked at.

Okay. I can do this. My memory is excellent.

"Watch the level of champagne at booth two. When a bottle is empty, open a new one and replace it. Standing order."

"Will do."

"Booth three just got their round, so you don't need to check on them immediately, but both one and four need to be served."

Calling the small sectionals that wouldn't look out of place in a millionaire's living room booths is weird, but what do I know? Maybe to the extremely rich, that kind of seating is a booth?

I walk quickly, but not too quickly, over to the group of women in booth four. There are two unfinished drinks on the table, but the rest of the glasses are empty or close to it.

"What can I get you?" I ask them, memorizing their order as they give it to me.

After relaying the order to the bartender nearest booth four, I make my way to booth one.

His booth.

He watches me approach with unnerving interest, trapping my gaze with his.

Nerissa is sitting several inches away from him now and nothing about their body language screams intimacy. That doesn't mean she isn't hoping.

I don't blame her. I'm irreparably broken in that department, and I'm still drawn to him.

Encased in a Brioni suit, tailored to fit his muscular form, he relaxes on the leather sectional, one arm slung along its back.

Yet the aura of leashed power surrounding him makes me think he could spring into action at any moment. From the heated look in his eyes, he might be springing in my direction.

My heart beats a rapid staccato in my chest while I struggle to get enough air. Who is this guy?

Instead of scaring the crap out of me like he should, my ovaries wake up screaming from their lifelong nap. I don't feel sexual attraction. Not to men. Not to women. Not to anyone.

Tell that to my now weeping vagina. What the hell is going on?

Unable to break eye contact with him, I stop when I'm a foot away from the table. This close, I can tell that his eyes are the color of gray.

I force words past my tight throat. "What can I get you?" My voice is a husky timber I have never heard from my own throat before.

Caspita! Could I sound any more ready to go to bed with this man?

"Are you on the menu?" he asks.

It's a totally cheesy line, so where is the ache in my core coming from? Why are my thighs pressing together with the power of vise?

"No." Very cool, Bianca.

At least smile, or something to let him know you get the joke. Even if it is at your expense. No way does someone with VIP access *not* know the servers don't fraternize with the club patrons.

"You sure?" he asks, his voice whiskey smooth.

My thighs clench tighter, and I go through an entire litany of Italian curse words in my head.

"I'm sure. Would you like a drink?"

He orders top shelf Frangelico in a rock glass. Nerissa James orders a specialty coffee I know we don't offer.

When I explain that, she gives me a mocking glance and says, "I'll just have a black coffee then."

Something tells me she knows Amuni doesn't do specialty coffees. Ignoring her petty power games, I get the orders from the remaining people at the table. The two men sitting on either edge seat of the sectional want sodas, their hyper vigilant attitudes exposing them as bodyguards.

The man sitting across from Mr. Gorgeous orders a mixed drink with a smile that doesn't reach his assessing blue eyes. That look crawls over my body like ants at a picnic and I have to suppress a disgusted shudder.

Mr. Gorgeous is deep in conversation with the skeevy guy when I bring the drinks back and doesn't look up when I place his Frangelico on the table.

That is not disappointment I feel.

I refuse to let it be.

Leaving, I notice booth two needs more bubbly. I drop one off and snag the empty bottle to put in the recycle bin. Fingers snap around my wrist as I'm returning from the kitchen.

I yank at my arm and spin around to face my assailant, still trying to get loose.

"What the fu—" Realizing it's the man from booth one, I cut myself off before I curse out a customer.

Letting go of my wrist, he puts his hands up, palms out, and smiles at me, even white teeth flashing in his handsome face. "I didn't mean to startle you."

I am right. He *is* tall. Really tall. I'm five-foot-four and he's got to be almost a foot taller than me.

"Do you need something?" I ask, rubbing my wrist with my other hand.

It doesn't hurt. It tingles. Where he touched me. What is happening to me?

He leans his shoulder against the wall, blocking my exit and creating a pocket of privacy for us. "When is your next break?"

"Not for a couple of hours. Don't worry, I can get you whatever you need."

"Two hours is a long time to wait."

Uncomprehending, I stare up at him. "You don't have to wait. I'll get you another Frangelico now, if you want it."

"I meant wait to taste your lips."

CHAPTER 3

BIANCA

The penny drops and I groan. "Why are all your pickup lines so lame?" And still so freaking effective?

"You think I'm lame?"

I give him a once over, ignoring the way my body wants to lean toward his. "You're gorgeous, I'll give you that, but you don't have game."

"No one has ever complained before."

Arrogant much? "And were you paying these women for their time?"

I can't believe I'm teasing him. I'm going to get myself fired and I need this job.

His laughter is rich and dark. It goes straight to my cooch, and I stifle a gasp as unfamiliar feelings ricochet through me.

"Sometimes. I'll pay you for some of your time."

I shake my head. "No can do."

He pulls a money clip from his pocket and pulls five crisp hundred dollar bills off. "I'll pay you five hundred to let me kiss you."

"Do you even realize what a creeper you sound like right now?" I ask.

His dark eyes narrow and his jaw tenses. "I am a businessman. Money talks."

"And you want me to listen."

"Yes."

"No, thank you. My time is not for sale."

As if he doesn't even hear me, he pulls another five bills off. "A thousand. For one kiss on your break."

"Now, you sound desperate."

He jerks away from the wall, towering over me, his relaxed demeanor gone. "I am not desperate."

"And yet you're offering me a thousand bucks for a kiss." I won't pretend that money wouldn't come in handy, but at the cost of getting me fired?

So not worth it.

"I prefer the expediency of transactions."

"Makes sense." I don't blame him. If I wanted sex, I'd probably like paying for it too.

You can't be betrayed when there are no expectations other than the give and take of a business transaction.

"I'm glad you think so," he purrs. "Take half now and I'll give you the other half after the kiss."

I ignore his outstretched hand and shake my head. "My kisses aren't for sale. Neither is anything else, in case you were wondering."

Though I'm hella tempted and that? Is so far out of the norm, I'm seriously freaked out.

"I need to get back to work."

His fingertips brush down my neck and instead of jumping a mile and taking off like I would with anyone else, I shiver. Pleasure sparks from one nerve ending to the next until I'm ready to press myself to him and offer my lips for that kiss.

I cannot believe this. My body is on a whole other wavelength when it comes to this man.

"Do you need something?" My voice breaks on the word *need* and I want to sink into the floor. "Other than to harass the help, that is." At least I end strong.

"You know what I need." His eyes burn into me with hungry fire, leaving no doubt what that is. "I'll pay you five thousand to sleep with me tonight."

"Are you for real?" We're up to five thousand? I shake my head even though I'd rather say *yes*. And *please*. "I. Am. Not. For. Sale." I enunciate each word of my refusal, making it its own sentence. "No."

"Do you want me to seduce you? Would you rather that than money?" He sounds intrigued by the idea, like I just increased my attractiveness to him.

Who is this guy?

Clearly someone who isn't used to being told *no* and taking it as a personal challenge when it happens.

"You're not as irresistible as you think you are," I inform him. Lying.

Everything about this situation should reinforce my lack of desire for physical intimacy.

The opposite is happening. My nipples are peaked and achy. My breasts feel heavy in my bra. My lips keep parting like they're getting ready for the kiss he wants. And I'm not even going to think about how wet the gusset of my panties is.

"I will exhaust you with orgasms," he promises me.

I roll my eyes, but my core clenches. "Why don't you try your luck with that lady at your table? She seems interested."

Che palle. Why did I say that? I don't want him to start macking on Nerissa James while I'm serving them their drinks.

His face twists with genuine revulsion. "Nerissa is my sister, or as good as."

Totally inappropriate relief floods me. The beautiful and successful Nerissa James is his sister. *Or as good as.* Which means she isn't really. The relief sours in my belly.

For whatever reason, that finally breaks the stasis in my body. Unwilling to give the gorgeous stranger a chance to offer me any more money for a kiss, or more...I scoot around him.

Because I might take it. And not for the money I legit need, but for the pleasure he promises. Pleasure I have never once experienced or craved in my adult life.

The next time I come to booth one to get drink orders, Franco, the man I *thought* was the big boss, is sitting with them. Tension invades my limbs.

Is the dark-haired Adonis part of the mafia too, or is this the club manager schmoozing a wealthy patron?

"Bring a chilled bottle of Belvedere, unopened. And shot glasses from the cooler," Franco says to me.

"Of course, sir. Anything else?"

"I'll have another coffee, and if you could bring it while it's still hot, that would be great," Nerissa says.

Franco frowns. "Your coffee was cold?"

"It was fine," Mr. Gorgeous answers before the woman can.

She smiles at Franco. "I'm sure your new waitress will get the hang of things."

The words sound like she's trying to be nice, but she's not. She's undermining me in front of my boss and she knows it. I'd like to pour the next cup of hot coffee over her head.

Forcing a smile, I say, "I'll do better."

Mr. Gorgeous is frowning, and the look isn't directed at me. "Knock it off, Nerissa."

"I only pointed out that my coffee was cold last time. If she served it like that to a regular patron, it would be a problem."

She's not a regular customer? How so?

I don't stick around to find out. If I do, I'm more likely to tell her where to shove her supposedly cold coffee.

The two years I danced on the pole, I forgot how much I hate customer interaction. It's one of the reasons I went for the dancing job in the first place. As long as I stayed up on the stage, I didn't have to deal with entitled or bitchy customers.

I return to the table with chilled vodka, shot glasses and a cup of coffee, still steaming.

Giving the hot drink to Nerissa first, I offer her the fakest smile in my repertoire along with it. Candi says that smile is as good as saying fuck off. I'm more likely to say *che palle*, but the meaning is pretty much the same.

Nerissa's eyes narrow. She's reading my facial expression fine.

I dismiss her with a subtle shift of my head and offer the vodka and glasses to Franco.

"You want to do the honors Salvatore?"

Salvatore. As in the *real* big boss, Salvatore De Luca?

Suddenly this whole situation takes on new meaning. He is testing the new girl, trying to tempt me into screwing up.

Che palle. What a jerk.

I know how serious the club is about the no turning tricks on the side, or dealing drugs. You'd have to be an idiot to try to deal drugs on mafia territory anyway. But Salvatore is trying to set me up to fail. To get fired.

Why? Does he do it to all the new servers? Or am I special?

It doesn't matter. I didn't fall for it. Even if I was close to doing so, he'll never know that.

Something inside me cracks. For the first time since puberty, I wanted to kiss someone.

No sloppy lips forcing mine apart, just hazelnut liquor flavored goodness that could set my body on fire.

But that someone isn't really into me. For all I know, Nerissa *is* his girlfriend and *as good as a* sister to him. After all, they *don't* share a last name.

I hold the drinks tray so tightly, my knuckles turn white.

"Would you like anything else?" I ask Franco, ignoring everyone else at the table.

My boss's gaze takes in the way I'm holding the tray and his eyes narrow. He thinks I'm annoyed with Miss Bitchy for complaining about my service. Or maybe he realizes I'm pissed at Salvatore.

Doesn't matter. I force my fingers to relax their grip and a smile that feels more like a grimace to curve my lips.

Franco gives a tiny nod of approval. "That's all for now."

I don't wait for someone else to stop me, but quickly turn away.

Was Franco in on the plan to test me tonight? Was Sierra? Is that why I got put on the VIP floor my third night on the job? Is this their way of weeding out servers who don't abide by the rules?

Hell, maybe there wasn't a plan at all. Maybe Salvatore De Luca gets his kicks out of trying to trip up unsuspecting servers when he's bored.

If that pile of rat pellets accosts me by the kitchen again, I'm suing this place for sexual harassment.

Letting myself fantasize about taking Amuni to the cleaners, I serve the other tables in the VIP lounge. By the time I circle back to Salvatore's table, rational thought is overriding my temper.

I'm not suing a mafia owned business. I like breathing too much.

CHAPTER 4

SALVATORE

Franco says my name and Bianca goes rigid. After exchanging a few words with Franco, she walks away from the table. Without looking my way once.

Call me arrogant, but this is not how women usually respond to learning who I am. They see a rich businessman, not the brutal capo. My wealth and power only make me more appealing to them.

Bianca's response is unique. And interesting.

Making no effort to hide the way I watch her, I track the sexy redhead's movements around the VIP lounge.

She doesn't return my obvious interest. Unlike before Franco revealed my identity as the club's owner, there are no furtive glances my way as Bianca walks between the tables and the bar.

She has a hurried, whispered discussion with the other server on the floor, but after an unsubtle look at my table, the waiter shakes his head. She's trying to trade with someone else to get out of serving us.

Why? Is she playing hard to get to increase my interest?

Women have been playing games to get my attention since my voice dropped. Only one woman's games caught me, but in the end it was her downfall, not mine.

Bianca is a novice compared to Monica. But this pretense that she's not interested in me is working. Damn it.

I only want her more.

"I don't think she's all that into you, Salvatore," Nerissa drawls.

I frown at my second. "Maybe she's avoiding your bitchiness."

"I wasn't being bitchy," Nerissa defends herself.

"You're always bitchy."

She shrugs. "It's part of my charm."

My bodyguard, Pietro, coughs in a poor attempt to hide his laughter.

"Your other *charms* make up for it," Juniper says, his eyes fixed on Nerissa's chest.

Nerissa picks up her coffee and looks over its rim at him. "One of them is how good my knife throwing skills are. Keep looking at me like that and I'll show you. I never miss the bullseye."

Instead of looking chastened like an intelligent person would, the man trying to offload a chain of decrepit bars smiles wider. "Youse only live once. Might as well do it dangerously."

Five-foot-eleven with her body toned with muscle and her shooting skills outstripping her accuracy with a knife, Nerissa killed to become made just like I did.

Juniper only sees my sister's beautiful exterior and is clueless about just how dangerous she really is.

Bianca arrives at the table and waits for Franco to acknowledge her before asking, "Can I get you anything else, sir?"

The urge to shoot Franco where he sits when she calls him sir is so strong, my hand goes to the gun in my shoulder holster.

"Sal!" a familiar voice booms from several feet away.

My jaw clenches. I do not go by Sal. That is my father. I am Salvatore and anyone with half a working brain acknowledges that fact.

The man approaching my table is proving himself to be lacking in that department on many fronts.

Pietro moves smoothly to his feet, making it possible for me to exit the booth if I want to. Nerissa groans. She doesn't like Lorenzo Ricci and now that she's my second-in-command, she can't avoid him like she did as one of my father's enforcers.

"Introduce us, Franco, I haven't met this one." Lorenzo is behind Bianca when he speaks.

He doesn't see the way she pales, a look of terror flitting through her gaze before she pulls concrete walls around her emotions, completely closing them off.

What the hell is going on?

Ignoring his demand to be introduced to my staff, I meet my fellow capo's gaze. "Lorenzo."

"Brought my friends to party. I knew you could fix us right up."

Considering that Lorenzo Ricci is in charge of drug importation, exportation and sales for *la famiglia*, he's not talking about getting them some Molly. Which he wouldn't get at Amuni anyway.

As one of our legit business fronts, drug dealing on premises is strictly forbidden. Just like my father before me, I have some inventive ways to discourage anyone thinking they can break that rule.

His gaze slides over Bianca's form as she hurries away without taking any orders or empties. "New meat?"

"My servers are not meat," I inform him. "If you are looking for companionship, take your friends to the Pitiful Princess or The Red Room."

That Bianca used to work at the former pisses me off for no accountable reason. What difference does it make if she's sold her ass to a hundred other men? I only want it for one night.

I've never fucked a virgin and I don't particularly want to. Pussy isn't like a bee's stinger. It's not a onetime use commodity.

Besides, sex is easier after a woman has learned how to find pleasure with her pussy.

His brows drawing together, Lorenzo fixes his gaze on Bianca's retreating back.

Only when she disappears down the hallway with access to the kitchen and bathrooms, does he look back at me. "I've got some business to discuss with you."

"I'm busy tonight." I indicate Juniper with an inclination of my head. "Call and we'll arrange a time to meet."

My role as capo is less than a year old, and some of the old guard are still struggling to adjust to my promotion. I could give two fucks.

If he wants to talk business, he'll make an appointment like anyone else.

Surprising me, Lorenzo nods almost affably. "I'll do that." He claps Franco on the shoulder. "Well, I gotta drain the dragon. Maybe we'll head to the Red Room after that. The music in here is better suited to teenagers."

Considering the drinking age in New York is twenty-one, teenagers are not Amuni's target demographic. But neither are men my father's age.

"More like drain the worm," Nerissa mutters under her breath as the older man walks the same direction Bianca went.

Suddenly I feel an urge to take a leak myself. I stand up and acknowledge Juniper. "Excuse me for a minute."

"Youse do what you need to," he says with a knowing look. "I'll keep your beautiful sist-ah company he-ah."

His New Jersey accent is thicker than when he started drinking. Not surprising considering the fact he drank at least a third of the Belvedere on his own.

BIANCA

My hands shake as I rush down the hall toward the restroom.

Che Palle. Why did Lorenzo Ricci pick tonight to come into the VIP area? Next shift I'll be back on the main floor, one server among many, and lost in the crowd of patrons.

Fuck my life.

I haven't seen that *stronzo* for six years and he hits on me the minute he lays eyes on me? I'm skeeved out and drowning in fear filled adrenalin at the same time. Because I still remember his threat when he threw me out of my family home.

Getting hit on by him is slightly better than having a gun shoved in my face, but only a little.

Back when I first started working at Pitiful Princess, I knew there was a risk that Lorenzo would come into the club and recognize me. But it wasn't a big one. I remembered hearing my dad say Pitiful Princess wasn't Lorenzo's style. The capo preferred The Red Room because it was more upscale.

One of the dancers there was his mistress at the time, which was probably the real reason. Regardless, the two years I danced the pole, Lorenzo never came into Pitiful Princess.

I wore a sexy lace Mardi Gras style mask as part of my costume, just in case though. The customers loved it, and I grew complacent. Even learning tonight that Amuni is owned by the mafia, I didn't worry about Lorenzo coming in.

He's old school. Amuni definitely is not.

From the first word he spoke, his voice went through me like an icepick. Instant recognition sent a jarring alarm clanging in my brain.

Get away. Get away. Get Away.

Shoving the door open to the ladies room, I hurry inside.

"Are you okay?" A woman reaches out like she's going to touch me.

I jump back and force a smile. "I'm fine."

It's a lie. I'm anything but. Doesn't matter. You don't let them see you sweat, even if they're trying to be nice.

"Are you're sure?"

I'm surprised at her continued concern. This is New York. Not some friendly small town. New Yorkers aren't heartless, but we do a good job of sticking to our own business.

Right now, this beautiful, rich lady is sticking her nose in mine.

It's weird.

"I'm sure." I figure there's a better chance she'll believe me if I say the words instead of nodding.

"Come on, Alisa, the guys are waiting." Her companion grabs the friendly woman's arm and drags her toward the door.

Getting my frozen limbs to work, I go into a stall. Not because I have to pee, but because I need a second of privacy and this is the only place I'll get it. I don't have time for a meltdown.

I don't indulge in them anyway. Crying never got me anything but a headache.

Lorenzo probably didn't even recognize me. Why would he?

The last time I saw him, he'd just executed my father and tossed me out on the street after threatening to shoot me if he ever saw me again.

That's pretty memorable.

Me? Not so much.

I was a teenager with bad hair and even worse dress sense. Don't forget the red, blotchy face from crying. He got to witness the last time I let myself cry in front of anyone else. How's he going to recognize me from that?

Okay. I'm alright. Stop panicking and get back to work.

When I come out of the stall, there are a couple of women at the mirror and sink. They don't notice me because they're too busy looking at the man standing near the doorway, glaring.

It's Lorenzo Ricci and the way his eyes narrow when they land on me, he's not in here because the men's room is suddenly out of order.

Oh, *merda*. Shit. He did recognize me.

Trying to brazen it out, I pretend ignorance and go to scoot by him. He won't do anything in front of witnesses, right?

Wrong. He grabs my arm and shoves me against a wall. "Where the fuck do you think you're going?"

When he looms over me, it's nothing like Salvatore, trying to get his freak on. This capo scares the hell out of me. He always has.

Fear makes me angry and I glare up at him, refusing to answer.

"What are you doing working for a family owned club?" he demands.

"I didn't know it was." Not until tonight.

Lorenzo glowers at me. "Does your boss know your dad was a rat?"

"Why would I tell anyone about my dad?"

"You keep it that way. You know what happens if you don't keep your mouth shut," he hisses.

My stomach rebels as every word sends a gust of Lorenzo's bad breath in my direction.

I don't react to his threat because I've been living under it since I was sixteen. And I don't react to him calling my dad a rat because it's true.

Not of the telling on the mafia to the FEDs kind, but the stealing money from his boss kind. That's what got Dad killed. The same weakness that left his daughters vulnerable to his debtors.

"Thirty days on a good probiotic will take care of that," I mutter, probably picking the least sensible thing *to* react to.

"The fuck are you talking about?" Lorenzo shakes me.

Pain shoots up my arm, but I don't react. Never let them see you sweat, especially when they are *stronzo* capos trying to intimidate you.

"Your bad breath. Mints help, but they don't treat the root of the problem. Sometimes a probiotic will." It worked for Candi when she got that godawful breath after trying one of her weird diets.

He makes a sound like a rusty door being yanked open. "Listen, you little bitch—"

"Get the fuck out of here, Lorenzo," Salvatore's voice cuts off the other man with the force of an axe being swung by Paul Bunyon. "I told you my servers are off limits."

"You don't belong here. You're not family anymore," Lorenzo hisses at me, squeezing my arm again for good measure.

His words don't hurt like he thinks they will.

I stopped being part of a family a long time ago. After the way my dad's buddies in the mafia made me pay his bad debts, I want nothing to do with the Cosa Nostra family either.

"We're just talking." Lorenzo's hold on my arm loosens so he can turn to face Salvatore. "Do you mind?"

"I fucking mind you ignoring me. Get the hell out of my club and don't come back."

"You can't ban me from this place," Lorenzo shouts, his face going florid with fury.

Taking advantage of his focus on the other capo and loosened hold, I yank myself loose and scoot under Lorenzo's arm. Salvatore blocks the doorway and my headlong rush out of the bathroom. Abruptly stopping in front of him, I wait for the younger capo to move.

He doesn't.

After several long seconds of silence, I school my features and look up at my boss's boss. The man who offered me a thousand dollars for a kiss and five thousand for sex, hoping to get me fired.

Though I've been thinking about it ever since, I still don't understand why.

"Did he do anything to you?" Salvatore studies me like he's memorizing every inch of my face.

He and Lorenzo are like two bulls snorting and pawing at the earth, ready to charge. I'm not playing the part of capeless matador caught between them.

No way am I going to tell him about my throbbing arm. "Can I get by?"

Salvatore's gaze doesn't break away from mine.

"I need to get back to work," I remind him.

With a jerk of his head, he moves aside just enough to let me by. Our arms touch, sending jolts of electric pleasure dancing along my nerve endings. I don't let that show on my face though.

Never let them see you sweat, especially not the boss.

CHAPTER 5

SALVATORE

W hen I reach the hallway, I don't see Bianca or Lorenzo. Is he hitting on her? Rage heats my blood as I slam the swinging door to the kitchen back.

The dishwasher looks up, startled, from a tray of glasses he's preparing for washing and sanitizing. His mouth gapes, but no sound comes out of it. No one else is in the kitchen. I spin on my heel and head to the bathrooms. If Lorenzo is in the men's room, there's no issue.

So, I walk right past it and shove the outer door to the ladies' room open. While two women fix their makeup and another washes her hands like nothing is happening, the asshole I'm chasing down looms over Bianca.

He's got her backed against the wall with his hands on either side of her head, speaking to her in tones too low to hear.

"Get the fuck out of here, Lorenzo. I told you my servers are off limits."

The older capo jolts like I hit him with the cattle prod I am known to use to drive a point home. Fists are good, but sometimes 5,000 volts are better.

He says something to Bianca and then turns to face me. "We're just talking. Do you mind?"

Does this slimy bastard really think I'm going to turn around and leave him to harass my staff? Not fucking likely. "I fucking mind you ignoring me. Get the hell out of my club and don't come back."

"You can't ban me from this place," Lorenzo yells.

That is where he is wrong. I own this club and he's not getting back inside. My crew don't bow to any other capo. When I tell the bouncers to keep him out, they will obey me.

Because they know how far I'll go to maintain order and obedience.

Bianca ducks under Lorenzo's arm and rushes toward me, her face that same expressionless mask she donned a few minutes ago. She stops in front of me. I wait until she looks up and meets my eyes.

"Did he do anything to you?"

Her shoulders tense, but nothing shows on that beautiful, stoic face. "Can I get by? I need to get back to work."

The words are reminiscent of what she said when I cornered her near the kitchen earlier. This time they are said with no breathless inflection. Her beautiful blue eyes hold no reluctant interest.

They reflect nothing at all.

I step to the side a few inches and she scoots around me. Her arm brushes mine, the scent of cherries and vanilla I noticed earlier teasing at my senses.

When she is gone, I give Lorenzo a sardonic lift of one brow. "What are you doing in here? It's got to be hard when you're too old to stand up and piss, but there are stalls in the men's room too."

Lorenzo's face goes florid. "You little shi—"

"Uh, uh, uh. Ladies present."

The women titter and one sends me a sultry look in the mirror. Her body is on display in a skintight mini dress and she's got curves in all the right places. Normally, I would wink and might even take her up on the invitation in her eyes.

Right now, I'm disgusted, and I turn away from her blatant interest to glare at Lorenzo. She and her friend ignored the way the other capo was forcing his company on Bianca.

Besides, my cock only wants one woman. The skittish server who high-tailed it out of here.

Putting my hand out toward the door, I indicate Lorenzo needs to leave. "Maybe you should start bringing your bodyguard with you so he can ensure you don't get the words on the doors confused again."

"Watch it, Little Sal. Making me an enemy isn't smart."

No one has called me Little Sal since I punched a made man in the nut sack at age eight when he did it. If Lorenzo doesn't watch it, I'll do more than punch his family jewels. I'll castrate them.

I let the imminent demise of his junk show in my eyes. "The ladies might be impressed with your posturing, *old man*. I am not."

"Severu is going to hear about this disrespect." Lorenzo takes a step backward.

My gaze flicks sideways to the women watching us and listening with blatant interest. Lorenzo left subtle behind a decade ago. He swaggers through life, throwing his weight around. Not only does he not care who knows about his connection to the mafia, but he revels in the fear it usually causes.

Stronzo. This guy really is an asshole.

And my patience is all used up. I grab Lorenzo by the back of the neck and shove him out of the women's restroom. He squawks the whole time.

"You better watch your back," he shouts as I strongarm him right into the men's room.

I toss him forward. "Piss and then get out of my club, Ricci."

He yells and windmills his arms, barely avoiding a fall against the black marble back wall of the urinals where a steady stream of water runs.

The man using the urinals cuts off his stream and shoves himself back into his jeans. "I'm outta here." He takes off without washing his hands.

Unsanitary.

Two men rush out of the stalls and wash their hands. *Grazie a Dio.* Casting a nervous glance our way, they hotfoot it out of the bathroom. A quick glance confirms the rest of the bathroom is empty.

Unless someone is standing on a toilet to eavesdrop on us. But this isn't a fucking afterschool special.

Lorenzo is puffed up like an angry chicken. I'm not calling him a rooster because he's a dickless piece of shit as far as I'm concerned.

"You cannot treat me this way. Severu should never have promoted you to capo," he sneers. "You are too fucking young and immature to respect the role."

I'm 31 not 14. "The fuck I care what you think. I'm a better capo than you. I take care of my people."

Lorenzo runs one of the most lucrative industries for the mafia, but he has men on his payroll that are forced to work a second job to cover rent. It's one of the reasons Severu is investigating the other capo.

Where is the money going, if not to his people?

"Who has been complaining?" Lorenzo demands.

Not once has he looked around to make sure we are alone. How pissed would Severu be if I killed the stupid son of a bitch?

"You think the rest of us don't have eyes?" I ask derisively. "We can see when your guys show up looking haggard from working two jobs."

"I don't coddle my soldiers like you and your dad. I expect them to pull their weight."

"Your men swear loyalty to *la famiglia* and in return, their don and capos take care of them. It's not coddling to pay a man what he is worth." I don't call him a stingy piece of shit.

He should thank me for the restraint.

I move until I'm looming over him like he was doing to Bianca when I found them. "You are banned from this club. Piss me off again, Lorenzo, and I will ban you from all of *my* clubs."

"You can't do that!"

"Watch me."

Without another word, I execute an efficient search of the bathroom stalls. No, it's not a movie, but I'm not a man to take chances either.

Something my father taught me.

When I'm done, having found the stalls empty of potential informants for the FEDs, I wash my hands because I've got no interest in becoming a walking petri dish. I leave the bathroom without saying another word to Lorenzo, who is still standing there glowering.

I guess he doesn't need to piss after all.

Returning to the main area, I signal the bartender that we want another round.

Bianca is at another table, talking to the patrons, but he'll let her know.

Impatience scores my brain like nails on a chalkboard. It's not good enough. I want her attention on me *now*. And I want her within touching distance if Lorenzo accosts her again.

I will get great pleasure out of knocking him into next week if he does.

She turns from the other table and I signal to her, indicating my booth with a tip of my head. She pretends not to see me and goes to another table to pick up empty glasses. Her back to me, she talks to the two men sitting there. Probably taking their order for the next round.

It pisses me off.

When she heads to the bar without looking back toward me, frustration is a louder beat than the club music in my head.

Reaching the table, my mood sours even further. "Where is Juniper?"

"He's dancing." Nerissa indicates the lower level with her thumb. "He asked me to join him. I declined."

Good. We want the man to sell us his string of bars, but if my second stabs him for being handsy, that's not going to happen.

Franco is gone too, but that's not a surprise. He is the club manager and it's a busy night.

Lorenzo comes storming out of the hallway and shouts at his companions. "Let's go!"

The two men and their arm candy jump up and scurry after the capo who is giving his bodyguard an earful. Typical. He probably told the man not to follow him because he wanted to try it on with Bianca.

When things didn't go his way, Lorenzo blames his bodyguard instead of his own obnoxious behavior.

"Something happen in the bathroom?" Nerissa asks. "Lorenzo doesn't look too happy and you look like you want to kill someone."

"I do. Him."

"Why?"

"Do I really need a reason with that *stronzo*?"

"Not in my opinion, but you're usually the cooler headed one between the two of us."

"He accosted Bianca in the bathroom."

"The curvy little waitress you've been making calf's eyes at all night?"

"Fuck you, Nerissa. I'm not a sap."

"First, eww, no thanks. Second, before tonight, I would have agreed, but you have it bad for the waitress and she's got no time for you." My sister smirks. "I never thought I'd live to see the day that my big brother got shot down by a working girl."

"She's not a working girl. She's a server." Bianca turned me down flat when I offered her five grand to fuck me.

Nerissa makes a dismissive gesture. "She worked at Pitiful Princess."

I'm not surprised she knows. As my second-in-command, it's Nerissa's job to oversee the strip clubs.

"Not all of the dancers sell extra curriculars," I say, wondering for the first time if Bianca is one of the extremely few that chose not to.

Nerissa scrutinizes me like she can tell what I'm thinking. "Right. And not all guys jack off after they discover what their dick is for besides pissing."

"Did she?" I ask, a powerful need to know pounding through me.

Nerissa shrugs. "Don't they all?"

My look tells her I don't appreciate her flip answer.

She sighs. "I don't know, okay? You know I don't deal with the dancers. I only recognized her because she was one of the only two plus size dancers we had there."

One of the only dancers with generous curves, and maybe the only one who didn't make money from offering extra-curriculars.

CHAPTER 6

BIANCA

My feet hurt and my brain is on a sluggish spin cycle when I finish my closing shift at Amuni.

Lorenzo never came back, and Salvatore finally left around two. It's just my luck that my night of training on the VIP floor brought me to the attention of two powerful capos. And not in a good way.

The tips might be twice what I earn on the main floor, but the extra money isn't worth it for this kind of stress.

In the employee locker room, I take off my uniform. It's a sleeveless mini dress, with a flared skirt and square neckline, cut low enough to show a couple of inches of cleavage. I am allowed to wear flats with it, but not tennis shoes.

My feet are thankful I splurged on a pair of black comfort-support ballet style flats before my first night as a cocktail waitress. They're doubly grateful tonight. Who knew that serving a smaller clientele would require so many more trips across the floor?

I'm not wearing either going home. Not when I have the walk to the subway station ahead of me and a ride on the F train alone at four-thirty in the morning.

"How was your night up on the VIP floor?" Armando asks, ignoring my partially undressed state.

I slip on a form fitting t-shirt that says, *I didn't mean to push all your buttons. I was looking for mute.* "Okay. I prefer the main floor."

"I hear that the VIPs can be demanding." He changes his shoes, pulling on trainers nearly as beat up as mine.

Despite looking so worn out, my tennies are comfortable. More importantly, they won't get me mugged for my shoes.

Pulling on jeans I got from the rag bin at a second-hand store, I ask, "You don't know? Didn't you train up there too?"

I thread my belt with a knife hidden in the buckle through the loops of my jeans. According to the psychology class I took, needing to have a weapon handy is a trauma response from what I experienced as a teenager.

It feels like a natural native New Yorker response to me.

"Nope. I've worked at Amuni for over a year and have yet to spend a single night serving VIPs. I hear the tips are great?" He makes it sound like a question.

I shrug as I shove my new shoes in the bottom of my backpack before careful folding my uniform and putting it inside too. I don't know the other server well enough to tell him I have twice as much cash on me right now than I went home with last night.

"Oh, yeah," he says, like I said something. "Your trainer probably took most of the tips. They wouldn't have let you serve tables on your own your first night up there."

He doesn't make this a question, so I don't feel the need to correct him, but I didn't have a trainer. I had assumed that was because I'd already done my first night with a trainer on the main floor. Only he makes it sound like I should have had one tonight.

"How was the main floor?" I ask. Not because I care, but because I don't want to answer any more questions.

"Busy. We could have used you. I didn't know the woman who took your place, but she's gotten soft serving the VIPs."

"You think? I ran off my feet getting to all the tables in my section as fast as they expected." Shoot. I should have kept that to myself.

"Yeah? Even with a trainer?" Armando asks me with unsurprising interest.

I need to think before I speak.

I hum, not wanting to lie, but not wanting to admit my lack of a trainer either. Because then he'll ask why I didn't have one and I don't know. I'll ask Sierra when I come in for my next shift though.

If she's in a better mood than tonight.

I zip up my threadbare, oversized hoodie that turns my curves from my neck to mid-thigh into a nondescript single shape.

I'm going for invisible because invisible means safe. When I flip the hood over my red hair, my armor is complete.

Almost.

Before sliding my arms through the straps on my backpack, I pull out my pepper spray. I never walk alone at night without it. Or the knife

"That backpack looks like it's ready for the garbage heap."

"I know," I say proudly.

It doesn't have any rips, but worn duct tape covers strategic spots making the bag look about ready to disintegrate. If you don't look like you have anything worth stealing, then no one tries to steal what you have.

More invisibility.

"The duct tape is a nice touch," he says admiringly.

I repay his admiration with my own. "Yours looks like you pulled it out of the trash heap." I wrinkle my nose. "It smells like it too."

"My mom's fish oil. Prick a couple of capsules and rub it into the zipper. Instant stink and my zipper doesn't stick."

"Smart."

Armando doesn't change all his clothes like I do, but he pulls on a worn flack jacket that covers the uniform.

The other waitstaff and kitchen staff who closed join me and Armando as we leave the locker room. We'll walk together to the subway station. None of the others ride the F train with me, but there's safety in the group for the walk.

I keep my pepper spray in my hand anyway.

We're almost to the door when I hear my name called. Turning, I see Sierra waving at me.

Wishing I had pretended not to hear, I trudge over. The others are going to leave without me and that will end up with me walking alone. Not for the first time, but I prefer going with the group.

I stop in front of Sierra. "Yes?"

"I wanted to know how it went up on the VIP floor."

Seriously? She called me back to chat about my night? I couldn't have told her when I came in for my next shift? Or better yet, she should ask the bartender for his opinion. She's going to anyway. It's not like she's going to trust me to critique my own success.

"Fine, but I'll be glad to get back to the main floor."

Sierra frowns. "Didn't I make it clear? You're assigned to the VIP floor now."

"But I'm new," I can't help saying.

"Are you saying you don't want the VIP floor?" she asks with disbelief. "You told me you need the money."

"Who doesn't?" Any of the main floor waitstaff would be thrilled to be assigned to the VIP level.

So, why am I, a new hire, getting the assignment?

Did Salvatore arrange this? But from what Sierra is saying, the decision to put me in the VIP lounge was made before I ever met the big boss.

"Just out of curiosity, is Mr. De Luca the usual honey trap you all use to weed out servers willing to take money on the side for sexual favors?" I ask, my annoyance at the capo surging all over again. "It seems like it would be beneath the general manager, though."

"I don't know what you are talking about. Are you claiming that Mr. De Luca offered you money for sex?" Sierra asks, doing a good imitation of shocked offense.

It's close, but I manage not to roll my eyes. Sure, she doesn't know what I'm talking about. "Did you need anything else?"

"I would like you to clarify your question," Sierra says.

"That will not be necessary. I'll take it from here, Sierra." That voice rolls through me like a swirl of hot fudge in my blood stream. "Bianca."

Sierra walks away without another word to me. This is why she held me back from leaving. Not because she cared how I found my first night on the floor, but because her boss told her to.

I turn slowly, knowing what I will see.

Salvatore De Luca stands way too close, looking as immaculately put together as he did at the beginning of the evening. Not a dark hair on his handsome head is out of place. His tie is gone, but he looks far from disheveled.

Black ink from a monochromatic tattoo is just visible on the strong column of his neck revealed by the open top two buttons on his shirt. His neatly trimmed beard frames his sensual lips.

I swallow in my suddenly dry throat. "Mr. De Luca."

"I wanted to make sure you are alright after earlier. It is not acceptable for one of our employees to be accosted in the bathroom."

"I'm fine." I'm not about to make a big deal about Lorenzo Ricci's actions.

He's the kind of man who holds a grudge and punishes those who cross him. My father's death is testament to that fact.

"Some might say your behavior earlier in the hallway was on par with Mr. Ricci's."

"Do you say that?" Salvatore asks.

I cock my head to one side. "Does it matter?"

"It does."

"Mr. Ricci scared me."

Tension fills the muscular man's frame. "Did he proposition you?"

"No."

"What did he want then?"

"I don't know." It's a lie, but a small one.

Lorenzo Ricci wanted to know if my new employers were aware of my father's past with the mafia. I'm not about to bring that up and I hope he doesn't either. He and Salvatore are clearly not friends.

"Thank you for making him leave me alone," I say, realizing I should have said it earlier.

"No thanks necessary. If he comes onto you again, you tell me."

So, Salvatore doesn't believe me that his fellow capo didn't proposition me. Not surprising, but it stings.

I wish it didn't. I should not care what this man thinks of me, other than as it pertains to my job.

Yeah. Right.

I care way too much.

"I'll tell Sierra," I promise. Not that I think the waitstaff manager will do anything about it.

"You tell me. Not Franco. Not Sierra. Not the head bartender."

"Um..." How am I supposed to tell Salvatore.

"Give me your phone."

"Why?"

Salvatore waits for me to comply without answering.

Sighing, I pull my phone out of my front jeans pocket with the hand not holding my pepper spray and offer it to him.

"Unlock it."

"Why?" I ask again, this time determined not to do what he says until he gives me an answer.

"I'm going to put my number in it."

"What? Why would you do that?" He can't mean his regular cell number.

He has to mean an extra he keeps around for calls from people outside his inner circle. He's a capo, for goodness' sake. He's not going to give me his main phone number.

"You can't tell me if Lorenzo bothers you again if you can't call me. I'm only in the club one or two nights a week."

"Wouldn't it be better if I told Franco? He could tell you if he thinks it's necessary?" Not that I plan to tell anyone because there won't be anything to tell.

Now that I know he's an Amuni patron, I will stay out of Lorenzo Ricci's way.

CHAPTER 7

SALVATORE

Why is Bianca arguing with me about this?

Getting my number is a privilege. How does she not know that? Her reaction to hearing my name tells me she's aware I am her boss's boss, even if she doesn't know I am a mafia capo. What other cocktail waitress gets offered my number?

Niente. Zilch. None.

"Unlock your phone," I tell her again.

The more she balks, the more determined I am to get my number into her contacts. Her number is already in mine. Ridiculous for what I planned to be a one night stand, but maybe the sex will last longer than one night.

It would be unethical to fire her just for having sex with me. Not that business ethics are a high priority for me.

Making no move to obey me, she stares up at me through narrowed eyes. "Is this another test?"

What the hell is she talking about? "Who tested you?"

Is that what Lorenzo was doing in the bathroom? Testing her about something? Why the fuck would another capo be testing an employee of one of *my* establishments? Lorenzo is one of the few arrogant enough to do it though.

"You tested me." She rolls her eyes. "Like you don't know it. Or maybe you think I'm so stupid, I don't."

"When did I test you?"

"Offering me money for sex." The look she gives me is all attitude.

"I can fire you as easily for insubordination," I warn her. "And that was not a test. I want to fuck you."

"Have you heard of sexual harassment? I mean I know you're practically a dinosaur, but it's been a thing for a long time."

The fuck I'm a dinosaur. I'm one of the youngest capos in the Cosa Nostra. "I'm only thirty-one."

"That's still almost a decade older than me."

She's right. Her application says she's twenty-two, old enough to drink and serve alcohol. And old enough to fuck.

"I have more stamina than the twenty-somethings you're banging." White hot rage burns at the thought of her letting another man touch her perfect curves.

"Nice to know," she drawls smartly. "But I think I'll keep my job, thanks. No dick, no matter how attractive the package it comes with, is worth getting fired."

Getting even backhanded confirmation she's attracted to me takes my semi to full in a few heartbeats. "I offered you five-k. That would tide you over while looking for another job."

"You aren't even going to deny that saying yes would have gotten me fired?" Her bright blue eyes flash with hurt, but she hides it as her too kissable lips purse in disapproval.

My erection pressing painfully against my trousers, my mouth salivates for a taste of her. I want to nuzzle into her neck and inhale her earthy scent from working all evening mixed with the cherries and vanilla.

"We don't let our staff moonlight in the sex trade." Even if they don't do it out of the club.

As a legit business front, we can't risk having Amuni employees that might bring the heat down on us for any reason. That includes sex work, or dealing in their off hours.

"And you say you weren't testing me. Right."

"It wasn't a test. I wanted you to say yes."

"And you didn't care if that got me fired. You are a piece of work, Mr. De Luca."

Unused to being looked at like a pile of dog shit she stepped in, I cross my arms and frown down at her.

"Salvatore," I correct, not wanting her to create distance between us with formality. "And you are still risking getting fired for insubordination."

"You think?" She couldn't look less impressed. "New York may be an at-will employment state, but you still can't fire someone for illegal reasons. And firing me for turning down your sexual advances is illegal in all fifty states."

"You're pretty damn knowledgeable for a twenty-two-year-old with no college education."

"Condescending much? I'm working on my degree."

I'm never surprised. I'm too cynical, but shock rolls through me. Is she lying? "You didn't say anything about going to college."

"When was I supposed to mention it? When I was taking your orders, or maybe when I was clearing the table of dirty glassware?"

It's not on her application, but I don't bring that up. Because it's not unheard of to hide an education. She might not have her degree yet, *if* she's telling the truth, but she would still be considered overqualified for a lot of jobs.

"What are you studying?" I ask.

"Business."

That shouldn't spark approval in me, but it does. We have that in common. And that shouldn't matter for a one-night stand either.

Will she be graduating in a few weeks?

That could explain her not putting her schooling on her job application. She needs a job while she's looking for one in her field, but she won't be staying at Amuni.

Disappointment twinges in my chest. Ridiculous. That is exactly what I want.

"You're twenty-two," I prompt.

"And you're not."

Smart ass. I almost smile. "When do you graduate?"

"Thinking of offering me a job behind the scenes?"

"No."

"That was fast." She shrugs. "Doesn't matter. I won't graduate for another year and a half."

"Why?"

Her look says *none of your business*.

Mine says *tell me anyway*.

Surprisingly, she does. "Most of the time I have to take the bare minimum number of classes to maintain my grants."

"I would think you'd want to get through school as soon as possible."

"Sure. I also want to live in an apartment with no roommates and work a job that doesn't leave me with sore feet at the end of my shift. But none of that is going to happen right now."

"Why?"

"You hire someone to do the books, don't you?" she asks condescendingly.

My eyes narrow and I cross my arms, taking a stance that makes made men nervous.

This little spitfire rolls her eyes at me. "Do the math, *Salvatore*. Working at night makes it easier to attend classes during the day, but there are still only so many hours in a day."

According to her, that means she has eighteen more months of juggling school and work. And she turned down five-k because she did the math and figured keeping this job is worth more to her than that.

She's pragmatic, smart and determined. Which is as much of a turn on as her luscious body.

"You're smart. You have scholarships." She has to.

A look passes over her pretty features I cannot read. "How I pay for school is none of your business, but I know what I know. You can't fire me for refusing to have sex with you. Not without risking financing my early retirement with a lawsuit payout."

Too bad one of the things she knows *isn't* that I'm a mafia capo. She wouldn't be spouting all this shit about reasons I can't fire her, that's for damn sure. She'd know that trying to sue me for sexual harassment would not go well for her.

My don would be pissed as hell if I drew attention with a lawsuit of that nature though.

"So, what's it going to be?" she asks borderline belligerent. "Are you going to fire me for turning you down or can I go home now and come back to work tomorrow?"

"I'm not going to fire you for refusing to have sex with me." I am not desperate, and I don't need to threaten women to get them hanging off my cock.

Even if I don't give a rat's ass about business ethics.

She's good at hiding her emotions when she wants to, but her shoulders relax a little and the tension around her eyes eases. She's relieved.

For all her bravado, Bianca does not want to lose this job, but she doesn't back down from me either. Her refusal to be cowed only makes me like her more.

This beautiful creature has the inner strength to be an asset to the mafia. Like my sister. Unlike my sister, I doubt Bianca could kill to become made though.

There's a reason, besides backward thinking and blatant chauvinism, that there are so few made women in the Cosa Nostra. They tend to seek resolutions that don't require bloodshed.

Nerissa would tell me believing that makes me a chauvinist too. My sister could be right, but like Bianca, I know what I know.

I also know those resolutions could well be better than the ones we employ so easily in mafia business.

Bianca turns and starts walking away.

I should let her go. We've established she's not going to relieve my aching cock tonight. She wants to go home. Alone. Walking the streets alone. Riding the train. Alone.

She does it every night. She's fine.

Cazzo.

I stride after her and grab her upper arm. "Come on. I'll take you home."

"Giving me a ride home isn't going to get your dick wet. I don't even have a bed." She tries to tug her arm away.

I tighten my hold. "Where do you sleep then?"

"I pay for one half of the pullout sofa." How much she does not like that arrangement is in every word.

"And the other half?"

"One of my roommates."

"You share your bed with a roommate? Is he the reason you don't want to fuck me?" I guide her past the door the other employees use to the exit for me and my people.

"Get over yourself. *She* doesn't swing that way and I already explained. I'm not having sex with you if it means losing my job. Besides..." Her voice trails off and I want to know besides what?

But I ask, "And if it didn't mean losing your job?"

I want to know the answer to that more.

Can I promise to keep her at Amuni after fucking her? My plan is to bed and forget her. Will I be able to forget Bianca if she's around to turn me on with every swish of her hips?

"Do you ever stop?" she demands, exasperated.

"Not when it comes to getting something I want." She might as well know that right now.

I want Bianca and I *will* have her.

"Does that mean I have more sexual harassment to look forward to in the future?" She doesn't sound worried by the possibility, or mad. More intrigued.

This woman.

"Probably." Honesty is probably a mistake, but I'm not going to pretend. I'm not hiding what I want.

The only thing I hide is my illegal business transactions as a Cosa Nostra capo from the FEDs.

I shove the door open to the alley behind the club.

My armored RS7 is waiting with my driver and bodyguard. The Audi is the fastest armored vehicle on the market and can make tactical turns in a very tight radius. Ideal for city driving and evasion.

Things are calm right now and the security level is green. Tail cars and additional security are at my discretion.

I choose not to use them. Nerissa bitches, but I am the boss. What I say, goes.

"How have you not lost your club in a lawsuit yet?" She grinds to a halt before we reach my car, tugging at her arm and trying to get loose. "I don't need a ride home."

"Most women want my attention," I inform her, ignoring her comment.

"How about you give it to one of them then?" She yanks at my hold.

"Get in the car, Bianca."

"I'm fine. I have my pepper spray." She holds up the small canister. "I'm dressed to avoid attention. I know how to get myself home safely."

"Tomorrow night, you can do just that. Tonight, I'm driving you."

"Pretty sure you aren't the one driving," she snarks.

"I can be, but my bodyguard won't like being relegated to the backseat."

"Listen, I get that in your rarified rich world with bodyguards and shiny black cars, you think you're doing me a favor."

"I am doing you a favor. This time of night, we'll get you home before the train will and you won't have to walk to and from the station."

"It's not a favor if I don't want it."

"Get your ass in the car, Bianca. I have better things to do than argue with one of my cocktail waitresses in an alley."

"You are super arrogant. Like you could give classes in it."

I don't repeat my demand but tip my head toward the open door of the car.

With a gusty, rich-men-are-such-a-pain-the-ass sigh, she finally starts moving again.

I tell my driver where we are going before sliding into the backseat with Bianca.

She's frowning at me. "How did you know my address?"

"You work for me."

"You looked it up?"

As good as. I read her application for employment. "Yes."

"What else did you look up?"

"I read your application." My phone buzzes and I pull it out.

The text is from Nerissa, wanting to know where I am. I tell her and then tap to access my curated newsfeed.

It's silent in the car. Bianca fidgets, zipping and unzipping her backpack, but she doesn't take anything out.

"You can text a friend to tell them I'm giving you a ride if that will make you feel better."

"No thanks." She huffs and unzips the backpack again. "Did you really read my application?"

"Yes." I don't bother to look up from my phone and I don't tell her I read it right after instructing Sierra to hire Bianca.

"So, you know I worked at Pitiful Princess. Is that why you offered me money for sex? You thought I was a sex worker."

I turn my head so I can see Bianca's beautiful features. "Were you?"

"No."

Shrugging, I look back at my phone. "I must have got it wrong then. I thought that strip joint let the dancers use the back rooms for clients."

There's no way she knows about my connection to the Pitiful Princess. No one outside my inner circle does.

"They do, but it's voluntary. Or it's supposed to be anyway."

That gets my attention. When I look at her, she's staring out her window.

"What do you mean supposed to be? Does the owner pressure you to offer extra curriculars?" I know he doesn't because I'm the owner.

No way is Nerissa pressuring women to sell their bodies. Besides, my second called it earlier. She has nothing to do with the dancers.

"Not the owner. Not even the general manager."

"Then who?"

She finally turns her head back so I can see her troubled expression. "Gino. Ever since he took over as assistant manager and got put in charge of the talent, he's been pushing me and Candi to offer lap dances with a happy ending at least, but he made it clear he wants us to do more."

"More?"

"Turn tricks. I shouldn't have left Candi to fight him alone."

"What do you mean?"

"The other dancers work in the back already. They're not happy about the extra ten percent he takes from them, but me and Candi are the only ones who refuse to touch the customers sexually at all."

"I'm sure your friend is fine. She's been saying no to Gino to this point." And she's not going to have to worry about him if he is taking the extra ten percent Bianca thinks he is and pocketing it.

"Right. He's already put her on the slowest nights. What happens when he cuts her dance time even more? She can't live on what she's making now, and he knows it."

"Is that what happened to you?"

"He went the other direction with me. He knew I worked short shifts four nights a week by choice because of school, so he put me on longer shifts and scheduled me six nights a week."

The sudden need to see her dance is riding me as hard as the desire to bury my cock in her tight pussy.

"What's the difference between giving a lap dance and following through with a hand job?"

"Are you really asking me that? What's the difference between doing a no contact lap dance and participating in a sex act with a stranger? You tell me."

I let her attitude slide because she's right. That was a stupid question.

"Besides, I didn't do lap dances." The glare she gives me would shrivel a lesser man's dick. "I was hired as a pole dancer and that's all I did. I worked the pole four hours a night, Wednesday through Saturday."

"Until Gino changed your schedule."

She jerks her head in an angry nod. "He thought he could force me into doing what he wanted."

The revulsion in her tone says that even if she hadn't gotten the job at Amuni, that was never going to happen.

"And your friend Candi?"

"She'll do lap dances, but she doesn't touch the customers when she does them and she doesn't want to sell her body. That's her choice," Bianca says fiercely.

Like maybe I'll argue with her.

I won't. The Genovese Family does not force women into sex work. Men either. There are plenty of women eager to work our clubs for the safety we provide in exchange for half their take.

We protect our own. Working for us, they don't need a pimp. No one to steal more of their money than the agreed upon take, or beat them when they don't make enough in a given night. If Bianca is right, Gino is acting like a pimp in one way at least.

Taking more than he should of their money.

"Of course it's her choice. Did you try talking to the general manager before looking for another job? Gino is probably trying to impress him by increasing the nightly take."

This woman and her looks.

The one on her face right now questions my intelligence. It should piss me off, but it's having the opposite effect. I'm so hard for her, I could pound nails with my dick and not end up with a piercing.

"You think he doesn't know Gino is pushing the dancers to turn tricks?" she asks with an eyeroll. "Yeah. Not likely. The GM is there almost every night. Maybe he's the one pressuring Gino to bring in more revenue."

I bite down on the need to defend Ugo. He's loyal mafia. No way is he aware that Gino is trying to force reluctant dancers to turn tricks. Nerissa is going to blow a gasket.

I see punishment and maybe death in Gino's future. Nerissa is not one of the women who looks for nonviolent solutions.

"You don't believe me." Bianca shakes her head. "Typical. You assume that because Ugo is upper management, he can't be dirty when we both know that usually means he *is* dirty."

I assume it because Ugo would have to be a fool to take the risk of pissing me off. No way in hell does he want to take a trip to The Box.

Not on any of the building schematics filed with the city, The Box is on a subfloor of the Oscuro building along with holding cells. It's where we keep, interrogate and torture our enemies.

If Bianca is right, that is where Gino will spend his last hours. If she's wrong and it's a matter of an overenthusiastic guy in a new position breaking the rules to impress the boss, he still has to be dealt with.

Nobody breaks my rules. For any reason.

CHAPTER 8

BIANCA

C andi: *The GM asked me a bunch of questions about Gino tonight.*
Bianca: *???*
Candi: *Like am I being coerced to work in the back rooms? That's the word he used. Coerced. Felt like I was talking to a lawyer, or something.*

Wow. For once, my plan worked. When I realized who Salvatore was, I also realized that if Nerissa is his sister, she's mafia too. Which means mafia owns the Pitiful Princess and even though I've never seen him in there, it's under Salvatore's control.

Even if his sister is the face of ownership at the strip club, Salvatore calls the shots. His insistence on taking me home gave me a chance to try to help Candi and I took it.

Bianca: *And?*
Candi: *I told him the truth. Figured it can't get much worse than only two weeknights on the schedule.*

Gino, that greedy pig, cut her from five to four nights and now two? *Stronzo*. Candi can't make rent on that.

Bianca: *Do you need money for rent?*

The nest egg I've managed to save is hidden in an offshore account, but I can transfer funds to my digital bank within twenty-four hours. It would be instant, but I filter the money through other accounts to obscure my connection to the offshore bank.

Just like my dad taught me.

The last couple years of his life, dad grew increasingly paranoid and insisted I learn how to hide my money, showing me how he set up similar accounts for Lorenzo.

Candi: *Looking for another gig.*

Which is not an answer, but I don't push it. Candi doesn't like to depend on other people any more than I do. She knows I'm here if she needs me.

~ ~ ~

After two days off, this is my third night back in the VIP room. I rush through putting on my uniform and ballet flats even though I have time before I have to be upstairs.

I *should* want to avoid Salvatore. Only, I can't stop my eyes from sneaking a peek at the entrance to the VIP area every few minutes when I'm working. I should *not* be disappointed by Salvatore's continued absence, no matter how panty-meltingly hot he is.

I don't do sex. Not ever. His absence absolutely should be a relief. It's not.

I'm nothing but hella relieved that *stronzo*, Lorenzo, is nowhere to be seen though. My phone buzzes as I put my backpack in my locker. I'm not due upstairs for ten more minutes. I like to be early, but I have time to check the text.

Candi: :dancing girl emoji: :celebrate emoji: *!!!!!!!*

Bianca: *What?*

Candi: *Gino didn't come in last night. The GM told us tonight the creep won't be back.*

Bianca: *That's great!*

Relief swirls through the stew of emotions I keep a tight lid on. Candi is going to be alright. Salvatore came through for me and he doesn't know I'm aware he's the owner of Pitiful Princess.

He didn't do it to butter me up enough to slide my panties off.

A little curl of warmth unfurls inside me.

Candi: *The GM redid the schedule too.*

Bianca: *More nights for you?*

Candi: *Yes! And get this. I don't have to pay the house a cut of my tips for the entire weekend to make up for my inconvenience.*

Inconvenience. What a tool. Losing her home because she can't make rent would be more than inconvenient for my friend. It would devastate her. Her mom and sister too. They rely on Candi to support them.

Her mom does what she can, but her arthritis is so bad, she can't make it down the stairs to the outside, much less hold down a steady job. She hasn't left the apartment in all the time I've known them.

Bianca: *Because Gino tried to force you to turn tricks?*

Candi: *Because he cut my hours to do it. The GM says Gino asking is okay and it's on me to say no.* :screwdriver emoji:

Candi clearly agrees with my tool assessment of Ugo. He has probably never been asked to do something by the one person standing between him and being able to make rent.

Candi: *But trying to force me by cutting my income is on the club.* :shocked face emoji: *$$*

That's something at least. Not having to give a cut of her tips will help Candi make up for lost income. But I'm still surprised at Ugo's generosity. I might expect him to offer a single night, maybe Wednesday or Thursday, but the whole weekend?

While most nights of the week, there's a steady stream of johns for the dancers who use the backroom, tips for dancers are way higher on Friday and Saturday. And Candi earns more tips than anyone else. The other dancers don't mind because when Candi dances, they make more money in the back rooms too.

She's got banging curves and this innocence that drives the customers wild with lust.

The GM must not realize how much she earns in tips on a Friday or Saturday night.

He wouldn't give up the club's cut for both days if he did. His bottom line is the business and how much Pitiful Princess earns for mafia. Which is why no one thought talking to him about Gino's behavior would do any good.

We all figured he knew.

Bianca: :party horn emoji: *$$*

Bianca: *Gotta go. Due upstairs.*

Candi: *Slay, girl! Get your* :moneybag emoji: *tips.*

Tips are good on the VIP floor. My new job is perfect except when I'm not watching out hopefully for a glimpse of Salvatore, like some love-struck teenager, I'm looking over my shoulder for Lorenzo. If he comes in again, I'm going to fake throwing up and go home sick.

Even when he doesn't come in, I spend enough time worried he's going to tell Franco, or worse, Salvatore, about my dad. No one in the mafia wants to hire the daughter of a rat.

Guilt by association is the Cosa Nostra motto. Or close enough to it.

Neither man comes in tonight.

With a celebration for some corporate suit getting promoted and a bachelorette party for Daddy's Little Girl, I'm run off my feet. I don't know if Daddy is her actual dad, or the guy she's marrying, but her and her posse order expensive drinks all night.

A party like this goes two ways. One, they tip generously. Two, they barely tip at all. When the women stay past closing and resist every attempt to clear them out, a sour feeling in my gut tells me it's going to be the latter.

"Che palle," I grind out under my breath when they are finally gone, and I see the small stack of cash left on the table.

It's not even a five percent tip. Cursing in Italian, the whole time, I clear the table before dropping the bartender's cut of my tip on the bar.

"Big spenders, not big tippers," I warn him.

He looks at the few bills and shakes his head. "Keep it, Bianca, you earned it. I was worried you were going to suck and screw things up for the rest of us when the big boss insisted a brand-new waitress be put in the VIP lounge, but you work hard and know how to interact with the patrons."

"Uh, thank you." I grab the bills he refuses.

I can't afford to play the oh-no-you-take-it game. I'm saving every penny I can so I can move away from New York and start a new life somewhere else as soon as I graduate from QC.

"What do you mean, the big boss insisted I got put up here? I thought it was Sierra's decision."

I saw Salvatore for the first time five nights ago *after* I got put in the VIP lounge, but why would Franco want me in here?

Salvatore makes more sense. That guy is used to getting what he wants. But how could he know he wanted me if he hadn't seen me yet? Maybe he saw me on the main floor? And waited to come up to the lounge until I was settled in?

"Mr. De Luca," the bartender says, confirming my unlikely suspicion.

Wow. Salvatore's maneuvering should piss me off, or scare me at the very least. It doesn't. He did me a favor, even if his intentions were purely selfish. That first night wasn't a fluke. I take home twice in tips what I did on the main floor.

Even on a night like tonight with the bachelorette party from hell.

And unlike with Gino, when I say no to Salvatore, he doesn't pull out the big guns to try to force me to do what he wants.

He expects me to cave to his hotness.

Which is kind of sweet. And thinking that means I should probably start therapy.

No matter how hot he is, or how much I'm starting to like the bossy capo with the cheesiest pickup lines ever, my vagina is dusty and wearing an out of business sign so old it's starting to weather.

Even if she acts weird around Salvatore, going from dusty to soaking my panties.

Soaking. My. Panties.

That does not happen to me.

It's after five a.m. when I finally clock out and change in the now empty locker room. I'm practically falling asleep standing up.

Sleeping during the day on the sofa bed is never great, which is one of the reasons I started sleeping on the floor of the closet in one of the bedrooms.

My roommates like having access to the couch and the television, so they're happy to let me sleep on the floor in there.

I feel safer in the closet too. It's also quieter and darker, so I get better sleep all around. Only the last two days the super has been doing some plumbing repairs that require access to the wall in the back of the closet.

It's no use trying to sleep in the other bedroom's closet. It's too small and the floor is covered with shoes.

One of my roommates offered her bed, but sleeping there makes me feel exposed. Deep sleep is impossible and my body is craving my bedroll on the floor of the closet. Even if it is stuffy and warm in there today.

The sun will rise soon and with it the temperature in our fourth-floor walkup. It's only May, but even seventy-degree days make for stuffy heat on every floor above the second one in our old building.

Summer will be way worse. When I graduate and leave New York, I won't miss the hot and muggy summers in the City.

Walking to the subway station alone isn't my favorite thing, but everyone else is gone already.

Throwing my shoulders back, and putting my head down, I walk with the confidence of a native New Yorker. A poor one with nothing to steal. My tips are inside a pouch tucked in my underwear and my phone is in the front pocket of my jeans.

If someone cuts the straps on my decrepit looking backpack, they're going to get my uniform dress and shoes. That's it.

Holding tight to my pepper spray in my left hand, my right hand empty so I can easily grab my phone or the knife from my buckle, I head toward the entrance to the subway station. My head might be down, but I'm fully aware of my surroundings.

So, when two dark shapes step away from the buildings on my right, I notice. Adrenalin floods my system, blowing away my exhaustion as they rush toward me. I quickly release the knife from my buckle with practiced movements as I pivot away from the hand reaching out to grab me.

I slash downward, slicing through fabric and skin with ease when another hand comes around my waist.

"Fucking bitch!" the man shouts. "She cut me."

Shifting to my right foot, I spin and I unload my pepper spray on my other assailant, hitting him with over five-million scoville heat units right in his face.

He screams, reaching up to rub his eyes, which is only going to make it worse, but I'm not about to tell him that.

A beefy, tattooed hand lands on my shoulder and I drop down, surge forward and slash upward, giving his right forearm a gash to match the one on his left.

I don't want to kill him. I want him to give up and go help his friend who is now sobbing and rubbing at his eyes with the hem of his t-shirt. This guy is tougher than his friend though. The cuts on his arms don't slow him down and he grabs me...or my hoodie.

Unzipping it, I peel right out of it and my backpack. The flight part of my fight-or-flight instincts finally kicks in and I start to run. Something heavy hits me in the back and knocks me forward onto my hands and knees. My pepper spray goes flying, but I manage to keep hold of my knife.

I roll and just miss the knife intended for my chest.

Che palle. These guys are playing for keeps.

And there are three of them, not two. Not good.

Rolling again, I use the momentum to shove myself to my feet, but the man with the knife is too close. I shuffle backward and a hand covered in blood crosses in front of my face before the attached forearm presses against my neck. He grasps my shoulder with his other hand in a bruising grip.

Reaching up I stab the forearm against my throat and slice sideways.

"Fucking vicious bitch." The arm loosens but doesn't leave my neck entirely.

I can breathe. That's what matters.

The guy with the knife waives it in front of my face. "Think you're so smart, bitch?"

"Smarter than you." Using the other man's hold on me as ballast, I swing my knee up and right into the knife wielding *stronzo's* nut sack.

His face blanches and he doubles over, wheezing.

I stab the guy holding me in the thigh this time and drag my knife upward, pulling it away when he bellows in my ear. He releases me finally and I jump sideways, spin and start to run, but the guy I kneed follows and manages to grab my upper arm.

Throwing myself forward, I try to dislodge his grip. He doesn't let go and my feet drag against the sidewalk as he pulls me back toward him. Then, suddenly, I am free and my body flies forward.

Pain explodes in my head as I collide with the ground. There is a gurgling sound followed by a thump behind me. With no time to worry about nearly knocking myself out, I shove myself back up to my feet and start to run again.

"Bianca, stop. You are safe," a voice that has played a starring role in my dreams the past five nights says harshly from behind me.

My legs stop moving of their own accord, my body reacting to the assurance of safety in Salvatore's tone even more than the command. That's what I tell myself anyway.

There is more scuffling behind me and wanting to see what's happening I start to turn.

"Don't," Salvatore barks. "You do not want to see this."

He's wrong. I do want to see my assailants laid out, but he's right too. Because if I look, then I'm a witness and that's not something I want to be. Not when a Cosa Nostra capo and his security team just took out three men.

"Not turning," I gasp out, winded.

The adrenaline giving me energy takes a nosedive and it's all I can do to stay standing, even more exhausted than before. I try to suck in air, but something in my chest hurts. Sweat drips into my eyes from my forehead. I swipe at it. Damn New York muggy weather.

Blood is smeared on my hands from my assailants. Assholes. It's so hard to get out from under your nails. That's a lesson you never unlearn.

I sway.

"Boss—"

Whatever Salvatore's man says is muffled and I can't make it out. My hazy vision goes black around the edges.

CHAPTER 9

SALVATORE

"Boss, there's blood on this asshole's knife. She might be wounded," Pietro says.

Bianca sways. I catch her as she crumples. She's bleeding like hell from a gash on her forehead and the back of her t-shirt is soaked with it.

Pietro reaches out like he's going to touch her and I jerk her backward, snarling.

He puts his hands up. "I won't touch her boss, but she needs a doctor. There's a rip in the back of her t-shirt and she's still bleeding."

Cazzo. We have to get the Lucchese soldiers off the street, but Bianca needs medical attention now.

I shove my handkerchief against the wound on her back and start jogging to the car. "Franco is still at the club. Call him and then wait here for backup."

Severu De Luca, the Genovese don, and my boss, will go nuclear over this.

"Already called him boss. The Audi is fast, but not ideal for disposing of bodies," my driver says.

A black metallic SUV slams to a halt right behind my SR7. Franco and two men jump out.

"Take the one still living to The Box," I bark. "Store the others on the sublevel until Severu decides how he wants this handled."

He'll want to make a statement with the bodies, but whether it is a pile of dismembered parts dumped on the don's front lawn, or something else is anyone's guess. Some people might think our don has grown soft since getting married, but the opposite is true.

Keeping Catalina safe makes my boss twice as deadly.

"Tell Severu I want to be there for the questioning," I yell toward Franco as I slide into the backseat with Bianca.

What are Lucchese soldiers doing mugging a woman on Genovese territory? Interrogating the *stronzo* my feisty server hit with her pepper spray will have to wait.

"Take us to the hospital and show me how fast this fucking car can go getting there."

We peel away from the curb as I press one of the black hand towels, we keep for situations like this, hard against Bianca's back over my handkerchief. I take another and press down on the oozing wound on her forehead.

She sucks in a breath and her eyes pop open. Her face contorts in pain, but she doesn't cry and she doesn't complain. Her silence bothers me.

"You will be alright. We're taking you to the hospital."

She names a hospital on the other side of the river. I tell my driver to take us to the Cosa Nostra hospital instead.

Her eyes narrow and I have no doubt that the woman in my arms would argue with me, except she loses consciousness again. Cursing out the Lucchese bastards who attacked her, I press harder on the towels.

Too bad there is only one still alive. He's going to pay in pain for attacking a woman in our territory.

For attacking this woman, he will pay double.

~ ~ ~

Bianca is not a good patient. She wakes up to argue with the doctor about treating her here, only to grudgingly give consent to treatment when the doctor explains that not doing so could result in a much longer convalescence.

She answers the questions about her health history grudgingly and asks her own about every damn test they want to run.

I make it clear to both her and the doctor that the tests *will* be done. Every last one of them.

"Bossy," she grumbles.

"Irreparable damage could be done to your spinal cord if we don't find out exactly where the knife went in," the doctor explains patiently.

"What knife?"

"The one you were stabbed with." I text Franco for an update and my driver to bring me a fresh suit.

Franco: *Street cleanup done. On our way to work.*

Good. New Yorkers aren't going to faint at the sight of a little blood on the sidewalk, but nobody needs to see the dead bodies. Witnesses are a mess to clean up. Even when you pay them off, you have to monitor them.

It's a headache.

They should be at the Oscuro building soon. I text Severu to give him a heads up.

Bianca is still arguing with the doctor. "He didn't stab me. One of them hit me in the back. It hurts, but I'll be fine."

I walk over to the bed and grab the hand not getting an IV and press it against my blood-soaked shirt.

The blood is starting to dry, but her hand comes away smeared with red. "You bled all over me and my car. You were stabbed."

Her eyes round and she blinks at her hands like she's trying to make sense of what she sees.

The nurse frowns at me. "Her hands will have to be cleaned again and what if some of that blood is from the other involved parties?"

Involved parties? Is this a nurse, or a lawyer?

I shrug. "She doesn't have any open wounds on that hand."

The nurse looks like she doesn't believe I checked. I don't care what she believes.

My phone rings. It's Severu. I go to the outer room to take the call and give my don a sit rep.

"She's in treatment. I need to get back in there before she tries to sign herself out of the hospital against doctor's orders."

"Why would she do that?"

"Why do women ever do the things they do?"

When I come back into the treatment room, Bianca is laying on her stomach and there is an imaging machine above her. I'm right and she's still bitching, but she's not moving so they can get their pictures. And she's not trying to deny treatment, so I don't intervene.

"There has been no damage to the spinal cord or major vascular structures."

"Then why the hell did she bleed so much?" I demand.

The doctor's explanation sounds like he's throwing out big words because he's getting paid by the syllable.

"In English," I demand. "Medical speak isn't one of the four languages I'm fluent in."

"Excuse me, but I'm the patient and I understood just fine." The defiant words seem to exhaust Bianca.

Refusing to tire her further, I don't argue. I will get my answers from the doctor later.

"Does she need a transfusion?" I ask.

"We can make do with plasma and fluids."

"What part of being a doctor at this facility has anything to do with *making do*?" I fist my hands to keep from grabbing him by his pristine white coat and shoving him against the wall until he apologizes to Bianca for merely wanting to *make do* with her treatment.

He can apologize after she's better.

"A transfusion would be best," he hurriedly adds.

"What's your blood type?" I ask Bianca.

"I have already ascertained that," the nurse informs me in a snippy tone.

What the hell is going on with this place? Have these people forgotten who their patients are and who pays their salaries?

Bianca doesn't seem to hear the nurse and says, "B negative."

Satisfaction I don't understand settles in me. "I'm B negative." I glare at the doctor. "You'll transfuse my blood to her. If she needs plasma after, you will take it from my stores."

I expect an argument from Bianca, but her eyes are shut and her breathing is even.

I walk swiftly toward the bed. "Is she sleeping, or passed out?"

I don't wait for the nurse or doctor to answer and jostle Bianca's arm.

She hunches her shoulder, winces when that hurts her and mumbles. "Leave me 'lone. Tired."

Her eyes don't open.

"Fix her." I let the doctor see his own broken body in my eyes if he doesn't repair the damage done to Bianca. "Give her what you need to not hurt her patching her up."

The nurse grumbles about treating a patient without consent, but the doctor instructs her to administer local anesthetic before irrigating the wound on Bianca's back, or doing anything else.

I insist on a plastic surgeon being brought in to do the stitches on both her back and forehead.

When Bianca wakes up, she immediately goes for the IV needle in her hand. I'm on the phone discussing the purchase of Juniper's bars with Severu, but I see the movement and grab her wrist before she can rip it out.

"No. You need the plasma." She's already had a pint of my blood.

"Is she awake?" Severu asks me.

"Yes."

"Find out why they targeted her."

"You could ask the Lucchese asshole I sent to The Box if he was still alive," I say in Italian.

Fury rolls through me in impotent waves. Since when does a made man bite off his own tongue and choke on his blood rather than face interrogation?

"Whoever sent them had them more afraid of our interrogation techniques than death," Severu says with disgust.

"Pretty sure you and Angelo are the reasons the other families fear being interrogated by us." Not that I can't inflict damage when necessary, but both the don and his head enforcer have torture down to a fine art.

And the New York underworld knows it.

Bianca gasps, drawing my attention back to her.

"Do you need something for the pain?" I ask her.

"You sound damn solicitous," Severu mocks me.

Bianca shakes her head. "I'm woozy as it is."

"Is it true that you insisted on giving her your blood for the transfusion?" my boss asks.

"We're the same blood type."

"And I'm sure they have pints of B or O negative on hand."

"No doubt." We keep a supply of O negative available at all times because it's the universal donor blood type. "I wasn't letting the doctor put some random guy's blood into her veins."

"That's how blood transfusions usually work," Severu says, sounding inexplicably amused. "You didn't have to use your private supply."

"I didn't." Not for the first bag anyway.

All capos and their inner circles in the Genovese Family keep plasma in cryo storage, refreshing the supply once a year, or after it gets used.

"You had the doctor take directly from your vein?" Severu asks, all humor leached from the tone that reveals nothing of his thoughts.

"She needed the blood." I'm glad Bianca doesn't speak Italian.

This whole conversation is not something she needs to hear.

"Is there something I need to know about her?" Severu asks.

I grimace at what he's implying.

I'm a capo. I don't get married without the don's approval. Not that Severu exercises his right of refusal. So far anyway and he's been don for over five years.

"Other than I want to fuck her until her throat is raw from screaming my name?"

Bianca squirms with discomfort again and I push the call button. She's getting pain meds, whether she likes it, or not.

Severu barks out a laugh. "It's like that?"

"It's like that."

"Sounds like she's got some healing to do before that can happen."

"Doctor said minimum two weeks before anything strenuous."

"You asked?" Severu's laughter lasts longer this time. "You have got it bad, Salvatore."

"You know how it is. You want what you can't have."

Cold water saturates my chest and down the front of my slacks. Shouting, I jump back and lose my grip on my phone.

"What the hell?" I demand.

Bianca looks up at me, her pallid face showing exhaustion and pain, but no remorse. "I knocked it over."

"And the lid slipped off too?"

"It was hard to get enough water, so I took the lid off."

Cazzo. I should have been paying attention. "I'll get you a new bottle of water."

This one had better be easier for her to sip from or the medical staff here will find out how unpleasant it can be to deal with untreated pain.

CHAPTER 10

BIANCA

The truth hiding reality rolls off my tongue like Mr. Ruhnke taught me. "Don't lie when the truth will protect you better," was one of his favorite sayings.

Since everyone who mattered in my life before him hurt me with their lies, I follow his advice whenever I can.

I did knock over my water bottle. Right down the front of Salvatore De Luca's expensive suit, which he must have changed because it looks pristine with no splotches of dried blood.

And I *couldn't* get as much as I wanted to use with the lid on.

Hopefully the ice water bath cooled off his libido.

The *stronzo* wants me because I refused him.

He's only taking care of me because he wants to use my body. I don't know what the deal is with his blood, but he probably wants me to feel more beholden to him.

Newsflash: I don't.

Who is going to pay for this swanky hospital he's got me in? The room I'm in is light years away from a cubicle in a public hospital ER. It's like the kind of hotel rooms my mom insisted we stay in for our family trips before she left my dad and me, taking my twin with her.

I told Salvatore to take me to the one covered by my insurance. I know I did, but did he listen?

No.

Well, I didn't sign anything agreeing to treatment and I'm not paying a dime for any of this.

My glare is wasted on him because he's too busy picking up his phone from where he dropped it on the floor.

"You still there?"

Pause.

"I'll talk to her."

Her has got to be me, but I don't know what he wants to talk to me about. Or who he's talking to. My guess is someone in the mafia because they're speaking Italian.

Whoever it is, Salvatore feels comfortable telling them he wants to have sex with me. Jerk.

If there was any water left in the bottle I found on the swing table by my bed, I'd trick him into leaning over and dump it on his head.

He doesn't know I speak Italian. Just like he assumed I didn't have a college education, he assumes I don't speak our mother tongue.

Okay, I have my mom's blue eyes and my grandfather's red hair. And maybe I do look more like my mom's side of the family than my dad's, but my name is Bianca Gemelli. You can't get much more Italian than that.

Salvatore should know that not all Italians have dark hair and eyes. My nonna's mother was blonde with blue eyes the same shade as mine. The same shade as nonna's.

My *bisnonna* came over from Italy to marry my great-grandfather. An arranged marriage. I shudder internally at the thought.

They still happen in the mafia, even now. One good thing came from getting kicked out of the Genovese Family by Lorenzo Ricci. No one is pushing me to marry some stranger for the sake of *la famiglia*.

Salvatore demands pain meds, which I tell the nurse I don't want, and another water bottle for me. "This one had better be easier for her to drink from."

"The bottles are designed to require minimum suction, Mr. De Luca," the nurse assures him.

"She had trouble drinking out of that one," he says like it's the nurse's fault.

Her face mottles under his tone. Is she scared, or angry at being spoken to like her life is on the line if I don't get a working water bottle?

"Do you need a towel?" she asks him politely enough.

Salvatore glowers down at his wet clothing. "Yes."

The nurse turns away, probably to get the towel, but she winks at me and gives me a subtle thumbs up. She knows the water bottle isn't defective. She assumes that I dumped the water on him on purpose. She's right.

I smile back.

"Don't smile at her, she's doing her job," Salvatore barks.

The nurse rolls her eyes and I have to stifle the urge to laugh. Not least because it will hurt if I do. Any kind of movement, including breathing, hurts right now. My whole body feels like one big ache and tomorrow is going to be worse.

The second day always is.

So, no laughing. Because pain, but also because I don't want to get the other woman in trouble.

"As a person who makes her living in the service industry, I will always show my appreciation for someone doing their job." My voice isn't strong, but I don't slur my words and Salvatore gets the message.

The nurse hands him a neatly folded towel.

"Thank you," Salvatore says shortly, still frowning.

Surprise flashes in the nurse's eyes, but her lips remain pressed together in a straight line. "As you said, it's my job."

It sounds like she's saying *you're welcome* but I have a lot of experience saying something that sounds like one thing, but I mean in a totally different way. The nurse isn't a pushover and she's not impressed by the capo's grudging appreciation.

Salvatore doesn't seem to care either way, which fascinates me.

My only experience with another capo is Lorenzo Ricci, as limited as it was. But my dad talked about Lorenzo. A lot. The older capo is not the type of man to let even the tiniest indication of disrespect slide. He would go ballistic if I spilled water on him too.

The nurse bustles from the room and Salvatore moves closer to the bed. "Why did those men come after you?"

"You'll have to ask them." He said something about a Lucchese soldier on the phone.

The Luccheses are another one of the Five Families in the New York Cosa Nostra and the family of the current godfather, Don Caruso. Why would their men mug someone in Genovese territory?

The Five Families are allies and sometimes rivals, but they usually stick to their own territories.

Salvatore is not impressed by my answer. "I'm asking you."

"I don't know."

Salvatore knows more about what happened than I do. I only know three men attacked me. He knows they are from a rival family.

"You must know something. Three Lucche—three men attacked you. What are you mixed up in that has made you a target?"

"Are you victim blaming?"

"I am asking you: Why were you targeted by three killers?"

They were a kill team?

"Maybe I wasn't the target." Talking is harder than it should be, dizziness making the words hard to string together.

Nausea makes my stomach roil too and I take shallow breaths, trying to control it.

Salvatore strides to the door, yanks it open and says something to someone outside. His voice is muffled and I can't tell what he says, but his tone is easy enough to decipher. He's angry and impatient.

I'm not surprised when a few seconds later, the nurse returns with a tray holding a fresh water bottle, a vial of clear liquid (probably the pain medication I said I didn't want) and a hypodermic.

"Give her something for the pain," Salvatore demands. "She can't talk without it hurting."

Of course, he's worried about my ability to communicate. Why else would a busy and powerful capo be hanging around my hospital room? He wants answers.

Too bad for him. No matter how easy it becomes for me to talk, I still won't have anything to say he wants to hear. I don't know why I'm the one lying here in a hospital bed. I don't live in Lucchese territory. I don't know any Lucchese made men.

The nurse prepares the hypodermic before approaching the bed. Her steady, compassionate gaze meets mine. "This is a mild opioid. It won't knock you out, but it will make you drowsy."

Even with my dad's history, I want that shot. I hurt.

But I shake my head. "No. I still have to get home."

Thinking of trying to deal with this pain in my current living situation would make me cry. If I let myself cry.

Bile rises in my throat and I take a hasty sip of water to settle my stomach. It doesn't work. The room is spinning around me.

Salvatore says something, but his words sound like they're coming through a wind tunnel.

"Are you feeling nauseated?" the nurse asks, her face too close to mine.

I don't like people close to me. Even medical professionals. Maybe that's why I'm feeling so sick. This whole hospital thing is triggering my need to get away from people big time.

I swallow, trying not to vomit.

"I'll take that as a yes. Is your heart racing?"

"Just anxiety." Something I have to live with.

She looks worried. "Are you feeling dizzy?"

"Room is spinning," I get out before clenching my teeth on the need to throw up.

"I think you're having a reaction to the local anesthetic."

"You were supposed to ask about allergies," Salvatore says in a deadly tone.

"I did, but a patient can be fine with a medication the first ten times they are exposed to it and have a reaction on the eleventh."

"Fix it!"

I don't know about the nurse, but my body wants to obey Salvatore's roar.

CHAPTER 11

SALVATORE

It's another harrowing forty minutes before the medical team have Bianca's reaction to the local anesthetic treated. It leaves her looking even more exhausted and fragile than before.

My response to her saying she still doesn't want the pain meds is not calm.

"The fuck are you talking about? You're not leaving the hospital." If she tries to get out of that bed, she will fall flat on her face. Before she can argue more, I tell the nurse, "Give her the codeine."

The nurse makes a point of looking at Bianca and pretending I am not standing right here. "Do you want this medication? I can give you the analgesic by itself, but it won't help as much with the pain."

"No strong meds." Bianca blinks, clearly trying to stay awake.

She needs rest. And to be comfortable. "You are in pain. You will allow the nurse to administer the drug."

The stubborn woman shakes her head at me. "I can't stay here."

What the hell does she think she is going to do? Go back to her shitty apartment and rest on her half of the sofa bed?

"You are staying," I tell her.

Despite the dark bruises under them, her blue eyes flash defiance at me. What the fuck is wrong with her? I'm her boss. I am *the* boss and she may not know I'm mafia, but she knows I own the club she works at.

She's still out of it from everything that has happened. That's why she's not thinking straight.

And it's the reason she needs to stay right where she is. In that hospital bed.

"Don't bother looking at me like that, Bianca. You are staying the night here and probably tomorrow too. And you are taking that damn shot. "

"That's not your choice." She's trying to sound tough, but her voice is so thready it makes my argument for me and if she wasn't so out of it, she'd realize it too.

Patience gone, I don't softshell this. "It is if I say it is." I zero in on the nurse. "Give her the pain medication, or look for another job, because you won't be working here any longer."

Getting her fired is the least I can do to her. And working at this hospital, taking care of the patients she does, she has to know that.

She squares her shoulders and looks me right in the fucking eye. "I am not one of your soldiers, Mr. De Luca. I have an ethical duty to treat my patient as *she* requires."

"Wow. I just got a lady boner," Bianca says, obviously impressed by the other woman's foolish bravery.

I'm done dealing with this woman. "Get the doctor in here now."

Alarm washes over Bianca's features.

"I'll take it if you're footing the bill for all this." She frowns at me and sweeps her arm to indicate the hospital room.

Wincing, she lets the arm fall back to the bed.

"Don't wave your arms around like that," I bite out. What the fuck is wrong with her? "You'll tear your stitches."

"Are you sure you want this?" The nurse holds the needle up for Bianca to see.

"Yes."

The nurse nods to Bianca and then gives me a baleful stare, "I will instruct accounting that all charges related to Miss Gemelli's care are to be billed to you."

Like that is some kind of threat. "I already took care of it."

Bianca's tired eyes show shock and then something else. Maybe gratitude? But then her expression turns mutinous. "I'm not having sex with you because you pay my medical bills."

That's one thing we agree on. "You'll let me fuck you because your pussy weeps for me and for no other reason."

BIANCA

Heat climbs up my neck and into my cheeks at Salvatore's crude words. I cannot believe he said that and in front of the nurse.

My ovaries are *not* swooning. Not.

Oh, yes, they are, my inner voice sings.

Pretending not to hear it or his arrogant, and strangely arousing claim, I focus on the woman prepping the syringe.

When she's done, she administers the medication through my I.V. port. "The codeine phosphate will act more quickly this way, but you'll have to take the accompanying analgesic orally."

I nod.

"It will take about ten minutes for the full effect, but you should start feeling relief immediately."

I feel woozy. And it's easier to breathe. So yeah. Relief.

Feeling thirsty, I reach for my new bottle of water, but my hand misses. Okay, really woozy.

Before the nurse can help me, Salvatore is there, grabbing the bottle and holding it so the straw is right in front of my mouth.

I take a drink and almost regret pouring my other water over him immediately. The cold liquid sooths my throat so much.

"Don't drink too much at once," the nurse warns me. "Some people get nauseated when they take opioids."

"Get her something for the nausea."

Frowning, I push the water bottle away from my face. "Don't be so bossy. I'm not nauseated anymore."

"But you might get that way. She should be prepared."

"We are always prepared, Mr. De Luca," the nurse claims. "If you could step aside. I need to give my patient the acetaminophen."

Salvatore puts his hand out imperiously. "I'll do it."

The nurse looks to me for permission and I give a small nod. She may not realize how deadly the capo's anger can be, but I do. He killed three men only a couple of hours ago because they were mugging someone on his turf.

The nurse hands the tiny paper cup to Salvatore. Only, instead of handing it to me like I expect, he slides one arm behind my shoulders and helps me sit up.

Then, guiding the cup to my lips with his other hand, he says, "Open up."

The position feels intimate, but it's not uncomfortable. For some mysterious reason, having Salvatore inside my personal bubble doesn't bother me.

"I could do this myself," I mumble anyway.

He ignores me and waits for me to obey him. The man is not going anywhere until I do. So, I open my mouth and he tips the pills into my mouth, and offers me the water bottle straw immediately after.

I manage to swallow the pills and take a few extra draws of water because I can. When I'm finished, he puts the water bottle down and settles me back against the bed, but doesn't step away from me.

Right. More questions.

"Okay, get it over with," I say with what should be a wave of my hand but ends up being a wiggle of my fingers.

Huh. Not sure how mild the opioid is if I can't even control my limbs properly.

"Get what over with?" Salvatore asks.

"Your questions." The words come out a little slurred and my eyelids grow heavy.

"You're not going to question her now?" The nurse sounds scandalized.

Or annoyed.

Maybe both.

"Leave." What patience the capo has is used up and he's giving the poor nurse a death glare.

With him the death part isn't a euphemism, so I shoo her which turns out to be another series of finger wiggles. "Go. It's okay. Gonna fall asleep soon anyway."

And Salvatore can blame himself for that. He's the one that insisted on the pain medication.

"Did you give her too much? She shouldn't be this affected by codeine. It's not as strong as morphine."

"Ooh, you wanted to ask your question and now you're gonna have to wait." I giggle.

"I gave her exactly what the doctor prescribed." Offense vibrates in every word of the nurse's defense of herself. "Your girlfriend lost a lot of blood, that can impact how strongly she will react to medications until her blood supply has renewed itself."

"She's on her second transfusion bag."

Alarmed, I manage to get my eyes open to stare blearily up at Salvatore. "Can't donate that much at once."

"You're not donating any blood," he tells me condescendingly.

"Not me. You."

"Mr. De Luca donated one pint of fresh blood and another of his stored plasma, Miss Gemelli."

"Not his girlfriend," I slur as my eyes close again and my body drags me toward sleep.

SALVATORE

Bianca sleeps through the nurse taking her vitals and a woman coming in to ask if either of us wants breakfast.

I'm reluctant to leave and order breakfast. Bianca needs looking after. The woman clearly doesn't take her own health seriously. She has a stab wound and gash on her forehead. Not to mention her rejection of the local anesthetic used on her. Her body needs rest.

If I leave, she'll probably try to check out the minute she wakes up again.

While I wait for my food and coffee, I check messages on my phone. Severu wants the three bodies delivered to the godfather, Don Caruso. Miceli is going to do it, but asks if I want to come along.

Hell, yes, I do.

Those Lucchese *stronzos* attacked one of my employees, outside of one of my clubs. Whoever sent them needs to know I'm coming for him.

Bianca moans and my head snaps up. Her eyes are closed, but she's frowning and moving restlessly on the bed.

I stand and go to her, saying her name softly. "Bianca."

She doesn't respond, locked in her nightmare. No dream would make her face contort in that rictus of agony. She's dreaming about the attack, I bet. Her head whips violently back and forth on the pillow and that can't be good for her concussion.

Mild, or not.

I lay my hand against her cheek, holding her head immobile. The zing of connection surprises me under the circumstances.

"Bianca, it is alright, little one," I tell her in Italian, leaning down so I am practically whispering in her ear.

She stops moving, her face losing some of the stress lines. I rub her arm and talk to her in Italian until she's breathing deeply, and her body shows only the relaxation of sleep.

"Boss, your breakfast is here," Pietro says from outside the door.

My men have strict instructions not to come into Bianca's room. She is only wearing a thin gown and no bra or underwear.

I found a stack of cash in a pouch tucked into her underwear when I undressed her. That was the first time the nurse gave me attitude. I told her Bianca is my girlfriend to get her off my back.

No way was I letting someone else undress her. Not even the nurse.

The cash is probably her tips from last night. I put it with the rest of her things in the closet.

"Let her through." Pulling my hand away from Bianca's soft skin, I turn to face the woman returning with my breakfast and point to a desk-sized table on the other side of the private room. "Put it over there."

But before I can sit down, Bianca gets restless again. I return to her, laying my hand against her neck, brushing my thumb along the underside of her jaw and speaking to her in low Italian. She settles almost immediately.

"Put my food here." I indicate the swing table by Bianca's bed.

After the woman leaves, I drag the chair closer and maneuver myself so I have one hand on Bianca's arm and the other available to feed myself. I speak to her between bites of food and sips of coffee, telling her about my plans to buy a string of bars and turn them into nightclubs.

To make my own mark on *la famiglia* and prove I didn't get named capo because of who my cousin is. Being my father's son will always influence my role within the family, but I'm *not* Little Sal. I am Salvatore De Luca and I can make those bars into something that will make millions for the Genovese Family.

I speak in Italian, too low for anyone outside her room to hear me. Not that I'm worried. I have men in the outer room that will make sure no one comes near the door without me knowing.

I'm taking my last sip of coffee when my phone buzzes. It's Franco.

CHAPTER 12

SALVATORE

I move away from the bed to answer. "What do you know?"

"I sent their pictures to the don's security team. They came back with names and their affiliation."

Most likely the request for information was forwarded to Catalina, the don's wife. No one outside my cousin's inner circle knows that his wife has more intel than the FEDs when it comes to organized crime families.

"Who do they work for?" I ask Franco.

We know they are Lucchese soldiers because of the tattoos on their left wrists, but we don't know what capo they are under.

The Genovese mark our people too, but we hide the symbol with other tattoos in ink only visible under black light. Every one of us from soldier to don is required to have the black light app on our phones, so we can confirm affiliation when necessary.

The invisible tattoos make us harder to spot by law enforcement and Severu has been pushing for all the Five Families to adopt the practice. Most have, but some capos still require a visible mark of loyalty.

Which narrows down who the capo is that the dead men worked for.

Before Franco can answer me, a moan comes from Bianca's bed. Shit. She kicks her blanket off and flails. She's going to rip out her IV. Rushing over, I grab her hand and settle her down before going back to my phone call.

"Who?" I ask again.

"Caruso's nephew."

Cazzo. There is no such thing as coincidence in the life. Bianca has nothing to do with those soldiers being in our territory. She was just in the wrong place at the wrong time.

Henrico (call me Henry because I'm a douche) Caruso thinks he should be the next godfather because he is his uncle's heir and will become Don of the Lucchese after the godfather's death.

But Don Caruso has already told the other Five Families that Severu should be made godfather upon his death. Even if Severu is younger than any Cosa Nostra godfather in the last hundred years.

The other dons will listen and cast their votes for Severu as long as nothing happens between now and Don Caruso's death that makes our family look weak.

Like not being able to protect our territory.

This morning, we killed the *bastardos*. A win. But if Bianca hadn't fought like a fucking warrior, she would be dead and we would still be looking for who did it. She kept her attackers busy long enough for us to drive by on the way back to my place.

It was good luck, but not coincidence, we got there in time. I instructed my driver to take a small detour by the club after Franco texted me to tell me that the VIP lounge closed late. A bachelorette party that didn't want to leave. I knew Bianca would be heading to the train and wanted to make sure she got there alright.

Nothing soft in that.

Once we have sex (repeatedly), this obsession with the cocktail waitress will abate. Amazing lay, or bad one, I'm not looking for a relationship. Especially with a woman nine years younger than me.

Offering her a ride home was just another opportunity to persuade her into my bed.

"You're going to have to get someone to cover Bianca's shifts for the next few weeks."

As long as her stitches hold and her concussion doesn't get worse, she could return to Amuni in only a few days. However, no way am I letting her go back to work where other men can ogle her gorgeous curves until we've had our fill of each other.

This jealousy is new. I'm a possessive guy. I don't share, but I also don't do relationships where that possessiveness lasts beyond a night, or two.

Once I bury my cock in her hot pussy, this need to keep her out of circulation will abate.

Franco's long silent pause makes me itch.

"You want me to keep her job open for her?" he finally asks.

"What the hell? Are we fucking heartless? She got mugged on her way home from working at Amuni. Even if those assholes hadn't targeted her for her connection to us, we wouldn't fire her for taking sick leave, would we?"

"Is this a trick question?" Franco asks, sounding amused. "That's exactly what we would normally do."

"Well, we're not doing it this time. And we need to take a fucking look at how we treat our employees."

"Says the man who intended to pay a waitress to sleep with him and then fire her for it."

I regret telling Franco my plans. "When you say it like that, I sound like a heartless jerk."

"Uh..."

"Okay, enough with the comedy routine." I was going to pay her 5K.

It would have been enough for her to live on while looking for another job. Probably.

"I wasn't joking, boss."

No, he is just telling it like it is. I am no soft touch. Not even close. Pops raised me to be hard and life did the rest. Whether the 5K would have been enough, or not, should not be a blip on my conscience.

But it's the clang of a five-alarm fire. "Keep her position open for her, or create one when she's ready to come back. I don't give a damn which. She's got enough to worry about without stressing over losing her job."

"Did you get religion, or something?"

Or something. "I'm Catholic like all good capos."

"Right, boss." Franco laughs. "The last time you were in a church was for the don's wedding."

There's no point in denying the truth, so I don't.

My cock is ruling my head right now, and worse, I'm letting it.

What the hell?

After I end the call with Franco, I take off my suit jacket and tie. Hanging them in the closet I can't help noticing Bianca's beat up bag and threadbare clothes. She's got multiple roommates and makes good tips, as the thick bundle of cash sitting on the shelf attests.

Why does she dress like she's barely getting by?

Does she have a drug habit?

Considering how opposed she is to taking pain meds, that's unlikely. But then what?

I ponder the conundrum that is the sexy cocktail waitress I will now have to wait two weeks to fuck vigorously while I kick off my shoes and remove my belt. After tucking both in the closet I cross the room to her bed, reaching her just in time.

She's already having another bad dream. Damn it.

Is it the codeine? I know from experience morphine can cause some pretty lousy dreams. I don't like how distressed she gets.

Bianca isn't going to sleep quietly without me. After putting my gun in easy reach, I don't feel a drop of guilt climbing onto the bed beside her. I put my arm over her waist and she turns her face toward me, inhaling like she's seeking my scent.

My dick grows predictably hard, but I ignore it, closing my eyes and willing myself to sleep.

BIANCA

A deep rumbly voice infiltrates my consciousness. "Leave her the fuck alone. She's sleeping."

"We need to take her vitals, Mr. De Luca," another male voice responds, this one softer and almost chipper.

The body underneath me tenses. "Get a female nurse in here then. You aren't coming near her."

Someone is with me? In the hospital bed? And I slept? How?

My head is nestled in his neck, and I'm laying half on top of him. A familiar scent of expensive aftershave mixed with a unique fragrance I have only smelled once. When Salvatore De Luca had me cornered outside the kitchen at Amuni.

Shocked, my eyelids fly open and I try to shove myself away.

His arm over my hip stops me going anywhere. "Relax, *dolcezza*. No one is going to hurt you."

Before my brain processes Salvatore's words, my body obeys him, going boneless and relaxing into him. What the hell?

How did he do that?

I tilt my head to look up at him and our eyes lock. Whatever he's thinking is hidden behind expressionless steel gray orbs. While I'm sure he can see the battle between nerves and confusion going on inside me.

Opening my mouth to tell him to let me go, a jaw cracking yawn comes out instead. I slap my hand over my mouth, wincing when the movement pulls something in my back.

"Do you need more pain meds?" He studies me, like he's making his own determination. "You only went into deep sleep after draping yourself over me."

Cheeks hot with mortification, I try to move again.

"Settle." He holds me against him while brushing my hair back from my face. "Are you in pain?"

"Not enough to need more codeine." I can't believe I slept next to someone else.

Not even next to. On top of.

A male someone too. One who makes no bones about wanting to sex me up.

I don't feel hypnotized, but this is weird. Even how relaxed I feel right now is freaking me out, but my body is not sliding into a panic attack. No, my heartrate and breathing are totally chill.

"Are you a vampire?" Aren't they the ones that are supposed to be able to hypnotize?

His gaze narrows. "Are you feeling alright? You have only had two doses of codeine and they were four hours apart."

It's the codeine. It must be. That's why I'm so chill like this with him. More than chill, I do not actually want to move.

My brows draw together in confusion. "I don't remember a second dose."

"You were asleep when it was administered."

"I thought they were supposed to wake me up."

"I woke up." He says it like him making medical decisions for me is a given.

It isn't.

"You aren't the patient," I remind him.

"I took responsibility for you."

"That's not how it works." Like at all. It doesn't matter who is paying the bills for my stay at this luxurious medical facility.

I am the patient and an adult. He isn't even related to me. He can't legally make decisions for me.

"It is here." He's complacent.

Me? Not so much. "I bet the nurse was pissed at you."

"She refused to administer the second dose without waking you. I called the doctor in to do it."

"You're a bully. You know that right?"

"I am the boss."

"But that doesn't make you a god." Not even if he is a capo.

"God would be less wrathful."

Caspita. What did he threaten the doctor with? "You didn't get the nurse fired, did you? I like her."

"No. She was watching out for you."

And he likes that? "You're a very confusing man."

"Not at all. I am who I am and everyone around me knows who that is."

Lie. Lots of people don't know he's a capo, or what that means if they do know. I doubt all his employees know he's a made man who has killed before.

"So, they all know you sleep in hospital beds with wounded waitresses?" I push.

"This is a one off. You would not settle. The codeine gave you bad dreams."

I remember some of those dreams and they have nothing to do with the codeine. "And you insisted they give me a second dose? Thanks a lot."

"You're welcome. As long as I stayed near, you slept fine, despite your dreams."

But why? I don't sleep well with anyone near. Not even my savior, Mr. Ruhnke. For sure not my roommates. And a man who wants to screw me? I shouldn't have slept a wink with him in the bed.

"How long since the last dose?" I ask.

"Two hours."

"I slept six hours?" With him in the bed? Repeating it isn't making it any easier to believe.

"You did."

"I'm sorry."

"For what?" His eyes try to see into my brain. "Did you bring those men into my territory?"

"You consider the area around your club your territory? That's pretty arrogant." I'm teasing him and I'm not sure why.

But he doesn't know that I know he's mafia. So, his claim *is* arrogant.

"Answer my question," he demands without responding to mine.

Typical.

"No, they didn't come to Manhattan looking for me. I don't know why they were near the club or why they attacked me. I told you." That I remember.

"What are you sorry for then?"

"Keeping you here with me. I'm sure you had better things to be doing."

"Sleeping here, or at my apartment." He shrugs, lifting my body with the movement. "It's the same."

"I'm sure your bed is much more comfortable than this one." And I doubt very much he's the kind of man to let women sleep cuddled on top of his chest.

"You'll find out soon enough," he assures me, his arrogance very much in evidence.

"Yeah, that's not happening."

"You don't think so?"

"No." But for the first time in my life, I might be lying when I say I'm not interested in sex. "You need to go."

"Are you trying to kick me out of your hospital room?"

"If I say yes, will you leave?"

"Doubtful."

I sigh and let my head drop back to that super comfy, and ridiculously *comforting* position nestled into the strong column of his neck. "Bully."

"I am looking out for you."

"Until I give you sex, which is not happening."

"Until I am not," he corrects me, sounding as surprised by his own words as I am.

Huh. "That doesn't sound like a one-night stand that ends in me losing my job."

"No, it doesn't, does it?"

CHAPTER 13

SALVATORE

W hy did I say that?

I don't do relationships. And if I did do a relationship, it wouldn't be with a barely making it cocktail waitress nearly ten years younger than me.

Yet, I practically promised not to fire her after we have sex.

"Will I be able to leave soon?" she asks, her breath puffing against my neck enticingly.

Now is not the time to get an erection.

Before I can answer, one of my men knocks on the door and then opens it a crack. "The nurse is here to take Miss Gemelli's vitals."

"A woman?"

"Yes, boss."

"You shouldn't have a let a man in here."

"I'm sorry, boss. He was a nurse."

I give a shit. "Orders are orders."

"Yes, boss." His voice is infused with a healthy dose of fear.

As it should be. I see to discipline personally when the refraction occurs under my orders. Unlike some of the older capos, I don't leave it to my second-in-command. My sister would enjoy it too much.

She is feared among my men, but my punishments are worse and I am feared more.

A woman dressed in nurse's scrubs comes into the room. She's younger than the nurse from early this morning, with bright blonde hair pulled up in a bouncy ponytail.

She smiles at me, paying no attention to Bianca. "Good morning, Mr. De Luca. Is it alright if I take the patient's vitals?"

Affront rolls off of Bianca and from one breath to the next she goes from lax and pliant to sitting up and glaring. "That question would be better directed toward me. I am the patient."

"I could take your vitals, Mr. De Luca," the nurse says in a flirty tone. "If you'd rather."

"Are you kidding me?" Bianca mutters under her breath.

She casts a glare up at me over her shoulder as if it's my fault the nurse is behaving like we're in a kink club and offering to play *doctor*.

"What part of me being in this bed with your fucking patient makes you think I'm open to your flirting?" I ask the nurse in clipped tones.

"You're not with her though. She told Amanda that she's not your girlfriend. We all understand why you said she was."

"Yes?" I ask in a tone that should clue her into how precarious her position is right now.

"Oh, yes. You thought you needed to say that so you would be allowed into the exam room with her."

I *had* said it to give my insistence on overseeing Bianca's care some legitimacy. That doesn't mean I enjoy having this woman bring attention to that fact, or knowing that she and her colleagues have been gossiping about me.

"You and your coworkers would be smart to keep your nose out of my business."

Instead of being frightened like an intelligent human being, the nurse looks like she just soaked her panties.

"Everybody knows you brought her in because you feel sorry for her. She was attacked outside your club, but that doesn't make it your responsibility," she says earnestly.

"There is no world in which I need your advice." I am done with this woman. "Take Bianca's vitals and get the hell out of here."

Finally, her smile drops and she blinks like she's going to cry. For fuck's sake.

"Do you even know how to take her vitals?" I demand.

"Y-yes. Of course. I'm trained."

"Trained as what?" I ask suspiciously.

"I'm a fully qualified medical assistant." Her eyes shine with suspicious moisture and I don't feel a spark of compassion.

"Get a fucking nurse in here and don't come back."

She turns and runs from the room.

"That wasn't very nice." Bianca presses the controller so the head of the bed raises.

Without her sharing my space, there's not really enough room on the bed for both of us. My reluctance to leave her is ridiculous.

"I need to go." Ignoring the weird twinge of conscience the words give me, I climb out of the bed.

With a look toward the bathroom door, Bianca shifts her legs over the side of the bed, doing her best to hide the pain the movement gives her.

"I am trained to read micro expressions," I tell her conversationally.

She shrugs, pretending that doesn't hurt either.

"Stop moving like that, or I'll instruct them to give you something to knock you out with your next dose of pain medication."

Fear flashes through her eyes. "No. Don't. I can't be unconscious here. Please, Salvatore."

It costs her to say please like that. Enough that she can't hide that either.

"You slept through the night," I remind her.

"Sleeping and unconscious are not the same thing."

No, they are not, but I don't expect her to make the distinction so adamantly. "Then, stop moving and hurting yourself."

"I won't heal if I don't move. Besides, I have to pee."

This woman. Even terrified of being drugged she can't help talking back.

"You argue with me more than anyone else." I put my arm out for her.

Sliding off the bed to her unsteady feet, she takes my arm without a word. At first, I'm uncertain about leaving her in the bathroom alone, but she is adamant.

So, I stand outside, with the door open, in case she falls.

She refuses to hold my arm walking back to the bed. But it's beyond her to get back onto the bed without help. Her solution is to stay up.

Mine is to lift her onto the bed.

She settles with the blanket over her.

"You're damn stubborn."

"Pot meet kettle." She rolls her eyes.

Rolls. Her. Eyes.

At *me*.

"You should do what I say," I inform her.

"Yeah, no. I am not one of your soldiers, capo."

Everything inside me stills. "Capo?"

Her expression does not shift from irritated. "Please. If you throw a rock in Manhattan, you can't help hitting someone that knows you're Cosa Nostra leadership."

"I do not know what you think you know." But I'm going to find out.

"I know that the medical facility caters to the Cosa Nostra, mostly the Genovese Family. I know that a De Luca is the don and your last name is De Luca. Even if I hadn't heard from someone that you are a capo, I would know you're connected."

"Not all De Lucas are connected to the mafia."

"No, but you are."

"Who told you I am a capo?"

"A friend."

I grab my gun and holster and put them on. "What friend?"

Were the Lucchese men there for her? Is she part of that mafia family? But if she is and spying for them, they would not have tried to kill her.

The knife wound wasn't fatal though, was it?

She sighs and closes her eyes, like she's tired and in pain. Which I'm sure she is. But giving into it like this? Feels timed.

"Does it matter who?"

"Yes."

Her eyes open and she bites her lip. "I don't want to get anyone into trouble."

"They are only in trouble if they spoke out of turn." Bianca is not wrong.

Probably half of Manhattan knows about the Genovese Mafia. Not that anyone outside our family has proof of syndicate ties. No one should have proof.

Do they?

"One of my roommates dated a guy named Marco. He knew a lot about the mafia in New York."

Fucking Francesco Jilani, Severu's former consigliere, had a made man running his security named Marco. My dad, the new consigliere, demoted Marco to foot soldier for being sloppy.

"Did you ever meet this Marco?" I ask, watching for any evidence of a lie falling from her beautiful lips.

"A couple of times. They broke up when he lost his job. Only I didn't know you could get fired in the mafia without...you know, *dying*."

"What did Marco look like?" I ignore her comment.

Unlike Marco, I don't have loose lips.

"Shorter than you. Thick like Franco, but with less muscle." She shrugs and winces. "Dark hair. Brown eyes. A couple of years ago, when I knew him, he wore a hipster goatee and his hair always looked like it needed a wash. He dressed the part though, complete with gold chains and silk suits."

Fucking Marco.

"You took a job at Amuni believing it was owned by a capo in the mafia?"

"I didn't know you were the owner when I took the job. I thought Franco owned it."

"He doesn't." Not even on paper.

Amuni is squeaky clean and one of my official business interests in New York. Like the chain of bars I'm buying from Juniper.

"When Armando told me the big boss was coming in I knew Franco didn't own the club."

"Armando is one of the servers?" I guess.

"Don't you know?"

"I own five clubs." Two nightclubs and three strip clubs in our territory. "I don't track every employee."

"He's a server on the main floor."

How did the waiter know I was coming in? Had Sierra announced it? Probably.

No doubt she believed my visit was me checking up on the running of my property and wanted everyone on their toes. When in fact, I showed up that night to see Bianca and to get the beautiful redhead into my bed.

My fascination with her is because she said no. Of course, it is. There's no other reason for the amount of brain space Bianca has taken up since that night.

"You didn't quit after learning I own the club," I observe. "And you think I'm part of a syndicate."

"Are you saying you aren't?" she asks.

This time, she's the one watching for any sign of dishonesty from me.

"No." I'm not saying I *am* either, but I'm not denying it to her.

I don't know why that feels important, but it does.

She nods. Her hand lifts to press gingerly at the bandage on her forehead. "Man, those jerks did a number on me. Speaking of, Mr. Not Going to Confirm or Deny Being Mafia, why do you keep asking me about them when they were probably there because of your organization."

"Only a fool would attack on territory claimed by the Genovese Family." It's still not a confirmation, but it's taking me further away from denial too.

"I heard you say something about Lucchese on the phone. Isn't that another mafia family in New York?"

"What else did you hear?"

She gives me a measured look I don't understand. "A lot of Italian."

Good. She might have picked a name out of my conversation with Severu, but she wouldn't have gotten anything else. And we talked about plenty in her hearing if she was awake longer than I realized.

"You still haven't told me why you continued working for a club you believe is owned by the mafia."

"You still haven't confirmed that you're a capo. I guess Marco was wrong about that, huh? I mean a capo wouldn't have brought an employee to the hospital, much less stayed the night watching over my dreams."

The hell is she talking about? The fuck I'm not a capo. I'm one of Severu's strongest captains.

"Marco was not wrong," I grind out.

A little flicker of triumph shines in her eyes and I know she played me.

"Reverse psychology? Really?" I demand.

She grins. "It worked, didn't it?"

"You played to my pride."

"Well, yeah." She's smug.

And gleeful. I'm charmed when I should be pissed.

"And now that you've admitted it, I can tell you that the idea of working in a mafia protected business felt safe."

Felt not feels. Because she was nearly killed on her way home from that *protected* business.

CHAPTER 14

BIANCA

The nurse who comes in to take my vitals is a huge improvement over the flirtatious medical assistant who acted like I wasn't even in the room.

When she's done I ask how soon I can get discharged. But Salvatore comes out of the bathroom looking like a GQ model before she can answer.

His suit and shirt are fresh and wrinkle free. I bet one of his guys brought him new clothes *again* while I was sleeping. The capo can't look anything less than put together. Salvatore's hair is smoothed into place with product that manages not to look greasy.

My dad always had the stereotypical Italian mafioso look. He could have been an extra on the Sopranos, with his slicked back hair, dark suit, shiny shoes and thick New York accent.

"All good?" Salvatore asks.

"Yes."

Salvatore does the clasp on his watch and looks at the nurse. "Make sure she gets some lunch."

He turns to leave without saying anything else. My eyes follow him while I bite back the need to say something. Anything. Like goodbye. Not as bad as the urge to ask him not to leave pushing against my vocal cords.

The nurse smiles at me. "The doctor should be in to talk to you soon. If she approves your release, we can have you on your way after you eat lunch."

Salvatore stops and turns around, his handsome face set in grim lines. "You will spend the night at least."

"Would you?" I demand, knowing he wouldn't.

The knife wound in my back hurts, but it didn't hit any organs or vital tissue. It's the equivalent of a flesh wound, only a little deeper. The doctor said it wouldn't take more than a couple of weeks to heal on the surface.

There's no reason I should have to stay the night in the hospital and I say so.

"You are staying."

"I am not."

"And if you get discharged after lunch, where exactly are you planning to go?" he asks mockingly.

"Home?" Why did I make it sound like a question? I clear my throat. "My apartment," I say more firmly.

"The apartment you share with five other people? The one where you sleep on a sofa bed in the communal living room?"

"I only have one apartment, Salvatore. We aren't all as rich as God with more than one place to live." I assume he owns multiple properties.

Even if he doesn't, his father does and the family home is still an option for the man glowering at me.

"You will stay right here." His expression dares me to argue.

Too bad for him, I'm not one of his soldiers. He can't tell me what to do. "I'm going home."

"Will the doctor release her if she has no one to care for her at home?" Salvatore's tone implies the nurse's answer had better be no.

Hugging the tablet where she recorded my vitals to her chest like a shield, the nurse takes a step backward. "I don't know, Mr. De Luca."

"And she can't find out while you've got her trapped in the room. Let her leave, Salvatore."

The look he turns on me is sulfuric. "You do not tell me what to do."

Save me from the egos of men.

I put my hands up in surrender only to wince and let the right one fall immediately. I'm not due for more pain meds for at least an hour and no way am I taking codeine again.

I need to stay alert to ride the train home.

Maybe I'll splurge on a rideshare. I assume my tips are with my clothes. I wonder what the nurse thought of my money pouch in my underwear when she undressed me.

"I'm not trying to boss you around." Like he does me. And everyone else, I'm sure. The man is a dictator. "I only wanted to point out that she can't leave the room with you standing there."

Salvatore steps aside without acknowledging my words verbally. "Tell the doctor we need her in here now. I have things to do today."

He's a capo. Of course, he has things to do. Him staying this long is surreal.

The nurse nods and scoots out the door, letting it close behind her.

"There's no reason for you to wait for the doctor's consultation. I'm not falling asleep sitting up like earlier."

"There is every reason because apparently you have no concern for your own wellbeing."

"I'm not about to check out against medical advice." Now that I know Salvatore has taken responsibility for the charges for my care here.

I have no intention of taking advantage, but neither am I going to leave if the doctor believes there's a genuine medical reason for me to stay. And Salvatore's general bossiness is not that.

"You are not checking out at all. Not until the wound on your back no longer requires care."

"That's ridiculous. That could take days."

"Two weeks at the very least," he corrects. "You could stay at my apartment. My housekeeper will keep an eye on you."

The look he gives me tells me that I wouldn't just be a house guest.

The look I give him tells him that's so not going to happen. "I already told you. I'm not paying for medical care on my back."

"And I told you that the only reason you're going to spread your legs for me is because your pussy is craving my big dick."

"Arrogant much?" I mutter while said ladybits react in a totally unpredictable way to him.

Again.

He shrugs. "It's not arrogance if it's true."

"I'm sure all men like to think their dicks are the size of the audience at a Taylor Swift concert, but reality says not."

"I'll have to stretch you to take me, but don't worry. I like playing with a woman's pussy to get her ready."

"What is wrong with you?" And what is wrong with me? Because those words should scare the crap out of me.

Instead, my vagina is all, *bring it on, bitch.*

"Nothing a few hours buried in your tight flesh won't fix."

Before I can blast him, there's a knock on the door. I *would* blast him, right?

A little voice in my brain says she has her doubts.

Salvatore's guy tells him that the doctor is here. The level of security Salvatore has in his life is unbelievable. Talk about stifling.

I don't remember Lorenzo's guys being so careful. I might have only met him that one awful memorable time before the other night, but I saw the capo out at restaurants and even attending his nephew's basketball games at the high school. His men weren't nearly as conscientious about not allowing anyone near him without approval.

Salvatore is the don's cousin. Maybe that's why his security is so tight. They must be trained to blend in because I didn't notice it at Amuni.

After checking the wound on my back and forehead and applying new bandages, the doctor asks, "Have you gone to the bathroom on your own yet?"

"No," Salvatore says.

As I say, "Yes."

I roll my eyes at him. "You insisted on helping. That doesn't mean I couldn't go alone."

For a minute I thought he wasn't going to leave me to pee in peace. He refused to let me shut the door, but at least he stepped away from the bathroom and out of my line of sight.

"Were you woozy?" the doctor asks me.

"A little," I admit grudgingly. "But that was the codeine. Once that's out of my system, I'll be fine."

"Why would it be out of your system? You are due another dose in an hour."

"I'll be staggering acetaminophen with ibuprofen," I inform him. Not that it's any of his business.

"Will that manage her pain sufficiently?" Salvatore asks the doctor.

The doctor flicks her gaze to me. "Only Miss Gemelli can answer that question. It is what she wants."

"Didn't you say you have things to do?" I unsubtly try to get Salvatore to leave.

He doesn't react to my words by so much as a twitch of an eyelash. "Will the ibuprofen prevent her from receiving the codeine if the pain becomes too much?"

"No."

He nods.

Why do I want to throw something at him? I'm not a violent person, but this man's arrogance is getting on my last nerve.

"So, once I've proven I can get to the bathroom alone, you'll discharge me?" I ask.

"Yes."

"Doesn't she need to have a bowel movement first?" Salvatore asks, like that's a perfectly normal thing to inquire about another person.

A person he barely knows.

"That is only true for patients who are put under general anesthesia." The doctor turns her gaze on me. "If you have someone to help you change bandages and you can take your pain medication orally, there is no reason for you not to go home."

"I've been taking the acetaminophen orally since I got here this morning. Taking the ibuprofen won't be a problem."

"Pietro will be in the outer room to take you home when you are discharged." Salvatore turns to go and this time, he doesn't stop.

His easy capitulation surprises me, but I'm sure not going to ask him why he's suddenly decided to let me make my own medical decisions. I'm just glad he is.

Again, he doesn't bother to say goodbye.

And I'm not disappointed.

It's doubtful I'll ever see him again. No way are they going to hold my job for me at Amuni. Not for the time it will take before I can go back to work.

At least with Gino gone, I can probably get my old job back at Pitiful Princess when I'm healed enough to dance.

My stomach rebels at the thought of dancing the pole in front of lascivious strangers, but I'll get over it. The attack this morning brought up some old feelings, that's all.

The doctor gives me an encouraging smile. "Once the codeine has worn off and you've eaten something, you'll feel more like yourself."

"You think so?" I ask hopefully.

"Yes."

Relief pours through me. Maybe I won't lose my job after all if I only miss a few shifts.

The doctor frowns, like she's reading my mind and she doesn't like what she sees there. "Remember, you lost enough blood this morning to need a transfusion. You'll be able to go to the bathroom on your own, but you still need a lot of rest while you're healing."

"Okay, sure."

My quick agreement doesn't appease her.

If anything, the doctor's expression turns to one of deeper concern. "You shouldn't work for at least two weeks. Three would be better. Things might look healed from the outside, but your body still needs extra energy to fully recover."

"We'll see." Though I'll have to get through Salvatore to go back to work at Amuni and I don't see that going well.

He's weirdly worried about my health.

I'm not going to be doing any semi-naked dancing right away either, not with stitches still showing on my face and back. "When will the stitches disappear?"

"They won't, but the surgeon will remove them in five to six days depending on how you are healing."

Right. Because I'm going to come back to the bougie hospital that probably charges more for a meal than I make in a day to have the "surgeon" remove my stitches. Millionaires like Salvatore may be able to afford this kind of medical care, but cocktail waitresses aren't so lucky.

The doctor must read something on my face because she says, "Check in with your primary care doctor in a couple of days and if you have issues, you can of course consult them instead."

"I will."

CHAPTER 15

SALVATORE

I stop in front of Pietro on my way out of the hospital suite. "When Miss Gemelli is discharged, you are to take her home."

"Yes, boss."

"My home."

Pietro rears back like I smacked him. "You want me to take the waitress to your apartment?"

"Yes. She needs help with her wound and her living situation is untenable for recovery. Your mom is good with stuff like that." Rosa has been bandaging my scrapes since I was three.

When I moved out on my own, she came with me as my housekeeper. Her husband maintains the fleet of cars for our crew and my father's, now they are not one in the same.

Pietro is their oldest and he's been on my crew since the beginning.

Their youngest is on my father's payroll, but their sister married a professor ignorant of the life. They moved to California when he got an endowed chair at one of the state universities. Her children will grow up to live normal lives without any knowledge of the mafia their mother was born into.

One day, when I have children, they will never know anything but *la famiglia*. Just like I don't.

Pietro grimaces. "Mamma will make sure Miss Gemelli rests, that's for sure. She'll stuff her with *healing* soup too."

"That's what I'm counting on." I don't need to be worried about Bianca when I should be focused on business.

Worried is too strong a word. I don't *worry* about potential bedmates. But she won't heal if she doesn't rest. If she doesn't heal, I can't slake this incessant lust I feel around her.

That's why I need Rosa watching over her.

"You're going to a lot of trouble for a piece of ass." Pietro looks at me like he's trying to figure out my angle.

My head of security who also leads my security detail is nowhere near ready to settle down. He knows I'm not either. When I marry it will be an alliance that is best for *la famiglia*. Emotion will have no place in my decision about a bride, no matter what my mother thinks.

"Bianca is more than a one-night stand. I think it will take at least a few nights to get her out of my system," I admit.

Pietro nods knowingly. "I figured. You spent six hours sleeping with her in that hospital bed, and you weren't banging. That's got to be a first."

It is. I haven't slept the night in the same bed as a lover for more than a decade, much less during the day.

Damn it. "Shut it. She had nightmares unless I was nearby." I'm not analyzing why I slept so soundly beside her. "Since she was attacked by our enemies because she works at one of the Genovese clubs, I wasn't going to abandon her to her nightmares."

"Uh, sure. Whatever you say, boss." Pietro doesn't look or sound convinced.

Giving him a pissed off glare, I double down. "It was a matter of expediency."

If a part of me is hoping that expediency is necessary again tonight when I can share her bed in much more comfortable circumstances, I'm not acknowledging it.

But until I get this woman out of my system, normal rules of sex and non-dating do not apply.

"Yeah. Okay. So, I bring this totally normal piece of ass to your apart—"

"Stop calling her a piece of ass," I bark over him. "Her name is Bianca." Thinking of him using it with her, I growl. "Call her Miss Gemelli."

Pietro salutes with a sardonic twist of his lips. "You got it. Miss Gemelli who is not just a piece of ass that you are moving into your place before you have even known the heat of her pussy."

"Do not mention her pussy." I grab Pietro by the neck. "Or any other fucking body part on her."

Although he is only two inches shy of my own six-foot-three, I lift until only his toes touch the floor and his face is beet red.

He nods the best he can in the situation.

"Do not look at her. Do not talk about her. If you so much as mention her gorgeous rack I will cut out your tongue." I drop him.

Coughing, he tries to suck in air. "I apologize, Salvatore," he gasps out. "It won't happen again."

"Good." I meet the eyes of the other men in the room, one by one.

I don't have to say anything. They bow their heads in obedience.

I told the hospital that Bianca is my girlfriend so there would be no argument about me staying in the room for treatment. Not that I would have let them keep me out, but the claim was the easiest path to my goal.

Now, I tell my men. "Get the word out. Bianca Gemelli is off limits."

"Yes, boss," they say in unison.

"Should I send one of the guys to get some of her things from her place?" Pietro has his phone open ready to send a text.

Thinking of her crowded living situation, I nod. "Tell him to pack up everything and give her notice."

"You think that's a good idea? Where's she going to live after?" Pietro asks, his voice still raw.

"Where I put her." When our passion fizzles out like it always does, I'll find Bianca someplace safer where she can have her own room.

First, she has to heal. Two weeks. At minimum. Before I can wreck her. Before she can wreck me.

Ignoring the speculation in Pietro's gaze, I leave.

~ ~ ~

Severu, Miceli and Angelo are waiting in the don's office at the Oscuro building when I get there.

Severu De Luca is my don. Miceli is his brother and underboss, and Angelo is Severu's top enforcer. Interrogator. Killer. Whatever the title, Angelo has as much power in *la famiglia* as any capo.

"What did you find out?" Severu asks me as soon as I enter the room.

I sit down in a chair across from his desk. "She doesn't know anything. They attacked her because she was in the wrong place at the wrong time."

"Is this Henrico Caruso making his move, or feeling out our reactions?" Severu asks to the room at large.

"He thinks he should be godfather when his uncle dies," Miceli says. "Hell, I don't envy the Lucchese family with him as their don. He'd be a goddamn fucking disaster as godfather to the Cosa Nostra."

"He will be godfather over my dead and decomposing body." The words are no surprise. Everyone in this office feels that way.

However, who says them is. Angelo is not a big talker.

"I have to meet with Don Caruso before I can sanction a hit," Severu says.

The only man our don answers to is the godfather and it doesn't sit well with my cousin. But he kissed the ring like every other don in the Cosa Nostra and he's loyal. Like we all are.

"You think Caruso would sanction a hit against his own nephew?" I ask, doubtful.

"No, but he'll have to offer restitution."

"Do we have video footage of the attack?" If we don't, Henry might claim the deaths of his soldiers were unprovoked.

Miceli does something on his phone. "Sent it to you. They come into the frame when they are already chasing the waitress."

In other words, there is no proof that she didn't do something to instigate the attack. "They fucking tried to kill her. No matter what they think happened out of frame, that was not sanctioned on our territory."

Severu nods. "Which is exactly what you and Miceli will say to Henrico when you return his men to him."

"I cut off their hands before I sanitized the bodies." Angelo steps away from the wall.

"Good." They dared to touch what is mine.

They will be buried with mutilated bodies for their mistake.

Angelo stops at the door. "The bodies are ready for transport in the Beemer."

Even with the large cargo capacity, three bodies will be a tight fit in the BMW's spacious trunk.

I stand. "Let's get this done."

Miceli nods, but Severu inclines his head. "A word, Salvatore."

The other two men leave the office and I wait to hear what my don has to say.

"With this incident, it is imperative that we get those bars."

In full agreement, I nod.

He's talking about the bars that Juniper is selling. My plan to buy them and turn four of them into nightclubs, providing income and a place to launder money, is now secondary to securing the properties for the sake of protecting our territory.

"Whatever the cost," Severu emphasizes. "I don't care if we have to buy all five to get the three we want."

Juniper owns properties in three of the five boroughs of New York, including Manhattan. Genovese territory. The others are in Brooklyn, Lucchese territory, and Staten Island, Gambino territory.

Severu plans to use the property in Staten Island to solidify his alliance with the Gambino don. He had the same plan for the one in Brooklyn, but that could change with Henry's recent aggression.

That bar might become leverage rather than a source of goodwill. So far, no one in either of the other families knows about the deal I'm making with Juniper, or his desire to sell the properties he inherited from his dead uncle.

The other two properties are outside the state, but I still want them. My cousin isn't convinced.

I'm determined to prove to him my plan is solid and good for *la famiglia*. "They'll all be good earners eventually. Having more businesses outside the city to launder money spreads out our risk too."

Severu nods. "Get it done."

Taking that for the dismissal it is, I go to leave.

My cousin's voice stops me at the door. "Catalina is having your parents over for dinner next week."

"Okay." His wife is something of an introvert, so having a dinner party is notable, I suppose.

"She wants you to come too."

I turn and look at Sev. "Why?"

"Does she need a reason?"

"I guess not." But my cousin isn't telling me something.

"Her sister is going to be there as well."

Cold chills run down my spine. "Your wife cannot be matchmaking. Her sister is too young for me."

Neither of us mentions that I'm five years younger than Sev and he was engaged to Carlotta a year ago when she was only nineteen. The ten-year age gap between him and his wife, Catalina, is big enough. Not that I'll say anything about that either.

I'm fond of life.

"Come to dinner. You can ignore Carlotta, but not my wife."

"I would never ignore Catalina." I like my cousin's wife and I respect her. She's strong and loyal. Her sister is neither.

Severu says I can ignore Carlotta, but if his wife is matchmaking, I don't like my chances. My parents are going to be there as well, which means my mother is onboard with this scheme.

"Bring a date if you want a buffer," Severu says, reading my mind.

An image of Bianca flashes through my brain, not that I'm bringing the woman I want to get into my bed and out of my head.

But a date is an excellent idea, especially if she's someone who will have no expectations after. Maybe Bianca *is* a good idea. My mother won't see a pole dancer turned cocktail waitress as wife material. So, I won't have to worry about her hounding me later about how things are going with Bianca.

And Bianca knows I'm not looking for commitment, or even anything longer than a few nights.

It started with me wanting one night, sure. But that won't be enough. For either of us. She thinks I didn't notice how she pressed her thighs together trying to contain her arousal, or how her pupils expanded with desire when I talked about fucking her.

I'd make a lousy capo if I was that oblivious. "Let your wife know I'll be bringing a date."

CHAPTER 16

BIANCA

The doctor is right. After I eat and the codeine has more time to wear off, I'm a lot more lucid.

Clear headed enough to feel the pain in my forehead and back every time I move wrong. The pain is manageable though, so I don't say anything to the nurse when she comes to check on me and offer me street clothes to change into.

I manage to get into the brand-new underwear and leggings, but no way am I going to manage the bra. It's the stretchy kind that fits more than one cup size, but the clasp is in the back. Not happening.

There's a thin cami to wear underneath the oversized off-the-shoulder t-shirt. Both are made of ultra soft fabric and don't irritate my bare skin. I don't know where the clothes came from, but I'm not upset to be going home in something other than my blood-soaked shirt with a knife slash in the back.

I don't see it, or my jeans, anywhere. My tennies are in my backpack, but I opt for the ballet flat style slippers the nurse brought with the new clothes. They don't require socks or bending to get on.

The leggings are the kind with slip pockets on the side of the legs. I take my phone (with cracked screen courtesy of the *stronzos* who came after me) and put it in one pocket. My ID goes in the other one.

My pepper spray is gone along with my clothes, all of which are replaceable, but I want my belt and buckle knife. After I tuck the pouch with my tip money into my underwear, I call the nurse and ask about my belt and buckle knife.

She doesn't know where they are. Apparently, neither does anyone else. I don't like being defenseless.

It will definitely have to be a rideshare home and not the train. No way am I riding the train without a weapon to defend myself.

After I go to the bathroom by myself, the doctor discharges me, as promised. The nurse goes through a sheaf of instructions for my wound care and follow up before I can leave.

Honestly, I don't know how I'm going to check the wound in my back for infection. Maybe one of my roommates will help. They're not bad people. Most of us just live very different lives from each other.

Some of my roommates are aspiring actors or musicians. The only person with a normal job is the primary renter's girlfriend. She teaches third grade and they share the largest bedroom.

She will probably check my wound and help me change my bandages if I ask.

"Are you ready to go, Miss Gemelli?" a deep voice asks when I come out of the hospital room.

Thinking I'm alone, now that the nurse is gone, I jump.

But I don't look toward the speaker. I'm too awed by the room I'm in. *Ma va'.*

I thought Salvatore's men were hanging out in the hall outside my room. But no. My hospital room is part of a freakin' suite.

This outer room has more space than the living room of the apartment I share with five others. There's a big screen TV mounted on the wall in front of a brown leather couch and chair. The four-person table for dining looks like real wood. There's even a full-size desk with a charging station on top and an executive desk chair.

Dark wood and rich colors make the room feel like a luxury hotel.

It's light years away from the rundown hospital room Mr. Ruhnke breathed his last breaths in. If I could have given him this for those last days, I would have.

He deserved it. I'm only here because the man who wants in my pants is a capo from one of the wealthiest crime families in the world, much less New York.

I let my gaze settle on the man near the outer door. A little shorter than Salvatore, he still exudes strength and power. There's no expression in his dark eyes. No smile meant to make the invalid feel better.

That might be a red flag for some people, but I trust no emotion over fake emotion any day. Besides, he's one of Salvatore's guys.

"I remember you." He was seated at Salvatore's table when I served them. "You were at the club with Salvatore."

"I was in the car this morning, too, but you were mostly passed out. The name's Pietro."

Even though I know passing out like that was the culmination of lack of sleep, adrenaline fatigue and the knock I took to my head, I'm still embarrassed.

When I get embarrassed, I get cranky.

"Hope you got the blood off the leather seats," I say with sickly sweet insincerity.

Getting blood out of leather is almost impossible.

"Not my job," he says with a shrug.

"Okay, well, whatever your job is, you probably want to get back to it." I wiggle my fingers toward the door, dismissing him.

His dark brows rise mockingly. "My job right now is to take you home."

"Not necessary. I already booked a rideshare and if I don't get downstairs, he's going to drive off without me." Technically the car shouldn't be here yet.

Because I don't risk stuff like that, I booked him to arrive fifteen minutes from now. Better to wait on him than not be there when he pulls up and chance losing my ride.

"Cancel it." Pietro grabs my backpack, which I'd been holding rather than wearing because *stab wound in my back*.

I try to snatch it back, but he's already out of the room and I'm hustling to keep up. Not so easy right now. "Hey, slow down. That's my backpack you're stealing."

There's not much in it, just my Amuni uniform and shoes, but it's *mine* and I want it back.

Pietro doesn't slow down, but when he reaches the elevator, he stops and waits for me at least.

When I reach him, I put my hand out. "Give it back."

"You don't need to be carrying anything right now."

"Listen up, bub. That's my backpack and you are not my boss. Give it here."

Ignoring my outstretched hand, he steps into the elevator when the doors open. Aargh!

There's no one else in the elevator and I'm not getting in there alone with him.

I turn and shout down the empty hall, assuming in a place like this someone is around to hear me. "Nurse! Doctor! He's stealing my backpack."

His eyes grow comically wide and he steps back out of the elevator, clearly intent on shushing me. Not going to happen. I start backing up fast, shouting for help the whole time.

"Stop that, Miss Gemelli. I'm not stealing anything."

Not having my pepper spray or knife has me on edge and his looming presence isn't helping.

"I'll take the stairs and meet you." It's a practical plan. "Just give me my stuff."

"You're being irrational. You aren't walking down six flights of stairs."

Six flights? Okay, yeah, that feels like a little much. "So, you take the stairs."

Pietro doesn't answer, but lunges for me.

Fight or flight adrenaline floods my system for the second time in less than twenty-four hours and I pivot, grabbing Pietro's arm and yanking so his forward momentum takes him into the wall opposite.

Not waiting to see how effective the move is, I turn and run, going left as soon as there's an opening. I get winded fast and have to slow down. Looking over my shoulder all I see is an empty corridor. No *stronzo* chasing me, but no one to help me either.

Giving up on the yelling, and moving a lot slower, I try to find my way back to the elevator. He's not going to be there waiting for me. Why should he?

He has your backpack. You know he's not stealing it. Salvatore told him to drive you home. He's just following orders.

I still don't want to get on the elevator with him and I'm willing to give up my backpack to avoid it.

Didn't I pass that doorway before?

I'm not lost. I will find the elevator. Or the stairs. I can make it down six flights. On my butt, scooting step to step maybe.

"Miss Gemelli." It's him. And he still has my backpack dangling from his meaty fist.

I glare. "Go away."

"No."

"Nice. My rideshare is probably gone and it's all your fault."

"Let me drive you home."

I shake my head and regret the movement immediately as the low-level headache I've had since waking up turns it up a few thousand notches to intolerable. My sprint down the hospital corridors didn't help either.

I need to sleep, but that's not going to happen and there's nothing I can do about it. Even if the closet is empty and available, sleeping is hard on a good day. Today is not one of those.

"I just want my backpack."

He shakes his head, looking at something over my shoulder.

I'm not falling for that trick. Only what if someone is behind me? I feel a sting in my arm that shoots pain deep into my muscle. A bee? A mosquito? How does a bug get into a place like this to fly around?

Trying to rub the sting away, I look over my shoulder. There are no flying insects, but I discover an orderly right behind me. I sidestep, putting distance between us without getting closer to Pietro.

The orderly is holding an uncapped hypodermic in his hand. Maybe he's a nurse? I don't think orderlies administer shots.

"You're not getting near me with that."

He puts his hands up in surrender. "Not coming near you."

Only then do I see the plunger is already depressed.

"*Bastardo*. You drugged me!"

"It's just something to calm you down."

"I don't need to be calm." Okay, maybe I did overreact to Pietro wanting me to get on the elevator with him. A little. "I want to go home. Point me to the elevator."

Pietro can keep my backpack. I don't care anymore.

Is that the sedative talking? How fast acting is it?

"I'll show you the way to the elevator," Pietro offers.

I shake my head and point at the guy who stabbed me with a needle. "You do it."

The man shrugs and walks past me. I scuttle back so there is always at least two feet between us, but I follow him. Pietro's heavy tread sounds behind me.

My shoulders tense, but I do my best to ignore his nearness. I've embarrassed myself enough for one day. As we get closer to the elevator, my legs feel wobbly but I don't stop walking.

The orderly-slash-nurse, whatever he is, pushes the button for the elevator.

"There you go. You got it from here?" The question is clearly not for me, but for the hulking mafia thug behind me.

"Yes."

The man in scrubs walks off without asking if I'm alright.

"Let's go." Pietro grabs my arm and tugs.

I yank away from his hold. Or I try to. It's more like a slow sidestep. "You go first. I'll take the next one."

"There's only one elevator on this side of the building."

I don't ask why. Probably something to do with mafia security. Why the orderly...I've decided he's an orderly because a nurse would be more concerned about my wellbeing.

What was I thinking?

Oh, yeah. Why the *orderly* guided me to the elevator reserved for the mafia is a mystery, but right now I'm too woozy to care. I just want to get to ground level.

There are taxis and maybe even my rideshare at ground level.

"I'll wait for it to come back." Go me for remembering what we were talking about.

"Salvatore's instructions are for me to take you home." When did Pietro get so close?

"Get away," I slur and close my eyes against the way the wall starts expanding and contracting.

SALVATORE

My phone rings on our way to Brooklyn. I check the screen and see it is Pietro.

I swipe the phone to answer and press it to my ear. I don't need Miceli and the other two men in the car to hear this conversation.

"Talk." I'm not big on greetings and my men know that.

"She's resting in your guestroom bed. Mamma will wait for her to wake up and feed her. She's saying she's going to stay until you get home."

Manaja. That means Rosa wants to talk to me, or she's worried about Bianca.

"Is something wrong with Bianca?"

"No." The word is a negative, but he doesn't sound convinced.

Why the hell should I be? "Tell me."

"We had to drug her to get her out of the hospital, boss." Pietro's tone is worried.

It should be. Images of killing my head of security six different ways flash through my mind.

"You drugged her?"

Miceli goes on alert beside me, settling his full attention on me.

Cazzo.

"Yes, boss. We had to."

"Why?"

"Miss Gemelli was hysterical. Yelling all sorts of shit about needing help, that I was stealing her stuff. I don't think she should have been discharged. The drugs are still playing with her mind."

"And you thought giving her more drugs was the answer?" How much would I regret killing one of my best friends?

"She wasn't going quietly, boss."

"You scared her."

"Not on purpose. One minute she's all sarcastic, pissed off woman, the next she's running and screaming for someone to help her."

"You made her run?"

"I didn't make her do shit. She went bananas the second I stepped onto the elevator with her backpack. I wasn't trying to leave without her."

"But she ran from you?"

"Yes."

"She was afraid of you?"

"Yes."

"So, you drugged her."

"Yes." Pietro says the last affirmative through gritted teeth.

He's pissed he had to drug Bianca to gain her compliance. He's used to women falling all over themselves to do what he wants. That's no excuse for drugging her.

"With what?"

"I had one of our guys give her a shot of K."

"Ketamine? What if it reacted with the codeine still in her system?" My insides turn to ice.

Bianca could have stopped breathing. Her heart could have stopped. Mine skips in my chest. *Cazzo.*

"She's breathing okay?"

"Of course. Better than when she was practically hyperventilating with hysteria."

"Get a doctor in to check her out," I bark. "If the K causes her any problems, I will give you twice the dose and leave you in an alley in Colombo territory to sleep it off."

It's not an automatic death sentence, but he won't make it home un-scathed.

"Manaja." He sighs. "I'm sorry, Salvatore. I didn't know how to get her to calm down."

"Words."

"I tried words. She just kept screaming."

"You didn't try hard enough."

"Did you want me to carry her out of the hospital kicking and scream-ing?"

I hang up without bothering to answer. We both know he had to touch her to carry her at all and I'll make him pay for that. As for the kicking and screaming, Pietro had to have done something to set her off.

Bianca never screamed once with me. Not even when she woke up with me in her bed.

CHAPTER 17

BIANCA

The first thing I notice is the silence. There are no street noises. No shuffling feet.

Only silence.

Am I still in the hospital?

Opening my eyes cautiously, I blink and then blink again, trying to make sense of what I see. I scramble to sit up and the wound in my back pulls, piercing me with a shard of pain.

I grunt and stop moving to breathe in shallowly through my nose until the fiery pain in my back settles to less than scream inducing levels.

Okay. Note to self: *no fast movement.*

With a lot more care than I used sitting up, I scoot off the big bed and stand up. My body lists from one side to the other and I grab the top of the headboard to steady myself.

This bed is ridiculous. If it was in either of the two bedrooms in the apartment where I live, there would be no room to walk or even open the closet door. But in this room? It fits fine.

Because this bedroom that I have never seen before is freakin' huge. And wow. Seriously elegant.

It's even more bougie than the Cosa Nostra hospital.

The heavy drapes on the floor to ceiling windows that cover one wall are a slightly darker shade of tan than the duvet cover. There are wood nightstands on either side of the bed with smooth lines, no decorative detailing.

Everything about the room is sleek and modern. Even the bench at the end of the bed. Covered in off-white leather, it has no tufting or ornamentation.

But it's what's sitting on top of the bench that has my heart beating faster.

With the sight of my backpack, everything floods back. Pietro's insistence I go with him. My ignominious flight. The unwelcome sedative.

Che palle. The *stronzo* had that bastard orderly drug me and then when I got woozy, Pietro freakin' kidnapped me.

Gingerly making my way to the windows, I cuss Pietro out under my breath and push one of the curtains aside. I catch my breath.

Looking down, not up, at the familiar New York skyline tells me that I'm in one of the taller skyscrapers and this apartment is way up. Maybe even penthouse level.

Clouds have moved in, bringing spring rain, but it's still light out, which means I was either out for only a few hours, or overnight and into the next morning.

A flash of memory from earlier plays in my brain. I reach down for my phone in the side pocket of the leggings I'm wearing. Relief gusts out of me in a big breath as my hands touch the hard lump of my phone.

I fish it out and the cracked screen lights up to reveal that it is 5:17 p.m. on the same day. So, I was only out a little over an hour.

Long enough to kidnap me from the hospital and bring me to this rich man's dream of an apartment.

And I know what rich man. Salvatore De Luca.

The controlling jerk.

He knew I wanted to go home. I still want to go home.

A red tide of anger rises, making my muscles tense and my heart beat fast and hard. I jab at the screen until I get into my contacts. Without waiting a single beat, I call Salvatore.

The phone rings twice before going to voicemail. I call again. Same thing, only it goes to voicemail immediately this time.

Yeah, no. I'm not giving up and the capo is going to learn he isn't the only stubborn person around here.

I dial again. And again.

He probably put his phone on do not disturb, but I don't care. I keep calling.

Finally, instead of the call going to voicemail, Salvatore answers. "What?" he barks.

Nice way to answer the phone, douchebag. "You had Lurch drug me!" I shout without preamble.

"His name is Pietro, not Lurch."

"I care." My voice drips with sarcasm.

"He did not have my permission to drug you."

I scoff, "I'm supposed to just take your word for that?"

"Yes." The call drops.

He hung up on me. Rude.

I immediately dial again.

"I'm busy," he barks instead of a greeting and hangs up again.

I cannot believe this guy. Who does he think he is? The president?

Reality bites me in the ass with the truth. He's a Cosa Nostra capo. Practically a god in his own mind, and lots of other people's. Of course, he thinks his time is more valuable than my mere human problems.

Too bad. I dial again.

SALVATORE

Miceli gives me a look when my phone rings *again*. He wants to know why I haven't put it on DND, or at least silenced the ringer.

Our situation is precarious.

Three dead bodies, wrapped in plastic, lay at our feet on the driveway behind the godfather's house.

He is also the don of this territory and taking them anywhere else would have been disrespectful.

A dozen of Caruso's men surround us with their guns pointed in our direction.

Our two soldiers' hands hang loose so they can draw their guns quickly, but Miceli gave the signal not to. The Genovese underboss looks bored, but I know better.

He's on high alert. Just like I am.

Neither of us is worried though. Killing us would trigger an all out war among the Five Families. Henrico Caruso might be stupid enough to risk it. His uncle is not.

That doesn't mean the situation lacks any danger. Twelve fucking guns are pointed at us.

That's why I answer the phone. I'm telling the godfather how unworried I am. We're in the right and we know it.

"Excuse me, I need to take this," I say to the godfather.

Respect flashes briefly in his eyes and he nods, giving permission. I step through his perimeter of guards and create enough distance none of them will overhear me.

Miceli can handle the explanation. I'm here because the aggression happened near my club and that makes it personal to me. He's still the don's underboss and spokesperson for the Genovese right now.

I slide my finger across the screen to answer. "Stop calling. I'm busy," I repeat, in case she didn't get it the first time.

"You had your thug drug and kidnap me, Salvatore. Excuse me if I don't care if you have business to attend to."

Flicking my gaze to the tense tableau less than twenty feet away, I frown. "Pietro is not a thug. He's the head of my security."

"Oh, I'm impressed. *Not.*"

"He was not supposed to drug you."

"But kidnapping me is okay?" she shouts. Then groans.

"Hurt your head yelling?" Which is exactly why she needs to be in my apartment and not her own.

She has too many roommates. With all that noise her headache will be constant.

"You cannot just kidnap me to your lair, Salvatore."

"I'm not a super villain. It's a penthouse apartment, not a lair."

"You're a Cosa Nostra capo. It's a lair."

In her mind that makes me a villain? She is not wrong. And still she works for me? She said it made her feel safe. In the past tense. Maybe my villainy now overshadows the security of working for the most powerful mafia family in New York.

"It's my home and you are safe there. Rosa will help with your wound care and make sure you eat."

"Who is Rosa? Your wife?" Bianca asks, clearly horrified.

"My housekeeper."

"You really had me brought to your *home*?"

"As opposed to?" I ask with more curiosity than I have time for.

"Your fuck pad."

"I don't bring women to my apartment to fuck them."

"Good to know."

"That doesn't mean I won't be fucking you there." A picture of her spread naked across my bed sends blood surging into my cock.

I don't have time for this.

"You won't be screwing me at all." Her ire is sexy as hell and her words do nothing to dampen my libido.

"I have to go." Right now is not the time to spring wood. "Stop calling me."

"Fine. I won't be calling you again," she says like it's a threat. "But don't expect me to be here when you finally deign to show up."

It's her turn to hang up but I smile. She's not going anywhere. My apartment door does not open without security clearance and the penthouse elevator does not move without it either.

Bianca won't be able to access either.

BIANCA

Walking like an old woman who needs a hip replacement, I cross the room and pick up my backpack. The pull of the weight in my hand turns the throb of pain in my back to a more acute sensation.

I was planning on getting some ibuprofen and acetaminophen on the way home. That didn't happen.

Because Pietro, the thug, kidnapped me.

Leaving is even more imperative. I need pain meds and I need them now.

The handle on the guestroom door turns easily, surprising me a little. I half expected to be locked in here.

Since I'm not, I pull the door open and step into the hall. I turn left, assuming that's the way out because about twenty feet down on my right, the hall ends in a large window with no covering. I bet it's bullet proof.

All the windows in this penthouse apartment are probably bullet proof. Or *impact resistant*. Whatever, no way does a mafia capo live here without taking precautions. Especially one with security as heavy as Salvatore's.

The hallway ends at a door, which I open, finding myself on a landing before a set of stairs. To my right is a reading nook that overlooks the large living room below. The back wall is lined with bookcases that reach the ceiling, their shelves filled with books and no nicknacks.

The temptation to check out the titles is huge, but I don't succumb. Even when I imagine Salvatore sitting in one of the comfy looking armchairs wearing a pair of black rimmed reading glasses and an open book in his hands.

Swoon.

I'm halfway down the stairs when a woman bustles into my line of sight. She looks so much like my nonna, only younger, that I freeze, trying to decide if she's real or the result of the knock to my head and the drugs I've been given.

CHAPTER 18

BIANCA

"*Mamma mia*. What are you doing child? You should not be out of bed." She rushes up the steps, muttering in Italian about the foolishness of youth the whole way.

Closer to my mom in age, this sweetly rounded, motherly Italian woman even sounds like Nonna. She stops in front of me, her hands out like she's going to catch me if I fall.

Or grab me to her in a hug.

I take a hasty step back but stop before she gets the wrong idea that I'm going back upstairs. "I need to go home."

"You need to rest," she counters, trying to shoo me back the way I came.

Gripping the rail tightly, I shake my head. "I'm leaving."

"What are you talking about? You are staying here where I can take care of you." She's bossy like my nonna too.

"You might as well give up. Mamma never loses an argument when she's got her mind set on something," a familiar voice comes from the bottom of the steps.

Tensing, I look down. Pietro.

Anger shoots up my spine and right out of my mouth. "You jerk. You drugged me! You can get arrested for that. Kidnapping is a federal offense too."

Not that I'm going to the cops about any of this.

Not even my attack in the wee hours of the morning. I'm sure those men are long gone and not in the leave-the-area-of-their-own-volition way.

Not Pietro drugging and kidnapping me. Though I'm freakin' tempted. It would be just my luck to file my report with a cop on the Genovese payroll.

So not happening, but the thug frowning up at me doesn't need to know that.

He rolls his eyes. "I didn't kidnap you. I told you I was bringing you home."

"To *my* home, not here. And you drugged me to do it. I'm not here of my own volition. That makes this kidnapping."

"Come, let's get you back to the bedroom. Pietro will apologize for drugging you and promise never, ever to do anything like that again to a defenseless woman." The look she shoots Pietro could incinerate concrete.

And I could swear she got it from the same storehouse of looks as my nonna.

If I revel a little in her son's wince and obvious discomfort at his mother's disapproval, who could blame me?

Knowing Rosa is on my side doesn't make me want to stay though. "I'm tired and in pain. Please let me pass so I can leave."

It's the wrong thing to say and I realize it almost immediately.

"Of course, you are tired. You need your rest as I have said. Pietro, bring up the pain relievers and a carafe of water," she orders her drug-happy son and then turns back to me. "Let's get you back upstairs."

It's clear she's not moving and I'm not about to push her out of my way. She might fall and then getting drugged again would be the least of my worries.

Pietro would probably kill me.

Still, I try. "I'm not going to be alone. I have five roommates."

"With that kind of chaos around you, how do you expect to get better?" she asks with clear disapproval.

I feel a little of Pietro's pain, and she's not even my mother.

"Mrs.—"

"It's Rosa," she says firmly, herding me up a step before I realize it.

I stop. "Rosa, please. You cannot hold me here against my will."

"I am not holding you anywhere," she says with clear affront. "Salvatore will return in a few hours. Take a nap and then you can talk to him about leaving when he arrives."

In other words, no matter what she says about not keeping me here, that is exactly what she's doing. I'm going nowhere without the capo's approval.

My stance on calling the cops might be shifting. Only what do I tell them?

A really nice lady is holding me in this totally swank apartment against my will? Sure, with the human trafficking problems in New York, I might get listened to. But then Rosa would get in trouble.

Maybe even arrested. While I don't care if her son, Pietro the thug, spends a night or two in jail, I don't want that for the woman who reminds me of my nonna.

It's not a rational response, because Rosa isn't my grandmother or any sort of relation. But I can't help feeling the way I do. She is so much like the woman that stars in the best memories of my childhood there is no way I'm going to do anything to hurt her.

Nonna died when Bea and I were twelve. If she'd still been alive, the stuff that happened when we were thirteen wouldn't have. And neither would any of what happened later, but her death was the first blow in the destruction of my family.

"*Per favore, dolce ragazza*, let me take care of you."

Tears spring to my eyes. *Sweet girl.* Just like my nonna used to call me. She called my twin, Bea, *bella regazza*. Pretty girl. Nonna always said we were both pretty and sweet, but that I was sweeter and Bea worked harder to be pretty.

It was true. Back then. Before.

I'm not sweet now. Not even a little. But Bea is still beautiful.

Unable to deal with memories that usually never see the light of day, I give in. "I'll go back to the room and take my pain meds."

Anything to get this sweet Italian mamma to stop using endearments with me. And taking the medication will make escaping easier too. I'll be able to move faster than I am right now. That's for sure.

Rosa and Pietro left me alone once. It's just bad timing they caught me coming down the stairs. They'll leave me alone again. Especially if I pretend to take a nap like Rosa suggests.

My plan would be foolproof except Rosa insists on helping me undress and put on a borrowed nightgown, so new she has to remove the tags. My phone and ID wallet end up on the bedside table before Rosa helps me into the bed.

Fluffing the pillows behind me so I can sit up in the ginormous bed, she gives me a motherly look that makes my heart ache. "I will bring you some food. You should not take pills on an empty stomach."

"That's not necessary. Really. I had lunch." I look longingly at my phone and then my backpack, once again resting innocently on the bench at the end of the bed.

"That was hours ago. And hospital food. Pfft."

Her disdain for the chef prepared cuisine I had for lunch makes me smile.

"Ah, that is good. You smile. You are feeling better already now that you are off your feet."

I don't argue. Just like nonna, Rosa isn't about to let facts get in the way of her perception of life. Nonna believed pastina soup could cure all ills and no doubt Rosa thinks the same.

She bustles out of the room to get me something to eat, but she comes back a couple of seconds later carrying the carafe of water she'd told Pietro to bring up. "We'll just put this here on the bedside table for you, but you need to eat some soup before you take the pain pills."

Half tempted to take the ibuprofen as soon as her back is turned, I nevertheless nod.

As much as I want to take the meds now - because hello, stab wound in my back and stitched up gash in my forehead complete with accompanying painful goose egg - I don't want to see the disappointment on Rosa's face when she realizes I didn't listen to her.

Which is ridiculous, because resemblance to my nonna, or not, Rosa is a practical stranger to me.

Nevertheless, I know I won't be giving into the temptation when she leaves. Which she does almost immediately.

Sighing, I pull out my phone and check my texts.

There's one from Candi. And another from Mr. Ruhnke's daughter-in-law. I read the message from her first.

Lynn: *Call me when you get a chance.*

That will have to wait. Contacting Lynn will never be at the top of my priority list, but right now I'm a little busy being held hostage.

Tapping into Candi's message stream, I smile. There's a gif of an ATM spitting out money sent early this morning, before the attack.

Candi: *Making Ugo regret letting me keep all of my tips for the weekend.* :smiling devil emoji:

Me: *Dance tonight like only rich guys are watching. $$*

I put my phone down when Rosa comes back into the room. She is quicker than I expect. She must have had the broth on simmer.

I smile at her. Pietro walks behind her, carrying a wood bed tray. The kind with legs that can sit over your lap so you can eat in bed.

Him, I frown at.

He rolls his eyes, like I'm oh so annoying. Which makes me smile inside, satisfied I've irritated him.

She takes the tray from her son and places it carefully over my legs. "This will help you heal faster than any drugs."

Casting a glare at her son to let him know she hasn't forgiven him for drugging me, she tsks.

Hiding my grin, I inhale the delicious aroma of the soup. I was right. Rosa's answer to all ailments is pastina soup. Just like Nonna.

The scent of chicken stock and garlic makes my nose tingle and my mouth water. "This looks yummy."

The large ceramic bowl is filled with tiny star shaped pasta and the light yellow of egg swirled in the broth to cook. A little convinced that both she and Nonna are right and the soup can heal anything, I scoop up a spoonful and blow on it so I won't burn my mouth.

Warm memories from my childhood play around the edges of my brain as I eat the soup with near reverence.

"Mamma's cooking will have you feeling 100% in no time," Pietro says, like he has anything to do with the delicious soup I'm eating.

I frown at him. "Do you need something?"

He spins on his heel and heads out of the room, muttering, "I don't know what the boss sees in her," in Italian as he goes.

"Pietro!" his mother admonishes.

"Don't worry, mamma. She doesn't speak Italian," he calls from the hallway.

Pretending ignorance of their exchange, I eat my soup. Apparently, I'm still not telling Salvatore I speak Italian. Which means not revealing it to his people either.

Even if it didn't give me a tiny sense of power in my suddenly out-of-control life, it is probably better for my health for Salvatore not to know I understood the parts of his conversation with the don I overheard.

He might want me to spend a night in his bed, which is so not happening right now, but he's still a Cosa Nostra capo with a brutal reputation. He wouldn't hesitate to finish the job my attackers started if he thought I was any kind of threat to the security of *la famiglia*.

After Rosa bullies me into eating nearly the whole bowl of soup and I take my pain meds, I'm yawning like I haven't slept in a week.

"I shouldn't be so tired," I complain.

Rosa helps me lay down and tucks the blankets around me. "Nonsense. Your body is healing. Rest is the best thing for you."

I would argue, but I can't work up the energy to lift my eyelids much less open my mouth.

CHAPTER 19

SALVATORE

"Are you finished talking to your girlfriend?" Miceli asks with a heavy dose of sarcasm when I return to the circle.

The godfather's men have lowered their guns, but not put them away. Progress.

"Maybe you want to explain to me how this is not an act of war on behalf of your don?" Don Caruso asks me. "Your cousin hasn't been very forthcoming."

We all know that Severu called the godfather and Caruso knows exactly why there are three dead bodies on his drive. He's posturing.

Why? Has he decided to withdraw his support of Severu as the next godfather and back his incompetent, hot headed nephew instead?

Henry Caruso looks like he just got a hand job he didn't have to pay for the first time in his life.

Cazzo.

"Three of your capo's men came into Genovese territory and attacked one of our own." I let Henry see his death in my eyes.

If not today, then later. Because his uncle isn't going to last much longer, no matter what the godfather wants us to believe by coming out of his house and away from his medical team.

I make no effort to hide how pissed off I am when I meet the old man's eyes. Yes, he is our godfather, and we swore an oath of loyalty to him. However, we are Cosa Nostra, not dogs to be led around by a leash.

He gives me a gimlet stare. "A cocktail waitress who shakes her ass for tips and doesn't even make your club extra money is hardly one of your own."

A red mist of fury drops like a curtain in front of my eyes at his dismissive attitude toward Bianca. Those *bastardos* nearly killed her.

Miceli, who has been relaxed since we arrived at the compound suddenly tenses, like he knows how close I am to saying something I shouldn't to the godfather.

"Amuni is one of our legit businesses," I remind the old man from between gritted teeth.

"Which makes this *puttana* even less one of your own." That's Henry sticking his broken-down oar into the water.

"Call my girlfriend a whore again and I will end you." I stare him down until he looks away.

"It is true then?" the godfather asks. "The woman is your girlfriend. I had heard that is what you told the hospital, but I dismissed it as provocative gossip."

Provocative because she's not in the life? Probably. I doubt Don Carusa has so much as flirted with a woman outside the Cosa Nostra in his entire long life.

His words aren't meant to chastise my choice in bedmates though. He's telling us that he still has his finger to the pulse of the Five Families in New York.

"I thought Captain Playboy didn't do committed relationships," Henry sneers.

I dislike the moniker Captain Playboy almost as much as being called Little Sal. But if I let the *stronzo* see how much I hate it, he'll use it. And I give my enemies nothing to use against me.

"She is mine," I say to the godfather, ignoring his grandstanding shit-stain of a nephew.

"What was she doing walking alone that time of the morning?" he asks, sounding genuinely perplexed. "I know things have changed since my younger days, but my mistresses never went without protection."

This admission of his age is more worrying than his nephew's play for power. Don Caruso just admitted he doesn't keep a mistress any longer.

Fuck and double fuck.

Severu's timeline for building the support he needs for his bid for godfather just got jacked.

"She's my girlfriend, not my mistress." And too damn stubborn and independent for her own good.

Not something I'm going to tell the godfather and his nephew though. Especially when Bianca herself has no clue she's now my girlfriend. I don't need to increase their interest in her.

But she's not a secret and I'm not married. So, not my mistress.

"Only a fool doesn't protect what is important to him." This time there's no question the godfather is censuring me.

Rather than worry about disappointing him, I will capitalize on his words. "I'm glad you see it that way, Godfather, since I killed the three men who tried to harm her."

Henry sucks in a breath. He knows his uncle just played into my hands and by proxy, Severu's. It's not a mistake Don Caruso would have made even a year ago.

If it is a mistake. Maybe he *wants* to sanction the hits.

"Regardless of their target, your capo's men were in our territory and they tried to kill someone without Severu's approval." Miceli's voice is pure ice.

Both of my cousins were raised not just to hide weakness, but to have none. As I was.

"Was it a hit?" I ask Henry, sure the answer will be no, but wanting to shake the other capo up a little.

He blanches and shakes his head vehemently. "No."

In his urgency to set me straight, he has just confirmed that his men were in Manhattan on *his* behalf to screw with us.

Does he realize that?

The dawning look of chagrin on his face says he does.

"Does your don seek reparations?" the godfather asks.

"Uncle—"

"Shut it," Don Caruso cuts his nephew off. "You need to control your men."

So, Henry has convinced his uncle that the men weren't there on his orders. Or at least that is what Don Caruso wants us to believe.

The godfather turns that gimlet glare on Miceli. "And your brother needs to prove his strength if he wants my support to take my place."

I ignore Henry's pathetic objections, as does everyone else.

Miceli shrugs. "Severu's inclination is to wipe out your nephew and all his men in retaliation for this act of aggression. I thought you would be against it, but if you're sanctioning retribution..."

Don Caruso goes nearly purple with fury, realizing once again he's left himself open. Oh, hell.

How the mighty have fallen.

He was once the scariest man in New York. Now he's barely keeping it together. If his nephew was any kind of a second, this entire conversation would have gone differently.

"My uncle said *reparations* not retribution," Henry is quick to correct Miceli.

Again, Severu's much better second ignores him, waiting for the godfather to speak.

"My nephew will pay a tithe to Severu for three months." He glares balefully at the wrapped bodies. "One for each man on his crew he could not control."

Henry glowers in impotent fury. "Did you have to cut off their hands? It's going to upset their families."

"You're damn lucky we didn't chop them up into bite size pieces and dump them in the river." Not that we dump bodies in the river.

We use a chemical bath under the floor of The Box for disposal. Enough time in that morbid soup and there is no body, much less DNA evidence left to trace.

"For the three months of the reparation tithe, we expect Lucchese soldiers to stay out of Manhattan." Miceli meets the godfather's gaze without
a single glance in his nephew's direction. "Any found in our territory will
not be returning for a proper burial, or otherwise, regardless of their reason
for being there."

"We have always had good relations between our families," Don Caruso
lies.

None of the Five Families can claim a history without bloodshed between them.

"And that will continue if there is no further aggression." Miceli's tone
makes it clear that this is the only concession the Luccheses will get from
us.

Next time Henry decides to rattle Severu's cage, he'll face the teeth of the
lion.

~ ~ ~

Rosa reads me the riot act about letting that poor, sweet girl get hurt
when I return to my penthouse.

"She should never have been walking to the subway alone." My housekeeper slams the cupboard closed after putting away a freshly washed pot.
"I thought the men in this family had more sense."

"We can't provide an armed escort for the employees, Rosa."

Rosa crosses her arms and taps her foot, frowning up at me. "And why
not? Are you saying you don't have enough soldiers to keep a couple
available to walk your employees to the train after closing?"

"They usually walk together." Which admittedly I only know because
Bianca told me.

"Then why wasn't she walking with them? Did you keep her late at the
club and then send her on her way without a second thought?" Rosa is as
good as any Italian mother I know at dishing out guilt.

Even my own.

"I wasn't there at closing. She had a table of customers that were slow to
leave."

"What?" Rosa is incensed. "You allow your customers to keep your
employees after closing hours? Are you a man, or a doormat?"

I don't bother reminding her that Franco is the Amuni's general manager. As far as Rosa is concerned, I am responsible for anything related to any of my businesses because I am capo.

She is right.

"I will make sure the female employees are escorted to the subway station after closing."

"What you think men can't get mugged? And what about employees whose shifts end before closing?" she demands, not giving an inch. "The streets of Manhattan aren't any safer at midnight than at four in the morning."

"All employees, whatever time their shift ends, will either walk in a group or be escorted. Happy?"

She smiles and pats my cheek. Like I'm ten fucking years old again. "You're a good boy, Salvatore. Now, go check on your guest. She keeps trying to leave."

I find Pietro standing like a sentry at the bottom of the stairs. When he sees me, his shoulders drop with relief. Which is not the emotion he should be feeling, knowing how badly he screwed up drugging Bianca earlier.

"Boss." He nods.

Without telegraphing my intention, I hit him with a left jab to his stomach, followed by a right cross to the head and a left uppercut to his chin. He falls like a damn tree.

I whip out my gun and have it pointing at the center of his forehead by the time he sits up. "You ever going to drug Bianca again?"

"No, boss." He shakes his head like he's trying to clear it.

I didn't pull my punches.

"Don't know how you're going to keep her here without drugs, unless you plan to chain her to the bed in the guestroom?" he asks hopefully.

An outraged gasp comes from behind me. "No one is chaining me anywhere."

Looking over my shoulder, I find Bianca standing on the top of the stairs. The light behind her turns her thin nightgown into a sexy peep show, revealing every luscious curve.

"Get the fuck back into your bedroom," I bark.

Then I whip my head around to see if Pietro is looking. He's got his gaze fixed firmly in the other direction. Smart man.

"You don't tell me what to do, Salvatore De Luca," the termagant shouts from where she is still standing at the top of the stairs. "I want to go home. Now."

She thinks she is going to give orders to me? Her capo?

Fucking hell no.

"Shit." Pietro jumps to his feet. "She's not in the life, boss. She doesn't know."

Now he's defending her?

"I don't need you defending me, Mr. Kidnapper!"

"You need to be quiet," my top bodyguard shouts right back. "I'm trying to help you."

"Why the hell are you trying to help her?" I press my gun against his forehead.

"Rosa," Bianca screams and then she's yelling at me. "Salvatore, what is the matter with you? What if it goes off?"

All of this shouting cannot be good for the headache she admitted to earlier. The woman clearly doesn't know how to take care of herself after being hurt.

Most people outside the mafia don't have my experience with it. That's why she needs to stay here, with people who do.

Rosa comes rushing into the living room. She's still wearing her apron. Is she not planning on going home tonight? What the hell is happening in my home?

"Salvatore?" Rosa asks, sounding a lot less worried than Bianca and it's *her* son I'm pointing my gun at.

Unlike the woman stomping down the stairs behind me, Rosa knows I won't kill him though. Not for pissing me off. If he's trying to get with Bianca, that's another story. I'll cut off his dick and then kill him.

"Are you and Bianca *friends* now, Pietro?"

His eyes widen and he swallows. "No, boss. It's not like that."

"What's it like then?"

"Am I not allowed to have friends?" Bianca's small hand lands on my arm.

"My men are not your friends." I think for a beat. "Rosa can be your friend."

"Tell me I'm still sleeping and this is some bizarre nightmare."

"I don't star in your nightmares," I inform her.

"You can't dictate my dreams."

"Bet me."

"Yeah, no." The eyeroll is in her voice.

I don't have to see it.

"Do you honestly think I'm going to be friends with the thug who drugged and kidnapped me and then stole my clothes?"

"Explain." I shift my body so Bianca in her unexpectedly revealing nightgown is standing behind me.

I ordered nightgowns intended to be modest so they would not make my already volcanic lust erupt and cause me to do something I would regret. Like seduce her and undo the painstaking efforts of the plastic surgeon to repair the wounds on her forehead and back.

The modest cut is deceptive however, because of the thinness of the cotton. And the buttons down the front make me want to undo them, kissing every silky inch of skin revealed as I do.

"She wants to go home and she's..." Pietro pauses, clearly struggling with what he wants to say.

"Resourceful?" Bianca asks with a heavy dose of sarcasm. "Smart? Unwilling to be trapped in my rich boss's penthouse?"

"She tried to go down in the food service elevator."

"How?" It has a shelf cutting it in half, making it impossible for anyone to fit inside.

"The shelf is not welded in."

It's not? That's a huge potential breach of security. And Bianca found it.

Wired to the security system, the food service elevator does not move without someone on my team knowing about it. The motion detectors in the shaft will draw attention to anyone who gets past the guard and locked steel door at the bottom and is foolish enough to try to climb the forty stories to my penthouse.

As irritated as I am with Bianca, I can't help feeling some admiration too. Nerissa couldn't have done any better herself.

"Get it fixed." I shift my gun away from Pietro and put it back in its holster.

Watching over the escape artist is its own form of punishment, I guess. Doesn't mean I feel bad about the bruises he'll have tomorrow from my punches.

He doesn't step back but his shoulders relax infinitesimally. "Already done."

Bianca tries to step around me. "But not before he took my clothes away."

I step to the side so she's still behind me. That nightgown might as well be made of plastic wrap. It shows everything.

"You are wearing a nightgown," I observe, wondering if I put my gun away too soon.

Pietro hastily explains, "Mamma helped her change again."

"You can't go around firing people just because I don't want to stay here," Bianca admonishes me. "Making your sweet housekeeper an accessory to kidnapping is just wrong."

That explains how Rosa convinced Bianca to change into the nightgown after her failed escape attempt. My *sweet* housekeeper lied.

CHAPTER 20

BIANCA

Any hope I had of Salvatore's return being the catalyst for getting me out of this ridiculous situation lay in ashes at my feet. The man is even more irrational and bossy than Pietro.

No wonder Rosa has been so stressed about me trying to get out of the apartment. Our boss is an ogre. I'm not sure why she doesn't want to get fired though. Working as domestic staff for Salvatore can't be a picnic.

But she'd practically been in tears when she begged me to put my nightgown back on and get back into bed. I'd decided then that I would wait for Salvatore to return and confront him without putting an innocent woman who reminds me of my nonna in harm's way.

Maybe getting fired entails more than just losing her job. Salvatore is a mafia capo after all.

A mafia capo who put his gun back into a holster on his belt. Not a shoulder holster, which would make what I'm about to do impossible.

My hand snakes out and I grab for the gun.

Salvatore is faster and his fingers clamp around my wrist like steel bands.

Che palle!

Keeping hold of my wrist, he turns and suddenly his entire attention is on me.

Fear thrills through me, but that's not the only reaction my body has to his fierce regard. My vajayjay gives a single, powerful pulse of want as wetness soaks my panties.

He inhales like he can smell it. He can't, can he?

That's not a real thing. Is it?

The predatory look that comes over his features says maybe it is.

Merda. Am I in trouble.

Because that look on his face is only making the situation between my thighs more acute.

"You tried to run away?" he asks, like he's my father and I've broken a house rule.

Too bad I have no respect left for father figures and his rules wouldn't apply to me even if I did. I'm not a member of Salvatore's household.

"It's not running away when I don't live here," I inform him.

At the same time, Pietro narks, "Twice. First, she tried to short the door lock mechanism."

"How?" Salvatore asks, looking like he wants to laugh.

If he does, I will knee him in the nut sac.

"I'm not sure what the plan was," Pietro says. "But I found an empty glass, a wet wall and a metal object wedged into the trim around the security panel."

Salvatore regards me with curiosity. "Metal object? Water? What was your intention? To electrocute yourself?"

"My intention was to open the door."

"The security panel is tamper proof. I could shoot it and it wouldn't crack."

Which explains why the metal cocktail stirring stick I pilfered from the drink's cabinet bent rather than breaking through the panel. I tried wedging it behind too, but it got stuck in the wood casing around the panel.

In a hurry because I could feel my time while Rosa and her son were otherwise occupied dwindling, I left it there and snuck into the kitchen to get a knife.

Which I now know would not have worked either, but when I found the dumbwaiter, I focused on using it. Pietro and Salvatore wouldn't fit inside, even folded up like a contortionist. I might not be model thin, but I'm a lot more compact than they are.

"Not sure how she thought she was going to call the elevator without access if she'd been able to get the door open." Pietro's patronizing tone makes me want to hide thumbtacks in his bed.

"I assumed the elevator has a button like normal buildings," I gripe. Not that I got anywhere near it.

"When that didn't work," Pietro, the snitch, continues. "She tried the food service elevator."

"Tattletale." I lean to the left so I can glare at him only to be reminded in vivid detail why moving like that is not a good idea.

"How the hell did she have enough time to do all that?" Salvatore spins to face his housekeeper and head of security, his body rigid with anger.

"I am your housekeeper, not jailer for your unwilling guests," Rosa says with wounded dignity. "I was relaxing in my room off the kitchen."

"Watching her soaps, she means," Pietro says sotto voce.

He's right. I could hear the sound of Rosa's program through the door. It was the only reason I risked taking the shelf out of the dumbwaiter with her so nearby.

"What were you doing?" Salvatore asks Pietro in a voice that gives me chills.

I have no idea what it's doing to Pietro.

"Working in the office with the door open. I *thought* Miss Gemelli was sleeping." He makes it sound like me faking sleep is worse than him kidnapping me.

I don't think so. "Yeah, I heard you on the computer when I tiptoed by."

The clickety-clack of a keyboard warned me to drop to a crawl going by the doorway. Too bad for him, stealth movement is one of my skills, honed by necessity in my teens.

"She heard you, but you didn't hear her?" Salvatore sounds less than impressed by his guard's observational skills.

I think Pietro got complacent, believing there was no way I could get out of the apartment without help from him or Rosa. Considering the fact, he brought the dumbwaiter back up to the penthouse before I could reach ground level and get out, odds are in his favor.

That doesn't mean I'm going to give up and remain a good little prisoner for them. "Salvatore, you have to let me go home."

"When was the last time she had pain meds?" Salvatore demands of Rosa like I didn't even speak.

I mean, I assume he's not talking to Pietro. Considering how special Salvatore is being about his guard seeing me in this nightgown. Which is perfectly decent, covering way more than my cocktail waitress uniform. It's a little thin, but it's hardly see through.

Not that I want to run around Manhattan wearing it, but still.

"Bianca has refused the acetaminophen she was supposed to take two hours ago." Rosa's voice rings with disapproval.

Apparently, Pietro got his tattling ways from his mother.

"Why did you refuse your pain meds?" Finally, Salvatore is looking at me again.

I'm only the person in question.

"The ibuprofen made me sleepy. The acetaminophen would too." Probably. It's not worth the risk.

"It did not occur to you that you are tired because your body is recovering from the trauma of this morning."

"Oh, so when you get into a fight, you nap the day away after?" I ask with sarcasm.

I don't think so.

"You did not get into a fight. You were chased down by three large men intent on doing you harm."

"And I fought back."

"Yes." Admiration reflects in the depths of his gray gaze. "Very well too."

"Not well enough." I would be dead if he hadn't shown up with his men. As much as it pains me to utter the words, I say, "Thank you for stopping them."

"Show your appreciation for me saving your life by allowing me to take care of you."

Right. He's not taking care of squat. My so called care is all on Rosa.

"Your housekeeper doesn't need extra work. I can take care of myself."

"Like when you tried to electrocute yourself opening my door?"

"Give me a break. I used my phone's silicone case to hold one end of the stick. I was never at risk of getting a shock, much less being electrocuted."

"For a pain in the ass, you're pretty smart," Pietro says from behind Salvatore.

His boss doesn't seem as pleased by the praise as I am. It's honest admiration after all and that is in short supply in my life.

My banging body gets plenty of approval, but that's different. This is my brain we're talking about.

"You do not care that he called you a pain in the ass, just that he said you are smart," Salvatore says with narrowed eyes.

I shrug and wince, questioning those smarts. How many times am I going to move the wrong way and add to the pain radiating out from the stitched up wound in my back?

"That's it. You are going back upstairs and taking your pain medication. All of it. Argue with me and I'll carry you."

I roll my eyes. Men. Logic isn't always their friend.

"How are you going to do that without hurting me?" If he wants me to take pain meds, it follows he doesn't want to add to my discomfort.

Salvatore doesn't bother to answer verbally but moves with the speed of the predator he is. Trapping my own arms in the process, he wraps one arm around my waist and the other around my hips right under my butt. Then he lifts, like I weigh no more than a child.

"This is ridiculous." I squirm, but I can't even move enough to pull at my stitches. "Put me down!"

He heads up the stairs with a smooth gait that doesn't jar me. Okay, maybe he's got the no hurting thing down. It stands to reason that a capo knows how to cause pain, which probably makes him expert at knowing how not to cause it too.

"I didn't do anything wrong, why am I being kept a prisoner?" I complain all the way to the bedroom.

I might have called him a few names in English that I usually reserve for my Italian muttering. He ignores all of it. The name calling. The demands. The appeal to his better nature, of which I'm increasingly convinced he does not have one.

"Is that your dick?" I screech as a hard bulge presses against my thighs. "This is turning you on?"

"Everything about you makes my cock hard, Bianca. Holding you so close to my body is only a bonus."

"I could have walked."

"But would you have?"

I turn my head away, refusing to answer because of course I wouldn't have come back up here under my own steam.

He releases his hold on my thighs and controls my slide down his body with his other arm.

"This is sexual harassment." And it is not turning me on to be so close to this man.

Even in pain and cranky about being held prisoner *for my own good*.

Not.

"I'm not your boss right now."

"That's not how it works, Salvatore. Besides, you're always the boss, aren't you, Mr. Capo?"

"Then perhaps you should learn to obey me?"

"You aren't bossing me into your bed."

"While that could be another kind of turn on, no I am not. When it happens, you'll come of your own free will."

When, not if. I shake my head. "Over confidence was Napolean's downfall, you know."

"It's a good thing I'm not a French dictator then, isn't it?"

I realize he is no longer holding me against him and step back, refusing to acknowledge the sense of loss I feel when we are no longer touching.

Yes, I want this man, but I'm not screwing him until I have full freedom of movement. And maybe not even then.

Though, probably? I am.

Because as annoyed as I am right now, the fact that his touch doesn't make my skin crawl is huge. That I can stand with my body trapped against his without having even a mini panic attack? Unprecedented.

I don't spend time along with men. At all. Not ever. There are two male roommates in our apartment, and when they are the only ones home, I leave. No matter what time it is, no matter what the weather is like, I'm out of there.

Right now? I want to leave on principle, not because being alone with this man makes me anxious.

He's a capo. A made man. He's a killer. A criminal. Dangerous.

He should scare the crap out of me, but he doesn't.

"You have a weird look on your face." He steps toward the bed.

I don't move. "Do I? It's probably my irritation at being kept a prisoner."

"You are not a prisoner."

"The locked door and inaccessible elevator says otherwise, not to mention my jailer, Pietro the thug."

"Again, not a thug."

"Maybe you need to rethink his position as your head of security. I got past him pretty easily." Because he underestimated me.

What if Pietro underestimates one of Salvatore's enemies? A sick feeling in the pit of my stomach says I never want to find out.

"He won't make the same mistake again."

I wouldn't like to have that anger directed at me, but then again, I'm making zero effort to avoid pissing off the mafia capo.

Huh. Maybe the knock to my head had more impact than the doctors thought.

Then again, it's hard to be afraid of a man who is currently straightening the sheets and duvet on the bed for me. He even fluffs the pillows.

"Uh, shouldn't Rosa be doing that?"

"You think I should leave everything to my housekeeper?"

"You don't?"

"No." He pulls the bedding back into a perfect triangle, so I can slide in easily.

"I don't want to lay down."

"You need to rest and trying to escape down food service elevators isn't helping."

"Maybe if I didn't need to escape, I could be sleeping right now." I yawn, highlighting how tired I am. "In my own bed."

Or on the floor of the closet. Which admittedly does not seem nearly as appealing as the bed Salvatore just made up for me.

CHAPTER 21

SALVATORE

Why is she still arguing with me? There are purple bruises under her eyes. That yawn is no sympathetic reaction either.

Her beautiful body needs rest.

And I need those curves safely tucked out of sight. "Do you need the toilet?"

"I'm not a toddler. If I need to go to the bathroom, I'll go."

"Do you need to go now?"

"No."

I nod. Good. "Then get in the bed." I'd much rather be saying those words under different circumstances.

"I want my clothes and I want to go home."

"Do you remember the doctor saying the dressing had to be changed with new antibiotic ointment applied daily? That even if you do everything right, the wound on your back could become infected?"

"Yes," she says grudgingly.

"Who is going to help you with that?"

"My roommates."

"Even you don't sound convinced. Why the hell would I be?"

"It doesn't matter if you are. It's my life."

"Which I saved. I have a vested interest in you not losing it to an infection that could be avoided."

"Are you kidding me? This isn't some tale in King Arthur's court. I don't owe you my life for saving it. Or my ass for that matter."

"I killed three men for you." Two to be accurate. One killed himself, but that's extraneous detail she doesn't need. "Even in the twenty-first century mafia that means I have a claim on your life."

And her ass as she so eloquently put it, but that argument can wait. She will come to my bed because she is no more immune to this pull between us than I am.

She bunches her fists and puts them on her hips, her eyes sparking fire I have to ignore.

For now.

"You might be right about my roommates, but I have a friend I can stay with."

"Does this friend work?"

"Of course, she does. Who doesn't work?" she snarks.

"Then she can't be with you all the time," I point out more reasonably than I would with someone else. I am used to being obeyed, but this woman challenges me. And it turns me on. "Here, you will always have someone with you."

"That's not the benefit you seem to think it is," she grumbles.

If I can't get her into the bed with logic, there are other ways. "Did you know that with the light behind you I can see the outline of your luscious tits and hips. I can't accept the invitation your hard nipples are making, but I promise when you are healed. I will."

She squawks and rushes to the bed, practically diving under the covers despite the pain it causes her, evidenced by her wincing. She pulls the duvet up to her chin and glares at me.

"You're damn shy for a woman who used to dance at a strip club."

"Sue me." She huffs.

I smile. "Not necessary. I find it intriguing."

"Don't."

"What?"

"Be intrigued by me."

"Too late for that." Much too late.

She caught my attention the first time I saw her fiery red hair across the club and hasn't let go of it a single day since.

"I'll stay the night, but tomorrow I want my clothes back and escort out of this apartment."

"If you won't stay here, then I will pay for your stay at the hospital." I'm not a monster. Well, not all of the time. "You cannot tend to that wound on your own."

"Candi can help me."

"The friend who works?"

"Everybody works, Salvatore. Even Rosa. She won't be with me twenty-four-seven and I don't need anyone to be. That would stress me out."

"Why?"

"I don't like being around people."

"And yet you share your apartment with five roommates."

"Six if you count my couch-mate's boyfriend."

BIANCA

Salvatore's eyes narrow, the space around him going still in some weird way.

A shiver goes down my spine.

Because his mask of urbanity is gone and he is pure predator. "He shares a bed with you?"

"Not with me. With her." Like I'm going to participate in a three-way when I'm not even interested in a one-on-one.

At least I wasn't. Before Salvatore.

Not sharing that little tidbit.

He stalks toward the bed, a prowling panther, ready to spring. "But you sleep on that same sofa bed."

"I pay for half of the sofa." Keeping a firm grip on the duvet covering me, I scoot to sit against the headboard. "I don't sleep there."

"Where do you sleep?" He lowers his powerful body to sit beside me on the bed.

Strange. There's just enough room. As if I somehow unconsciously made space for him when I scrambled into the bed to get covered. Like I want him near me, or something.

Salvatore's big hand drops onto my duvet covered thigh and stays there.

My nipples grow achingly hard and I have to fist my hands so I don't try to soothe them. There are tingles in my core, his nearness sparking a strange electric current through me.

There is none of the usual panic that having a man in my sleeping space would cause. Just like at the hospital.

It's all I can do not to embarrass myself completely and lean forward to inhale his scent.

The hand on my thigh squeezes. "Where?"

"Where what?"

His smile is pure masculine arrogance. I lose my train of thought and he assumes he's the cause.

He is, but I'm not stroking his ego and admitting it.

"Where do you sleep in your overcrowded apartment if not in the sofa bed you pay for?" he asks.

Oh. Right. "The couple that sleeps in the main bedroom lets me use the floor of their closet."

"You pay for half of the sofa bed, but you sleep on the floor." He speaks slowly, like maybe he's got it wrong and he's giving me a chance to interrupt and set him straight.

I can't. "It's not as bad as you're making it sound. I don't sleep well with other people nearby." Or not at all.

"You slept with me."

I have no explanation. "The pain meds," I say, but don't believe it.

Neither does he by the look on his handsome face.

"You are telling me that you have a bed in the closet?" he asks with narrowed eyes.

"More like a yoga mat, blankets and a pillow." I mean, it has been my bed for a couple of years, but it's not really *a* bed.

"Even better." Sarcasm saturates his tone and the air around him is redolent with that panther-about-to-pounce energy.

And instead of having a panic attack, my ovaries are sending out all sorts of *get me some of that* signals.

When other women claim they can't resist their lovers, I judge them inside my head. Every single time. Of course, they can resist. It's their body.

Only my body is awash with chemicals sending messages to my brain I thought were on the blocked list.

Desire. Want. *Need.*

No, I'm not going to give in to these feelings, but for the first time, I want to. And if I didn't have stitches in my back and forehead, it might be a different story about the giving in.

More like enthusiastic participation.

Both terrified and exhilarated by that truth, I stare in silence at Salvatore. Can he tell what I'm thinking?

The banked anger in his steely gaze says he's not thinking about sex right now. For once.

And I can't get my ladybits to shut up about it.

How the tables have turned.

"You were going to go back to that apartment to heal? On an old yoga mat on the closet floor?"

"Some of us make do with what we have, Salvatore." If Mr. Rhunke were still alive, I would be able to stay with him.

But two years ago, the man who saved me from homelessness at sixteen had a stroke that left him first paralyzed and then dead. His family evicted me so his younger son could move into the rent-controlled apartment.

After Mr. Ruhnke's death, and having no other option, I moved into an apartment with five strangers, including one man who officially lives there and one who does not.

Life. It's full of twists you don't see coming.

Like me being here.

"You making do would have ended up with you in the ER, or worse." Salvatore looks at me like he's trying to figure out my brain.

Good luck with that. I still don't understand what drives me sometimes. "What's worse than the ER?"

"Your roommates not noticing you in delirium from infection and you dying of dehydration."

"Man, you have a talent for coming up with the worst-case scenario, don't you?" Maybe it goes along with being a capo in the mafia.

Death feels like the natural go-to.

"It's a gift."

"Was that a joke?"

"Capos don't joke."

"Uh huh. Pretty sure that was another one." What the heck is going on?

Who is the humorous version of the man determined to get me under him? Or maybe he wants me on top? X-rated images of different positions with Salvatore play like an unruly porno in my head.

"Candi isn't going to ignore an infection." But neither am I willing to put that stress on her.

Not when she's home she has her little sister and arthritic mom to take care of. Going to stay with Candi would not be fair to her.

Accidenti.

I'm not about to share that revelation with Salvatore. Once he lets me leave, I can just go home. To my many roommates, one of whom will hopefully be willing to help me with the daily dressing.

"Does Candi have a guest bedroom?" Salvatore asks, like he can see right into my brain.

"Not exactly."

"What exactly?"

"A twin bed." In a room she shares with her little sister.

"You would rather put your friend out of her bed than stay here?" Salvatore asks, the look on his face judging me.

"No." I chew on my lip, thinking.

This is too much for just a one-night stand. His concern makes no sense. Even his bossiness. Why does he care so much? He could sit back and wait for me to heal and then pounce.

I'm pretty sure we both know I want him.

"You're not used to allowing others to help you."

"Are you saying you are?" Not likely.

"We are not talking about me."

"We kind of are and your need to take care of a perfect stranger."

"One. You are not perfect."

"Another joke?" Seriously?

"Two," he says smoothly as if I did not interrupt him. "You are not a stranger. You work for me."

"For Franco, technically," I have to interrupt.

Though we both know that as the club owner Salvatore has the power to fire me just like Franco.

One dark brow raises. "We both know that technically, everyone who works at a Cosa Nostra club in this territory works for me."

"That makes your attempt to coerce me into bed even more skeevy."

The long suffering look he gives me is everything. "I don't coerce women into bed. I offered to pay you. You turned me down."

"Go me. I bet you're not used to women saying no."

"It doesn't happen. Maybe that's why I want more than a single night now."

Oh no. No. No. No. I did not supercharge his desire to screw me by turning him down.

Only, I think I really did.

And my vagina is not unhappy about that. Which, considering my past, is some kind of sexual miracle. But wanting and being able to do something about it are two very different things.

CHAPTER 22

BIANCA

"What do you mean you want more than a single night?" Is he talking about dating?

"We will discuss that when you are feeling better," he says blithely. "Have you considered that once Rosa knows about your living situation, she'll worry herself sick about you?"

"And I suppose you're going to tell her the minute you get the chance."

"I would prefer my housekeeper not believe I kidnapped you with no reason."

"I thought you didn't approve of kidnapping."

"I disapproved of Pietro's use of a drug to gain your compliance."

"But it was okay to kidnap me?"

"Considering the situation you were returning to in order to convalesce, forced compliance should not have been necessary."

And was therefore okay? Judgy much? "Convalesce. Who talks like that?"

"Educated men?"

"Here I thought all you learned in the mafia was how to intimidate and kill people, not to mention kidnapping." My sarcasm is as thick as his judgment.

"As my father's second, that was definitely part of education. However, I got my degree in business and then my MBA because I knew that his second-in-command wasn't all I would be."

Right. He's probably known since he was a toddler that one day he'd take over as capo from his father.

"Please tell me Pietro isn't your second."

"Nerissa has that privilege."

Privilege, right. Of course, he thinks it's some kind of honor to intimidate, kidnap and even kill on his behalf.

"Your sister is your second-in-command?" That's not the mafia I remember.

He shrugs. "Miceli is underboss to our don and his brother. It's a solid system. Keep it in the family."

"What does Nerissa's husband think about being married to a capo's second?"

"My sister's not married."

"But her last name is different than yours."

"She joined our family when she was fifteen."

Apparently, that's all the explanation I'm going to get, but it's more than I expect.

"Aren't you worried about telling me this stuff?" It's a real turn around from the man who didn't even want to confirm he is a Cosa Nostra capo.

Now, he's telling me mafia stuff, not to mention a pretty personal piece of information about his family dynamic.

"You witnessed me kill a man."

"According to you, three men." And he's decided that somehow makes me trustworthy?

Or maybe that's the real reason he had me kidnapped. To stop me going to the cops. "It happened behind me."

"You'd still make a credible witness."

"Are you going to kill me to keep me quiet?" Has all this talk about getting me into bed been a smokescreen?

Only if he wanted to kill me, wouldn't I already be dead? Why go to the trouble of having Rosa help tend to my wound? "Is that what this keeping me in your apartment is really about?"

"No."

"You need time to get rid of the evidence."

"The *evidence* was gone by the time you woke up the first time in the hospital."

"Except me. I'm not gone."

"You're not evidence either."

"You said it yourself. I'd make a credible witness."

"To a crime there is no evidence was ever committed."

"Oh."

"It is safe to say your brain doesn't travel the same tracks as mine."

"Duh. Not part of the mafia." Not anymore anyway. "Let me get this straight. Since I witnessed a crime there is no evidence for, you have decided it's okay to tell me who the Genovese underboss is."

"Are you trying to imply Marco didn't already? If he mentioned me, he definitely spilled the beans about Severu and Miceli."

"You are not wrong."

"So, I'm not telling you anything you don't already know."

"And you're so arrogant you think you know everything without even asking me to confirm it?" That tracks.

He shrugs, not bothered by being called arrogant.

It figures. "Did you really threaten to fire Rosa if I didn't cooperate?"

"Does it matter?" His eyes bore into mine.

I'm not trying to hide anything. Right now. So, I look back. "Yes."

"Why?"

"If you'd fire her for something like that, I'd know I can't trust you."

"You *can't* trust me."

"You know what I mean."

"Not sure I do. I don't trust anyone outside *la famiglia* and few within."

Which is a pretty clear way of saying he doesn't trust me. "You don't need to trust a woman to have sex with her."

"No."

"But I do. Need to trust a partner, I mean. I couldn't let a man into my body that I didn't trust." I'm not sure I can ever let a man into my body that way at all.

"What if I lie and say no, but the real answer is yes?"

"What if you don't lie to me?"

"No," he says with conviction. "Rosa is like a second mother to me. My own would disown me if I fired her."

His words ring true. But then so did Rosa's. "She lied to me?"

"Did it work?"

"You know it did." It had to have been the tears.

They convinced me. Not to mention her too believable manner. Huh.

Salvatore shrugs. "Rosa is a smart woman and she didn't want to cause you further stress, but you weren't being reasonable."

"Wanting to leave my prison isn't unreasonable."

"My apartment is not a prison."

"Right. You've got other places to keep prisoners."

"Do you really want me to confirm that?"

"No. Your thug drugged and kidnapped me, so you know...even a penthouse can feel like a prison under the right, or wrong, circumstances."

"Pietro deeply regrets drugging you."

"But not kidnapping me." It's not a question.

Salvatore doesn't regret it. Why would his guard?

"You were heading back to a yoga mat on the floor and planned to take a rideshare to do it. You might as well put a sign out welcoming infection."

"You are such a drama llama."

His eyes widen fractionally, and the edges of his mouth start to curve before he stops the smile forming. "No one has ever called me that before."

"No one has insisted on taking care of me since Mr. Ruhnke had his stroke." And maybe Salvatore is a tiny bit right.

I might be reacting to him wanting to do it slightly irrationally. I'm feeling more emotional than usual. I blame the drugged kidnapping. So, basically, it's Pietro's fault.

"Who is Mr. Ruhnke?"

"Someone I used to know." I should call his daughter-in-law to find out why she texted. "I need my phone."

Salvatore looks around like he expects the device to materialize. "Where is it?"

"Pietro took it." When I made my empty threat to call the cops after my failed escape attempt in the dumbwaiter.

"I will see you get it back."

"Thank you."

"Will you stay and allow your body to heal in an environment conducive to it doing so?"

"You sound so formal."

His expression is not amused.

"You're actually asking me now?"

"Yes."

"And if I say no?"

"I will arrange for you to return to the hospital or a rehabilitation facility until you are healed."

He is really determined to take care of me.

Doing my best to pretend I don't notice that warm sensation in the center of my chest, I nod. "I'll stay."

SALVATORE

A tormented scream yanks me from my uneasy doze and I'm jumping from my bed with my gun in my hand before a second one shatters the nighttime silence.

Bianca.

Adrenalin spikes and I rush to her room, slamming open the door without knocking. Jerking my head from side to side I look for the threat, but no one else is here.

Two of my men guard the penthouse at night from inside and two more in the hall. Another team patrols the parking garage and the lobby.

None of them would come up here, but that scream.

Cazzo.

I am ready to kill and there's no one to shoot.

"No!" Bianca flings herself to the side.

The covers are twisted around her and she's fighting them, trying to kick her feet. Tears track a silver streak down her cheeks in the near dark.

She's having nightmares again.

Yesterday's attack is still affecting her.

Reparation isn't enough. I want retaliation. If that *stronzo*, Henry, or any of his people make the mistake of coming to Manhattan, I will get it too.

I won't disobey the godfather and hunt them in their own territory, but if they come to ours, it will be the last mistake any of them make.

It only takes a few seconds to tug the duvet and sheets away from Bianca. She doesn't wake, even when I say her name.

There's only one way to calm her down. The same as at the hospital. But no way in hell am I sleeping in a guestroom bed in my own house.

Picking her up, I hold her against my chest, but she's still trying to thrash. Then she turns her face into my neck and inhales. Her body goes limp.

How? There's no white knight in my gene pool. We're mafia back five generations.

And this sweet woman finds solace in my nearness. There's something wrong with her olfactory senses. My scent is that of a predator. It should frighten her, not calm her down.

My presence brings terror and submission, not this...this peace.

Carrying her into my bedroom, I dismiss how right she feels in my arms. My cock is aching and hungry for her. It doesn't want any other pussy. That's all this is.

Until I fuck Bianca a few times and get her out of my system, my lizard brain is going to approve of her in my arms. And I can't bang her if I can't touch her.

That's all this is.

Settling Bianca into my bed on her side, I make sure she's not irritating her wound. She rubs her face against my pillow and a soft little sigh puffs from between her parted lips.

I climb into the bed and pull the covers up over both of us before putting my hand on her hip. She squirms until her arms are pressed up against my front and her head is tucked under my chin.

My cock is hard, like it has been all night, from knowing she's in the room next to me. In a bed. In my home. Where she belongs.

For now.

For now, I repeat to myself.

Despite the arousal pulsing through my veins, my body relaxes and the pull of sleep finally takes hold.

~ ~ ~

I wake a couple of hours later to a quiet moan.

"Bianca?"

"What are you doing in my bed?" she whispers.

She's in my bed, but she'll figure that out soon enough. And probably start yelling at me about it. I'd like both of us to get a few more hours of sleep before that happens.

I ask the smart speaker what time it is and realize Bianca is past due for her acetaminophen.

"Stay there. I'll get your meds and be right back."

When I return with the pills and a glass of water, she swallows them without argument. I tell the smart speaker to set an alarm for when she needs her staggered dose of ibuprofen and climb back into the bed.

"I suppose you're going to tell me that I was having a nightmare until you got into bed with me." She's still whispering.

"If you already know, there's no need for me to tell you."

"I'm too tired to argue." She turns so her back is to me.

My muscles bunch with the need to pull her against me, but because of the still raw wound on her back, I won't. I settle onto my own back, but somehow my right hand makes it onto her thigh.

Her breath catches, but then the tension drains out of her body. "I don't sleep with men."

"With a bed in the bottom of a closet, I'm not surprised," I say drily.

"It's not that." She sighs. "Never mind. But..." She pauses and then says, "Thank you, Salvatore. I don't know why you're being so nice to me. Why you are willing to be my woobie blanket, or why my subconscious feels safe with you, but I appreciate you helping me sleep."

I don't know how to respond to her gratitude.

Women thank me for screaming climaxes and expensive gifts. They don't thank me for being *nice*. I am not a nice man.

And what the fuck is a woobie blanket?

CHAPTER 23

BIANCA

My fifth day at the penthouse, I decide enough with the nightgowns.

Today I am getting dressed.

The only problem is: I still don't know where my clothes are. So, I ask Rosa when she brings up my breakfast.

To Salvatore's room.

I go to sleep alone in the guestroom bed every night, but wake up in Salvatore's massive bed every morning. Again, alone. But memories of him taking care of me linger along with his scent on the pillow.

My super-hot, violently dangerous nurse makes sure I take my pain pills in the middle of the night.

And he touches me. Not intimately. But his hand is always connected to me somewhere on my body. My hip. My shoulder. The back of my neck. Whenever I wake it's there and I sleep better and more deeply than I have since my nonna died.

I don't know why he carries me into his bedroom and shares his bed with me when he is not getting the one thing men seem to want. Sex.

It feels like connection and that's even scarier than Salvatore, Cosa Nostra capo.

Every morning, he's gone when I wake up though and doesn't return until after I fall asleep. Which isn't that hard since I fall asleep so easily right now, it feels like I have narcolepsy.

It's weird. I usually doze at best. Sometimes I can't sleep at all at the apartment, but although I'm sleeping more than ever, I'm exhausted.

I can only be grateful I took my last final the day before the attack. There's no way I have the focus or energy to attend classes. Even if I could do it without Salvatore having a meltdown.

Who probably thinks that QC is as rife with germs waiting to attack my healing wounds as the closet I sleep in at the apartment.

Wearing street clothes will be a signal to my body to stay awake.

"I put them with the rest of your clothing." Rosa lays the tray on a table by the windows.

"The rest of my clothes?" Salvatore must have sent one of his men after some things for me to wear.

I wish he'd said something. I've been living in these thin cotton nightgowns. Even though I am not allowed to shower, Rosa gives me a clean one to put on after I get my wounds checked by the doctor every day.

Washing myself with a fluffy wash cloth isn't cutting it and today, I'm taking a shower. The doctor said on Sunday it would probably be okay, but she would prefer I waited one more day.

That day is done.

I'm getting clean. Today.

"They are in the guestroom dresser and closet." She presses a button that draws the drapes back to reveal the stunning view of New York from Salvatore's corner bedroom.

"Oh, okay. Thank you." I never even thought to look in what I assumed was an empty dresser and closet.

Why would I? I don't live here.

Which makes what I find in the guestroom after breakfast so astonishing.

The dresser is full. My entire, though yeah sparse, collection of t-shirts, yoga pants, and jeans are mixed in with clothes of the same size with the tags still on them. "Did you buy me clothes, Rosa?"

"That's all Salvatore." The older woman straightens the fresh bedding on the bed. "He had everything delivered."

Salvatore bought me clothes? Rosa must be mistaken. But then where did the soft t-shirts with smartass sayings on them come from? Or the designer jeans mixed in with the ones I got from Goodwill?

Maybe he told one of his guys to do it. I grin at the thought of Pietro being forced to shop for my clothing. That would explain the t-shirts. Though, they fit my personality to a *t*.

Is it a pun if you only say it in your head?

When I open the drawer with bras and panties, my cheeks heat and I fervently hope Pietro *did not* buy these for me. I've never owned a pair of La Perla panties in my life. Now I have seven. With matching bras.

They're all ridiculously feminine and sexier than anything I own.

I could live for months off of what was spent on this drawer alone. Also, I haven't had underwear to wear since Rosa took the pair from the hospital away with the first nightgown to wash. Only, apparently, I did.

Lots of them.

Pride makes me reach for a pair of my cotton panties that came in a pack of five, but my fingers slip along the soft satin of a pair the same blue as my eyes and I cannot resist them.

I grab the panties and matching bra before I can stop myself. Slamming the drawer closed, as if that will negate my choice in underwear, I inhale a deep breath.

The t-shirt I grab is silk and the same shade of blue with pink lettering that says, *I'm not responsible for what my face does when you talk.* The yoga pants I pick are mine and one of my most comfortable pairs.

Opening another drawer, I stop in stunned amazement. The man even bought me socks. My five pairs of well washed black ankle socks reside in a single small stack next to a plethora of ankle and no-show socks in every color. The drawer is practically stuffed.

Feeling like I'm selling my soul, I pull out a pair of pink fuzzy slipper socks. But I'm already going to be wearing over $500 worth of underwear, what's a pair of cozy socks compared to that?

"I'm a little afraid to look in the closet," I admit to Rosa.

The look on her face says I have reason to be worried. Which only makes it impossible to ignore my curiosity.

But it's not the dresses hanging in the walk-in closet that have me sucking in a breath and forgetting how to let it out. It's the neat rows of shoes and other items. This is not picking up a few things from my place so I have something to wear, which considering all the shopping Salvatore did, is a complete waste of energy.

And yes, now I accept Salvatore did the shopping. No way would he let one of his men buy me underwear when he wouldn't even let a male nurse near me at the hospital.

All of my things are here. Not just my clothes. Everything. My box of keepsakes sits on the top shelf next to my pillow. My yoga mat is rolled up and leaning against the wall. My bedding is folded and stacked neatly in one of the closet cubbies.

My school bag empty except for my laptop and charger sits lonely on another shelf. I already sold my physical textbooks back for the semester. Ebooks are more convenient, but since they can't be sold back, the more cumbersome but economic physical books are usually what I end up getting.

I don't own a lot, but what I have is here. If I go into the attached bathroom and start opening drawers, I bet I'll find my makeup, my toothbrush (even though I've been using a new one straight out of the package since I arrived), and everything else I kept stored in my bathroom basket in the apartment.

"Did they bring my food from the fridge too?" I ask Rosa sarcastically.

She looks at me reprovingly. "I told them not to bother, but I purchased items similar to what you had."

Similar, but not identical. Rosa isn't going to buy store brand pasta. *Accidenti*. She's not going to buy dried pasta at all.

Even the tiny star shaped pastina in her soup tastes fresh. "No wonder my coffee tastes perfect. You got my cinnamon dolce creamer."

"Bite your tongue." Rosa is scandalized by the suggestion. "I put real cream and cinnamon with a dash of vanilla in your morning latte."

There's only one thing missing. The African violet Mr. Ruhnke got me that first year he helped me. He showed up with the plant and a used grow light, saying it was good to have something to take care of.

He'd been right. That plant is like family to me.

I'll need to call one of my roommates. It's due watering tomorrow. But what if they water from the top, or give it too much? Maybe Salvatore will give me a ride back to my apartment now that I'm doing better.

"Why?" I walk out into the bedroom and wave my arm, encompassing the dresser, the made bed with the covers turned back invitingly. "Why all this?"

"You need to heal, *dolce ragazza.*"

"It doesn't take all my worldly goods to help me get better." But if they're all going to be here, I really wish my violet was among them.

"Salvatore does not like your living situation."

She cannot be saying what I think she is. Salvatore would not move me out of my apartment without even asking me.

Who am I kidding? He's a capo.

He thinks he's at least a minor deity. Of course, he would.

"How and where I live is none of his business." I say it as much a reminder for myself as for Rosa.

Being looked after, even if it is by an arrogant mafioso is dangerously appealing. Independence is woven into the fabric of my being, but being alone is not the same as being independent.

And I've been alone a long time. No safety net. No one to rely on when even my independent nature bows under the weight of life.

"Are you sure about that?" Salvatore's smooth tones have me spinning around to see him.

He's leaning against the doorjamb, his big body encased in a tailored suit and a cool expression on his features.

My heart surges with an erratic beat. Heat and want coalesce between my legs. My nipples tighten and poke against the thin cotton of my nightgown.

Why this man and no other? Why does my body go nuclear for him? Why does he make me feel safe?

My response to Salvatore is primal and rooted so deep in my atavistic instincts, logic has no hope of influencing it.

"What are you doing here?" I hold the pile of clothes in front of me like a shield.

His eyes say he notices and that he knows what I'm hiding behind that shield too. Hard nipples, aching for a touch they have never experienced.

Gah! The scream inside my head does not make it past my lips.

A tiny tilt of his too handsome mouth says he's amused. He knows. All of it. That I'm wet for him and can barely breathe past my desire for him.

"I live here," he drawls.

"But you're never home during the day." Okay, maybe I'm not qualified to make that statement.

I've only been staying here a few days.

"I'm not?"

"But..." My voice trails off because I don't know what I want to say.

My brain is too busy cataloguing every inch of the gorgeous capo determined to keep me locked in his penthouse like some kind of princess in a tower.

Until I heal.

But the fact all my worldly possessions are here indicates his plans might last beyond that and not just for a night of hot and steamy sex.

It's ridiculous. Salvatore doesn't want me living with him. He can't. We barely know each other.

But you're here now.

I shush that little voice inside my head. *Remember*, I tell it, *he's a mafia prince and I'm no princess*. Not anymore.

If I could be tossed away as easily as Lorenzo threw me out of my home and the mafia, abandoned by both my parents, I never was one to begin with. No matter what my parents claimed.

"The doctor is here to examine you."

Looking past his shoulder, I don't see anyone. "She is?"

"She's waiting in my bedroom."

"Why your bedroom?"

Not bothering to answer, Salvatore leaves.

The sound that comes out of me is not pretty. That man. Could he be any more irritating?

CHAPTER 24

BIANCA

"Give me these," Rosa says with a smile. "I'll put them in the bath-room for you."

I let the bundle of clothes go but shake my head. "I'm not going in there like this."

I'm not even wearing panties for crying out loud.

That didn't bother you last night when you were cuddled up against Salvatore in his bed.

Shut up, inner voice. No one asked you.

Rosa disappears into the bathroom and returns a second later with a blue silk robe. I'm starting to sense a theme here.

It's thin, but something is better than nothing. Pulling it on, I'm not surprised by how soft it is against my skin, but I am startled by how opaque it is. Tying the belt in a bow, I immediately relax a little.

I head to Salvatore's room, where the doctor is waiting for me. Again. Why here?

The previous visits with her to check on my wounds have been in the guestroom.

When I reach the penthouse's primary suite, I step inside and ignore the sense of being in my own space that it gives me. Sleeping so well has made my brain associate this room with comfort and home.

But I don't have a home and haven't had one in so long, it's not worth thinking about.

This is *not* my space. *Not* my room. *Not* my home.

But you want it to be.

Ignoring the thought with more bananas than an ice cream sundae, I smile at the doctor. "Thank you for taking the time to come here and check on me."

"It is her job," Salvatore says dismissively.

"Yeah, no. Doctors don't make house calls anymore, Salvatore." I don't look at him because if I do, my body is going to go haywire again.

"They do for me."

"It is no trouble, Bianca. You're one of my best patients. If only they were all as cooperative." Her smile invites me to share the joke.

The sound of disbelief Salvatore makes adds another layer onto the annoyance I feel toward him. "You find Bianca to be cooperative?"

Why do I desire a man who irritates me as much as he turns me on? Hormones and primal libido have a lot to answer for.

"Your houseguest has complied with every instruction I have given her."

"Too bad you didn't *instruct* her not to recuperate on the floor of a closet."

The doctor gives me a concerned look. "You've been sleeping on the floor of the closet?"

I look at Salvatore only long enough to singe him with my glare. "No. That's where I sleep usually."

"But not anymore," Salvatore says bossily.

Like he gets to decide.

"Well, it's a good thing you're sleeping in a bed with clean sheets. Your wounds are healing very nicely with no sign of infection."

"Your pronouncement is premature." Salvatore's voice is so cold it makes the doctor shiver.

Or is that fear?

He moves closer so I can't help seeing him in my periphery. "You haven't even checked her over yet."

"Let's get to it then, shall we?" The doctor indicates one of the chairs by the window. "Why don't you sit down, Bianca?"

Her things are already on the table where I ate my breakfast earlier.

Eager to get away from the too-sexy-for-my-own-good capo's proximity, I quickly walk to the chair and sit down. The doctor starts her exam with the healing gash on my forehead.

"Your skin is knitting together nicely. The plastic surgeon did an excellent job. I doubt you'll have much of a scar, if any at all."

"Plastic surgeon? You didn't put the stitches in?" I ask, confused.

I don't remember talking to a plastic surgeon.

"Mr. De Luca insisted your wounds be seen to by a plastic surgeon after my colleague cleaned them and determined the depth of the damage in your back."

Her colleague? She's not the doctor who saw me initially? Now that I think about it, I remember a male doctor talking to me when I woke up the first time in the hospital.

Considering how over the top Salvatore was about the male nurse who tried to take my vitals, having this doctor assigned to my care is his doing for sure.

"Why a plastic surgeon?" I let my gaze settle on Salvatore finally because I need to see his expression.

Not that it does me any good. He might as well be wearing a mask for all the emotion he's showing. Until I look into his eyes.

Molten metal stares back at me, heating my body with their intensity.

But when his voice comes out, it is cool and emotionless, just like his too gorgeous face. "I assumed you would prefer no scars."

"I do," I whisper.

There are enough scars inside, my outside doesn't need to match.

"There is your answer."

Because I want it? That's his answer. My ovaries swoon.

"Your forehead is healing nicely and you can leave the bandage off now. The plastic surgeon will be here Wednesday to remove the stitches."

"That's not a full week for healing. Is that wise?" Salvatore asks.

"Plastic surgeons don't like to leave stitches in longer than five, six days max because it significantly increases the chance of scarring."

When Salvatore doesn't say anything further, the doctor looks at me questioningly. "Do you want him to remain for the examination of your back?"

The question startles me. Does the doctor think the capo will leave his own bedroom if I say no?

Do I?

I narrow my eyes at Salvatore. "Will you leave if I ask you to?"

Tension immediately fills the air between us, but Salvatore grudgingly nods. "Yes," he says from between gritted teeth, like it pains him.

I'm tempted to roll my eyes at his reaction, but part of me, the vulnerability that hides behind stubborn snark, likes how invested he is in my wellbeing. This isn't only about sex between us.

If it was, I wouldn't be here, in his home, to heal.

Fear wars with comfort inside my chest, making it ache.

"You can stay." It's not like he's going to see anything but my back.

I don't like being naked in front of others. Even when I'm dancing, I always wear something. I'm known for my creative outfits that reveal what I want them to. On the stage, I feel removed and in control.

Here, not so much. The doctor hasn't complained yet that I don't take off my nightgown for the exam.

Like the previous exams, I unbutton the front of my nightgown. Then I untie the silky robe and allow both to slide down my shoulders and upper arms. I keep the fabric over my chest, but my back is on display for the doctor.

And Salvatore.

His heated stare sends frissons of responding desire through me. Unfamiliar excitement I can't act on, even if I want to.

At least not until I'm healed.

The doctor carefully peels the gauze and paper medical tape away from my back. "There's no sign of infection."

Of course there isn't. Rosa checks it six times a day. She insists it's necessary because of the risk of infection to a knife wound. I comply because she reminds me of my nonna and her concern brings back good memories.

Rosa applies the prescribed salve and changes the bandage for fresh, sterile gauze every time too. It feels like overkill to me, but she says Salvatore will be furious if it gets infected.

Considering how weirdly concerned he is for my health, I believe her.

"This cut is healing just as quickly as the one your forehead." The doctor sounds happy.

So, I smile.

"Good," Salvatore says.

Could he make the affirmation sound grumpier?

"You no longer need to bandage this wound either, but continue the use of the salve once a day."

"It only needs to be applied once a day?" I ask.

The doctor's lips twist wryly, like she knows about Rosa's zealousness. "Technically, yes, but it certainly doesn't hurt to apply it more frequently."

Yeah, no. Rosa is going to have to dial it back a few notches. I have the doctor's recommendation on my side.

"Can I take a shower?"

I don't ask for my sake, because I already know it's okay and that I *will* be bathing.

I ask for Salvatore's. I don't like his chances of coming out unscathed if he tries to tell me I need to settle for another session with a soapy washcloth.

Every inch of my skin itches with the need to get clean.

"Yes, but no direct spray on either wound. You do not want to soak them until they are closed fully, so no baths or swimming."

"I haven't had access to a pool since high school," I say with a laugh. "And it's been longer since I had a bathtub where I live."

Specifically, since I got booted from my childhood home at sixteen.

"You have access to both here but using them will have to wait until you are healed." Salvatore talks like I'm going to be here long enough for that to happen.

"I'm sure the plastic surgeon will have further instructions when he removes the stitches." The doctor starts packing up her things.

I'm surprised he allowed the plastic surgeon to operate on me and say so.

"The time it would have taken to wait for a qualified female surgeon to arrive would have taken too long."

"Too long for what?" I wonder out loud.

"Healing without a scar," the doctor offers.

I'm still not sure why that's so important to Salvatore. "Are you that turned off by imperfection?"

"No. It is simply a matter of making sure you get the best care."

Do I believe him? I think I do.

Does that make me intuitive, or foolish?

"If that's all, I'll be going." The doctor smiles at me.

I nod.

Rosa appears in the doorway. "I'll see you out, doctor."

When the other two women are gone, I shake my head. "I swear Rosa's psychic. She always knows just when to come into the room to tidy it, or when to show up to escort a guest back downstairs."

"Have you had other guests?" he asks, sounding suspicious.

"You're kidding, right? You think there's even a remote possibility that a visitor came to your apartment you weren't told about?"

"There'd better not be."

"Don't worry. I'm sure Pietro would rat me out in a nanosecond."

"It's not being a rat to tell me what is happening in my home."

"About that."

"Che cosa?" He grimaces. "What?"

I roll my eyes. "I know what *che cosa* means."

"I suppose you have been around enough Italians to pick up a phrase or two."

It's all I can do not to roll my eyes. "You could say that," I say wryly.

Only my entire childhood. I could tell him I speak Italian fluently, but I'm having fun seeing the perfect capo get it wrong. Besides, I don't want the questions that would come after revealing my fluency. Like, how did I learn Italian? Who are my parents? Where is my family?

People can be nosy, and Salvatore is more intrusive than anyone I've ever met. Comes with being a capo, I guess.

"About what?" Salvatore prompts, his tone bordering on impatient.

"Do you have somewhere to be?"

"In fact, I do."

"Oh. Well, then you better go."

"Ask your question."

"Bossy."

"Bianca," he says warningly.

"It's just, you keep talking like I'm going to be here longer than a few days to recuperate. You bought me enough clothes to triple my current wardrobe—"

"Which is not saying much."

"Every piece of clothing I owned, I paid for, so get over yourself about how many pairs of jeans I have."

"Had. And it was one."

"It *was* two, but you had my clothing thrown away at the hospital." It's a guess, but none of the clothes I was wearing during the attack are in the guestroom.

"They were covered in blood and your shirt was torn."

"Blood can be washed out and tears can be mended." I puff out a breath of frustrated air. "Never mind, that's not what I'm asking about."

He gives me a look that says, *get to the point already*.

"Not only did you buy me a ridiculous amount of clothing, but you had your guy pack up all my stuff from the apartment."

"And it did not even fill the trunk."

"The fact he only had to take one trip is not the point. It's that you moved me out of my apartment. Without talking to me about it, which we will get to. But you moved me in here, like we're..." My voice trails off.

I don't know what we are.

"Right now we are friends."

"Are we really?"

"What else would you call it?"

"I don't know what to call it," I admit with exasperation.

His warm hand cups my neck and reaction tingles along my nerve endings. "I'm not ready to let go of this thing between us."

"Thing between us?" I ask incredulously. "What thing? You mean the *you want to get me into bed* thing? Or the *you had me kidnapped and then forced me to stay at your apartment to recuperate* thing?"

"Do not pretend you don't want to open your sweet pussy for me as badly as I want to be inside it. Your pulse is erratic from this simple touch."

"Again, not the point. I can't suddenly be living with you." And that's not something I should have to mention. "Who does this? You're a capo! You can't move a perfect stranger into your home."

"My *secure* home," he points out, rubbing in the fact I couldn't leave without help, despite my best efforts. "And we have addressed the perfect stranger concept. You are neither."

"You are not cute. We aren't dating. We don't have a relationship. We haven't even kissed."

His eyes darken. "Do you want to change that?"

"No." Then more honestly, I admit, "Maybe, but I—"

I don't get to finish my thought because his mouth takes possession of mine.

My brain shorts out. He's kissing me. And I like it.

Why did I think his lips would be hard like him? They're not. They are soft.

His scent surrounds me, the heat from his body drawing me to him like a moth to a flame. Though I feel more like a butterfly, coming out of my chrysalis to bright sunlight and a new life where touch is possible.

Where having a man touch me without throwing me into a tailspin is possible.

Where warm lips mold to my own so perfectly moisture burns at the back of my eyes.

Salvatore does not grab at me, or squeeze my boob until it hurts. There is no sweaty stench. No cruel demands.

Just touches that makes my soul sing.

He traces the seam of my lips with the tip of his tongue, sending shivers of delight through me. I always thought if I were to be kissed like this, with tongue, it would sicken me.

It doesn't. The opposite happens and I revel in how good every tiny touch between our mouths feels.

Salvatore nips my bottom lip and I gasp.

CHAPTER 25

SALVATORE

Bianca's lips part like I want them to and I take advantage of the opening to push my tongue inside the warm heat of her mouth.

Vanilla and cinnamon slide across my tastebuds along with a sweetness that is uniquely Bianca. My dislike for dessert forgotten, her sugary essence becomes my new favorite flavor.

She doesn't respond, her own tongue unmoving, but she's not trying to push me away either. Her body is almost preternaturally still as she seems to be relishing our connection as much as I am.

But I want more.

Lifting my head, I order, "Kiss me back."

Her lids snap open but her pretty, blue eyes are unfocused, nothing in them to indicate she registers cognition of my words. Knowing the barest touch of my lips affects her this way feeds my already healthy ego.

Only I will see her like this. No one else.

Right now, my brain taunts me, *until she gives herself to the next man.*

It won't be enough for her to leave Amuni. I need her out of New York after this thing runs its course. My primal nature will never allow another to touch what I have claimed as my own.

But I can't keep her. I am capo. I marry to further the interests of *la famiglia*. That is my duty.

In the future.

Right now, she is my pleasure.

"Bianca." I rub my thumb along her bottom lip. "Kiss me back."

Confusion flares in her gaze. "How?"

She wants to know how I like it? *Cazzo*. Why does that turn me on so much?

"Like this." I kiss her again, harder this time, forcefully thrusting my tongue into her mouth.

Hers slides against my own, making no effort to eject the marauder. Because we both want this. For however long it lasts.

My cock strains against my slacks, the pantleg not tailored to make room for my oversized erection. Because I'm not a teenager who gets hard when a sexy woman walks by.

Bianca sets my control over my hormones back fifteen years.

Groaning, I deepen the kiss as I pull her body close, pressing her stomach against my aching dick, teasing myself with what I cannot have. Yet.

Her soft little moan is almost my undoing. I want to rip the silky robe off her and her nightgown with it.

If I don't end this kiss, I'm going to do exactly that and she's not healed enough for the kind of sex that will lead to. But even as the thought forms her lips finally start to move under mine and I am lost.

Her mouth moves perfectly against mine with just the right amount of pressure, just the right amount of softness. She's the best fucking kisser I have ever laid my lips on.

Her body presses even more tightly against me. Hands that have remained at her side bury themselves in my hair, grabbing two clumps to yank my head closer.

She's too short. Sliding a hand under her ass, I lift her up so nothing can break our kiss. Her legs dangle. But then they come around my torso, locking like a vice, her years dancing the pole evident in the strength of their grip.

The only barrier between her hot, drenched pussy and my skin is my rapidly soaking shirt.

Cazzo.

She's not wearing panties. How often has she been naked under the nightgowns?

Without permission from my brain, my free hand slides under the thin cotton and over the silky skin of her ass. My middle finger dips between her swollen, wet pussy lips. No thought to hesitate, I spread her honey to her clit and rub there, my thumb pressing inside her hot tunnel.

She goes rigid against me. Does she want me to stop?

Fuck that. She wants this as much as I do. She's not trying to break the kiss. She's just not moving. Not her body. Not her tongue. Not her lips.

Then a switch flips inside her and she starts riding my hand like a rodeo queen. Her lips are suddenly eating at mine like she's ravenous and her tongue meets mine, thrust for thrust.

This woman is going to be a tsunami between the sheets. Or against the wall. In the bath. Wherever the hell we decide to bang, which my libido demands will be *everywhere.*

Her pussy soaks my hand as her vaginal walls clamp around my thumb, her nearly instant climax making her muscles spasm so tightly I feel like a boa constrictor is around my torso.

I don't stop moving my finger on her clit, forcing another orgasm to follow the first and she screams into my mouth, nearly biting my tongue.

Turned on to the point of madness, I reach down to undo my slacks so I can shove my cock into her right where stand.

"Salvatore!" That is not Rosa's voice.

It's my mother.

Managgia la miseria!

Bianca is still too out of it to realize we've been interrupted by the one person who could stop my rampaging libido right now. Even my father's presence wouldn't. But I'm not burying my cock in Bianca's heat in front of my mother.

"What are you doing to that poor girl? She's supposed to be resting." Of course, my mother knows all about my houseguest.

She and Rosa are thick as thieves.

Breaking our kiss, I surreptitiously slide my hand out from under Bianca's nightgown and robe.

Her eyes still closed, she mewls, trying to capture my lips again with her own.

I want to destroy something.

She's so hot for me, she doesn't even realize my mother is here.

"Shh...*bellissima*. We must stop. We have a guest." I look back over my shoulder. "Give us a minute, mamma. We'll meet you downstairs."

Skepticism twists my mother's perfectly painted lips. "For shame, *mi figlio*. If I leave you now, that young woman is going to end up flat on her back on your bed. And considering her recent troubles, that is the last place she should be."

The only saving grace to that little speech is that my mother spoke in Italian.

Bianca makes a sound of distress and it's not sexual need this time. She realizes we are no longer alone. Her legs unlock from around me and she tries to throw herself from my arms.

With no intention of allowing her to hurt herself further, I keep my arm tight around her hips. "Calm down, you're going to hurt yourself."

"I'm going to *murder* you if you don't let me down this very second." The anger and embarrassment blazing in her eyes is a potent combination.

She might actually try to do it. Maybe strangle me with those amazingly strong thighs of hers? The thought does nothing to deflate the log in my pants.

Which is why, after I carefully lower Bianca and make sure she is steady on her feet, I don't turn to face my mother.

Besides, there is a wet spot on my shirt my mother does not need to see.

All she could have seen was us kissing passionately. From her angle she can only speculate that my hand was buried between Bianca's thighs.

CHAPTER 26

BIANCA

Mortified does not begin to express the scope of my humiliation at being caught by Salvatore's mother while getting fingered by him. I have never been so embarrassed in my entire life.

Worse, I resent the intrusion with every fiber of my being. For the first time in my life, I enjoyed a man's touch. Salvatore made me come. Twice.

And I want more.

Which is terrifying enough to have me backing away from him as fast as legs still shaky from my climaxes will carry me.

"Uh...you need to..." I waive my hand toward his mother, who smiles kindly at me.

I want to sink through the floor. But I also want to find a place to revel in my newfound sexuality.

Sex can feel good. I know that on an intellectual level, but after my experience at sixteen, my body has always equated sex with humiliation, pain and fear.

Of course, we weren't actually bumping uglies, but his thumb was inside me and I liked it. A lot.

I just want to be alone to revel in that a little.

Why isn't he leaving? He has to realize his mother won't go anywhere until he does.

My gaze skitters down his body, yanked to a stop with a force stronger than even my will when I reach the noticeable wet patch on his shirt just above the waistband of his pants. I did that. My arousal soaked his shirt.

I should be even more embarrassed. But the awe I feel at the evidence of my own sexual desire pushes everything else out.

Salvatore pulls his jacket together, buttoning it and only then do I notice the pipe straining against his pants. If the monsters in my past had been that big, they would have split me in two and killed me.

For the first time, not even a tiny part of me wishes they had.

"If you keep looking at me like that, I'll never be able to turn to face my mother," Salvatore says without a trace of embarrassment.

He may not want his mother to actually see the erection that looks painfully constricted in his tight-fitting trousers, but he's not ashamed of it. Not even a little.

"Eyes up here, *cara*."

My gaze snaps to his and I do enough blushing for both of us.

His gorgeous mouth is twisted in a smirk. "Are you going to be alright?"

I nod, no words at the ready.

He nods too and then turns, severing the tether between us. My heart burns. Like he literally took a knife and cut our connection.

Dio mio. I have to get out of here.

"Come, mamma, you can explain why you dropped in without calling first downstairs."

"I can't drop in on my favorite son? Never say so," she scolds him.

Salvatore offers his arm to his mother. "I am your only son."

Isn't he going to wash his hands? His fingers must smell like me. Like my juices.

The thought sends another burst of arousal pulsing through my lady-bits. *Che palle*. I am in so much trouble.

Mrs. De Luca looks back at me before they exit the room. "Come downstairs after you have taken a moment to freshen up, my dear."

Without waiting for a reply, she turns her head to face forward again and lets Salvatore lead her from the room. She just expects me to obey her.

Like mother, like son.

And like her son, Mrs. De Luca will learn that I'm not great at being told what to do.

I scurry to the open door and peek around it to see mother and son disappear down the hall. Once their voices fade entirely, I make a beeline for the guestroom. It is blissfully empty when I get inside. Slamming the door shut, I press the lock and then lean back against it.

Closing my eyes, I replay the kiss that turned nuclear.

My first ever orgasm.

I've never even masturbated. The attempted assault on Bea happened when we were thirteen and just starting to have hormone driven urges. What happened to Bea and the aftermath that followed turned off any instinct I had to explore my budding sexuality.

That might have changed later. Maybe. I don't know.

But then that horrifying, painful night happened when I was sixteen, two weeks before I watched Lorenzo execute my father. It's all wrapped up in my subconscious as one trauma because I spent those two weeks in a fog of pain and disillusionment, abandoned by everyone I trusted.

Equating sex with agony, abandonment and betrayal, nothing about it or my own sexuality interested me. At least until I met Salvatore.

He sparked a reaction in me that I didn't believe I was capable of feeling. And now, he's given me my first climax and my body is still humming from it.

Tugging my nightgown and robe up my thighs, I slide my own hand down over my stomach, reveling in the sensation of skin-on-skin contact. Even if it is my own.

Maybe especially because it is my hand on my body causing this pleasure. My fingers brush over the hair at the top of my mons and I shudder. It's as if every individual hair follicle is sensitized. Do other women feel this when they touch themselves?

I could ask Candi, but I might combust from embarrassment if I do. Even if I'm pretty sure she would answer without hesitation.

My hand drops lower and I slip two fingers between my folds. The wetness coating my most intimate flesh is copious and silky. This is what Salvatore felt when he touched me, this slippery liquid covering plump labia.

If I slide my finger inside my vagina, will it feel as good as his? Unable to resist finding out, I press my middle finger inside. It's not nearly as thick as his thumb but I still feel it in my tight channel.

Sliding my forefinger in beside my middle finger, I shudder. That's closer, but it still isn't the same.

That unfamiliar feeling of euphoria is starting to wash over me again though. I want it. The loss of self for the brief time my body drowns in ecstasy. Pushing my heel into my clitoris, I slowly fuck myself with my fingers.

The climax hits me by surprise and my knees try to buckle. I press back against the door, not ready to give up this feeling of bliss. I don't stop touching myself until I have wrung every last drop of pleasure from my body.

I've never done drugs. Not even weed. But friends have described a really good high like the floaty feeling I'm experiencing right now.

The monsters stole this from me along with my innocence, but Salvatore De Luca, dangerous mafioso, gave it back.

I have never had any desire to touch the part of myself I consider soiled, or let anyone else near enough to do it either.

Self-help books and Mr. Ruhnke's wisdom did a lot to help me realize what happened to me didn't make *me* dirty. It made the men who did it monsters.

But I have yet to find the inner sex goddess Candi says we all have. Well, until now.

Until a capo burst into my life with his brutal good looks and refusal to believe I don't want him as much as he wants me.

I guess today proved without a doubt that he is right.

SALVATORE

"So, you have a house guest." My mother pauses and studies my face, seeing inside me as much as anyone can do. "That you kiss in your bedroom."

Never let it be said that Ilaria De Luca is not as adept as any made man at interrogation. Her techniques don't include torture, but they are damn effective.

"He was kissing her?" Rosa asks, her tone scandalized.

"You knew I had someone staying, or you would not be here now." I speak to my mother, but give Rosa a look meant to quell.

Her complacent expression shows a woman of stronger mettle than most of my men. "You did not tell me to keep your involuntary guest a secret from your family."

"She is not here under duress," I grind out.

"She is free to leave?" Rosa sounds surprised. "That is not the impression I got when you instructed me not to use my access to open the apartment door for her."

"Is this true, *mi figlio?*"

How does my mother manage to imbue five words with so much disapproval?

"Bianca does not know what is good for her. She was going to return to a tiny apartment she shares with five other people, six if you count the roommate's boyfriend. She doesn't even sleep on the pullout couch she pays for. Bianca sleeps on the floor. She would have been back in the hospital in a matter of days. If her roommates even noticed she was ill. She could have died," I say with exasperation.

The whole time I am talking, my mother's eyes grow rounder and rounder. "Have my prayers been answered? Is this you showing concern for the welfare of one of your girlfriends?"

"I don't have girlfriends," I remind my mother. And if I did, she wouldn't be a pole dancer, turned cocktail waitress.

"More's the pity," Rosa mutters.

Mamma pours me a cup of coffee before serving herself and Rosa tea from the other urn on the tray. "What do you call a woman living with you if not your girlfriend?"

My obsession.

Rosa takes a sip of her tea and says, "His kidnap victim who he forces to sleep in his bed."

Managgia la miseria. These women.

"Is this true?" my mother asks with brows raised.

I am not about to explain Bianca's nightmares. She deserves her privacy even if Rosa does not believe I deserve mine.

"I did not kidnap her. That was your son," I remind my housekeeper-slash-second mother.

Bianca's suggestion of taking her to a fuck pad is sounding better by the minute. Not that I have one, but a penthouse suite at the Ritz-Carlton will do.

"On your orders," Mamma chides. "We did not raise you to shirk responsibility, Salvatore Enzo De Luca."

Shit. My full name. Mamma is going to mount a rescue mission any minute if I don't calm her down.

"She agreed to stay."

Mamma looks questioningly at Rosa who shrugs. "If she has, I didn't hear it."

If? Fucking if?

That is it. I have had enough. "When have I ever lied to you?" I demand of my mother. And then I glare at Rosa. "*If* you find it so onerous to work for someone you clearly don't trust, perhaps you should cease doing so."

"Are you threatening to fire your housekeeper again, Salvatore?" Bianca asks lightly with a teasing smile from the archway of the living room.

Mamma's head snaps up and she turns to watch Bianca's unhurried progress across the room.

Her long red hair pulled back in a wet ponytail, my soon-to-be lover's luscious curves are encased in one of the snarky t-shirts I bought her to replace the one destroyed in the attack. The snug fitting yoga pants she's wearing with it send my heartrate spiking.

She's not wearing shoes, though she has several pairs in her closet. Both new and old. Instead, she's got on one of the pairs of fuzzy slipper socks that looked too comfortable to pass up.

I don't need a lot of sleep, so I woke well before Bianca that first night she was here. Unwilling to leave her to her nightmares, I worked on my phone and ended up ordering Bianca clothes after checking my email.

Ensuring she would have adequate clothes to wear was surprisingly gratifying.

The smile playing at the edges of her mouth is even more so. If I had known giving her an orgasm would put her in this good of a mood, I would have found a way to eat her out at the hospital.

"Hello, Bianca. It is a pleasure to meet you." My mother stands and offers her hand to Bianca. "Since my son did not see fit to introduce me upstairs, I am Ilaria De Luca. You will call me Ilaria."

Shock reverberates through me. My mother is a stickler for propriety. Very few outside of our family are given permission to use her first name. Rosa being one of them, but even Pietro calls her Mrs. De Luca.

"Thank you, Ilaria." Bianca smiles and shakes my mother's hand before sitting beside me on the sofa.

Right beside me. Her thigh presses against mine.

What the fuck is going on?

"Would you like coffee, or tea, Bianca?" Mamma asks.

"Coffee please."

Mamma pours Bianca her coffee and hands it to her before giving me a gimlet stare. "You threatened to fire Rosa?"

My housekeeper is offering the cream and sugar to Bianca and apologizes for not putting the doctored creamer she made specially for my houseguest on the tray.

I shake my head. She's more solicitous of Bianca than she is of Nerissa. Not that my sister tolerates being coddled, but this is ridiculous.

My mother taps the side of her teacup once with her fingernail, her signal to pay attention.

Meeting her eyes, I let my irritation reflect in my own and don't try to keep it out of my voice either. "No, I did not threaten to fire Rosa. She lied and told Bianca I had to get her to cooperate."

Rosa shrugs. "It worked. The child needed her rest."

So, it is okay for my housekeeper to decide what is best for Bianca, but not me? Fuck that noise.

I am capo.

CHAPTER 27

BIANCA

S alvatore is so angry; steam should be coming out of his ears.

Neither his mom, nor Rosa appear worried.

But it's the hurt lurking behind the furious capo façade neither of them seems to see that concerns me. I arrived in time to hear both Rosa and Ilaria question his truthfulness. He doesn't like it.

At all.

Which tells me three things. One, he expects to be believed. Two, he isn't used to having his honesty questioned by either woman. And three, he doesn't lie to his family.

That last one is a leap, but it fits what I know of him so far.

"I've only known Salvatore a short time." I smile toward him before meeting his mother's eyes. "But he doesn't strike me as a man who lies."

"I'm a Cosa Nostra capo, of course I lie." Tension vibrates from his big body.

Glancing toward him, I bite my bottom lip. The look he's giving his mother and Rosa dares them to deny his claim.

Something about that defensiveness tugs at my heart. It's as if he wants them to admit he lies when he has to. Which is not the same as lying for convenience, or to the people that should matter most.

I know. I've been the recipient of those lies. Salvatore is nothing like my father.

Che palle.

Give a girl an orgasm and suddenly she's looking at you like you're some kind of superhero and your feelings matter.

To be fair to myself, that orgasm was pretty spectacular and it wasn't isolated, not to mention my first ever. It's bound to impact me more strongly than it would someone who is used to having them.

"I'm sure you do," I pat his thigh. "To your enemies. Not to family."

Salvatore goes still, that predator about to strike aura surrounding him again. Then he turns his whole body to face me without dislodging my hand.

He studies my face like it's a map he has to memorize. "How is it that you realize that truth, but my own mother and the woman who is as close as family do not?"

Ilaria makes a sound of hurt disagreement and Rosa mutters something about never being too old to be questioned by the women who love him in Italian.

Salvatore ignores them both and waits for me to answer.

"Even when you knew it would piss me off, you told me the truth." I don't mention what that truth was.

I get the feeling neither of the older women would approve of his offer to give me five thousand dollars to have sex with him. Especially if they knew that me taking the money would automatically mean losing my job.

Now that I know how good sex can feel, I'm rethinking my position. Not the getting paid part. The actually having sex part.

He knows exactly what I'm talking about though. I can see it in his eyes and the way they travel from my lips to my chest. The La Perla bra fits my DD boobs perfectly and makes them look amazing. Which he is definitely noticing.

It's also surprisingly comfortable. I wouldn't expect him to get the cup size wrong, but the band size is another matter. Most men are clueless and think 36 is the norm. There are a lot of bralette tops at Pitiful Princess that are too big around the band for most of the dancers and too small for both me and Candi.

Either he checked my other bras, or he has excellent size guessing skills, because Salvatore got it right.

Ilaria taps on her teacup and Salvatore's gaze snaps to her, his mouth tipped down in a scowl. "Yes?"

"I did not accuse you of lying."

"The De Lucas take responsibility for their actions, mother. You looked to Rosa for confirmation of my words, implying you believed I could be lying." There is no give in Salvatore's tone.

Whatever hurt he's feeling is buried down deep now and the only face he's showing is that of arrogant capo.

And still, I just want to climb in his lap and rub myself all over him. How long is Ilaria planning to stay? Will Salvatore be returning upstairs with me when she does?

"You had the girl kidnapped," his mother defends herself in Italian.

"English, mother. It is impolite to speak in Italian when not everyone present understands the language."

As much as I enjoy knowing something Salvatore doesn't, this is getting ridiculous.

"There is no need to worry about only speaking in English around me," I say in Italian.

"You speak Italian?" Salvatore demands, his deep tones filled with shock.

I shrug, the pull on my stitches negligible at this point. "My father's family was from Italy."

"Where are they now?" Ilaria asks.

"They're all gone." The Russos in Detroit are just names to me, not family.

I've never met any of them. While I might have distant relatives among the Genovese *famiglia* if I do, I don't know who they are either.

Ilaria gives me a look filled with compassion. "I am sorry to hear that. Family is important."

"Why didn't you tell me before now?" Salvatore's voice drips with suspicion.

He's not talking about my family being gone. He's still harping on *me* not telling *him* I understand Italian.

Really? I frown at him. "You just assumed I didn't speak the language. Considering how many Italian speaking people there are in New York, I wouldn't think you'd be so quick to dismiss the possibility."

"You aren't part of *la famiglia*."

"There are plenty of Italian American's who aren't." And he's right.

I'm not part of the mafia, not since Lorenzo kicked me out of my home, cutting my ties with the Genovese Family when he killed my father for being a traitor.

"You should have told me. I discussed sensitive information in front of you."

"It's not Bianca's fault if you didn't show enough sense to mind what you said around her." Rosa's staunch support warms me.

But it's having the opposite effect on Salvatore.

His gray eyes are icier than a glacier. He opens his mouth, and my gut tells me the words that will come out aren't going to be pleasant for Rosa to hear.

I like Rosa. I don't want Salvatore to hurt her feelings.

I also don't want Salvatore hurt by more criticism from his mother, or housekeeper. He's clearly not used to it.

It still surprises me that I believe the arrogant capo can be hurt, but I do. I know what I saw when I got in here, even if he's got his top dog face on now.

I jump in to say, "You said it yourself, I witnessed you killing my attackers." Not that I actually watched, but for the sake of this discussion we'll go with it. "Not much you could talk about that would be more sensitive than that." I do air quotes as I say *sensitive*.

His eyes narrow and I just know this conversation isn't over. How disturbed am I that I'm looking forward to arguing with him later?

"You will tell my mother you are here of your own volition," he demands, apparently ready to shift back to the original volatile topic.

"Bossy much?"

"Bianca," he warns.

I roll my eyes, but then I meet Ilaria's eyes. "Pietro kidnapped me and I wasn't happy to be here at first."

Salvatore lets out a frustrated breath.

"I'm being honest here, Salvatore. Your mom knows Pietro drugged me and carted me back here like an abandoned puppy."

"Pietro drugged you?" Ilaria demands.

I nod an affirmative.

Then she shows she's got a temper every bit as volatile as my nonna's ever was and starts yelling. When she's done, Salvatore's face looks like granite and Rosa is dabbing at her eyes in shame for her son's behavior.

Are these women for real? They are married to made men. Their sons are made men. Even Ilaria's daughter is made. *Dio mio.* Nerissa is Salvatore's second.

What do they think happens in mafia business?

"I have dealt with Pietro's overzealousness in carrying out my orders."

"He did," I agree.

With panty melting efficiency. Not that I will ever admit seeing him dole out punishment to his top bodyguard turned me on.

Definitely disturbed.

Before another argument can erupt, I say, "I have agreed to stay here while I heal."

"Not under duress?" Ilaria probes.

That granite line of Salvatore's jaw goes diamond hard. *Accidenti.* His mother does not know when to quit, but I also like that she's watching out for me like Rosa. I am not alone here and ultimately, if I want to go, they will help me, I realize.

Even if Salvatore forbids it.

I let my gratitude for her concern shine in my eyes. "He actually used logic. I guess the risk of infection to knife wounds is high, even those that have been treated at the hospital."

At least that's what I take the doctor's warnings to mean. And sleeping on the floor of a closet, no matter how clean I keep my little spot, isn't the best way to avoid it.

And even if I had wanted to leave before, now that I've experienced sexual pleasure with Salvatore, I definitely don't. I want to explore what else my body can feel with someone who doesn't trigger a panic attack when he gets intimately close.

"I have to admit that you didn't look like you were here against your will upstairs." Ilaria winks at me.

She winks.

Like we're friends and are sharing a joke. Heat blooms in my cheeks while embarrassment crawls like a spider up my spine. I'm more grateful than a dancer taking off her heels at the end of the night that Salvatore's big body blocked his mother's view of mine.

I would die if she'd had a front row seat to his fingers inside me.

Which doesn't look good for me going back to pole dancing if I have to once my wounds heal. I haven't had the nerve to ask Salvatore if I'm fired, or not. But the chances of Franco holding the job open for a brand new cocktail waitress are worse than the odds of the guy obsessed with watching you dance turning out to be your soulmate.

This self-consciousness about my body has to stop.

But then getting caught by my lover's mother while his thumb is buried in my wet vagina and his fingers play with my clit isn't the same thing as dancing on a stage where no one can touch me. Where I choose what to show and when.

Lover? Did I just think of Salvatore as my lover?

Because of one, probably super tame for him, sexual experience in his bedroom? I need to slow my roll.

Or stop it all together.

He's not my lover. Not my boyfriend. Not even my friend with benefits. We barely know each other and me temporarily living in his house doesn't change that.

You go on telling yourself that, girl. The man brings you to his bed every night. He touches you like he has the right to. And you let him.

My groan is spontaneous and loud. And it has the two older women and Salvatore all staring at me.

"Uh, sorry about that." Hiding in my coffee cup, I take a slow sip, but eventually I have to set it back down.

No one's attention has moved from me by a single iota. I stifle my sigh, like I should have the groan.

"Do not be embarrassed. I should not have come upstairs unannounced," Ilaria says soothingly. "Not when I knew Salvatore had a guest staying here."

"Bianca merits courtesy and I do not?" Salvatore does not sound impressed.

Ilaria takes a sip of her own tea, pointedly not replying to her son's question.

Oh, man. There are some complicated relationships going on here. Do they even realize how much push-pull is happening between them? Ilaria is Salvatore's mother, but he is *her* capo.

Having grown up in a mafia family, I know that means that family, or not, she is supposed to treat him with deference and respect. Is it because he's only been a capo for about a year?

Or maybe it is because she is his mother, and that role gives her special license to treat him like a human being.

She's also the wife of the consigliere. I'm not sure where that puts Ilaria in the mafia pecking order. Despite my dad's pride in being (distantly) related to the Detroit don, our family didn't interact with anyone in the Cosa Nostra higher ranks.

The first day I actually spoke to Lorenzo was the one when he kicked me out of my home.

He was rude to Salvatore at the club too. Not that the younger capo allowed it. If Salvatore gave me the look and warning he did Lorenzo, I would probably piss myself.

I guess taking over as capo isn't all that easy, even if the role is inherited.

CHAPTER 28

SALVATORE

Not for the first time, I question the wisdom of keeping Rosa as my housekeeper now that I am capo.

It doesn't surprise me that she called my mom and told her that Bianca is staying here. They are like sisters.

But it is not acceptable either.

Neither is either woman questioning my word when I told them that Bianca is not here under duress. If I needed to keep her here against her will for the good of *la famiglia*, I would. I am capo.

And I would not hesitate to tell either woman that is the case, like I did not hesitate to tell Rosa to keep Bianca here that first day. For Bianca's health and safety.

The welfare of the people under my authority rests on my shoulders.

My mother and Rosa can get as pissed as they want at me. Ultimately, my word is law. The only voice with authority to override mine is Severu's. As his underboss, Miceli can override me only when speaking directly on behalf of the don.

My father is consigliere, which is a position of great influence, but he does not have the authority to override my will either. So, why the hell do my mother and Rosa think I would stoop to lying to them?

I don't need to.

But it is obvious neither woman sees things that way. Rosa will never give me the unquestioning loyalty I need from a member of my household staff. She loves me, which she believes gives her leeway to question my actions and motives and share her concerns with my mother.

It does not.

I'm going to have to fire her. I don't like it, but I trained my entire life to be what I am and there's no room for sentimentality in a capo's decision making.

She does not see her actions as disloyal, but they are.

And I cannot let that stand.

Which means I need a new housekeeper.

But not today because you also need someone here to watch over Bianca. What is more important? Her wellbeing or demanding the respect due you as capo?

There is no contest. I'm not like that loser Lorenzo. I don't need to throw my weight around to feel the heft of my position. Rosa will have to go, but not until after Bianca has healed.

Her brand of disloyalty is not dangerous for *la famiglia*. Or even me. It is simply unacceptable.

"If you two are finished convincing yourselves that I have not suddenly started participating in the flesh trade," I stand. "I have work and Bianca needs her rest."

"You're leaving?" Bianca asks, surprising me.

I expected the feisty beauty to argue with me about her need to rest, not question whether, or not, I am sticking around.

"No." I have phone calls to make in my office.

Juniper is dragging his feet about finalizing the sale of the bars and I want to know why. Money should be enough to convince him to sign his properties over to me, but if it isn't, I'll persuade him in other ways.

Taking possession of those locations as soon as possible is key to Severu's bid for becoming the next godfather. The sale needs to happen. Now.

"You are so dramatic, Salvatore." My mother shakes her head. "No one accused you of human trafficking."

Bianca gasps, like she's just registered what I said. "You would never."

"No, I would not." That is not something we allow in our territory, but how is she so certain of that?

"I'm sure your mom and Rosa never meant to imply that either." She gives them a reproving look, her tone admonishing.

The urge to smile startles me. But her defense pleases me and for once Bianca's ire is directed at someone else.

"Of course, not. My son is too honorable a man to participate in business so heinous." Mamma's righteous indignation is overdone for a woman who as good as accused her capo of lying.

Rosa manages to look wounded despite being the one to tell my mother I force Bianca to sleep in my bed. And mamma soaked it up like a sponge, only too eager to believe the worst of me.

"Salvatore is a good man," Rosa says with a pointed look at me. "We all know this."

Most of the time, both women see me through the rose-tinted lens of love and willful obliviousness. They spend their lives ignoring the seamier side of their husbands and children's lives.

Par for the course in the mafia.

However, I am *not* a good man. I do heinous things. What I do not do is: buy, sell, or keep sex slaves.

I put my hand out to Bianca. "Come."

"I am not a dog, Salvatore. You could ask." Crossing her arms over her chest, her beautiful eyes narrow at me. "We just established I'm your guest, not your prisoner."

I am a capo. I do not ask. And no matter how much I want to fuck this woman, it isn't going to make me into some tame lapdog.

"Do whatever the fuck you want," I say and turn to leave.

"Salvatore." My mother's tone is admonishing. "You did not kiss me goodbye."

In no mood to show familial affection, but also unwilling to disrespect her, I return to give her a perfunctory kiss on the cheek.

"Goodbye, mother," I say in Italian with a glare for Bianca.

She should have told me she speaks the language.

Bianca rolls her eyes like she knows exactly what I'm thinking, and she's not impressed.

This woman.

If my cock didn't see her as true north, I would not say another word to her while she's healing. Better yet, I would send her to stay with the Gallos and Rosa could watch over Bianca in her home. Then I could I hire a new housekeeper immediately, killing two birds with one stone.

Not going to happen. *Manaja.*

I don't make this kind of effort for bedmates. Not fucking ever.

"We will see you at the don's for dinner on Thursday," my mother says smoothly.

Like she can't feel the black cloud of temper hovering over me right now.

"We'll be there."

"We?" my mother asks pointedly.

"I'm bringing Bianca." As long as she has the doctor and surgeon's approval to leave the penthouse.

But since the doctor was going to let Bianca check out of the hospital only to go to that tiny apartment with more roommates than square feet, I doubt she'll have any objections.

"What? Bringing me where?" Bianca demands.

"My cousin's wife invited us for dinner."

"The don's wife knows I'm staying here?" she asks, her beautiful face creased in confusion.

"I told Severu I'd be bringing you," I explain. When I never explain.

My mother makes a sound of surprise and Rosa tuts. Ignoring both of them, I turn to leave. Again.

"Aren't you even going to ask if I *want* to go to dinner at a mafia don's house?" Bianca asks, her tone critical.

"No."

BIANCA

Salvatore walks out of the living room without looking back.

"He doesn't date a lot, does he?" I ask Rosa wryly.

The man has no clue.

"My son doesn't date at all," Ilaria answers for the housekeeper. "And yet he wants to bring you to a family dinner. Just how long have you known Salvatore?"

"Less than two weeks," I answer honestly, as bewildered by Salvatore's pronouncement as she clearly is.

Ilaria looks at Rosa like she expects the other woman to have the answers.

But the housekeeper shrugs. "I don't know what is going on with him. Since that she-devil, Monica, he keeps his heart closed off. He doesn't bring women here, but he won't let this one go."

Not comfortable being talked about like I'm not in the room, I insert, "Maybe he feels bad about the attack." And who is Monica, besides being a *she-devil*?

Also, I'm pretty sure that it's not Salvatore's heart involved. It's the impressive lead pipe in his pants, but I'm not about to say that to his mother and adopted aunt. I've done enough blushing for today.

"Why should he?" Ilaria asks. "He didn't attack you."

It occurs to me that Ilaria does not know the attack was from another Cosa Nostra family.

The Five Families are all part of the same syndicate. That doesn't mean they all get along. Cousins fight. So do the different families. But they always stand as one against an outside enemy.

At least that's what my dad used to say to explain the rivalry between the different families.

Rosa hmms. "Pietro said the attack happened when Bianca was late leaving Amuni."

She and Ilaria give me identical looks of censure.

Going from having no mom to two. It's a lot. Not that either are my mom, or ever likely to be by marriage, no matter what kind of stories they are telling themselves.

But the mom vibe is strong.

"I didn't have a choice," I defend myself. "The patrons wouldn't leave." And they'd been lousy tippers.

The knock on the head didn't make me forget that.

"Franco should have made them leave," Rosa says, disgruntled.

Ilaria nods. "Salvatore needs to talk to him. Employees shouldn't be put in such dangerous situations."

"I had a word with him already," Rosa says. "He promised to tell Franco not to allow the employees to walk alone to the subway station without an escort."

Wow, that is quite a concession. Is there a heart under that gruff capo exterior after all?

Content to listen to the older women chat, I sip my coffee and revel in being downstairs.

But the third time I smother a yawn, Rosa tsks. "It is time for you to rest."

Ilaria agrees and with both of them adamant, I take myself back upstairs.

The open door to Salvatore's office draws me like a beacon.

CHAPTER 29

BIANCA

His jacket and tie gone, his shirtsleeves rolled up, Salvatore sits back in a burgundy leather wingback office chair talking on the phone.

The sight of the black ink covering his muscular forearms locks me in place. I have seen tattoos peeking out of the neck of his dress shirts, but his forearms are covered. And it is seriously hot.

Do they cover his whole body, or just his arms?

He sleeps in boxer shorts, but he's always gone before I wake in the morning and there is no light to see him by when he wakes me up to take pain meds.

"Tell your boss I expect a call back today," he says into the phone and then swipes to end the call.

Steel gray eyes trap mine. "Finally decided to let your body rest?"

"I can't sleep the days away."

"That's exactly what you should be doing while your body heals. Getting as much sleep as possible."

"I've been sleeping too much," I argue. And when he's not here, that sleep isn't exactly restful anyway.

"Take a nap before lunch and I will take you up to the rooftop garden to eat."

"You have a rooftop garden?" Awe colors my tone.

Sue me. I know some buildings in New York have them. I've seen pictures but never been anyplace that had one, much less been allowed to visit it.

"Yes. Worth taking a nap to get to see?"

"If I take a nap now, can I go to my apartment later?"

"No." He looks ready to lecture me on the germs inherent in an apartment shared by so many people again.

I put my hand up. "Stop, Salvatore. I'm not moving back until I'm fully healed but there's something I need to get."

"My men got all of your things."

"They missed something."

"What?"

I don't want to tell him. He'll think it's ridiculous to be so worried about a plant, but I am. "My African violet."

"Where is it?" he asks.

It's that simple? No question about whether I really need it? Or why a plant is important enough to me to go get it?

Not willing to look a gift horse in the mouth, I tell him.

He pulls out his phone and sends a text. "Pietro will pick it up this afternoon."

"Tell him to be careful with it," I say, panicked. "If he hurts it, I'll—"

"He knows how to transport delicate plants. Don't worry," Salvatore interrupts before I can think of a threat dire enough toward Pietro.

"He does?" Does Rosa keep houseplants?

"Yes. You'll find out why after your nap."

In the rooftop garden? Curiosity and interest piqued, I nevertheless don't let this opportunity to bargain go by. "If I nap like a good girl, I want to go for a walk in the park tomorrow."

"I already acceded to the retrieval of your plant."

"If your guys had done their job the first time, it would already be here. They grabbed everything else. I want to go for a walk in the park."

He frowns, the muscles in his forearms flexing and distracting me. "You can walk in the garden."

"Even if it spans the whole building, that's still not the same as walking in the park."

"You don't need to tire yourself out getting fresh air."

"I'm used to working, Salvatore. My body needs to move."

"I have a gym. Once you're approved for mild exercise, you can use it."

"I'm already approved for mild exercise. The fact you and Rosa want to keep me wallowing in bed is beside the point."

"You will find that what I want is never beside the point, Bianca. I am capo."

"And I am an adult woman, capable of making my own decisions. I chose to stay here. I am not a prisoner. Remember?"

"As much as I might enjoy tying you to my bed, I don't want to keep you prisoner."

The image sends heat flooding through me. And not of the embarrassment variety.

"Don't think that you can start bossing me around since you gave me an orgasm."

Salvatore's gaze heats and he stands up. "Maybe you need another climax to help you sleep."

"What? No." My ladybits disagree and let me know with a thrum deep in my core.

He comes around his desk, moving with the grace and determination of a tiger stalking its next meal.

I should not have let Mr. Ruhnke talk me into watching so many nature documentaries. My imagination is slotting Salvatore into too many scenes I watched with the old man.

Of their own volition, my feet start moving backward, but instead of going out the door into the hall, I bump into the wall beside it.

Oof.

His grin is as predacious as his sensual glide toward me. "Your mouth says no, but those diamond hard nipples crowning your gorgeous tits are telling me that's exactly what you need."

Each word hits me right in the vagina, sending wetness gushing into my La Perla underwear. Everything down there pulses with anticipation for the pleasure he's offering.

My nipples are as hard as he says. And tight. They tingle with the need to be touched.

What is happening to my body? "I don't react like this when I dance the pole."

"That's because you were never dancing for me."

His words send my imagination spinning in another direction as an image of me dancing the pole in an empty club, except one patron. Him. In my mind's eye, the spotlight isn't on me. It's on him.

Suppressing a shudder of want, I say, "You're so arrogant."

"Is it arrogant if it is true?" He stops scant inches from my body. "Put your hands on me, *bella mia*. Show me you want this."

My hands clench. Can I touch him? Can I do what he wants and show him *I* want more pleasure?

His fingers curl gently around my wrist and he lifts my fist to place it against the hard muscle of his chest. Needing to explore in a way I never have, my fingers unfurl from the fist and splay across his pec.

Heat emanates through his shirt. The heel of my hand is over a small nub. His nipple. Hard like mine. Rubbing my hand in a circle, my heel and palm pass over it.

Strong fingers clasp my nape. "Yes. Like that, Bianca. Touch me."

I want to. So much.

So, I do, mapping his chest with my fingertips as I inhale his masculine scent. When my hand travels lower, it's like the appendage belongs to someone else.

To a curious and sexually open woman.

My fingers curl around the hard bulge I find angled toward his belt. Angled because this monster penis would be sticking out of his waistband if his belt wasn't in the way.

My core clenches and I shiver with atavistic recognition of what his hardon represents. The urge to merge two bodies in the most fundamental way. My mind might not be ready for him to be inside me, but my body is going nuclear at the thought.

Tracing his length from root to tip, I squeeze when I reach it, the column of flesh stretching my hand.

He groans, thrusting his hips forward. "*Cazzo, bella mia*. I want you."

"I..." I'm not sure what I want.

Him? Yes. But am I ready for penetrative sex? Pretty sure I'm not.

"I know." He groans again. "We have to wait. If I fucked you the way I want to right now, every one of your stitches would tear."

Why does that turn me on instead of frightening me? Memories from my past should have me trying to get away from him. They flicker dimly, like an overexposed reel under the hot sun of his passion.

My body is on meltdown and all I can think of is ways we could do the deed without ripping stitches.

No, Bianca. Bad idea. You don't even know if you could go through with it. You might freeze up at the last second and what if he doesn't stop?

That thought finally chills the raging inferno inside me and my hands still.

Salvatore inhales deeply. "Yes, you are right. We must stop." He steps back and looks into my eyes, his nearly black with lust.

A sound of need that I have never made before comes from my mouth.

Jaw looking hewn from granite, his gaze traps mine. "That doesn't mean I can't help you relax enough to sleep. Let me make you climax."

And all the air whooshes from the room.

The muscles in my neck jerk my head up and down in a nod without any input from my brain.

Salvatore doesn't hesitate. Careful not to jostle my back, he lifts me into his arms, and carries me into the hallway. I think he's going to go right past the guestroom, but he stops and sort of step pivots before pushing the unlatched door open and carrying me inside.

Was he going to take me to his bedroom? Did he change his mind? Why? He touched me in there earlier. What is different about now? Is it because I'm going to sleep after? Only he carries me to his bed nightly for me to sleep beside him.

My thoughts go static when he lays me on the bed and begins to undress me. Like this is normal. Like having a man take off my socks is nothing out of the ordinary for me.

It so is.

He pulls my leggings down my thighs slow inch by slow inch while he stares at what he reveals. I know what he sees.

I'm a dancer, so my body is strong, but that hourglass shape so popular in the middle of the last century? I've got it. I'm curvy.

The emcee called me the big girl with the juicy thighs whenever I got introduced on stage at the Pitiful Princess. Men appreciated my jiggle but I didn't care. I didn't dance for them.

I danced for myself because I love it. And I danced for the money I needed to support myself. For tips that went into savings toward my dream of leaving New York. It didn't matter how lasciviously the customers looked at me, it didn't touch me.

Salvatore's gaze burns through me though, setting my insides alight with desire. His eyes caress my body and leave shivery pleasure in their wake. He leaves my panties on and helps me into a sitting position so he can remove my shirt.

I don't know why I don't offer to help, but I don't. Letting him undress me feels nice. Like he's pampering me. Surprisingly, I enjoy that feeling. It is turning me on in ways I don't expect it to, as well.

His hands skim up my sides and cup my bra covered breasts. My nipples poke against the soft lace, begging for attention.

Caspita! What this man does to me.

"This looks better on you than I expected and I knew your gorgeous tits were going to look amazing in it." He fingers the bra strap. "La Perla should pay you to model their lingerie, but if they did, I would have to kill the photographers who looked at you to take the pictures."

I laugh breathlessly. "And all the men that saw me dance the pole at Pitiful Princess?" I tease.

Salvatore's face goes dark and his eyes are filled with death. "Give me names and I will take care of them."

Pretty sure *take care of* is mafia speak for kill. "You should be joking, but I don't think you are."

He shrugs. *"Sei mio."*

CHAPTER 30

BIANCA

My world shrinks down to his molten gray gaze as my breath stills in my chest.

You are mine.

Sex talk. That's all it is. All it could possibly be.

For a second though, my entire being thrums with the idea of belonging. Not being alone. Having someone who claims me as theirs, that I can tell the world belongs to me too.

It's ridiculous of course. We've known each other eleven days. He wants to have sex with me.

He does not want to keep me.

Only a fool would take his words to heart and I am no fool. I learned my lessons the hard way and they stuck because of it.

Doesn't stop my body from vibrating in anticipation of the pleasure it knows is coming though. Whatever the future holds, Salvatore is determined to send my ovaries into the stratosphere in the present.

He squeezes my breasts and I suck in air as sensation that borders on pain turns into pure ecstasy as his thumbs brush over my turgid nipples. My hands land on his hard, muscular shoulders.

"I want you to take your shirt off." I don't ask him to take his slacks off.

Because one, I don't know if I'm ready to see his naked body. Touching him through his trousers is sexy but safe. And two, even a novice like me can see that he's on the edge of his control. I'm not giving him a reason to tip over. Especially when I don't know if him trying to penetrate my body will send me into a freakout, or not.

He lightly pinches my nipples. "I cannot nap with you."

Jolts of sensation travel straight from my nipples to my pulsing vagina.

"I know, but I want to see you." At least his chest and arms.

"You do it." He rolls my nipples between his thumbs and forefingers. "My hands are busy."

My body electrified with pleasure, I don't wait for a second invitation. I start unbuttoning his shirt, taking in his hairy chest as it's revealed to my greedy eyes.

His pecs ripple as he reaches around and undoes the clasp of my bra and peels it away from my heavy breasts.

"Perfect," he says under his breath.

Warmth unfurls in me, but I don't look up from my task. His chest is covered in dark hair that vees down his abs until it disappears enticingly into the waistband of his trousers.

Sliding my fingers through his chest hair, I am startled by how soft it is. There's black ink under it on his right pectoral, but the image is hard to make out at first because of the hair he allows to grow over it.

After a couple of seconds of intent appraisal, I realize it's a viper. A dead one. I ruffle his hair to get a better look. The shading is done so perfectly, that it takes a second to realize what I thought were scales at first are parts of letters.

His hand traps mine against his chest. "Forget the tattoo. Touch me *bella mia*."

Mouth dry, I nod. But I saw what the letters spelled out. A woman's name. Monica.

The name of the woman Rosa mentioned downstairs.

What does she mean to Salvatore? Hot jealousy spikes inside my chest knowing he has her name inked permanently into his body. Even if it is mostly covered by his silky black chest hair.

Is she dead? Is that why the snake is dead? Why a snake? Why her? Who *is* she?

"Stop thinking about it. She doesn't matter. She'll never matter."

That's pretty definitive. "So, no girlfriend?" I ask just to be sure.

If I'm going to keep letting this man touch me intimately, I need to know there aren't any other women. I know it's not forever, but this physical closeness means too much to me for it to be any other way.

"I don't date. How would I have a girlfriend?" His hands slide down my back and he caresses my butt.

First outside the underwear, and then beneath it.

Losing my ability to focus, I demand. "Say it."

"No girlfriend. There is only you."

The words zing along my nerve endings like an electric current, leaving pleasure and anticipation in their wake.

"Now you say it."

"What?" I ask, barely tracking as his middle finger slides between my butt cheeks.

The tip of that finger taps my pucker. "You are mine."

I jerk as new sensations pour over me.

"Say it," he demands with another tap.

Dio mio.

"*Io sono tua,*" I gasp out. *I am yours.*

He growls in primal approval. Then he's laying me back on the bed sans bra and seconds later I'm without my panties too. My thighs clench in response.

Not sure what about that thigh clench triggers him but he growls again, lifting and bending my knees so my thighs spread wide.

His finger runs down my slickened slit as he inhales the crotch of my panties. "Your pussy smells like heaven." His gaze settles between my spread legs. "And looks like it too. *Dolcezza.*" He shakes his head and adjusts the giant bulge in his slacks. "So fucking sweet."

There is no warning before his face is buried between my legs. Nothing about this reminds me of the past. It is Salvatore pleasuring me, not taking his own from my unwilling body. He inhales deeply and a guttural sound comes from deep in his chest.

Dio mio. I am going to die, and he isn't even touching me yet.

His tongue stabs into the heart of me and I gasp in shock, a moan following right after. It feels good. Better than good. This is bliss.

That marauding tongue pistons in and out of my overjoyed vagina like a mini dick and it's all pure pleasure. Every glide brings more noise tumbling from my lips until a deep thrust makes me shriek.

Salvatore lifts his head and smirks, his lips glistening. "Good thing I locked the door this time, or we'd have Rosa in here wanting to know what I'm doing to you."

His words only half-register. I'm still pulsing from the bliss of his tongue in my most intimate place.

"Do that again," I order.

"It would seem I am not the only bossy one in this relationship."

I don't dwell on his use of the word *relationship*, but I notice. How can I not? Even with my brain and body fully occupied by sensation.

"Salvatore..." His name is another demand while my hips tilt upward in a silent plea.

"Your wish, *bella mia*..." His head drops, but his tongue does not thrust back inside me.

Instead, he slides it up between my labia, sending shivers of delight along every nerve ending until he reaches my clit.

He circles it. Over and over again. Teasing me with hint after hint of what I *could* be feeling.

"Do it," I demand, my voice hoarse with need.

But he ignores me, sliding his finger inside me and dragging more of my wet arousal out only to spread it down to my bottom. This time when his fingertip presses there, it slides in a little.

In automatic reaction, my thighs try to slam together but his head is in my way.

"Salvatore?"

He pushes his fingertip inside me.

Dio mio. It doesn't hurt. Not even a little. It feels good. Amazing. I should definitely not be enjoying this. Should I?

Why not? If it feels good. That's Candi's voice in my head and I like it better than the shrieking surprise of my own panicked inner voice.

Then Salvatore's tongue finally centers on the throbbing and neglected bundle of nerves at the apex of my labia. And both voices splinter into shards of nothingness as my brain goes static from an overload of pleasure.

Bucking up, I try to get closer to Salvatore's mouth. He nips and sucks at my clit, one of his hands traveling up my body to squeeze my breast and pluck at my nipple. Ecstasy sparks along the direct neural pathway between my nipple and my clitoris, creating a feedback loop that makes it all bigger.

So much bigger.

Suddenly, every muscle in my body contracts and I scream as pleasure so intense it borders on pain rushes over me. My body bows and Salvatore's hands grab my hips, supporting me as he continues to feast on my most intimate flesh.

The agony of intense pleasure goes on and on until it's too much. I try to drop my hips, but his hold stops my body from moving away from his mouth.

"It's too much," I gasp out.

Salvatore's tongue softens, but he doesn't move his mouth. He continues to stimulate over sensitized flesh until only moments later, I feel a second cataclysm building inside my core. He nips my swollen bundle of nerves and ecstasy detonates through me like an erupting volcano, leaving devastation in its wake.

My muscles lock, my uterus cramps, adding to the pleasure he's forcing into my body with his mouth.

My juices are running down my crack and he uses my arousal to lubricate my sphincter so his finger can slide inside that dark, secret place. Another orgasm crashes over me, sending me into blissful oblivion.

CHAPTER 31

SALVATORE

Bianca goes boneless. The kind of boneless that comes with unconsciousness.

Something I am well acquainted with. Although, usually when I knock someone out, it is not with pleasure.

Sitting back on my heels, I enjoy the view before me without a shred of guilt.

She is mine.

That pretty pussy, lips plump and flushed from her climax, is mine.

Her thighs are spread wide, revealing how those delicious nether lips shine with her cream. She squirted the last time she came, and her juice is so damn delicious, I'm salivating for more.

But the whole point of this exercise was to relax Bianca enough to sleep. Her somnolence and the relaxed state of her body is proof I did my job.

I swipe the back of my hand across my mouth and then lick the pussy juice off of it. *Merda.*

She tastes like honey with a little bit of spice.

Miceli claims to have read some kind of study that said when two people are sexually chemically compatible, their arousal excretions taste good to the other.

Miceli is always reading weird shit like that. It's why he and Catalina get along so well. He's the brother she never had and he's the only one in the family who wants to know as much random shit as she does.

I thought he was talking out of his ass, but there is no hint of the underlying sourness I usually taste when going down on a woman. I don't find it unpleasant, but this?

It's fucking ambrosia.

Bianca's eyes flutter open, her blue gaze unfocused. "You can touch me whenever you want, if it will end in pleasure like that," she slurs.

Then her eyelids drift down again.

What is she dreaming about to prompt her to say that? It sure as hell is not the nightmares that keep waking her since those *bastardo's* attacked her.

My primal instincts growl in satisfaction at her words while lust prowls like a beast inside me, insisting I take her up on the offer and get myself off with her body. But I am no boy to allow my sexual need to dictate my actions.

My self-control is legendary.

Except around her.

I force that inner voice into silence. I can control myself. To prove it, I undo my slacks and shove them and my boxers down my hips so I can jack myself off. I will not go near the bed. I will not shove my aching dick in her tight, sweet pussy.

But fuck if I will wait one more minute to come.

Spying her panties on the floor, I grab them and shove them in my face, letting her fragrance drive my arousal higher. Then I wrap that soft silk around my cock, rubbing up and down with the pressure and speed I know will take me over quickly.

I'm leaking so much precum that I soak the panties with only a couple of swipes up and down my shaft and over my sensitive head. Shuddering, I hold back from coming, reveling in pleasure more intense than anything I have felt with a sex partner in a long time.

If ever.

I am not even inside her beautiful body, but watching her sleep? Her heavy round tits tipped with nipples still erect from her climax, and her pink pussy lips beckoning me, desire explodes in my blood like a roman candle.

My balls ache with the need to come. Squeezing harder, I increase the speed of my hand on my cock.

Ecstasy roars up my shaft exploding in streams of cum that land in pearly pools on her soft, smooth skin. A few drops shoot as far as the tops of her breasts, one small streak landing on the base of her throat, marking her as mine.

Using her panties, I swipe one warm puddle up so our scents are mixed on the silk and stuff them in my pocket. Then, using my fingers, I rub the rest of my cum into her skin so she will smell my primitive claim while she sleeps and it will imprint on her subconscious.

While my fingers are still wet with my release I gently rub them over her lips. Her nose wrinkles, but then my knees nearly buckle when the tip of her tongue comes out to swipe over where my fingertips have just been. Her lips smack and a soft smile plays at the edges of her mouth.

This woman is going to be the death of me.

My cock is still ready for action, but I shove it back into my boxers and then zip up my slacks where a dark wet spot from earlier shows just how turned on this woman makes me.

Using all my vaunted self-control I move Bianca under the covers, turning her onto her side to take pressure off her wound. Not that she seemed to notice it while my mouth was feasting on her.

I hide her too tempting body from the predator in me that wants to strip out of my clothes and join her. No matter how much I want to, I cannot bury my cock so deep in her body, she will feel me for the next week.

After I tuck the blankets around her, I lean down and kiss her forehead, lingering to inhale her sweet fragrance underlying the heavy scent of sex. It makes me want to do things I do not do with women.

Touch? Yes. Fuck? Definitely.

Hold in my arms while she sleeps? Never before. Not even Monica.

The need to protect Bianca, to keep her near, to know she is safe is constantly in the background. It is why I was there the morning she was attacked. Knowing she left work late and had no one to walk to the train with drove me to instruct my men to take me on an alternate route home. The one that made sure I would see her walking between Amuni and the subway station.

I am not like this.

I do not worry about my playmates. I do not think about women when I should be working.

She is an outsider. Off limits for the long term. Understandable that my libido does not care, but my primal need to protect and possess isn't hampered by that truth either.

Managgia la miseria!

No matter what Bianca wants to claim, she is just as affected. My scent calms her nightmares. *Mine.*

She shies away from other men, even when she is working, she keeps a barrier up between herself and everyone else. Except me.

Does she realize that?

It has to be some kind of pheromone compatibility. I bet Miceli's article talks about that too, but no way in hell am I asking my cousin about this shit.

He'll start thinking I'm getting serious about Bianca.

I'm not.

I can't.

After Monica, I vowed I would never again consider commitment to someone outside *la famiglia*. It's too risky. If I had told Monica the truths I planned to, she could have destroyed me and maybe even my pops. Instead, I had no choice but to destroy her and the man she partnered with.

They say your first kill is your hardest. I did a damn good job of hiding how true that was for me from my father and my uncle, the don. Executing the woman I had sex with and told I loved only hours before? Had been hell.

But that hellfire had forged me into the strong capo I am today. I no longer feel remorse when I have to kill for my family.

I will not let Bianca, another outsider, be my undoing. Or put *la famiglia* at risk for her.

That doesn't stop me wanting her, or needing to possess her. She is mine until the lust that burns like a thousand suns between us goes out.

If it ever does.

Deliberately stepping away from the bed where Bianca sleeps so peacefully, I ignore the taunting inner voice.

Then, in defiance of the desires I cannot seem to control with her, I go into the adjoining bathroom where I wash my face and hands, before patting myself dry with a hand towel. I do *not* sniff the towel before tossing it in the hamper.

Refusing to acknowledge how I immediately miss her taste on my lips and scent under my nose, I grab my shirt and pull it on, only to be inundated with the perfume of her pussy dried into the fabric from earlier.

I rip it off on my way to my bedroom. Seeing my empty bed only darkens my mood.

Bianca should be sleeping there, not in the guestroom.

Fucking inner voice is as much of a meddler as Rosa.

I stomp into the walk-in closet and drop my shirt with Bianca's juices in the hamper only to grab it back out again. I shove it against my face and inhale, my still hard cock pulsing with renewed need.

I fold it up so the spot that has her essence is protected from the air and tuck it into a drawer. After I pull on a fresh pair of slacks, I put the panties with our mingled scents into the pocket.

I count it a win when I don't hesitate to drop my dirty slacks into the pile for the dry cleaner.

Why not? They only have your cum on them. Not her delicious juices.

Fucking inner voice. My phone rings as I finish buttoning my new shirt.

Juniper. Finally.

I swipe to answer.

"De Luca," I say by way of greeting when I want to ask why the hell it has taken him two days to return my call.

We're supposed to meet later today. Why do I think he's not calling to confirm the appointment?

"Hey, Salvatore."

"Juniper."

"Uh..."

My sixth sense for trouble sends the hairs on the back of my neck to standing attention. And I walk-jog to my office, where I grab one of my Bluetooth earbuds and put it in my ear. I never wear both.

I need to be aware of my surroundings at all times. When I see people jogging on the streets, oblivious to the noise around them, I cringe. The least of the dangers around them is getting knocked down by someone they don't hear coming.

If Bianca had been wearing earbuds on her walk to the subway, she never would have reacted quickly enough to fight off her attackers until I got there. She would be dead.

The thought sends rage spiking through me.

"When are we signing papers?" I ask Juniper bluntly as I text Nerissa.

Salvatore: *Get a fix on Juniper's location. Now.*

Nerissa: *Do you know if he is with his phone?*

"About that," Juniper pauses.

I remain silent, letting him hang.

Salvatore: *He's talking to me on it now.*

"I got a better offer," Juniper finally admits, like my silence forced the words out of him. Weak. "No hard feelings. It's just business. Right?"

His death is going to be my business if he doesn't sell me those bars. "Who gave you the better offer?"

I don't ask what the offer is because it doesn't matter. Juniper is selling those bars to me at our agreed upon price, whether he signs the papers or we forge them after dumping the body.

"It's a property development group out of Boston. They offered me nearly twice what you did. How could I turn them down?" His hopeful tone tells me two things.

One, he hasn't signed papers with the developers. Two, he's hoping to drive the price up even further.

Nerissa: *Got a lock on his location.*

Salvatore: *Pick him up.*

Nerissa: *Ninety minutes out by car.*

Fuck. It would be too easy for him to be in the City to meet me like he promised.

Salvatore: *He's in Trenton?*

Nerissa: *At home.*

Not his store? Until his windfall inheritance, Juniper's only property was a rundown corner shop in East Trenton. He probably doesn't think he needs to worry about the shop, with the money from the property sale coming in.

Especially if he expects to drive the price up with rival bidders.

Black fury rolls through my body, but I control it, like I control all my emotions when necessary.

CHAPTER 32

SALVATORE

"Are you trying to jerk me around to get more money?" I demand over the phone to Juniper.

"No, man." He pauses. "I mean, if you want to outbid the developer, I'll listen to any reasonable offer."

Fucking Juniper.

My phone dings.

Nerissa: *Helicopter?*

Reaching the area by helicopter would take thirty minutes instead of ninety. I do a quick calculation in my head, accounting for Nerissa and her crew getting to the helicopter, the flight and then driving to Juniper's home. Assuming we can source a vehicle and have it ready at the landing site.

Best case it saves her team thirty minutes in real time to reach him. Worst case, it takes as long, or longer than the drive.

The Irish control Trenton. Calling on our connections in the area to source a vehicle prevents this from being a clandestine snatch and grab with the local mob none the wiser.

Getting approval from Trenton's mob boss to land the helicopter and do business in his territory alone could take longer than the drive south.

Cazo.

Salvatore: *No helicopter.*

Nerissa: *Roger that.*

Salvatore: *Keep the tracker on his phone live.*

Nerissa put the tracking app on his phone when he came to the club. She is going to enjoy *encouraging* him to keep our bargain. I'd do it myself, but he pissed her off with one too many innuendos uttered while leering at her tits.

Bad choice, Juniper, not checking your phone for spyware.

He is babbling about land values and development potential the whole time I'm texting with my second.

"Youse can't expect me to take the first offer that comes along. That's bad business, man."

"You want me to believe some developer from Massachusetts contacted you out of the blue to offer you twice what I did?" I let disbelief I do not feel infuse my tone.

This offer is legit. I can feel it in my gut. But who are the *stronzos* willing to outbid me?

"I'm not lying. It's Stellar Holdings. They're big in Boston."

More dark fury brews with the rage already bubbling like lava in my gut.

Stellar Holdings are big all over the East Coast.

Except New York.

Owned by the Lombard family, who are still known in our circles as the Lombardis, Stellar Holdings is one of the front corporations for the Boston Cosa Nostra.

What are the Lombardis doing messing with New York real estate? The whole fucking state is off limits to them without the godfather's approval. Buying in the City could be construed as an act of aggression against the Five Families.

No way is the Lombardi don that foolish.

Which means he is working under the auspices of the godfather, or with one of the other Families.

"Who contacted you?" I ask Juniper as I text an update to Severu and request an information dive by his wife.

"Does it matter?"

"Answer the damn question," I bark.

"Okay. Shit, cool your jets, *amigo*."

Juniper is not Latino. Neither am I. Does he think amigo is Italian?

"You are not my *amico*," I stress the proper Italian word for friend. "We are business associates."

"Nothing to stop us from being friends is the-ah? Me and your sist-ah got a thing, if youse know what I mean." His New Jersey accent is thickening.

Either he's drinking, or he's nervous.

"My sister certainly has a thing for men who keep their word in business," I inform him.

"Hey, hey, hey...I'm not breaking my word. We ain't signed nothing yet."

"We shook on our deal." In the mafia a handshake is as good as a signed contract and in some cases, more binding.

The consequences of reneging are more severe than anything the courts could impose. Those outside the life learn quickly that when they make a promise on a handshake, *we* expect them to keep it. Regardless of whether they know we are connected, or not.

"Look, I gotta go. Youse take some time and think about if youse wants to up your offer."

"Do not fuck—" The call disconnects before I can finish telling him not to fucking hang up on me.

Stronzo.

Maybe I won't allow Nerissa to teach Juniper the error of his ways.

I'll reserve that pleasure for myself.

Twenty minutes later, I get a text from my second.

Nerissa: *We lost the trace on his phone.*

Salvatore: *WTF? How?*

Nerissa: *He could be in a dead zone.*

Our spyware utilizes GPS data, which is accessible even when a phone is out of cell tower range. There are few places it would not continue to send out signal. But they do exist.

Salvatore: *Where was he when you lost him?*

Nerissa: *The NJ Turnpike. He exited and five minutes later, we lost signal.*

The New Jersey Turnpike could take him to Manhattan, or Boston, depending on what he does when he reaches the I-278 interchange. If he stays on the interstate headed north.

Nerissa: *There are two helipads near the exit.*

Someone is flying Juniper north, and it's not us. Whoever it is has technology on their helicopter to block GPS transmissions like we do.

He's on his way to meet with Stellar Holdings.

Fuck.

I send a quick text to Juniper.

Salvatore: *I want those bars. I am willing to pay.*

The greedy bastard better not make a deal with the Lombardis without letting me make a counteroffer. Assuming they give him the chance. If I had my hands on him, I wouldn't.

I text my don.

Salvatore: *We need to track a helicopter heading from New Jersey to Boston.*

Salvatore: *Scratch that. Probably New York.*

The paperwork has to be filed in each county where the bars reside before the transfer of ownership is complete. If Stellar Holdings know about my offer, they'll want to file with the county clerk's offices immediately.

It's not something that can be done online.

I text Nerissa instructing her to send teams to each of the courthouses involved to be on standby to stop the filing of the paperwork.

Nerissa: *On it. Where will you be?*

Salvatore: *Here.*

Where the hell does she expect me to be? Until we know where they are headed first, there's no point in me leaving the penthouse.

Nerissa: *You keeping watch over your unwanted houseguest?*

Pissed off by the out of bounds question, I make no effort to explain my actions, or lack thereof.

I'm waiting for the intel from Catalina and a conference with Severu before deciding on next steps.

The Lombardis would not risk a Cosa Nostra civil war.

It would be guaranteed destruction for them to go up against New York's Five Families. Which means they are working with one of us and believe the decision to buy property in our territory will not blow back on them.

One of the bars is in the Gambino territory, the other is in the Lucchese territory. Either family could have learned about the property sale. Or any of the other families, for that matter.

The don's wife has scary mad skills for gathering information. Her being the best does not mean she is the only one with the intel though.

If the Lucchese family is involved in the deal, my path forward is limited. Especially if the godfather is behind Stellar Holdings' offer. Why would Don Caruso hide his interest behind an outside company brokering the deal though?

Maybe, like me and Severu, he does not want the other Five Families to know about the bars changing ownership before it's a done deal. He's the only member of the Five Families that could broker a backdoor deal like this through another mafia without incurring the wrath of the other families.

That doesn't mean he is the only one who *would* do it, however. I can think of a couple of dons and three times as many capos who are arrogant enough to believe they won't be found out until the leverage is in their hands.

The godfather could have plans to use ownership of the properties as leverage himself. It's something he would have done back in the day.

Not so much lately, but maybe he's more on top of things than our last meeting would imply.

Nerissa: *Getting this deal signed and sealed should be your priority.*

Stuffing down my rage at her insolence, I call her. This is not happening over text.

"Who the fuck do you think you are to question my priorities?" I ask as soon as the call connects.

I don't yell. I keep my voice even, but there's no question I am pissed.

"Getting these properties under our control is more important than you getting your rocks off," Nerissa says, disapproval dripping from her tone.

What the actual fuck?

"Who is in the SUV with you?" I demand.

Her punishment will be commensurate with how many of her team overheard her disrespect.

Her pause says she realizes her mistake. "I'm alone in the back with the privacy panel up."

Do I believe her? "Put me on video call. Now."

Her angry face pops up on the screen. "Are you really checking to see if I'm telling the truth?"

"Show me."

Eyes narrow, her mouth set in a firm line, she turns the phone so I can see that no one else is in the backseat with her and that the privacy panel is in place. "Satisfied?"

"You do not chastise me." My words are clipped, my temper too close to the surface.

This is the third woman in my family to challenge my authority and integrity as their capo today. I'm not sure what I'm going to do to fix this problem, but none of us are going to enjoy it.

"Mamma said she caught you kissing the little stripper in your bedroom." Nerissa's words prove she is either obtuse to my growing fury, or unimpressed by it.

Neither is acceptable from my second-in-command.

"Bianca is not a stripper." Why I need to address that point before the issue of respect, I don't know, but I fucking do.

"You don't deny kissing her."

"I have no need to. Mamma did not *catch* me doing anything. She walked into my bedroom unannounced and *found* me kissing Bianca."

And doing other things my mother has no idea about because the angle of my body blocked her view of my fingers buried between Bianca's leg.

"Who I kiss, fuck or put in my bed is not your business, or hers." I can't be any clearer without breaking out the hand puppets.

"I thought you were smarter than that." Nerissa's condescending tone is the last straw.

First, she questions my priorities. Now, she's disparaging my decisions and my intelligence? Not happening.

"And I thought you were smart enough not to disrespect your capo," I bite out.

My word is law. My actions not up for her scrutiny.

"You're also my brother."

From boss to brother. Fuck. All the women in my family do think they are immune to my status.

"Ask Miceli how often he disrespects Severu. I'll give you a hint, it starts with zero and ends with never."

"I mean no disrespect."

"Then shut your mouth because it's leaking out around your tongue."

"Salva—"

Too pissed to continue this conversation, I tap to disconnect the call. When my phone rings seconds later, I send Nerissa to voicemail.

She texts next.

Nerissa: *I am sorry, capo. It won't happen again.*

Salvatore: *It won't if you want to remain my second.*

Something is going on with the women in my family and it's crystalizing around my very much wanted houseguest.

CHAPTER 33

SALVATORE

Thirty minutes after I hang up on Nerissa, Severu calls with information on the helicopter. It is headed for Boston, not New York, which gives us time we didn't think we had.

He also updates me on what Catalina has uncovered. "Henry Caruso's mother is a Lombard. Her brother is the current CEO of Stellar Holdings and their cousin is the don of the Boston Cosa Nostra."

"If Don Caruso is behind the offer from Boston, I cannot kill Juniper and forge his signature on the sale documents." A frustrated sigh gusts out of me. "Even intimidating him into taking my offer could cause a rift between you and the godfather."

"His behavior at the meeting with you and Miceli has already made that rift." Severu's tone matches my cold and even one.

Miceli might be the only other person who would realize it, but our don is as furious as I am.

"Do you think Don Caruso decided to back his nephew to replace him as godfather?" He knows what is best for the Five Families, and Henry Caruso is not it.

But a man changes when he is staring death in the face. Sometimes for the worse.

"Our godfather's interest in his legacy could be stronger than his concern for the longevity and prosperity of the New York Cosa Nostra," Severu says, mirroring my thoughts.

"He has to know that shifting support from you to Henry won't get him voted in by the Five Families council."

"Our godfather isn't thinking as strategically as he once did," Severu says heavily.

"I can't argue with that." A shift in his support will complicate the battle for the position of godfather and could lead to a bloody civil war.

A war Severu will win, but not without cost to *la famiglia*.

Out of respect for Don Caruso and fear of Severu's power, the other dons of the Five Families will back Severu as things stand. My cousin Giulia is married to the underboss in Las Vegas. Severu will get their vote as well. Chicago, Boston, Detroit and New England remain noncommittal. But with the Five Families behind Severu, it doesn't matter.

He has the majority. Remove Don Caruso's support, and the same two dons arrogant enough to try a backdoor deal with Juniper through a third party would put themselves forward for the position. Chicago and New England's dons probably will too.

There's a chance they will anyway.

None of those dons are happy about a man as young as Severu stepping into the role of godfather. The other dons are all at least twenty years my cousin's senior. Even Henry is ten years older than him.

And not a damn one of them would lead the Cosa Nostra into the future as well as my cousin.

"We need to know who is behind the attempt to outbid you with Juniper."

I agree before hanging up.

Catalina and Domenico Bianchi's tech wizards dig deep to figure out which of the Carusos is involved in the property deal with Stellar Holdings.

Juniper's phone records show he is in contact with a phone registered to Stellar Holdings, but there is no record of who that phone is assigned to.

This does not surprise me. We don't keep records like that for the FEDs to find either.

There is no obvious link between Stellar Holdings and a particular Caruso either, Henry's family ties notwithstanding. Which in itself could be an answer. If Don Caruso were in contact with Boston's Cosa Nostra, there would be phone records to show it.

Maybe.

But we do know that with his family connections, Henry could be in contact through his mother or another unofficial channel, making him the more likely suspect.

My phone beeps and I see I have multiple texts. Two from my second and the other from Juniper.

Nerissa: *Juniper's phone tracker is working again.*

Nerissa: *He is in a moving vehicle headed away from Stellar Holdings headquarters.*

Juniper: *Don't worry, amigo. I'm busy tonight but tomorrow you can make me another offer.*

While I'm still typing a response, another text comes in.

Juniper: *You're going to have to up your game though. Tell that sister of yours to be a little nicer, yeah? Stellar Holdings really know how to treat a guy.*

I will get the deeds for the bar properties, but Juniper may not going to live to enjoy the money.

I text Nerissa.

Salvatore: *Keep me informed of his whereabouts.*

Then I text Juniper, picturing myself putting a bullet hole in the center of his forehead the whole time.

Salvatore: *Great. Looking forward to it. Don't worry. We know how to take care of our friends.*

And our enemies.

The alarm I set to remind me to wake up Bianca for lunch goes off. My fury banks as satisfaction settles in my chest.

Bianca did not wake up screaming in the past two hours.

When I walk into the guest bedroom, my beauty is on her side, the covers shoved down to her hips. One arm is tucked under the pillow and her other rests over her belly, leaving her gorgeous tits on display.

My cock wakes up, ready to party.

Shaking my head, I approach the bed and the curvy Siren lying there. There's no time to have sex right now. Taking time out for lunch is pushing it, but I have to eat and I'll have my phone with me. I can monitor information as it comes in.

Right. No sex. You might as well eat at the desk in your office after you wake up Sleeping Beauty.

Okay. Sexual gratification is not totally off the table. I don't have to be sitting at a desk or a table to monitor my phone. I set my phone, screen up, on the nightstand.

There. Problem solved.

Focusing on the buffet of temptation laid out before me my cock strains against my slacks. I reach out and cup one of Bianca's lush breasts, brushing my thumb over her nipple. It stiffens as quickly as my cock, turning the color of a raspberry almost instantly.

So fucking pretty.

My mouth waters for a taste of those sweet peaks, but there is something I want to taste even more.

Not wanting her to wake just yet, I carefully tug the blankets down until her entire body is exposed to my gaze. The scent of her arousal and the cum I rubbed into her skin earlier clings to her, sending hot desire pounding through my veins.

Cazzo. This woman turns me on like no other.

And you thought one night would be enough?

I shake off the thought but can't dismiss the one that comes right after. *A month of nights will not slake this lust.*

That should put a lid on my libido. Allow me to wake Bianca without touching her.

It doesn't.

I prefer to keep sex transactional. Bianca will not allow it. I still want her.

It has been more than a decade since I spent more than a couple of nights with the same woman. Yet Bianca has been in my bed for the last four nights. I have never allowed another woman to sleep in my penthouse, much less my bed. And I fucking moved her in.

Bianca is the exception to too many rules.

And knowing that does nothing to dampen the raging inferno of need inside me.

Fuck.

Rules be damned. I want to taste her sweet honey and that's what I'm going to fucking do.

My mind flips through scenarios that don't put her on her back. I should have gone for a different position earlier. I won't make the same mistake now.

The stitches come out tomorrow, but that does not mean she is healed.

With a detour to lock the door, I make my way around the bed.

My movements are stealthy as I climb onto the firm mattress, barely causing any disturbance. Who knew my training to be a made man would come into use in a situation like this?

But the idea of waking Bianca up with my tongue buried between her legs is too much temptation to resist. She gave me permission to touch her whenever I want, as long as I give her an orgasm, which I fully intend to do.

At least one of us will be satisfied this afternoon.

Salivating for another taste of that sweet, juicy pussy, I lie down on my side and gently lift her leg so I can rest my head between her thighs, my mouth pressed against her pussy lips. She mumbles but does not wake and I grin before licking her from her perineum up to her clit.

Her faintly tart, but mostly sweet, earthy flavor bursts across my tongue. Delicious.

Caressing her gently with my tongue, I stimulate her so she grows wetter and wetter. Little mmming sounds drop from her mouth and her hips cant against my face, but her limbs are still loose from sleep.

I could spend all afternoon feasting on her, but there's too much happening right now with the Juniper deal. Wanting her to wake on her orgasm, I simultaneously slide two fingers inside her slick, hot channel and suck her swollen clit.

Her tight vaginal walls clamp around my fingers and she wakes with a cry, her cum soaking my hand.

Bianca tries to close her legs in reflex, but my head is in the way.

Gripping her thigh with my free hand, I pull my mouth away from her still pulsing pussy. "Do not move. If you move, I stop."

She's good for at least one more orgasm and her body knows it, even if her mind has not caught up yet.

CHAPTER 34

BIANCA

My body reacts to Salvatore's words on a primal level before I even parse what he's saying in my conscious brain.

I go completely still, the only movement in my body my lungs sucking in and expelling gusts of air.

I woke from a dream about Salvatore to an orgasm courtesy of his mouth and fingers. Ecstasy is still sparking along my nerve endings. His tongue against my clitoris is too much, but do I move to stop him?

No, I do not.

Before I fell asleep, I told him he could touch me whenever he wants. As long as it ended in this carnal bliss.

I can barely believe I said that. Wasn't sure I'd even managed to utter the words I never expected to say, I was that out of it. But I did and I cannot regret it.

This kind of pleasure drowns out everything. Physical pain. Memories. Worries. All of it.

My second climax hits me like a freight train and I scream. Salvatore's name.

With a final kiss to my nether lips, he shifts his head from between my thighs and scoots backward off the bed.

"What was that?" I ask, still panting.

His grin is predatory. "You needed to wake up to eat your lunch and take your pain meds."

"So, you thought, hey, I'll wake Bianca up with my mouth on her?" Is this guy for real?

He wipes his fingers over his lips and then licks my juices off of them. "Can you think of a better way?"

The earthy gesture sends another pulse of remembered ecstasy through my lower half.

"You could have nudged me, or jostled my shoulder, or I don't know...said my name loud enough to wake me." I'm a light sleeper.

At least I usually am, but I slept through him taking the covers off of me and getting situated with his face up close and personal with my ladybits.

"This was more fun."

"For me maybe." He hadn't climaxed before, and another impressive erection is tenting his slacks now.

"I enjoyed it, trust me, Bianca. But if you are offering to return the favor, I will not turn you down."

Am I? Do I want to taste him? I think I do.

Oral isn't something the monsters that ripped my virginity away forced on me that night.

This is something of myself I can give that no one has taken from me. Salvatore never has to know he's my first blowjob. Unless I really suck at it. Then he might figure it out.

But I want to try.

I sit up and scoot around so I'm sitting on the edge of the bed, my feet dangling over the side. "I'm offering."

I don't try to sound sultry. Pretty sure I couldn't pull that off. But I don't hide how much I want this either.

He comes around the bed with flattering speed and stops in front of me.

Putting the side of his hand under my chin, he lifts my head so our eyes meet. "Are you up to this?"

The ice around my heart that has protected me for so long melts a little more. This man.

"I want to taste you too."

"I can get myself off." He makes the offer but shifts a little closer.

I smile. "Not necessary."

"Brava ragazza."

Something unexpected shivers through me when he calls me *good girl*. I want to be good. For him. And only him. The rest of the world can take me as I come.

All gentleness vanishes from his gaze and his hand snakes around my nape to grab my hair in a tight grip. "Take me out."

Desire gushes from my core at his demand and the hold he has on my hair. Because it makes me feel safe. Like everything else, he has this under control.

After undoing his belt and then his slacks, I slide the zipper down carefully so I don't catch the tented silk of his boxers on the teeth. I push the slacks down his hips first, paying no attention when they fall to the floor around his feet.

I'm too focused on the monster dick barely covered by the silk boxers in front of me. Pulling the waistband away from his body, I gasp as his erection surges up, the leaking tip an angry purple.

Eating me out did this to him. Making me come turned him on so much that there's a dark, wet spot on the front of his boxers. Inhaling his scent, I push his boxers down. Because of the elastic, they get caught on his hips.

I don't care.

His erection is bobbing in front of my face, tempting me to taste. To touch. To smell. I lean forward and inhale, taking in the unique scent of his precum only to jerk my head up and stare at him.

I've been smelling this since I woke up. "Did you come on me after I fell asleep?"

"Yes." There's no apology in his eyes.

I don't want there to be.

"Good."

"Cazzo. You are perfect for me *carina."*

A smile is flirting at my lips as I press them against his rigid column of flesh. I kiss him. *Hello, Salavatore's sex.*

Eager for a taste, I flick my tongue out and lick him from root to tip, swiping my tongue over the pearly essence beaded on his slitted opening. Tang slides over my tastebuds with a hint of salt.

More. I want more.

Licking and swirling my tongue all over his bulbous head, I lap up every bit of it I can get.

He's swearing in Italian and I think that's Russian? Is that Arabic? Not even sort of willing to stop what I'm doing to ask, I let the litany of incomprehensible words pour over my head.

Then I open my mouth as wide as I can and take him inside. My lips stretch as he immediately hits the roof of my mouth. Flattening my tongue against the underside of his hardness, I caress the warm, velvety skin.

"Cazzo!" His grip on my hair tightens and he pulls my faced forward, pushing more of his dick into my mouth.

He hits the back of my throat and I gag a little.

"That's right, my beauty, gag on my cock like the good girl I know you are." He says it all in Italian.

Which makes it hotter somehow.

"Open your throat for me. Let me in."

For a panicked second, I don't know if I can trust him enough to do it, to give him control of my airway like that. But then I just...do.

He pushes forward as I swallow and relax my throat. He roars as loud as any lion and then groans pushing more of his sex down my throat.

Power surges through me. I am a sexual being capable of giving and receiving pleasure. My past has not neutered my sensuality. It may have been in hiding, but it is still there.

Salvatore pushes deep, stretching my throat and the last bit of air exhales through my nose. My airway completely blocked, I put my hand on my throat to feel him inside me. A shudder works its way up my body.

He is inside me. I didn't think that I would ever allow this to happen. And I'm not just allowing it. I want it.

So much.

Laying his hand over mine, he slowly pulls his hips back until his hardness is in my mouth, not my throat. I inhale precious air through my nose and suck on his large sex, hollowing my cheeks around him.

"Cazzo," he groans. "That's good, *brava ragazza."*

The mix of English and Italian is endearing. And hot.

I swirl my tongue around his erection before I suck on him again, repeating this over and over, getting more and more of his precum to savor.

"Your mouth is so fucking good, I am not going to last," he says gutturally.

The words of praise add another layer of pleasure to what I am doing. Unbelievably, my clit is pulsing with the need to climax. *Again.*

Salvatore surges forward. "Take my cum, Bianca."

Air expels through my nose as he pushes into my throat again and then no air can move in or out. Only hot, viscous fluid jetting down the back of my throat.

"Swallow," he demands.

But I'm already doing it, taking his essence into my body. He's still coming as he withdraws so his semen pulses onto my tongue and spills out the corners of my mouth.

The way he is looking at me, he did it on purpose. He likes seeing his cum on me. No wonder he released on me when he masturbated earlier.

Will he do it again? When I can watch?

Does it make me a freak if I ask him to?

Not wanting to release him yet, I breathe through my nose and savor his taste. He swipes at the corner of my mouth with his thumb before pushing it between my lips as he withdraws his sex.

I suck his flavor off his thumb, my hand sliding between my legs and rubbing my clitoris with my middle finger. His big hand covers mine, his rougher finger sliding over my slick nub, sending shards of ecstasy through me.

"Come for me *brava regazza."* Pushing his heel against my finger, he thrusts two fingers inside me and hooks them. "Now."

I see stars. Entire super novas. As my body explodes for the third time since waking from my nap.

My head falls forward against him, my heart racing from the pleasure, my lungs sucking air like a spasming vacuum. His hand lands on the back of my head and he holds me like that as my breathing begins to slow and my heart no longer feels like it will beat out of my chest.

His phone rings, the sound a shrill interruption to the private cocoon we have created between us, his world intruding.

He swears, his fingers tightening their grip on the back of my head, but then he lets his hand fall away.

"Take a shower while I answer that." He caresses my cheek before stepping away.

I don't watch him as he picks up the phone. I jump up and hightail it into the bathroom, needing a minute of solitude to process what just happened.

What I did. What I let him do. What I *wanted* him to do. I crave that hardness inside me and not just in my throat. Vaginal walls contracting at the thought of him claiming the most intimate part of me, I force myself to step into the shower and turn on the water.

It is only a few seconds before the water is hot enough to step under. Steam begins to fill the space around me as I run my hands over my tingling body.

My mind playing both this morning and just now on repeat, I let the hot water soak my hair before washing it for the second time today. I use extra conditioner and leave it in while I wash the rest of my body, taking inventory of how things feel different and yet the same.

My skin is sensitized but it is also still *my* skin. Washing my vulva with the hot water, my fingers slide through the silky slickness at my core. I shudder.

That feels so good.

I'm tempted to pleasure myself again, but Salvatore said something about needing to eat lunch. I am ridiculously reluctant to lose the chance to spend time with him, so I quickly finish washing and turn off the shower.

Salvatore leans against the wall, his eyes locked on me like lust filled missiles. "If only we had time to do all the things I want to you."

"I thought we needed to wait to do them until I am more healed," I tease breathlessly, grabbing a towel to dry off.

"Until I fuck you through the mattress? Yes." He pushes away from the wall, coming to stand in front of me. "But there is so much pleasure to be had without putting your healing wounds at risk."

Things like putting his head between my legs while I am on my side? That's a pretty amazing way to wake up. Heat pools in my core as the memory of waking to an orgasm plays in my head.

Salvatore's body tenses and the air between us thickens with want. "Stop thinking about it."

"What if I don't want to?" I drop the towel and look up at him through my lashes.

Who *is* this woman?

His hands clenched in fists at his sides, he shakes his head. "No." But then belying his denial, he yanks the towel from my hand. "You are a lot of temptation for such a tiny thing."

"I'm hardly tiny." Okay, five feet, four inches isn't exactly tall, but it's not a shrimp either.

And if one of the strippers from Pitiful Princess was on the other end of a teeter-totter, I'd send her flying.

I like my body, but it's not tiny.

He makes a sound like I'm oh-so-annoying and turns me around so he can dry my back. "Compared to me, you are."

Well, I guess that's true. Still. Not tiny.

"Your presence takes up all the space in the room and my thoughts," he mutters the last bit. "Does that make you feel better?"

"Yes."

He finishes his gentle pats on my back with the fluffy towel. "It's a little red from earlier, but the stitches look fine."

"It's probably just red and has nothing to do with earlier." Plastic surgeon, or not, skin takes time to heal.

"Probably? You don't know?"

"As you pointed out so adamantly, I can't see that spot on my back and can barely reach it with my fingers." Not that I'm about to touch it. I don't want to accidentally pull on the stitches.

Removing the gauze bandage before my shower was easy. I just pulled on one corner of the medical tape. If being on my back earlier had caused any damage, the gauze would have been stuck to my back with blood.

It wasn't.

He carefully dabs the towel around the cut. "Does it still hurt?"

"A little."

"I shouldn't have had you on your back earlier."

"It doesn't hurt any more than it did when I woke up this morning," I tell him honestly.

"Rosa told me you refuse to take pain meds during the day." He brushes the towel over my butt cheeks, one at a time.

It feels like a caress, and I have to stifle the moan that wants to come out. "It's not unbearable and I don't like taking meds I don't have to."

The air shifts from movement behind me and then he's drying my legs, pushing them apart to gently wick moisture from between my legs. I'm not sure all of it is water from the shower.

A soft whisper of lips at the base of my spine and then Salvatore stands and taps my bottom. "Get a move on, or I'm going to be eating a lunch wrap in the car on the way to Oscuro and you are going to miss out on your time in the rooftop garden."

"Why can't I go up with Rosa?" He says I'm not a prisoner, but he sure wants to control my comings and goings.

Not that there's actually any *goings*.

"You don't want my company?"

A week ago, sheer self-preservation would have forced me to say *no*. Now? I can't deny the truth to a man who not only saved my life, but has taken very good care of me since, and keeps my nightmares at bay.

Impossible not to crave his company.

The best I can do is hold back saying how much.

CHAPTER 35

BIANCA

Access to the rooftop garden is via a set of stairs at one end of the terrace off the living room.

The view from the terrace is impressive enough, and Salvatore has to tug me by the hand to keep me going.

But from the roof? *Accidenti*. The 360º view steals my breath right out of my chest. This is my city and seeing it like this does something weird inside my chest.

Our family home had been in East Rutherford because my dad couldn't afford the cost of living in Manhattan on what he made working for Lorenzo. However, everything important in our lives took place 30 minutes away by train. In Manhattan. Genovese territory.

I'd gone to school here. Even after mom left and dad put me in public school, he fixed it so I attended one in Manhattan. Every dance lesson and recital happened here. Every job I'd held. The three years I lived in Queens with Mr. Ruhnke were the same. It was a place to sleep, just like the apartment I lived in with my roommates.

This is my home.

For the first time, I acknowledge moving away is going to be hard.

Leaving Salvatore's home might even be harder and it's not because of the luxury. Though breathing in the fresh air on the rooftop and basking in the warmth of the sun's rays isn't a hardship.

The sky, not even visible from the street in parts of the city, is blue with puffy white clouds.

The rooftop garden itself is as incredible as the view. Statuary are placed among the plants and shrubbery laid in a way that reminds me of the pictures I've seen of the formal gardens at the home where my *bisnonna* grew up in Italy.

Salvatore leads me to a large rectangular wrought iron table set for two in the shade of a freaking conservatory.

I can't call this elegant building with carved white wood dividers between beveled glass windows a greenhouse. It looks like it belongs attached to that same Italian villa.

Again, I feel that punch to my gut from how rich Salvatore and his family must be to own something like this in the middle of New York.

He pulls a chair out for me, and I sit down. His spot is at the head of the table to my right. Despite the size of the table and grandeur of the garden, it feels intimate.

My ovaries swoon a little and I grit my teeth against renewed arousal.

What is this man, this mafia capo, doing to me?

Salvatore presses something on the wall of the conservatory. When the wall slides back to reveal a familiar opening, I realize the dumbwaiter comes all the way up to the roof. The only thing I'd been interested in, when I was trying to find a way out of the penthouse, was going down.

He withdraws two covered plates and places them on the table as well as two glasses and a pitcher of Rosa's freshly squeezed lemonade. I've watched her make it. The housekeeper crushes mint leaves before pouring the hot lemonade over them and then chills it after.

It's delicious and my mouth waters for a taste.

I pour some in each glass before taking the lid off my lunch and smiling. "Rosa must believe I'm getting better. This is my first lunch here that does not include pastina soup."

Asparagus spears lay over a bed of pasta farfalle aglio e olio. I used to beg my nonna to make the bowtie shaped noodles because they are my favorite. And I like them best served this way, tossed in olive oil, garlic and grated parmesan. A fat link of grilled sausage is arranged in a neat line of slices to one side.

If we were eating inside, the meat would not be on the same plate as the pasta, but I guess some rules get bent for outdoor dining.

"It is my favorite. This is her way of apologizing for calling my integrity into question."

Even as I store the bit of information that we share the same favorite pasta, I wince at the anger lacing Salvatore's tone. "I'm sure that's not how she meant it."

"Never mind Rosa, or my mother, if she's the next topic on your conversation list. I want to enjoy my lunch." He gives me a pointed stare.

I shrug. "If you say so. Only I think you love both women and you're mad at them right now, but you'll realize eventually they're doing their best to look out for you."

A harsh bark of laughter erupts from his mouth. "You are lousy at following directions. I would punish one of my soldiers for disobeying a direct order like that."

"It's a good thing I'm not one of your soldiers then because I don't like orders," I sass.

His hot gaze sweeps over my body. "It is indeed."

Three guesses what he's thinking about and the first two don't count, girl. My pesky inner voice holds more snark than any words I say out loud.

From any other man, the insinuation would get a big eyeroll from me. But Salvatore's eyes on me sparks a very different reaction, one I don't attempt to hide from him.

There's no reason to. I'm going to enjoy the physical intimacy while it lasts and hope that the sensations he wakes in me do not go dormant when our relationship, such as it is, inevitably ends.

We talk about my business courses over lunch and what I hope to do with my degree when I get it.

"I've been saving up and I'm going to move away from New York."

"Why?"

The better question is why I have stayed at all. At first, I had a place to live, which made going to college more doable. Then after Mr. Ruhnke died and I got thrown out, I was already set up with financial aid at QC.

To establish residency for instate tuition somewhere else could take up to two years. With no guarantee the grants I receive would transfer, or that I would be able to get others.

And maybe a tiny part of me has always hoped my mom or sister would reach out, that I would be invited to move to Boston to be with them.

"I want a home with a yard," I say, answering the why of leaving. "A life that doesn't require working two jobs just to make ends meet without a roommate."

"You don't have to leave New York to get that, just move outside the city."

"It's not always that easy." Now that Lorenzo knows I'm still in the City, my need to move far, far away is growing by the minute.

I'm pretty sure I can't go back to Amuni and risk running into him again. My only excuse for sticking around after that first confrontation is desperation. I need the job, but I need to be safe more.

Weird how getting attacked and stabbed reworks your priorities.

Are you sure it's not having a gorgeous, rich capo moving you into his penthouse and promising to help you get settled when you move out?

"There you are!" A woman's voice cuts across my mocking inner voice. "I brought you this dead plant Pietro was carrying around like it's a freakin' Faberge Egg."

Dread bubbles upward until it's choking me at the words *dead plant*. Salvatore told me he would send Pietro for my African violet.

"He should have just thrown it into the trash." Nerissa plops a bedraggled African violet in a large margarin container on the table with zero care. "It's not an orchid. What do you even want with it?"

I grab Vee. Yes, I named my plant. Vee for violet. Not inspired, but it works. I talk to Vee too. When I'm alone.

Looking for some sign it can be saved, I brush the end of a stem where it's obvious a flower has been violently torn off. My roommates haven't killed her, but the violet is knocking on death's door for sure.

"What did they do to you?" I ask Vee, drawing my own conclusions from its condition.

The loss of its beautiful ceramic pot hits me like a blow in the center of my chest. Mr. Ruhnke gave me the pot made by a local artist when I graduated from high school. It means...meant...almost as much to me as the violet.

Someone must have broken it, and they rehomed my violet in this plastic container. How much damage to the roots did they do?

A quick look at the bottom has me groaning. No holes for water drainage also mean any watering done was from above. And the soil is moist. Too moist. The leaves that aren't curled and brown at the edges are too pale a green for a healthy violet.

"How could they do this much damage in a week?" I wonder out loud.

Salvatore looks from me to the plant with a frown. "Who?"

"My roommates. Who else? If I had to take a guess, they broke the pot, overwatered when they replanted it in the butter tub and put it in the windowsill to *help it recover*." Queens has fewer skyscrapers than Manhattan and being on the fourth floor means our apartment gets several hours a day of direct sunlight on our south facing wall, the only one with windows in it.

Usually, I keep my plant on a table far enough away from the window for sufficient indirect light. I give it two hours a day in the windowsill, but any more and the leaves lose their dark green color and the beautiful deep purple flowers fall off their stems.

Any less, and pretty much the same thing happens.

"They broke the pot?" Salvatore frowns. "On purpose?"

"No. Of course not, but when they have parties, it can get pretty wild." I always make sure to put Vee someplace safe before the party goers start showing up.

After the near disaster when I put it on top of the fridge for safekeeping, I started putting Vee on the top shelf of the closet during their parties.

Looking at the butter tub, my heart squeezes with grief. Mr. Ruhnke picked out the ceramic pot especially for me. It was glazed the same blue as my eyes with gold specks that he said reminded him of light that shines from inside me.

I don't feel very shiny right now. I feel like the connection I had to the last person to really care about me is both suffocating and drowning in that awful little plastic container.

Nerissa puts her hand out. "Give it to me. I'll throw it away. When you leave, you can get another plant. It's not as if that one is some rare genus of violet, or something."

I shrink back in my chair, hugging the near dead plant to my chest. "It's the only one of its kind because my friend, Mr. Ruhnke, gave it to me."

I have managed to keep it alive for six years. I'm not about to throw Vee in the trash now.

Also, why is a mafia soldier talking about the plant genus?

Maybe I'm being a little judgy here, but botany isn't something I would expect Nerissa to have studied. I'm only familiar with the term because of all the research I did on how to care for an African violet in a city apartment.

"Sentimentality." Nerissa sneers the word.

I've been living with her brother, the capo, for nearly a week. She does not intimidate me.

"Not all things have to be worth tons of money to have value," I sneer right back.

Nerissa's dark eyes flare with surprise before she masks it. She's not used to people standing up to her.

The look on Salvatore's handsome face can only be described as pride and he's directing it at me. "Who is Mr. Ruhnke?"

He's asked this before, and I never gave him a full answer. Sexual pleasure seems to have loosened my tongue though, because now I want to.

"My father died when I was sixteen. I didn't have anywhere to go." Not anywhere I was wanted.

An old ache echoes through my heart. I once asked Mr. Ruhnke if it would ever stop hurting. He said some wounds never heal completely, but they get easier to live with.

After today, I finally believe him. Because the slashes carved into my soul when I was sixteen are finally not the deciding factor in my life experience. It is amazing. And a little scary.

Maybe the way my parents abandoned me when I needed them most will get more bearable too. Right now, though, every time I think of that period of my life, anxiety and pain rip my heart to shreds all over again.

My solution? Don't think about it.

Yet, here I am, ready and willing to revisit it to explain the importance of the African violet to Salvatore.

"No family?" Nerissa's stance softens slightly, and her expression turns almost sympathetic as she sits down across from me at the table.

"No." None that wanted me. "I tried a shelter, but I couldn't sleep with everyone around me."

The reasons for that I am *not* willing to revisit mentally, much less go in to verbally.

"What did you do?" Salvatore asks, his own expression back to the stoic mask of capo.

I recognize it for what it is now. A protection, similar to the façade of uncaring I wear most of the time myself. I'm not sure why he needs that protection right now though. This story is my pain to bear.

Neither of them asks why I didn't go to social services. It's the mafia way. We don't trust outsiders and we especially don't trust government authority.

The realization I still think like I'm in the life hits me hard. Maybe I didn't leave my mafia roots as far behind as I thought I did.

CHAPTER 36

BIANCA

"I started sleeping between the dumpsters behind my high school."

"Bet you didn't sleep much," Nerissa says, like she knows.

I shake my head. "It was Manhattan, not the Bronx, but that didn't mean it was safe."

Sometimes, I marvel that I survived those first weeks without a home without suffering more physical trauma. Maybe my dad made a better guardian angel in death than he had a protector in life.

"So, you grew up in Manhattan?" Nerissa asks.

She's not as clever as she thinks she is. I recognize fishing when I hear it.

"I went to school in Manhattan."

"Where did you live?" Nerissa asks bluntly, clearly aware that I hadn't actually answered her question.

Changing my last name at eighteen makes this question a safe one to answer. "Before my dad died, we lived in East Rutherford."

Thirty minutes by train and forty-five minutes by car from Manhattan, it's in New Jersey, a territory that does not officially belong to any of the Five Families. Lower ranking soldiers can afford to live there without fear of stepping on another don's toes.

So can a lot of other people.

"How does Mr. Ruhnke come in?" Salvatore asks.

"He was the head janitor. He found me sleeping between the dumpsters one morning." I had finally gotten exhausted enough to sleep past the sunrise that usually had me packing up and getting out of there before the cleaning crew arrived.

"What did he do?" Salvatore asks when I stop talking, lost in my memories.

I shake myself, physically dislodging the tendrils of fear those memories still evoke. "He gave me a safe place to sleep and made sure I had what I needed to survive."

"He took you home to his wife?" Nerissa asks. "And she wasn't furious? I mean..." She gestures to me. "You're sex on a stick. You would have been a real temptation to a man even back then."

No doubt Nerissa considers her words a compliment, but they only bring back more devastating memories that have nothing to do with my savior. I don't let a flicker of that show.

Knowledge is power. And I don't want this hard woman having any power over me.

"Mr. Ruhnke wasn't like that." Not like the monsters that still invade my dreams. "Anyway, his wife was dead already and he didn't take me home with him."

More feral than a stray cat born in the streets, there was no way I would have gone to his house with him then. That came later, when I moved in with him so he didn't have to move in with his oldest son after Mr. Ruhnke broke his hip.

Officially? I was Mr. Ruhnke's ward and caregiver. Unofficially, I was the daughter he'd never had that he liked way more than his daughter-in-law.

Who I have yet to text back. Oh well. It's not like we're friends.

"He called social services on you?" Salvatore demands, his tone implying he finds my gratitude for that fact incomprehensible.

"The system isn't all bad. There are some amazing foster families out there." Candi's mom, who was actually her foster mom, is one of them.

"There are also nightmares," Nerissa says, like she has personal experience with that.

I nod. "True. But Mr. Ruhnke didn't put me in the system."

"What did he do?" Salvatore asks, like he's getting impatient for the answer.

I smile. "You're way too used to being catered to, you know that, right?"

"I am capo. The world moves at my direction."

Nerissa gasps. "Why would you trust her with that, Salvatore?"

"She already knew," Salvatore tells his sister. "Marco dated one of her roommates and had loose lips."

"Did you tell papà?" Nerissa's frown is downright scary.

I'm glad I'm not Marco.

Salvatore jerks his head in affirmative. "Yes."

There's a wealth of meaning in that one word. Marco is definitely in trouble with the consigliere. His punishment for being so candid about *la famiglia* isn't something I even want to contemplate.

I would feel bad for him and my part in getting him in trouble if he hadn't been such a jerk when he was dating my roommate.

"Marco likes to throw his weight around." In more ways than one.

The boyfriend that takes my spot on the sofa sleeper is a huge improvement over the violent mafioso.

"Enough about that *stronzo*. What did this Ruhnke guy do, if not put you in the system or offer you a home himself?"

"He did offer me a home." The only one I was able to accept at the time. "Mr. Ruhnke fixed up a supply closet in the basement of the school for me."

Then he put a new lock on the door in front of me and gave me the only keys to it so I could sleep at night without being afraid someone would come in.

"You lived in a janitor's closet?" Salvatore asks, his voice dark with disapproval.

"There are worse places," Nerissa says before I can.

I nod in agreement again. "Between the dumpsters on the cold ground was one of them. I had a bed. A desk. Heat. A place to shower. Food."

"What did the janitor expect in return?" Salvatore asks suspiciously.

"For me to bring my grades back up." My straight As has turned into Ds and Fs that year.

I'd stopped trying to keep my grades up when I realized my best attempt at being the perfect daughter wasn't going to convince my mother to make a place for me in her life.

"Was that all?" Salvatore's tone is skeptical.

Looking away from him, I push the remaining pieces of farfalle around on my plate. "His only other rule was for me to stay safe."

Mr. Ruhnke was adamant I couldn't sell drugs or my body to earn money. Which was never going to happen after my experience living with my dad.

Only I'm not sure what he would think of me becoming a pole dancer after he died. As long as I was safe, I think he would have approved. And I did stay safe, even when it meant finding another job.

I could not have foreseen the job at Amuni would put me back on Lorenzo's radar.

"He insisted on paying me an allowance, just like I was really his kid," I add.

Even after Mr. Ruhnke finally convinced me to contact my mom and she gave me a ten-thousand-dollar payoff to leave her and my sister alone.

Ten thousand dollars felt like a fortune to a sixteen-year-old. Five thousand dollars two years later wasn't nearly as impressive.

After Mr. Ruhnke sat me down and went over what it would cost to rent my own place, buy food and pay utilities, I realized that initial ten K wouldn't last more than a few months.

With roommates it could last longer, but at that time, roommates were not an option for me. For lots of reasons.

SALVATORE

For her to stay safe.

Why do those words hit so hard? And why do I have this inexplicable urge to find Mr. Ruhnke and thank him?

Standing from the table, I put my hand out.

Bianca hugs the bedraggled violet more tightly to her ample chest.

"Bring it with you."

Her beautiful blue eyes narrow in distrust. "Where?"

"To the conservatory."

"I knew it was too bougie to be a greenhouse."

Her words make me smile.

"That's the De Lucas," Nerissa says snarkily. "Full of pretentious airs."

"Since you are a De Luca, I guess that means you are too." Bianca sasses my sister as she skirts around the table to join me.

She shows no fear of my intimidating second-in-command. Her courage impresses me.

I like the way Bianca calls Nerissa a De Luca too. Even though my sister never changed her last name from James, Bianca doesn't question that my second is also my family. I told Bianca that Nerissa is my sister and she believed me.

Because my beautiful lover trusts me on a gut level whether she's willing to admit it, or not.

Pulling her by the hand, I lead her into the warm humidity of the conservatory. The light, temperature and moisture in the air are kept precise for the very rare, very expensive orchids residing in pots throughout the space.

Bianca pulls her hand from mine and I have to force myself not to grab it back. She walks to the nearest orchid and fern grouping. Her fingertips hover above the petals of my Koki'o Orchid, as if she knows how rare and fragile it is.

After the barest brush over one of the perfect green leaves, her hand drops.

"It's beautiful." Bianca's head turns first to the right and then to the left. "They're *all* beautiful and every pot is unique."

Her brow furrows as she slides her fingers across the uneven glaze on the orange and gold somewhat misshapen pot holding my Shenzhen Nongke Orchid. It is the most expensive specimen in my collection but isn't much more impressive than the pot it is in.

Only blooming once every four to five years, the rest of the time, it looks like any other orchid plant with light green foliage. The last time it bloomed, I sold each flower for more than I paid for the plant.

I am, after all, a businessman.

"That is my mother's first attempt at throwing and glazing ceramic," I inform Bianca.

"And you have it in here."

"Housing my most expensive specimen."

"That's sweet."

"I am not a sweet man." My mouth twists with distaste on the word *sweet*. I'm glad Nerissa didn't follow us into the conservatory to hear that.

"If you say so." Bianca's tone implies she doesn't agree.

I suppose it is alright if *bella mia* thinks I am sweet. "Don't call me that in front of others," I order.

"I can think it, but I can't say it?" she teases as no one is allowed to do to me.

"Yes."

"Fine." She points to my Shenzhen Nongke Orchid. "Is that what Nerissa meant by a rare genus?"

"It's one of them. Every orchid in here is difficult to obtain, but none as unique and scarce as that one." I bought many of them on the black market.

Not this one though. The first in my collection, I purchased that one directly from the Shenzhen Nongke Group for nearly a quarter of a million dollars. More than I would have paid if I had been willing to be put on the waiting list.

I was not.

I bought it to save a woman from being expelled from a university she did not actually attend. The woman, I killed, but the orchid I kept.

"And you put it in your mother's pot."

"At my father's request. He rescued the pot from the garbage after finding my mother in tears."

"Because it didn't turn out the way she expected?" Bianca asks.

"She considered it ugly, a complete failure and told my father she was never going to work with ceramics again."

"But her fingerprints are hidden in the clay, her DNA mixed with it under the glaze. He didn't want to let the pot be destroyed," Bianca says dreamily.

"I'm not sure my father thought of it that way, but he has never liked seeing my mother upset."

"So, he asked you to plant one of your orchids in her pot?"

"Yes. And ugly, or not, it works for what it was intended to. Putting that orchid in it was fitting." There are many ugly things in my world.

Torture. Death. Greed. Human weakness.

What I did that resulted in me being the final owner of the orchid, was one of ugliest of them all.

Necessary in my world. But ugly. I'm capable of heinous acts others could not stomach to see, much less perpetrate. It makes me a hell of a capo, but not a good man.

"After I planted the Shenzhen Nongke Orchid in it, papà arranged for mamma to visit my conservatory."

"Did it make her happy?"

I shrug. "She went back to learning to cast pots, paint and glaze them."

"So, it worked."

"Yes."

"That's really romantic."

"If you say so." My lips twist wryly. "No question, my father is soft for my mother."

Their marriage was arranged, like so many in our world, but they fell in love and my father has never taken a mistress. My mother treats him like a king and she is his queen.

There was a time I thought I would have that. Now I would rather slit my own throat than be that gone on a woman.

Bianca frowns. "You say that like it's a bad thing."

"Weaknesses can be exploited."

"Is love and devotion a weakness?" she asks like she really doesn't know the answer.

"It's fucking inconvenient. His need to make her feel better ended up with me having to repot every plant in my conservatory." Orchids and ferns alike.

"Because your mom kept giving you pots?"

I nod. "My dad said if I threw one away, he'd set fire to my conservatory to hide my cruelty from my mother."

Pretty blue eyes wide with surprise, Bianca throws her head back and laughs, her red hair rippling over her shoulders.

I wait for her to finish.

She's still smiling when she says, "It sounds like you're pretty soft for your orchids."

"I made more than a million dollars on the flowers from the last blooming cycle. The plants might not cost what a Faberge Egg would, but your Mr. Ruhnke could retire on what I would get for selling them."

She sobers. "Not soft, just practical."

"You'd make a mistake to believe anything else."

The look she gives me is unreadable as she reaches out to touch my Shenzhen Nongke Orchid's pot. "There can be beauty in ugliness."

"You think?"

"Don't you?"

"I don't think about things like that." Especially not whether this woman could find any in my scorched soul.

Bianca walks from one orchid pot to the next. "Mr. Ruhnke never got a chance to retire, but I think even if he had, he would have been more impressed by the ceramic pots made with love than the rare plants living in them."

Mr. Ruhnke is dead? Fuck. No wonder the plant means so much to her.

Opening a cabinet under the bench I use to prune and replant when necessary, I pull out two pots. "These are mamma and Rosa's latest gifts to my conservatory. Which do you want for your violet?"

Bianca stops running her hand over the smooth sides of a pot glazed in tans and creams.

Her eyes take in the two I am holding with longing. "You are giving one of those to me? But your family made them."

"It would make either woman happy to provide a new home for your plant."

She looks down at the bedraggled African violet.

"I don't think Vee is going to survive my roommates not so tender care." Bianca's voice is light, like it's a joke, but her eyes darken with grief.

The violet can be saved, but it will take effort.

"You named it?"

She shrugs. "It's the only living thing reliant on me."

And that means she gives a plant a name? As expensive as my orchids are, I have never considered naming any of them. If I did, I would call the Shenzhen Nongke Orchid, *Betrayal*.

"Which pot?" I lift both for her inspection, putting us back on track.

"But..."

"Choose, or I will choose for you Bianca."

"You're so bossy."

"We've discussed this. It's in my job description."

"You are not my capo though."

I am your everything. The words are on the tip of my tongue, but I don't let them past my lips. I am her *temporary* lover, nothing more.

My brain rebels against that reality and I frown. "You work for me. You live in my territory. *I am your capo.*"

"Uh, I'm pretty sure that's not how it works. Besides, I don't live in Manhattan. I live in Queens."

"Not anymore."

"That's right. You had your soldiers move me out of my place without my say. And just where am I supposed to go when this thing that isn't a thing between us ends?"

"I told you, I'll make sure you have someplace to live where you don't have to sleep on a closet floor."

She looks down at the violet held closely to her chest. "I would prefer not to return to an apartment filled with plant assassins, but I doubt I can afford anything you would find acceptable."

"Leave that to me."

"You want me to trust you?" Disbelief replaces the grief on her face.

"Why so shocked?" Doesn't she realize how many people rely on me? Trust me? How much *she* already trusts me? "My word is good."

"I'm sure when you make promises to your mafia brethren, you keep them."

"I keep every promise I make."

"If you say so."

I'm starting to dislike that phrase, but especially the way she says it. "I shouldn't have to."

"Only in your world is that true. The rest of us have to earn trust and only give it when it's proven we can."

She cannot be that naïve. "That is not true. Too many people trust without proof of worthiness."

"I'm not one of them."

Neither am I. It doesn't matter though. "You will trust me."

"The pot with the lemons and blue swirls," she says, avoiding a reply to my statement. "It reminds me of my nonna's dishes."

I set Rosa's pot on the bench and return mamma's to the cabinet. "I'm not surprised. It's a popular pattern in Southern Italy and Sicily. Rosa made this as practice before making pieces to replace those lost over the years in the dish set passed down through her family."

"It must be amazing to be able to do something like that." Bianca sounds wistful.

"If you would like to try it yourself, I am sure my mother or Rosa will teach you." Probably both, considering how much the women like my temporary roommate. "Give me your violet."

Bianca approaches me reluctantly. "You really think Vee can be saved?"

"Yes. Haven't you ever had to nurse a plant back to health?" I have had orchids show up worse for wear, despite paying more money for them than some people spend on a car.

"This is the only plant I have ever owned."

"I, on the other hand, have all the experience necessary." I waive my hand around to indicate the healthy orchids and their shade ferns. "Trust me with your plant, Bianca."

She hands me the little butter tub. Our fingertips brush as I take it from her. Electric current travels up my arm from the contact.

This woman and what she does to me.

I put the plant down on the bench beside Rosa's pot and turn back to Bianca. She's looking up at me like I'm something amazing, her blue eyes glowing with approval.

I pull her against me and claim the mouth I find irresistible, kissing her until we are both panting and I'm wishing I'd turned the windows opaque when we came in. I've come with her twice already and my body is still clamoring for more.

When we fuck, it is going to measure on the Richter scale.

That is just sex though.

This? I picture the bedraggled plant on the bench behind me. This is something else.

Why in the hell am I insisting on nursing her unimpressive, garden variety African violet back to health?

Nerissa is right. We could replace it with another just like it easily.

But it wouldn't be the plant a dead man gave her.

Manaja. "Go finish your lunch while I re-pot Vee."

She's got me calling the plant by a name now.

"Uh...okay. I'll just go spend time trading barbs with your sister. Sounds like fun."

"You'll survive." My voice is brusque as I shove down the need to warn my underboss to be nice to my lover.

Merda.

I am not soft for this woman.

That is a weakness I will never indulge in again.

CHAPTER 37

BIANCA

Nerissa has her own plate of nearly finished food in front of her when I come out of the conservatory. Putting her phone away, she watches me with cold eyes as I walk toward the table.

Finishing what is left of my lunch loses its appeal at the look on Nerissa's face. Instead of sitting down, I decide to explore the rest of the rooftop garden.

I'm trailing my fingers in the water of a small fountain when I hear the sound of steps on the white gravel behind me.

I turn with a smile, expecting to see Salvatore.

It's his sister. *Che palle.*

My smile slips from my face. "Hello, Nerissa."

"Miz James."

"Really?" I ask, rolling my eyes and shaking my head at the same time.

Her perfectly shaped brows draw together in a frown, her dark brown eyes as cold as Central Park in the dead of winter. "My brother may be mesmerized by your pussy, but I am not."

"Uh. Good?" I don't want this barracuda anywhere near my ladybits.

"I'm not letting any *puttana egoista* take advantage of my brother."

Selfish bitch? "I'm really getting the feeling you don't like me."

Nerissa's...excuse me, Miz James. No. Fuck that. She's going to call me a bitch?

Nerissa's eyes narrow. "You think you've hit the jackpot with my brother, worming your way into his home and playing on his sympathy."

I match the other woman's judgmental gaze with a dismissive glare. "First, I didn't worm my way anywhere. Pietro kidnapped me on your brother's orders and Salvatore refused to let me go home."

"Because he felt sorry for you," she inserts.

"Anyone else, and I'd say sure, but you know your brother better than me. Do you think the capo does anything he doesn't want to do? That he could be influenced by pity? Because I gotta tell you, I have my doubts."

"He wants to fuck you."

"Yeah, I got the memo."

"Playing hard to get isn't going to get you an engagement ring.

"Wow, that went from blinding him with my magical vagina to trapping him into marriage by withholding it. Pick a lane, why don't you?"

"When my brother marries, it will be to a mafia princess who can carry De Luca heirs and make the Genovese family stronger." Nerissa looks at me with something close to sympathy.

Wow. Okay, maybe not a raging bitch then.

Not an ex-pole dancer. I get it. "Listen, Miz James, I get the protective sister thing." I've played that role and with a lot more reason to. "But I'm not looking for any man to be my *jackpot*. I can take care of myself."

"My brother—" she starts to say.

I roll my eyes. Hard. And interrupt her, "Read the room, Miz James. Salvatore is a rich and powerful capo. I am a cocktail waitress. My vagina isn't capable of casting the spell you think it is."

And also, how many times is Miss Possessive Pants going to call Salvatore *my brother*? It's starting to feel a little pathological.

"My brother..." There she goes again. "Is not going to get taken in by a hot body and pretty face. I won't let him."

And she thinks he needs her protection? Does she know her brother?

"Your compliments leave a lot to be desired."

"It's not a compliment. You're used to trading on your sex appeal, but unlike Daryl Ruhnke's family, I won't let you take advantage of Salvatore."

Okay, definitely a raging bitch with a side of stooping low enough to scrape the ground.

"Shut your nasty mouth about Mr. Ruhnke. I never took advantage of him." I never did anything to get Mr. Ruhnke to help me, especially not what Nerissa is implying.

I'll never know why I was the one kid he chose to help. I sure wasn't the only teenager at that high school who was struggling, but Mr. Ruhnke picked me, and I'll always be grateful.

That doesn't make me a leach. It makes me lucky.

Then it hits me. "I didn't tell you Mr. Ruhnke's first name."

I never used it. At first it was a sign of respect and a way to keep emotional distance. Later, it meant something else. He told me when I said Mr. Ruhnke it sounded the same as when his sons called him *dad*.

I never called him anything else after that.

"How do you know his name was Daryl?"

"The same way I know his family are still furious about how you took advantage of an old man."

She looked him up? How? We were only in the conservatory for a little while. "Seriously, how did you find all that out so fast?"

The look she gives me. "You were in there with Salvatore for thirty minutes."

I was? It sure didn't feel that long to me. That kiss though. It could have lasted hours and I wouldn't have noticed.

"The name of your high school is on your employment file," Nerissa says dismissively. "Finding the janitor named Ruhnke that worked for them wasn't hard. A quick search on social media did it. One of the posts that tagged him was by his son after Ruhnke's death."

Then she found the son's phone number, or more likely work number considering what time it is, and called him. If she wasn't such a nasty minded troll, I would have a lady boner for her efficiency and tech savvy.

"If you try to play my brother, you'll get burned," Nerissa warns me darkly. "Just ask the last woman who tried to milk him for money. Oh, wait..."

My lips zipped, I refuse to take the bait.

The second gives an exaggerated look of having just remembered something. "You can't." She pauses dramatically. "Because she's dead."

Okay. There's a lot to process here.

First, Nerissa is a bona fide drama queen.

Second, a woman tried to make Salvatore De Luca her mark? Was she living under a rock? Anyone in New York knows you don't mess with the De Lucas, even if you don't know they're Cosa Nostra.

Third, that woman is dead.

And Nerissa is just itching to tell me about it. So, of course, I don't give into the curiosity burning like a hot coal in my chest.

"Who do you think killed her?" Nerissa demands when I remain silent.

"I don't know." But my brain is spinning with the possibility of what she's implying. "Your bitchy tongue, maybe?"

"You little..." Nerissa takes a threatening step toward me.

I instinctively fall back into a defensive stance, ready for her attack.

"What the fuck is going on?" Salvatore barks as he powerwalks over the gravel path toward us like an avenging demon.

"Your sister was just about to tell me about the woman you killed. I mean, I guess I'm making an assumption it's just the one." Two assumptions really because I'm also assuming Nerissa is implying Salvatore killed the dead woman.

I mean his second as good as said it, but it's still an assumption.

The look Salvatore gives his sister is lethal.

I expect her to drop from a heart attack any second.

Showing she's got more fortitude than I give her credit for, Nerissa glowers right back at her brother. "You already told her about you being a capo and she witnessed how you handled the men who attacked someone in our territory."

Not attacked *me*. But *someone in their territory*. A distinction I'm sure is important to the second.

"So, you decided it was okay to trust an outsider with my secrets?" Salvatore asks with glacial disgust.

Nerissa's face changes, and she looks sick at the realization of what she'd been about to do to make a point.

I'm not doing so great myself. The reminder that Salvatore considers me an outsider hurts in a way that it shouldn't.

Not if this thing between us is just sex.

Then Nerissa's whole demeanor changes and she smiles at me.

The smile of a hyena just before going in for the kill. "Do you know why my brother keeps rare orchids?"

Clearly, it's not for the money he earns on the blooms. A million dollars might be life changing for someone like me, but for him? It's basically pocket change.

"You ask a lot of questions you can't wait to give the answers to." I make a gimme motion. "Go ahead. Tell me."

Salvatore looks like he's going to say something to stop her, but he doesn't.

He wants me to know too.

"Every day he tends to them is a reminder that we cannot trust outsiders. That *he* should never trust a woman just because he's fucking her."

I don't know how the orchids connect to the dead woman who tried to pull something over on Salvatore, but somehow, they are his constant reminder not to trust another woman like her.

Another outsider. Another woman like me.

My gaze shifts to him, as my heart seeks assurances my brain insists I don't need for *just sex*.

But the avenging demon is gone. In its place is a man so aloof, there might as well be ten-feet-high steel wall between him and any possible emotion he could ever feel for me.

My heart proves my brain wrong. Because that hurts. A lot.

SALVATORE

I harden my heart to the flash of pain in Bianca's blue eyes. She needs to remember this thing between us is physical and transitory.

We both do.

My preoccupation with her has to end. Forcing myself to look away from my beautiful redhead, I let my sister see the fury and disappointment fighting for supremacy inside me.

She winces and her mouth opens. Probably to apologize to me. I do not fucking care.

I put my hand up. "Shut it."

Today is not the day for my second to go rogue. It looks like Nerissa did not get that memo though.

There is one sorry she needs to say that I want to hear. "Apologize to Bianca."

"For what? Telling her the truth?" my sister asks incredulously.

"I heard your whole conversation." Or at least most of it.

I started listening in the second I realized that my sister was no longer at the table. I have listening spyware installed on all my crew's phones and devices, but she and Pietro are the only ones who know.

Choosing to confront Bianca when she knew I could listen had to be deliberate on Nerissa's part. Did she think I would be swayed by the garbage she spewed?

"I didn't say anything wrong."

"I disagree. Ignoring for a moment what I stopped you from telling her, you disrespected a guest in my home. You made unfounded accusations against Bianca and you *will* apologize to her for them."

"They weren't unfounded."

"Did it sound like I was making a suggestion?"

Nerissa's lips twist like she's sucking on sour candy. "I am sorry if I disrespected you, Bianca."

Before Bianca can reply, I shake my head.

"Do better," I bark.

This is no longer only about Nerissa's words to my lover, it is about Nerissa's respect for me as her capo.

Showing more smarts than she has so far today, Nerissa's head snaps to the side so she's looking at Bianca. "I am sorry for accusing you of being a leach."

"I wouldn't mind if you included calling me a selfish bitch in that," Bianca goads.

My lips twitch but I don't let myself smile.

"I should not have called you that," Nerissa forces out from between clenched teeth.

She does not like apologizing. We have that in common.

Bianca nods. She's not offering forgiveness for an apology given under duress, but she's not turning her back on it either. Admiration for her dampens some of my rage toward my sister.

"Go to my office and wait for me," I say to Nerissa.

It's time to remind her that being family does not make her immune from the expectations of mafia hierarchy or discipline.

Without another word, my second turns smartly and heads toward the stairs down to the terrace.

"Don't be too hard on her. It's her job as your sister to watch out for you, even when you don't want her to."

Bianca's words hit me on the raw. How the hell is she standing up for Nerissa after my sister did her best to warn Bianca off?

The idea that Nerissa could have succeeded fills me with rage. Bianca isn't from this life. Learning I killed my ex would terrify her. Not that Nerissa left much doubt about what happened.

Bianca is too smart to miss the implication of my second in comand's disloyal words. Why isn't she bothered? She's angrier about the implication that she took advantage of Ruhnke than worried I killed my ex.

She's not afraid of how I handled Monica's betrayal because Bianca has no intention of betraying me, *or* sticking around.

Inexplicably, that knowledge fills me with more fury than my second's insubordination.

Bianca doesn't care if Nerissa doesn't like her. She sure as fuck doesn't make any effort to get along with Pietro. She's made it clear she doesn't want to be here and only stayed because she finally accepted that she couldn't care for the wound on her back by herself.

Despite me promising to help her get settled, she'll probably start looking for a new place to live as soon as the surgeon gives her a clean bill of health.

My hands fist at my sides, every muscle in my body rigid with tension. If she tries to leave me, Bianca will find out the difference between being a prisoner in my home and a guest.

How does that make you any different than the human traffickers you despise? The voice in my head sounds uncomfortably like my mother's.

But I know I'm different. I'm not keeping Bianca as a sex slave. I will never force myself on her, but she isn't leaving until she's fully healed and has a decent living situation to go to.

Until I'm *ready* for her to go.

And if that never happens?

Slamming the door on that question, I barely control my rage at my sister for creating this situation and Bianca for not caring about it.

"How the hell would you know?" I demand of Bianca harshly. "You don't have any family and how I deal with mine is none of your business."

Bianca blinks, that stoic façade cracking to show hurt at my words before her face is once again wearing the emotionless mask I'm coming to hate. "My family circumstances don't matter."

"They do if you think you know more about a sibling relationship than I do." I have a sister.

Bianca has no one. She said so herself.

"Transitioning to capo at your age can't be easy," she says, ignoring my jibe. "Navigating relationships that are both family and professional makes it even more complicated."

Why is she trying to reason with me?

She wants to leave. My success as capo doesn't matter to her. Neither do I.

"How I treat my soldiers has even less to do with you," I grit out, ignoring the truth of her words.

"You're right, it's none of my business, but that doesn't make my observations any less valid. Maybe you should talk to Severu. It seems like he's faced a lot of the same challenges."

She's still trying to be reasonable. Nice. While my temper is overheating like a nuclear reactor with a broken cooling system.

I am not running to my cousin like a whiney child. "You know too fucking much about the Genovese Family. I'm going to tell my father to cut Marco's tongue out."

Or I'll do it for him. I smile at the prospect.

"*Che palle.*" Bianca shakes her head. "I've never seen a smile that scary."

She looks impressed, not scared. Fuck. This woman!

"Come on. I've got more important things to do." At least that's what I'm telling myself.

Why does it feel like nothing is as important as this woman?

That is fucking madness and I am not going there. *La famiglia* comes first, last and always. It is the mafia way.

"I'll stay up here for a while." The way she says it, like it's her decision to make slices through the last tether on my temper.

Striding forward, I reach for her. She tries to evade me, but she's not fast enough and I swing her up into my arms.

"My orders are not suggestions." No matter what the women in my family seem to think.

Shock of all shocks, Bianca does not squirm, or try to get down.

She pats my fucking chest. "Okay, caveman. But you're going to spoil me into thinking I don't have to walk anywhere with this kind of service."

She's laughing at me. It's in her tone. Her eyes have lost that dead look and sparkle with mirth. At my expense.

I like it so much better than the fucking mask, I don't tell her off for it.

CHAPTER 38

SALVATORE

I don't hesitate to tear a strip off my second after leaving Bianca in her room with an order to rest though.

"The fuck are you thinking? Talking to me like that?" I pound my fist on the desk.

My second is fucking lucky she is my sister because I will not deal with her the way I did Pietro. But I have no doubt when she finds out what her punishment is, she'll wish she'd gotten off with a couple of punches.

"I meant no disrespect, Salvatore. I apologized. I shouldn't have said things the way I did."

"You shouldn't have said those things at all."

She looks ready to say something else and I slice my hand in the air. "No, you do not fucking speak again. Your earlier disrespect is the least of my worries."

I wait to see if she's going to try to interrupt again, but this time Nerissa's lips remain sealed in a flat line.

Good. "You were about to tell an outsider something you shouldn't even tell one of our own without my permission. That's the closest anyone on my crew has *ever* come to betrayal."

Nerissa winces, guilt and affront both glinting in her dark eyes. "I would never betray you," she says forcefully.

"What would you call it?"

Her shoulders slump, the anger draining out of her. "A mistake. I shouldn't have brought Monica up to her, but Salvatore, I don't want to see you hurt."

"You think she can hurt me?" My disbelief makes my tone even sharper.

"Anyone can be hurt when they fall for somebody. Even you. If Dad's people hadn't investigated Monica at Uncle Enzo's request, who knows how much money she would have taken you for before she disappeared with her partner."

Reminding me of my idiocy in the past isn't improving my mood. "I'm thirty-one, not twenty anymore. And Bianca isn't asking me for money."

"Not yet, she isn't." Nerissa holds up her phone, like it's proof of something. "I checked into Bianca's past. Did she tell you that Daryl Ruhnke is dead?"

"Yes."

I want to shut my sister down, but I am capo. I cannot allow emotions to rule me. So, I wait for her to continue. I will hear everything she discovered.

"I called his son at work. He told me how Bianca took advantage of his elderly father. Ruhnke paid her an allowance. It's not hard to guess what she did to earn that money."

"Ho detto basta." I bark. That is enough. "Bianca told us about that."

She'd said it made her feel like one of his children, something she'd clearly treasured.

"Why did she tell us? Was it to soften you to the idea of taking care of her financially?"

"You are so far off base, you're not even on the playing field. Bianca categorically turned down my offer of five thousand dollars for a single night of fucking." No way would she have doled out sexual favors for a measly few bucks every week. "She did not have a sexual relationship with a geriatric for money."

"Salvatore...listen to me," Nerissa insists. "Bianca convinced that geriatric to leave her fifty-thousand dollars in his will. She refused to sign it over to the family even though she has no real right to it."

"Cazzate!" What kind of bullshit is this? "If he left the money to her, it's hers."

Fifty thousand is nothing. To me. Fuck.

What portion of a school janitor's estate would fifty-thousand dollars be?

But if she has a fifty-thousand-dollar nest egg, why was she so worried about losing her job over taking money for sex? Was turning me down part of a long game to soak me for cash?

My gut rejects that idea. It doesn't fit who she is.

Or who you believe her to be.

"Did Ruhnke's son say anything else?" I force myself to ask.

I am not weak. I don't hide from the tough shit.

"He wanted me to convince her to meet with him and his brother and sister-in-law."

"What did you tell him?"

"To fuck off. I'm your second-in-command, not his damn messenger."

That sounds like my sister. Short tempered and unwilling to give an outsider the time of day.

"You didn't think it was strange that he was willing to tell a complete stranger about his family business?"

"Outsiders tell grocery story clerks their life story."

"He obviously had an agenda. He wanted you to convince her to meet with the family."

"That doesn't mean he was lying about the will."

"It doesn't mean he was telling the truth either." I shake my head.

My sister is usually much more cautious about believing unconfirmed intel.

"Give me some credit, capo. I planned to order a copy of the probated will."

"I am only going to tell you this one more time: I am your capo. I am not a twenty-year-old with dreams of true love and a house full of blonde babies. I have not been that man since the night I killed Monica."

"I know, Salvatore, but—"

"Zitto." Shut up. "Investigating Bianca's past was smart."

Nerissa's lips don't tilt into a full smile, but her expression turns pleased, and she relaxes.

I tap on the desk once. "Telling me about your intention to do so would have been smarter."

I tap again, this time more forcefully. "Almost telling her about Monica was not smart at all."

I tap a third time. "Assuming the intel you gathered was the only side of the story and confronting Bianca about it was short sighted, something my second cannot be."

Giving my second the benefit of the doubt, I ask, "Did you ask Bianca about the inheritance or for further information on the allowance?"

Maybe I missed enough at the beginning to misinterpret the conversation I overheard.

Nerissa swallows audibly and shakes her head.

"You thought scaring her with a story from my past about how I handle thieves was a better approach." It's not a question.

"She pissed me off."

I can imagine. Bianca has snark down to a science and my sister is used to being deferred to. Even before I made her second-in-command, she was a top soldier on my father's crew, not to mention his daughter.

"And that excuses you revealing mafia secrets?"

Nerissa's jaw sets stubbornly. "I was trying to watch out for you."

She still thinks she is in the right. When she is so fucking clearly not. Why?

"Did papà tell you to run a background check?" I know the order didn't come from Severu.

My cousin would have had his own people do it. The same team I'm working with right now to figure out who is trying to outbid me for the bar properties. And he would not hide doing it either.

He would tell me.

Nerissa's expression says it all.

"You are no longer on the consigliere's crew. You are on mine," I inform my second.

As if she could forget. Except, she did exactly that. Launching an investigation into Bianca without consulting me first.

"I know that, Salvatore. You have my loyalty. That's why I did what I did."

"No, you did it because you think I am weak. And stupid."

"No." Nerissa's tone is adamant, her expression horrified. "He's our father, Salvatore. Of course, I did what he asked."

"We are the damn mafia, Nerissa, not a fucking family company. I am your capo and my word is law. He is counselor to our don, that does not make his orders supersede mine."

"I know that."

"Then you know what has to happen. If I let you get away with this shit, I *am* weak." And we both know I am not.

Contrary to what her actions imply.

She clasps her hands behind her back. "Do what you have to do."

"For the next two months, your pay will be split between the top tier soldiers as a bonus for their loyalty."

Nerissa sucks in a shocked breath.

The punishment is a blow to her pride. She can easily live without that income, but for the next sixty days, she will be reminded of her disloyalty to me.

So will the rest of our soldiers.

Nerissa will lose respect from our crew and will have to work to regain it. She will have to fight to keep her position as my second-in-command.

Like I fight with every action, every decision, and every reaction to maintain the fear and respect my crew and the rest of the Cosa Nostra have for me.

She fucked up and now she will have to fix it. With them. With me.

That knowledge is dawning in her eyes.

"And Nerissa? If you ever call Bianca a bitch again, I will take it as a personal slight against me."

"She's not your wife, or even your girlfriend!" Nerissa argues.

"She is my girlfriend. She is living in my home. She is mine."

My sister's eyes go wide and then she scowls. "Have you told mamma and papà?"

"They are both aware she's living here." No way would my mother have kept that information from my father.

"Salvatore."

"Basta!" I raise my hand. "Do you understand?"

"Yes," my sister grits out.

We both know what happens to soldiers shortsighted enough to blatantly disrespect their capo like that. And it's not something my sister wants to experience.

"And Nerissa," I say before dismissing her. "I will have her background investigated, but not by you. If I find out you disobeyed me on this, being demoted and returned to our father's crew will be the least of your worries."

BIANCA

The temptation to eavesdrop on the conversation between Salvatore and his sister is strong, but I resist.

Mostly because I need to process. Not nap. Process.

I don't like the pain I felt when Salvatore referred to me as an outsider. Later, when I could tell he was trying to, if not hurt me, at least shut me down, I felt more compassion for him than anger on my own behalf.

Whether or not he wants to admit it, the war he's fighting inside himself over how to respond to his family as brother vs. capo is plain. Yes, he got short with me, but how obvious was it that he was compensating for his frustration over Nerissa's behavior?

I can hardly blame him for dismissing my advice on handling a sibling when he doesn't know I have one.

The way he rubbed my nose in my lack of family sucks though. Almost as bad as his sister's implication that I somehow took advantage of Mr.

Ruhnke. Nerissa's words were cruelly similar to what Mr. Ruhnke's adult children said when I moved in with him.

It wasn't about me. No matter how they want to paint it.

He'd fallen and broken his hip at work. He needed help while he recovered. His daughter-in-law wanted him to move in with her and his son and their kids while he recovered. Mr. Ruhnke loved his grandchildren, but he didn't want to live with them.

His younger son offered to move into the family home in Queens to watch over it. Only, Mr. Ruhnke confided he was worried that while he was convalescing, his kids would pack the house up and put it on the market.

His children had been pressuring him for years to sell the house, divide the proceeds between them and move in with his oldest son's family. They insisted Mr. Ruhnke didn't need all that space and with the proceeds from the sale, his oldest son could afford to buy a larger house to accommodate them all in a nicer neighborhood.

It was win-win. Except Mr. Runke hadn't wanted to move from the home he'd shared with his beloved wife and raised his children.

So, with a mix of fear and determination, I pushed myself to get over my aversion to sharing my space with another person. I was determined to stop his sons from forcing Mr. Ruhnke to leave his home of forty-two years.

It worked and he got to stay in his home until his death.

If his daughter-in-law thinks I'm answering her text after her husband trash-talked me to Nerissa, she's delulu.

It's bad enough they kicked me out of his house the day after he died, but they didn't let me attend the funeral either. I owe his family nothing.

For the sake of his memory, I've been polite to them and respected their wishes about the funeral, but I'm done being nice.

Whatever they want they can suck it.

Maybe it shouldn't matter to me if Salvatore thinks I'm a greedy scammer, but it does. Whatever lies they told Nerissa about me, she's going to repeat to Salvatore.

Che palle. I should have listened in on their talk in the office. Then I could be ready to defend myself.

Because I want him, even if he is an ass sometimes and over-the-top protective pretty much all the time. His touch does not spark panic, but desire.

Until I met him, I assumed having a partner, much less a family was totally out of reach. My mom and sister may never be my family again, but if I can have sex with a partner, I can build my own family.

Yes, I can go the single parent route. I've thought about it and in every realistic scenario, I'm in my forties by the time I build up enough savings to be financially secure enough to adopt. That's not too young to become a parent, but it means living alone, without a family, for at least two more decades.

But if I can let a man into my personal space, I can hope for something other than being alone. I could be a part of a family again, even if it's just the two of us.

Continuing sexual exploration with Salvatore is the key I never thought I'd find for the lock on the door holding all those possibilities on the other side.

Keep telling yourself it's all about the future and not about having Salvatore in the now.

Can you muzzle your own inner voice?

Okay, so I want Salvatore. So, I have feelings for him that make no sense. It's too soon. He's too arrogant. He's tactless, bossy, grumpy and part of the mafia I got kicked out of like garbage.

And so damn sexy, my ovaries have learned a whole new set of dance moves for him.

I feel safe with him. He makes me feel like nothing and no one can hurt me when he's around.

Even Nerissa's words only pierced so deep because he was there and part of me knew he would show up any minute and shut her down. Which he did.

I can fight my own battles. I've been doing it a long time. I don't need some billionaire mafia prince to take care of me.

But having someone stick up for me? Since coming to stay in Salvatore's place, I've discovered that feels amazing. And when he does it, little chinks of the wall around my heart fall away.

That scene on the rooftop ripped out more than a chink of my protective armor though. It left a big chunk of my heart unprotected.

I'll just have to rebuild the wall. Because Salvatore wants my body for a limited amount of time.

And I can't let myself get emotionally invested to the point that walking away from him will leave me as uninterested in other men as my past trauma.

It starts by taking back some of my control.

First, I'm going back up on the roof and soaking in more spring sunshine. Second, Salvatore isn't carrying my sleeping body into his bedroom tonight.

Because I'm going to be there already.

If he wants me to sleep in his bed, he doesn't get to say when that happens. It's either when I want it to happen too, or not at all.

You'll give up sleeping deeply for a point of pride? I don't think so.

For once, my inner voice is talking garbage. Because, yeah, I so will give up sleeping with Salvatore if he thinks it's only going to happen on his say so.

He might be capo, but he's *not* dictating all the terms of our physical relationship.

It is *not* transactional.

It *is* temporary.

It is *not* limited to the times he wants to touch me.

It *is* going to happen when I want to touch him too.

And I *am* sleeping in his bed.

CHAPTER 39

SALVATORE

I'm exhausted and still angry when I return to my penthouse that night.

After my meeting with Nerissa, I went to Oscuro to meet with Severu, Miceli, Angelo and my dad about the Juniper situation. The don, his underboss, his head enforcer and his consigliere all had something to say about it.

My receptivity was not high.

Resentful of my dad's interference in my life through Nerissa, I put his advice under the harshest scrutiny. When he tried to corner me after the meeting and scold me for disciplining my second, I told him to fuck off.

The argument that followed drew blood on both sides. He brought up my past.

My reply still rings in my head and I hope it is ringing in his.

"If you don't think I am fucking fit for my job, then advise our don to replace me, consigliere. Otherwise stay the fuck out of my business. As long as I am capo you will show me the respect I am due. If you ever undermine the loyalty of one of my people again, I will kill them, no matter who they are, and then I will fucking shoot you."

I didn't threaten to kill my father. We both know even I'm not capable of that. I won't kill my sister either, but I wasn't willing to admit that to him. So, I let the threat stand as I spoke it.

The look on my father's face told me he believed my words. All of them. Because I am the man he raised me to be.

He was a good father. However, he was always capo first, father second. I am a good son and brother, but I am capo first, like he taught me.

I don't even stop at my room before heading to the guestroom. I want to see Bianca. Feel her skin against mine. Breathe in her scent.

If I don't, I'm going to kill someone.

Rosa told me that Bianca went back up to the roof and stayed there for two-and-a-half hours. She ate dinner with Rosa in the kitchen and then retreated upstairs. Rosa thought to rest, but my check on the guestroom smart television shows Bianca watching it until a little after ten o'clock.

Rosa left after dinner, leaving only security to watch over Bianca, so of course I checked in on her. That I could only do so by checking her phone's activity and the smart TV, irked me.

Pietro needs to up his game. He's the head of my security and clearly, he should have installed cameras in the interior of the penthouse by now.

Everywhere but my bedroom.

I'll tell him tomorrow.

My eyes adjust quickly to the dark in the room, the light from the hallway enough to illuminate the empty bed.

There is no light coming from the attached bathroom and I don't hear anyone peeing, or breathing for that matter. I check the small room anyway.

It is empty. The closet is empty. Where the fuck is she? Did she decide to sleep on the roof? There are chaise lounges she could use, but it's not fucking safe up there.

What if someone got past the motion detectors around the perimeter? What if a sniper got a bead on her and thinking she's important to me, took her out?

My thoughts are spiraling as I sprint back down the stairs and through the door to the terrace.

"Is she up there?" I demand of the guard on duty out here.

"Who? Oh, you mean Miss Gemelli? She's upstairs, boss."

"She is not fucking upstairs. Her room is empty."

"Did you check the other rooms?" my soldier asks.

My racing heart thumps louder in my chest. I locked my office, didn't I? She wouldn't go snooping anyway. Why would she?

But memory of leaving my office includes watching my sister walk away with stiff shoulders. It does not include shutting and locking the office door.

Fuck.

I run back up the stairs and to my office, but Bianca isn't in there.

Is something wrong with her bed? Did she change to a different guestroom for a reason?

I check the other guestrooms on this floor. They are all empty. If my security let her leave the apartment, I am beating the shit out of every single one of them.

I'm heading back down the hall toward the stairs when a sleepy voice from my doorway halts me in my tracks. "What's going on Salvatore?"

Spinning to face her, I stare, my mouth hanging open like a new recruit on the first day of training.

She's wearing my t-shirt instead of the nightgown I know Rosa left out on Bianca's bed.

"I didn't mean to wake you up." Those are not the words I should say.

I should be asking her what the hell she's doing sleeping in my room. But fuck if I don't want her there.

"You galloped up and down the hall like a herd of rampaging elephants and expected me to sleep through it?" She yawns, covering her mouth.

I want to tug her hand away so I can see her pretty pink tongue.

"I didn't gallop." I ran. My movements might have lacked my usual stealth.

"Whatever you say." She turns back into the room. "Are you coming to bed, or do you have some more late night exercise you need to do?"

I can think of some exercise that will keep us both awake, but then she yawns again.

"Did you skip your nap this afternoon?"

"I'm not a downy haired baby, Salvatore. I don't have scheduled afternoon naps."

"You are definitely all woman," I say with appreciation for how my t-shirt stops midthigh, revealing her sexy as hell thighs.

"Put a pin in that thought for tomorrow," she says with a cute wink and another yawn before climbing back into her side of the bed.

Her fucking side.

Of *my* bed.

You started this by carrying her in here every night. Don't pretend you weren't going to do the same damn thing tonight.

"Why didn't you tell me you were going to sleep in here?"

"You mean none of your minions told you?"

"Security is not allowed upstairs while you are here."

"Okay. Well, now you know."

"I thought you ran away," I admit.

"I am too tired to explain everything wrong with that statement. Come to bed."

"I'm not the only bossy one in this relationship."

She groans and waves her hand. "Noted. Goodnight."

This is the first time I've seen her voluntarily give into her need for sleep. The first time she's even admitted she is tired.

That's another layer of trust right there.

I'm smiling as I walk into the bathroom to take a shower.

BIANCA

The sun shining through the big windows wakes me and the smell of coffee brings my eyelids fluttering open.

The spot beside me on Salvatore's bed is empty.

"What time is it?" I ask Rosa as she puts my coffee down on the table where she usually puts the breakfast tray.

Did I sleep so late there's no time for breakfast?

"Nine o'clock."

"Wow, I slept in." Even with all the sleeping I've been doing since arriving here, I usually wake around seven.

Salvatore is never here, even that early, so his absence is no surprise. It's disappointing though. I was too tired last night for more sexual adventures, but if he were here, I'd be totally down for them now.

"The surgeon will be here in an hour to remove your stitches." Rosa smiles at me. "You've got time for a shower. Do you want to eat here or on the terrace?"

I get a choice? "Terrace, if that's not too much trouble."

"No trouble at all. It saves me a set of stairs."

I'm on my second cup of coffee and eating my breakfast when I hear the sliding door open.

Expecting Rosa, my warm smile turns to something else, something more, when I see Salvatore striding toward me. That explains the second coffee cup on the breakfast tray.

"Good morning, *bella mia*. How are you feeling today?" His gray gaze roams over me, like he's looking for any sign I am not 100% while he takes the chair closest to me at the round table.

The table here is smaller than the one up on the roof, meant for more intimate meals. Not that he kept his distance during lunch the day before.

"Great. I slept in until nine." Duh. He knows that.

Rosa would have told him.

"I know. The temptation to wake you as I did yesterday from your nap was strong."

Tingling between my legs from his words, I pour him a cup of coffee and doctor it the way he likes before placing it on the table in front of him.

"If you're going to wake me up like that, I'm happy to take another nap." Even if, for the first time since the attack, I am full of energy and not at all sleepy.

"If I'm here to wake you, count on it."

My body responds predictably to his promise. I'm going to have to change my panties soon. "It's a deal."

However, the reminder that he has a job and spends very little time at his penthouse during the day deflates me. What are the chances he'll be here when I wake up from a nap?

He takes a sip of his coffee and gives me a look of approval. "You remembered how I like it."

"That's what I'm trained to do." Remembering the preferences for a regular customer is a necessary server skill if you want to make good tips.

"You're saying you remember how Nerissa takes her coffee from that night in the club?"

I frown at the mention of his underboss. "She wants it extra hot."

Salvatore must see something on my face because he asks, "What did you do?"

"I put that second cup of coffee in the microwave for a minute before serving it." Fresh coffee isn't supposed to be microwaved, but I wasn't giving her another excuse to complain.

He shakes his head. "She could have burnt her tongue."

I shrug. "She wanted it hot. I gave it to her hot."

"You weren't worried about her leaving you a tip."

"Give me a break. Nerissa wasn't going to tip me regardless." If the drinks had been on her tab, I would have been stiffed.

But they were on Salvatore's and he tips generously.

"She thinks I'm too into you."

"Does she vet all your sex partners?" I can't help asking.

"You're the first one, but to give her credit, you are also the first woman I have brought to my penthouse. I don't do overnights."

Which means he does not move women in on a whim. "Why me?" I put my hand up. "Don't give me the spiel about me needing someone to take care of me."

Yes, he offered to send me to a rehab facility or pay for me to stay in the hospital, both of which were ridiculous options in my opinion. But he wants me *here* in his home and he's made no bones about it.

"The plastic surgeon will be here soon," he says completely ignoring my question.

Maybe he doesn't know the answer. Any more than I know why this man makes me feel safe and triggers my libido, when no one else does.

"I still can't believe you've got a surgeon doing house calls."

"There's no reason to take you into the hospital for something as minor as removing stitches."

Which is pretty much the opposite of how normal people interact with medical professionals. If Salvatore wasn't involved, my stitches would have been put in by a doctor I would never see again. If they weren't the dissolving kind, I would see a nurse to remove them.

I suppose plastic surgeons do things differently and those that serve clients as wealthy and powerful as men like Salvatore, making house calls isn't out of the norm.

But it still feels weird.

CHAPTER 40

BIANCA

The surgeon, who identifies himself as Dr. Anders-Powell, examines me in the guestroom next to Salvatore's private gym downstairs.

The reason for the change of location for my exam becomes apparent pretty fast.

The surgeon leans over me to take a look at my stitches and brushes my hair back from my forehead. Fervently wishing I'd put my hair away from my face in a ponytail or braid, it's all I can do not to jerk away from his nearness.

In only a few days, I've become too used to not fighting my own reactions. Spoiled to no one but Salvatore invading my personal space and having more alone time than I have since living in the storage closet in my high school's basement.

I'm not mentally prepared for the surgeon's nearness and him touching me.

Salvatore growls and the look he gives the surgeon is borderline violent. "If you need Bianca's hair moved out of the way, tell me and I'll do it."

"Or he could, I don't know, tell *me*," I point out drily.

"I will need her hair pulled back to complete the exam and remove these stitches," Dr. Anders-Powell says to Salvatore, paying no attention to my suggestion.

"If you can wait a minute, I'll run upstairs and grab a hair tie." And put my hair up into a ponytail while I'm at it. "It will make it easier to remove the other stitches too."

My hair is long enough that it will interfere with the examination of the wound on my back otherwise.

"Stay put." Salvatore pulls his phone out of the inner pocket of his suit jacket and taps something on the screen before putting it away again. "Rosa will bring you a hair tie."

No one says anything while we wait for the housekeeper. She arrives a minute later carrying a brush and some hair ties.

I put my hand out. "Thank you."

"I should have thought of this before the surgeon arrived." She moves around to stand behind me, both items still in her hands.

Knowing it's useless to insist, I let my hand drop. The capo isn't the only bossy person around here.

"That would have been preferable, yes," the surgeon agrees, clearly unhappy with the delay.

What a tool.

He's all polite fawning to Salvatore, but the rest of us don't rate courtesy.

"If you were aware it was necessary, you should have provided preparation instructions ahead of time." Salvatore's critical tone makes Dr. Anders-Powell flinch.

Because I'm annoyed by how the surgeon is treating Rosa, I don't point out that it's only necessary because the capo doesn't want the other man touching me more than absolutely necessary.

And that is when the penny drops.

Salvatore's soldiers aren't allowed upstairs while I am here. That is what my lover said. Now I get that he meant absolutely no men are allowed up there, not even a medical professional.

Over protective, much? Or is that possessive?

Both seem excessive for a temporary sex partner. The whole one-night-stand thing is already blown out of the water, but it's not like I'm living here. Well, okay I *am* living here, but only because of my healing wounds.

Right? If that hadn't happened, Salvatore would have been happy with a single night of screwing. At least that's what his offer of five-thousand-dollars implied.

And because of my hangups, it never would have happened, no matter how attracted to him I am.

Our forced cohabitation worked a miracle in my reactions to him that I'm still not sure I understand.

Rosa finishes pulling my long red hair into a smooth, high ponytail and pats my shoulder. "There you go."

I smile up at her. "Thank you."

"My pleasure *dolce ragazza*." She leaves without another word to the two men.

The surgeon steps forward, leans close, and presses his fingertip to first one side of the gash and then the other. "Good. No blood seepage. It's healing nicely."

I force myself not to wince from the sting. It's not that bad. Dr. Anders-Powell removes the first stitch. It pulls a little, but that's all.

Doing a good impression of a brooding romance hero, or a cranky capo, Salvatore leans against the wall nearest me. "Does that hurt?"

"Not really."

"And when he pressed around it?" Salvatore asks, his tone definitely on the cranky side.

"Nothing much." If not for the wound in my back, I wouldn't still be taking pain meds. "I barely know it's there most of the time."

"Then we did our job," the surgeon congratulates himself. "I am going to put Steri-Strips on to make sure it doesn't open again and undo my work."

"Can I shower with them on?" I do not want to go back to cleaning myself with a washcloth.

"Yes, but keep your wound out of the direct stream of water."

That's better than the first few days after coming here from the hospital. "Okay, thank you."

"How long will she need to wear them?" Salvatore asks.

"The Steri-Strips can take up to ten days to fall off. If they don't by the fourteen-day mark, contact my office and I will send a nurse out to remove them. If the scab has not fallen off the wound in her back, new Steri-Strips will need to be applied."

"When can I take a bath?" The beautiful jetted tub in Salvatore's bathroom taunts me every day with how much I want to luxuriate in it.

Just once.

I would settle for the tub in the guestroom bath too.

"Not until the final Steri-Strip comes off."

I sigh. Too bad. I'll probably have Steri-Strips on my back for three to four more weeks. I'll be long gone from here before I can indulge in a soak in one of Salvatore's big tubs.

I never assume the best-case scenario. Less disappointment that way.

"I need you to remove her top and bra for me to examine her back," Dr. Anders-Powell tells Salvatore.

Crossing my arms, I glare at the surgeon. "I'm perfectly capable of taking off my own clothes."

"No," Salvatore barks.

I roll my eyes at Mr. Cranky. "I've been dressing and undressing myself for years."

An animalistic sound comes from deep in Salvatore's chest. "You are not taking your top and bra off in front of him."

Che palle.

I should be pissed at Salvatore's over-the-top possessiveness, but that growl sends my vagina into spasms.

Having a very different reaction to Salvatore's threatening behavior, the surgeon jumps away from me.

"I will do it in the bathroom where I can grab a towel to cover my front," I tell Salvatore.

I'm no more excited about being nude from the waist up in front of the self-important doctor than Salvatore is about me doing it. I'm not about to flash Dr. Anders-Powell my boobs if I don't have to.

Yeah, I know. I am sure a therapist would have a field day with my career choice as a pole dancer considering how much I don't like being undressed in front of other people. Salvatore being the confusing exception.

Or maybe a therapist would tell you that dancing the pole was as much about taking back your power as making money.

Since when did that little voice in my brain get so smart? About the time I read my tenth book on recovering from trauma maybe.

For the first time it occurs to me that the two years I spent dancing on stage, not ignoring my sensuality but not being vulnerable to it either helped me to heal.

So, when I met Salvatore and my ovaries started their impression of a Mariachi band, there was space in that healed spot inside me to explore those feelings.

Regardless of my subconscious reasons for taking the job at Pitiful Princess, I'm pretty sure I don't want to go back to dancing at a strip club. Even if I could get the same terms of employment I had before that *stronzo* Gino took over the dancers.

The attack brought back memories I don't want to keep reliving. I'm afraid the leering customers will trigger them now too.

"Need I remind you both that I am a medical professional? I am not about to look lasciviously upon Miss Gemelli's bare breasts." The surgeon's voice is loaded with affront.

Salvatore shifts away from the wall, the air around him filled with predatory menace. "Do I need to remind *you* that what I want, I get? And I don't want you looking at any more bare skin on my lover's body than absolutely necessary."

His lover.

My ovaries swoon like a teenager at a K-Pop concert.

"Perhaps you should get a different sur—geon..." Dr. Anders-Powell's voice breaks and goes high as Salvatore takes a step toward him. "T—to consult on this case."

"Maybe you should do your fucking job before I decide your services are no longer required." The threat in Salvatore's tone is unmistakable.

If Salvatore decides to fire the surgeon, the results will be longer term than losing income from one patient.

Finding Salvatore's threatening attitude hot is wrong. I know it is, but that doesn't stop my vagina getting wetter and wetter. My clitoris is throbbing for his touch too.

How quickly has my body adjusted to sexual pleasure?

"If you want to help me take off my shirt and bra..." I let my voice trail off in husky invitation.

The surgeon gives me a judgy glare but I don't care what the self-important douche-canoe thinks of me. I'm pretty sure this whole situation makes me a freak. I still want Salvatore to follow me into the bathroom.

And I'm not ashamed of that.

His eyes devouring me, Salvatore orders the surgeon, "Go to the living room and ask Rosa for some coffee."

"I have other appointments today." The other man's bravado is back now that Salvatore's attention is fixed on me.

My capo does not look away from me when he says, "You leave when I say you leave."

The surgeon makes a sound of disbelief.

"Take it from me, Salvatore is not talking out of his ass." The penthouse is a fortress. No one comes in or goes out without the capo's approval.

What initially pissed me off is just cause for another level of arousal now.

I don't wait to see if the plastic surgeon obeys Salvatore. He's smart enough to have gotten a medical degree and savvy enough to have landed himself a job at one of the most exclusive hospitals in the country. He's got to have enough sense not to goad a deadly predator like Salvatore any further.

Big hands land heavily on my shoulders when I cross the threshold to the bathroom, moving with me as I step over the tile in another pair of fuzzy slipper socks.

Stopping when I'm in front of the sink vanity, I am mesmerized by the image in the mirror.

My own blue eyes stare luminously back at me as I take in the tall, gorgeous capo with dark hair and olive toned skin decorated with sexy as sin tattoos standing behind me. My own skin is only a shade lighter than his, our Italian heritage obvious, if only to me.

We look like a pair that belongs together.

I shift my gaze to meet his and gasp at the desire turning his gray irises molten.

Whatever this thing is between us, it affects us both. Strongly.

"You are too damn tempting." His hands slide down my arms, making pleasure spark in every nerve ending along the way.

"Your fault."

"No, *brava ragazza mia*. It is all you."

His good girl.

Ovaries swooning yet again, I shake my head. "Agree to disagree."

Salvatore slowly tugs the loose oversized shirt I'd intended to simply lift for the exam up my overheated body. First, he reveals a wide slice of skin above the waistband of my leggings, then the underside of my breasts covered in red lace.

Stopping his movement, he scowls. "You were going to let him see you in this?"

Then the shirt rises so my entire chest is exposed along with the sexy style of the La Perla demibra. It barely covers my engorged nipples, but the cups support my ample breasts surprisingly well.

"I didn't plan for my shirt to go any higher than an inch or two above the knife wound." I'm still not convinced it needs to.

"Next time he comes to examine you, you wear a sports bra," Salvatore growls.

My thighs clench with need but I give him a look in the mirror that lets him know just how ridiculous I find his suggestion. "Yeah, no."

His eyes narrow and I can't help poking the bear. I'm not afraid of being eaten by the apex predator. In fact, I'm looking forward to it.

"If I wore something like this when I was dancing, I would have gotten double my tips," I gasp out between panting breaths, my body on fire for his touch.

The sound he makes as he rips my top off over my head sends thrills through me. My panties definitely need changing now.

"You are never dancing for other men again."

I know he doesn't mean it like it sounds. He's not laying claim to me or my future. He can't, but we can enjoy each other while I'm here.

"Does that mean you want me to dance for you?" I ask in an honest to God purr.

I didn't even know my voice could do that.

His hands dive into my demibra and he grabs my fleshy mounds. For all his ferocity, he does not squeeze so tight they hurt, but kneads them and plucks at my nipples until I moan with needy lust.

Leaning down, he growls into my ear, "Yes, *brava ragazza mia*, I want you to dance for me."

Shivering from the sensation of his hot breath in my ear, I lift my arms and clasp them behind his head while I press my butt back against him.

I crave the pleasure he gives me. I want him inside me, and I'm so turned on, that doesn't even scare me a little.

He pulls one hand from my breast and slides it down my torso until he reaches the stretchy waistband of my leggings. Running his finger along the waistband, he teases me.

"Touch me, Salvatore. Touch me now," I demand.

"Be a good girl and ask me nicely."

I shudder. "Please, *il mio lui*, touch me." *My him. My man. My guy.*

"Say that again," he demands in a hoarse voice.

He likes me laying claim to him, maybe even as much as I like when he gets possessive over me.

"*Il mio lui,*" I repeat. "*Sei mio.*" You are mine.

Salvatore goes nuts, ripping my leggings and underwear down and off along with my socks. He lifts me up onto the vanity, so my butt is on the edge of the sink and my feet planted wide apart on the countertop.

CHAPTER 41

BIANCA

My knees frame my raspberry tipped breasts and my thighs are open wide, revealing my most intimate flesh.

My capo's eyes burn back at me from the mirror, his gaze fixed on my flushed slit wet with invitation. Around it, my swollen nether lips glisten with my juices, a tiny nub peeking from the top of my labia.

"Look at that beautiful pussy, so wet and ready for me and that engorged little clit, just begging to be touched." He moves one big hand down my thigh and over my mons while his other arm holds me tight so I do not fall.

His forefinger and middle finger split to slide down on either side of my clitoris. His big, masculine hand goes lower until both fingers dip into my slit before drawing my arousal back up, coating my labia and clitoris with his now slick fingers. He does it again and again, driving the sensations coiling inside me tighter and tighter.

Squeezing his fingers together, he pinches my pleasure button as he rubs up and down along my now slippery flesh. Ecstasy explodes outward from the bundle of nerves and I cant my hips upward.

I need more.

That final cataclysmic eruption I know is coming.

"Touch your tits, *brava ragazza mia.*"

Letting go of my hold on his neck I cup my breasts and moan at how good it feels. I brush my thumbs back and forth over my sensitive nipples, sending frissons of ecstasy directly to my core.

My climax hits with unexpected power, and I scream Salvatore's name as my hands convulsively close over my sensitive breasts. It feels like every muscle in my body contracts and pleasure washes over my body in wave after wave.

He touches me through it until I go limp. The only thing holding me upright is his arm around my middle.

I'm floating in post-orgasmic bliss when I feel his hand moving behind my back. Then I hear the sound of his zipper lowering and his hot erection slaps against my spine.

His hand comes between me and the velvet covered steel and he starts jerking off. I want to help him, but in this position, there is nothing I can do but watch us in the mirror, my legs still splayed lewdly.

"Look at that soaked pussy." His hand moves faster. "And those perfect tits. My pussy. My tits. *Tu sei mia!*"

Aftershocks of pleasure roll through me at the intensely possessive claim.

"Say it," he demands.

"Io sono tua." I am yours.

I am afraid that my plan to get over my sexual hangups has backfired. Because even when I leave, I am still going to belong to this man.

"Capo mio." I barely whisper the words, but he hears them.

And they send him over the edge.

Warm fluid bathes my skin and he keeps jacking until I feel it all across my back.

He rubs it in with leisurely strokes. "You will smell like me and that fucking doctor won't be able to miss that you are mine."

"Okay, caveman," I tease, but secretly I like knowing that just as much as Salvatore's ferocious expression says he does.

He's careful only to rub the viscous fluid into my skin and stays away from the gauze, which he removes before finishing undressing me by taking off my demi bra.

"I'm not going out there naked," I tell him.

The ferociousness in his expression takes on a more demonic cast. "You think I would let you?"

"Considering how this got started in the first place because you didn't want Dr. Anders-Powell to see my naked upper half, I'm going with a no."

Salvatore pulls out his phone, tapping on the screen for several seconds. Other than his cock hanging out of the opening in his slacks, he's still fully dressed.

Unreal.

"Next time you are getting completely naked," I tell him. "I like seeing your tattoos."

"Done," he immediately agrees.

We both wash our hands, but neither of us mentions him washing the cum off that he rubbed into my back. I'm drying my hands and contemplating putting my messy underwear back on or going commando under my leggings when there is a knock at the bathroom door.

Salvatore opens it without letting whoever is on the other side see past his big body blocking their view to the bathroom. "Good. Thank you, Rosa."

He shuts the door, his hands filled with one of his button up shirts, and a new pair of underwear and a freaking sports bra for me.

Laughter bursts out of me.

"He does not need you to be without a bra to examine the stitches that are at least two inches below the band."

"I can just wear the red bra," I challenge.

"If you want the underwear, you put on the sports bra."

"That is blackmail."

"Is there anything in who I have shown myself to be that makes you think I would hesitate to use blackmail to get what I want?"

Still smiling, I shake my head. "Nope. But don't think that because you won this round, you'll win the next one."

His sardonic look says he thinks just that.

Too bad for him, I'm not easily led. The next time I'm examined by the doctor, I'll have on a damn thong and the demibra that *doesn't* cover my nipples.

"I don't like that look on your face."

I grin. "Probably because you know it means I'm plotting against you."

"Plot away, but remember, I play to win."

"I never doubted it, but so do I." Which is pure bravado on my part, because I have never once played games with a lover.

I've never had a lover, so it tracks.

Pulling up my leggings after I put on the new underwear, I scrutinize his shirt. "I don't think you got anything on you. Why do you need to change shirts?"

"This isn't for me." He holds the shirt toward me.

Ten minutes later, I'm on the chair, straddling Salvatore's lap and facing him, wearing both the sports bra and Salvatore's shirt backward so my arms and front are completely covered but the shirt is open in the back.

Salvatore is holding the edges of the shirt so it is open just enough for the surgeon to see my healing wound.

Dr. Anders-Powell tsks when he sees us, but wisely says nothing critical. You'd think after what happened in the bathroom Salvatore would be less possessive, but it's the opposite.

My nickname for him fits to a T as he plays the role of grunting caveman with a side of menace to perfection.

"It is healing very well. You should barely see the scar after six months, but it may take longer for it to heal completely." His fingertips run over the skin on either side of my wound.

Salvatore's arms shifts and I hear flesh slapping against flesh. "Watch it!"

I look over my shoulder to see my capo holding the surgeon's wrist in what looks like a painful grip.

Smacking my lover on the chest, I remind him, "He has to touch me to take out the stitches, Salvatore."

"I can take them out," Salvatore claims. "I've done it for myself before."

But he releases the other man's wrist.

"You demanded a plastic surgeon because you wanted your girlfriend to scar as little as possible," the surgeon says with afront. "But by all means, remove them yourself."

I wince internally. Taking that attitude with a Cosa Nostra capo isn't going to end up well for the surgeon.

"You tell me exactly how to do it and if Bianca still has scars six months from now, I will carve the same marks in your fucking face. Are we clear?"

The next ten minutes are fraught with tension. Not Salvatore's. He's confident he can do this. Not mine. I don't really care if there's a scar even a year from now.

But the surgeon's voice shakes as he gives my bossy lover instructions on how to remove the stitches and apply the Steri-Strips after.

"You need to thoroughly cleanse the area with an alcohol swab," he instructs Salvatore.

Salvatore tenses. "You only wiped over the area on her forehead once. Do we need to redo it?"

"Her forehead does not reek of efforts at copulation."

It's all I can do not to laugh at the man's prissy attitude. I smell like Salvatore's cum and I like it. Sue me.

"What kind of fool do you take me for? I didn't spread my cum over the scab." Something in Salvatore's tone tells me that once the scab is gone and the only thing left behind is a scar, it won't just be the anti-scarring cream he'll insist on rubbing on the pink ridges though.

I'm a freak, but the idea of him marking me that way sends a shiver of desire through my sated body.

The plastic surgeon winces at the word *cum*. "Be that as it may, cleanse the area thoroughly, but do not rub and do not disturb the scab."

Salvatore starts muttering about officious pricks in Italian and I press my face into his neck to hide my smile.

CHAPTER 42

SALVATORE

Two texts come through back-to-back as the surgeon is leaving.

One is a regular text from my don. The other is on the secure group chat with Catalina and the tech guys on Domenico's crew that have been working with us to figure out who is trying to steal the bar properties from under our noses.

Severu: *Call me.*

Group Text (QC): *Confirmed Henrico Caruso behind the Stellar Holdings bid.*

Group Text (DTC1): *Sending details via secure link.*

QC stands for Queen Catalina, because she is both my cousin's queen and the queen of gathering and analyzing information. The FEDs only wish they had someone as good as Catalina on their payroll.

DTC stands for Domenico's Tech Crew. 1 is his top guy, but they are all good.

We don't use names on our proprietary chat app. It's an extra layer of security, allowing us to talk mafia business. We still use coded communication if the information we're exchanging is too volatile.

My phone dings with another notification for a new email message.

Turning to face Bianca, I cup her nape and tug her forward. "I have to make a call."

"Okay. I'm going to go change my shirt."

"Leave it on." I like the idea of her wearing my shirt.

She rolls her eyes, but doesn't answer.

Leaning down, I kiss her soft mouth and inhale our combined scent. *Cazzo.* I have to go, but for the first time in memory, I don't want to jump to my don's bidding.

Kissing her one last time, I force myself to step away.

This woman is a fucking disaster for my self-control.

I wait to call Severu until I am in my office and the secure link is pulled up on my computer.

There are statements for a bank account we didn't uncover in our initial search. It is a joint account for Henry Caruso with his cousin Matthew Lombard. I know the Lombardis Americanize their names because of their political connections, but Henry is just a tool.

He acts like he's ashamed of his Italian heritage, or maybe it's his connection to the Cosa Nostra he is trying to hide. Unlike his family in Boston, pretending not to be connected is more likely to put him under scrutiny in New York, than if he stuck with his given name.

And this brain trust is our godfather's choice of successor to run the Lucchese Family?

"Why didn't we find this on our first pass?" It would have saved us the time looking into the other Families.

"We needed a thread to tug on to unravel the layers of obfuscation," Severu replies. "We got that in the copy of the earnest money agreement from Stellar Holding's offer."

Nerissa's team broke into Juniper's office at the convenience store while he was busy with the woman Stellar Holdings sent home with him. An effective watch dog for a man like him with the side benefit of gaining his favor.

It's not a job I would give one of my crew. That's not how we operate. A willing sex worker could keep him occupied without having to know why though.

I wonder which one the woman with Juniper is.

If she's made, she'll be more cautious around our people. And more dangerous if she figures out our plan.

"Nerissa is planning to dose Juniper when they prefunction at his place." Waiting to drug the man until they reach the strip club has too many variables that can go wrong. "She'll give his babysitter a knockout dose to keep her out of the way for the rest of the night and Juniper enough to make him malleable."

Neither will remember the night before. One of the benefits of Rohypnol.

I scroll down to the seven-fucking-figure earnest money check accompanying the offer for the bar properties. It doesn't list any individual names, only the company, Stellar Holdings.

It reveals two things immediately though:

1. Stellar Holdings is willing to pay well above market value for the properties.

2. Juniper's greed is the only reason he didn't sign that offer.

He thinks he can get more money out of me.

"Once Domenico's people had access to the account and routing numbers," Severu says. "It was just a matter of time before they found the actual names associated with the account."

"Why not use one of the company's usual accounts. It would have given them another layer of security?" I ask.

Our guys are exceptional hackers. They would have unraveled all the threads no matter how layered, but it's something we would do if we were trying to hide our involvement in a deal. Few hackers have the skills of Domenico's crew.

"My first thought is that they don't want The Lombardi to know they are partnering on this deal," Severu replies.

"You think Matthew Lombard is acting without the approval of his don?"

"Yes, I do. Now that we know it's Henrico and not our godfather involved in the attempt to purchase the properties, it's highly unlikely that the Boston don would sanction the action."

"The potential for blowback is too big."

"Buying land in our territory is an act of aggression that would not be ignored."

"You aren't going to ignore the attempt, are you?"

"No. Matthew will be punished in a manner commensurate with the crime, or his uncle will have to deal with me."

That is why Severu will make a good godfather. He doesn't hesitate to act. His show of force isn't always as blatant as torturing a man to death, but he never leaves his opponents in doubt of how badly they fucked up.

I scroll down with my mouse, marveling at Henry's cursory effort to hide his actions. "This leaves no doubt about who is working with Stellar Holdings."

There's a clear trail between Henry Caruso liquidating and shifting assets into the account. Technically, his actions are not against mafia protocol. As long as he takes full possession of the New York properties.

If his cousin maintains even a small stake in them, Henry is guilty of treason to the Five Families.

"Since Don Caruso is not involved, you have full freedom to proceed as planned," Severu tells me.

While Henry can buy property in New York by any means necessary, so can I.

Unfortunately for Juniper, I have no intention of outbidding the other capo. I have other ways to make him abide by our original agreement.

And if he squawks after, I can silence him for good. Once the properties have gone through transfer of ownership. With two other Cosa Nostra families involved, keeping a low profile with this is imperative.

We operate so effectively because we operate under the radar.

~ ~ ~

Bianca is dozing in the sun when I find her on the rooftop. She's wearing my shirt, the right way around, and the sleeves rolled up. Possessive pleasure rolls through me at the sight.

I'm making no effort to hide my approach, so I'm not surprised when her eyes pop open.

The smile that comes after sends 150 joules of reviving electric current through my heart. Enough to start the organ all over again, this time with feelings I've walled off for over a decade.

My step falters for a second, but I force my feet forward, dismissing the fanciful thought.

I cannot have feelings for this woman, but I can enjoy her while she is here. And make sure she enjoys being here too.

"Hi." She pulls her knees up and wraps her arms around her legs. "All done with your phone call?"

"Yes." I finished with Severu a few hours ago, but had a lot of work to catch up on.

Figuring out the Juniper angle has taken up time I don't have in my busy schedule.

"I have a business meeting tonight at Pitiful Princess."

Her eyes light up, but then dim. "Oh. So, you'll be gone. You didn't have to tell me."

"I am aware." I answer to no one for how I spend my time. "Do you want to come?"

"To a business meeting? Is that wise?"

Probably not. But I'm no neophyte soldier. She won't see or hear anything I don't want her to. "Your friend Candi is on the schedule. I thought you might want to see her."

"That's really nice of you?"

"You don't sound so sure."

"I'm just trying to figure out your angle."

"I have to have an angle?"

"Is this like a date with work stuff thrown in? Are those the only kind of dates a busy capo can go on."

"You can think of it as a date if you want."

"But you don't?"

"It's an opportunity to spend time together and for you to see your friend."

"That would be great. Really," she says like she's not sure I believe she thinks that. "I haven't seen her since I quit working there."

"You text every day though."

"You went through my phone?"

I shrug. "I'm a nosy guy."

More like security conscious, but she doesn't need to know that after tasking Pietro with doing a background check on her, I decided to do my own investigating.

Yes, Nerissa got in my head.

So, I did my due diligence, pressing Bianca's finger to her phone to unlock it while she was sleeping. Domenico may be the capo in charge of online money laundering and tech security, but I know my way around a phone.

Not that I found much.

There are no apps, hidden or otherwise on her phone. No social media. No internet history with a login page for her college. The phone is old and pay as you go. She probably deals with any apps or websites that require higher bandwidth on her laptop.

But it requires a password to access. If necessary, I'll have it hacked, or just demand she unlock it for me.

I did a quick Google search of her name on my own phone. No social media accounts popped up, which makes sense, considering her former occupation. She probably felt safer having no online presence.

There are phone numbers for Pitiful Princess, Gino and Ugo. I delete Gino's contact information after blocking his number. That *stronzo* is never talking to her again.

Her former roommates are listed in her contacts along with names that are clearly other dancer's stage names, including her friend Candi. There are no numbers associated with family though, supporting her claim that she is alone in the world.

Her call log is short. Apparently, she doesn't like to talk on the phone. And the only person she texts regularly is her friend Candi. Those texts were illuminating, but not condemning.

I saw a text from Ruhnke's daughter-in-law too. I had to unblock the number to read the text stream. It isn't long. And there is not a single mention of money or Bianca's inheritance. I blocked the number again and put Bianca's phone back where I found it on the charger.

"That is an invasion of my privacy, Salvatore."

"You are living with a mafia capo. There is no such thing as privacy when it comes to me staying on top of what is happening in my home."

Her eyes narrow. "Do you have surveillance cameras in the penthouse?"

"Only outside the access points." For now. "I value my privacy."

She snorts. "But no one else's?"

I consider it and then shake my head.

"You are something else. I can't believe you just admitted that."

"Would you rather I lie to you?"

She sobers completely. "No."

"Do you want to go tonight?"

"Yes. What time?"

"We need to be there by nine, but I thought we could get dinner first."

Bianca jumps up from the lounger. "It *is* a date."

"We both have to eat, *bella mia*."

"Stop trying to be such a grouch and just admit it is a date."

"I already said you are free to see it that way if you want to."

She shakes her head like I'm the most annoying person ever. No one treats me like that.

It should piss me off, but I feel my mouth curving into a smile instead.

Her eyes widen, like my smile surprises her. Then she grins. "I am calling it a date and since it's a date, I need to go get ready."

"You're fine in what you are wearing." More than fine. She's delectable.

"Yeah, no. I am not wearing a man's shirt and leggings on a date." She grabs her phone and looks down at it. "How long do I have?"

"An hour." Which I had planned to spend naked with her.

"*Caspita!* Are you kidding me? An hour? I won't be able to wash my hair, but I am definitely taking a shower."

"You want to wash off my cum?" I demand.

"I've enjoyed getting little sniffs of your sex scent all afternoon, but no, I don't particularly want to go to a strip club smelling like a guy's cum."

"Not a guy, mine."

"You know that. I know that, but any random customer at Pitiful Princess won't. They'll probably assume it means I'm available to take clients in the back."

"I will kill anyone who touches."

Her laugh cascades over me and she pats my chest, which is becoming a habit of hers. "No need for such drastic action, caveman. No one's coming near me with you by my side."

"Then why wash my scent away?" The primitive core of all made men craves marking her as mine.

"Better safe than sorry."

"You stay by my side."

"If that starts now, you're going to have to follow me to the bathroom for my shower."

It will be an exercise in temptation, if not downright sexual torture, to watch her naked body under the falling water without touching.

I am right behind her.

CHAPTER 43

BIANCA

A fter the most sensual shower of my life, where I am not ashamed to admit, I put on a show Salvatore will not forget soon, I rush through putting on my makeup, so I have time to style my hair.

I use the straightener to make big curls in the waves that cascade down my back. The whole time, Salvatore watches. He doesn't talk, and he checks his phone every time it dings with a notification, but the way his attention stays on me regardless is unnerving.

Going into the walk-in closet, I riffle through the hangers, trying to decide which dress is perfect for a not-date of dinner and going to a strip club after. I've never owned sexy designer dresses like the ones hanging in the guestroom closet. I've never owned so many dresses at all.

Not even when my mom and dad were still married and she made sure Bea and I had the latest styles "appropriate to our age" to wear every season. At thirteen, the need to go clothes shopping every few months was annoying.

I'm pretty sure I would find it no more exciting now. My mom and Bea have way more in common than I have with either of them, despite Bea being my identical twin.

The LBD is always a good choice, right? I grab a short black number to wear and carry it out of the closet.

Salvatore looks up from his phone. "Wear the blue one."

"I like this one." Black is easy to accessorize.

"I've been imagining you in the blue one since I bought it." He looks at me like he's imagining me naked, not wearing the blue dress.

"What is up with that anyway? You bought me a whole freaking wardrobe."

"I didn't know what you would need."

"So, you got me everything?"

He shrugs, which I interpret as *pretty much*.

"What do I get if I wear the blue one?" I ask.

His gorgeous face goes blank. "What do you want?"

That's easy. "No getting lap dances or tucking tips in the dancer's panties."

He can tip through management. A lot of the customers that appreciated my dancing designated tips for me on their bar tab. It wasn't my favorite because I had to wait to get the tips on my paycheck, but it works.

Salvatore's face clears and he smirks. "Feeling possessive?"

"Feeling like I have no desire to be one of the many women I've seen in the club watching their dates have eyes all over other women."

"I wasn't planning on doing either." His heated look sends tingles through my nether regions. "Only a fool would spend the evening watching someone else with you sitting beside him."

Warmth fills my chest that I do my best to ignore. "Those are pretty words for a man who insists this is not a date."

He shrugs. "The truth is the truth."

If only. There are so many shades of truth and honesty. There is so much about me that he doesn't know and so much about him that I have no clue about.

"You're going to tip though, right?" I ask after replaying his answer in my mind. "That's how dancers make their money. Or does the boss not tip on principle?"

"No one at Pitiful Princess outside of Ugo knows I own the club and I want to keep it that way."

"Okay." It's not like I'm going to announce the club's connection to the mafia, much less that he's a capo who owns several clubs in Manhattan for his Family.

I have a fully developed sense of self-preservation.

"You can tip the dancers on my behalf."

"I get to decide how much each dancer gets?" I ask suspiciously. I'm not looking at some kind of threesome energy.

"Yes, *bella ragazza mia*. You decide how much to tip."

Any dancer who makes a play for Salvatore while I am there isn't getting a dime. I'll have Candi spread the word.

"You look very pleased all of the sudden."

"Worried?"

"No. Intrigued though."

I just grin and go back into the closet to grab the blue dress.

Salvatore takes me to one of the hot restaurants in Manhattan I never thought I'd see the inside of as a server much less a patron. He silences his phone and tucks it into his inside suit pocket.

He'll feel the vibration of a notification, but I still appreciate the effort.

We talk about my life with Mr. Ruhnke over dinner.

"You moved in to stop his children from forcing him out of his home?"

"Yes." Still leery about living with another person, I installed my own lock on my bedroom door with a deadbolt and kept the only keys.

It wasn't safe if there was a fire, but I would never have slept otherwise. The past two years dozing in a closet and only sleeping when I knew all my roommates would be gone proves it was a good move.

"No wonder he left you money in his will."

"What? No. Mr. Ruhnke didn't leave me anything." If I hadn't had my savings, I would have been in real trouble when his children evicted me from Mr. Ruhnke's home after he died.

Salvatore's eyes narrow. "That is not what his son told Nerissa."

"The lying little weasel. I'm glad I blocked all their numbers now."

"You are saying he didn't leave you fifty-thousand dollars?"

"If he had, do you think I would be living in an apartment with five other roommates and my roomie's boyfriend that didn't pay rent?" The idea of having that money blows my mind.

I could have finished college faster and be planning to move away from New York already. Chances are, I would never have taken the job at the Pitiful Princess either. And I wouldn't have moved on to Amuni...or met Salvatore.

Suddenly the idea of a $50,000 windfall two years ago doesn't look so shiny.

"You no longer live there."

"Thanks to you, I don't live with plant assassins," I snark. "Is that what you want to hear?"

"Appreciation from a beautiful woman is always appreciated."

"Watch it, Salvatore. You're slipping into cheesy line territory again." This time though? I'm totally down with the idea of showing that appreciation in a fun and physical way.

He doesn't take the bait and our conversation moves on to how badly mobster movies get it wrong.

But I'm still thinking about what Mr. Ruhnke's son told Nerissa. Unless Salvatore called him and talked to him too?

Doesn't matter. What does is that he claimed Mr. Ruhnke left me $50,000 in his will.

What if he did? What if they have spent two years trying to hide that fact? What if that's why his daughter-in-law wanted to get ahold of me?

I only stop thinking about it when we reach Pitiful Princess. Walking in, the familiar scent of sex and alcohol mixed with perfume and perspiration hits me. I remember the first time I came into the club, when I auditioned for the job of pole dancer.

The smell of vagina clung around the stage and the pole, even though it was wiped down with disinfectant between each dancer's sample set.

That same earthy odor is under all the other scents in the club now. Wednesdays are not our...*their* busiest night, so there are only five dancers on the T-shaped stage in the center of the room and two on the four small circular stages mixed in with the tables.

There are three poles down the center of the stage that the dancers share. All three are being used by the strippers. The two poles on the ends of the cross part of the T are reserved for dedicated pole dancers. Like I used to be.

Both are occupied by dancers I don't recognize who are also dancing stripper style. Friday and Saturday nights there will be a dancer doing exotic flow in heels like I used to do on one of the dedicated poles. The other will have a dancer doing exotic hard in heels.

I never got into the faster paced and more physically demanding style of exotic hard dance.

Wearing a hot pink corselette that barely confines her boobs and matching six-inch stripper heels, Candi is performing on one of the circular platforms when we walk in. Her long brown hair is up in a high ponytail so she can whip it while she dances.

One of the patrons watches every move she makes, with the clear hope her breasts will pop out of the corselette. It's not happening. I know the brand of body tape she uses and there will be no accidental exposure.

She has routines that include stripping down to a g-string, but she reserves them for the weekend, when tips are highest.

There is an empty table with a *reserved* sign on it near her stage.

Waitresses, whose only uniform is a g-string and pasties, weave between the tables. One of them approaches, walking with a roll of her hips that makes her boobs jiggle. She's good with makeup because the contouring she's done makes her C cups look like my DDs.

I would be impressed if she wasn't eyeing Salvatore like a hungry cat. "Let me show you to your table, sir," she purrs.

I am the only woman allowed to purr for *my capo*. At least as long as I'm living in his penthouse.

I texted Candi to tell her we were coming and to spread my warning.

Did this server not get the memo? Or does she think she can convince Salvatore to leave her a big tip anyway? The dancers come from a lot of different backgrounds, but they learn fast how to spot wealthy patrons.

We've all been schooled in rich people's shoes, suits and watches. Not that I needed the schooling after being raised until I was thirteen by my socialite mom, not to mention a dad who always tried to dress like he was a capo and not a soldier.

Salvatore looks like the billionaire that he is in his bespoke suit (no tie), black silk hand-tailored dress shirt, Gucci oxfords and Patek Phillipe watch.

This chick is going to miss out on the brass ring if she makes a play for the golden goose.

"Lead the way." Salvatore slides his hand around my waist, keeping me close as we follow the naked and contoured ass of the other woman.

Ignoring the view, his gaze flicks side to side to make sure I don't come into contact with any of the other customers. A man leers at me and Salvatore, hooks his chair leg with his foot dumping him on his back as we pass.

Servers rush to help the man cursing loudly and throwing threats in Salvatore's direction. Somebody whispers in his ear and the angry man goes silent.

"Stop rubbernecking, *bella mia*. He's not that interesting."

"No but your caveman tendencies are kind of hot." I slide my arm under his suit jacket and around his torso.

My happy feelings evaporate when I see who is approaching the table from the back of the club.

Nerissa.

Looking elegant in a silver jumpsuit and heels that makes me feel gauche in the blue dress that made me feel beautiful and sexy only five minutes before, she walks confidently toward us.

Ugh.

The general manager, Ugo, is with her. So, Salvatore's business is club related? Still not sure why they're taking their meeting here and not some-place else. Especially with Salvatore so insistent on keeping his connection to the strip club under wraps.

"You weren't kidding when you said it wasn't a date," I gripe. "You could have told me your sister was going to be here."

He pulls a chair out for me. "Is that a problem?"

Candi's back is to us as she slides into a slow split looking to the side over her shoulder toward the other side of the club. I'll have to wait to say, "Hi," until she is done with her set.

So, I sit down.

"Why would spending the evening with the woman who called me a selfish bitch and accused me of trying to scam you be a problem?" I might understand Nerissa's protectiveness toward her brother, but I don't have to like it.

"She will not call you that again."

"You sound very certain."

"Because I am."

I don't get a chance to ask how because Nerissa and Ugo arrive at the table.

CHAPTER 44

BIANCA

Salvatore might be convinced Nerissa is done name calling, but the look she's giving me isn't filled with warm fuzzies.

She turns a no friendlier look on the waitress that led us to our table. "A round of tonight's rum special for the table."

The server looks hopefully toward Salvatore. "Would you like anything else?"

"No."

"You've been given our order. Bring enough drinks for the entire table," Ugo instructs her, indicating the empty chairs. "There will be others joining us."

The cocktail waitress finally leaves.

"What is she doing here?" Nerissa demands of her brother with a head tilt toward me.

"Watch your tone," Salvatore barks. "She is here as my cover."

Nerissa leans between us toward her brother. "Your cover?"

"A man like me doesn't come to strip clubs alone," he says in a low tone only the two of us can hear. "It was her, or a group of our men pretending to be my friends. This was easier and more believable."

"I guess the fact that your supposed girlfriend used to work here makes your patronage of a club like Pitiful Princess more credible too," Nerissa muses quietly.

The little bubble of joy that has been floating inside me all evening begins to deflate. I am his expedient cover. This really isn't a date.

"But the only people who think she's your girlfriend are our family and the hospital staff," Nerissa points out.

I really wish I wasn't privy to this conversation. I was having fun, but now the evening is tainted with the knowledge I'm being used. I thought Salvatore wanted to spend time with me, even if he did have to work.

"Which means everyone in the Family knows," Salvatore says wryly. "But I took her to dinner at Per Se to be seen."

So, we could be seen as a couple.

Even dinner was part of the cover. I thought that at least was the date part of the evening. I knew Salvatore had business, but dinner was just us.

"The car with Juniper will be here shortly. His date from Boston is currently sleeping off the effects of her pre-function drink," Nerissa says quietly in Italian, apparently mollified by her brother's explanation for my presence.

"Hello, Bianca, it's good to see you again." Ugo slides into the chair beside me. "If you ever want to come back to work, you'll be welcome. The customers miss you."

Yeah. That is not happening. No matter what the future holds with me and Salvatore, I've gotten what I needed to from exotic dancing.

His smile seems genuine, but he doesn't offer his hand. My own smile is noncommittal and hiding the turmoil roiling through me. I don't offer to shake hands either.

"Nerissa, you sit there. Ugo, move over a chair." Salvatore's tone demands instant obedience.

Because Ugo and Nerissa work for him, he gets it. After the shuffling, there are two empty chairs left at the table.

I lean toward Salvatore and ask quietly, "More scheming for whatever you all are doing here tonight?"

"I don't want another man sitting next to you."

This show of possessiveness would have turned me on five minutes ago. Now, it's just annoying.

I lean back in my chair and speak loudly enough to be heard over the music by the others at the table. "Get over yourself, Salvatore. I'm not going to trip and fall on some other man's dick just because I'm sitting beside him."

Ugo turns his head, pretending interest in what one of the servers is doing at a table nearby. Nerissa snorts a laugh she tries to cover, but there's no missing the amusement in her dark eyes.

Salvatore's not laughing though. "I didn't say you would."

"Didn't you?" I stand up. "Excuse me."

Salvatore grabs my wrist. "Where are you going?"

"To see Candi."

Done with her set, my friend has exited her stage via the climb down on the other side that looks like part of the club's décor. Our table is close to the stage, but the route she has to take through the other tables means she's still making her way toward us.

Suddenly, I have no desire to talk to her in front of Salvatore and his people.

"You can catch up here at the table."

"No."

"Why not?"

"I don't want to." I tug on my arm. "Don't worry. Her break only lasts fifteen minutes. I'll be back to play my part in your little farce then."

"It is not a farce. You *are* my girlfriend." He makes that last claim loudly enough to be heard at the surrounding tables.

Candi hears it because her eyes go wide and she gives me a thumbs up sign.

"Who is not on a date with you." I yank at my arm. "Yeah, that tracks." My voice is heavy with sarcasm.

"We'll go on a date tomorrow."

"To dinner at your don's? That's some date, Salvatore." I roll my eyes.

"I'm starting to like her," Nerissa says, but her tone is sarcastic.

I give her a look, one brow lifted. "Yeah? Is it because your brother is so willing to use me?"

I speak in Italian like she did earlier. I'm not willing to mess up Salvatore's *business*, whatever that is, but I'm not pretending everything is fine either.

"I am not using you," Salvatore snaps, tugging me into his lap.

"Che palle. Let me go," I demand, squirming to get up. "I'm your cover to be here. How is that *not* using me?"

A hard bulge under my hip tells me my movements are turning him on.

"No lap dances, remember?" I ask scathingly.

"You are the only one I would want one from," he says in a sexy growl.

I shove against his chest and shock of shocks, he lets me stand up. Only he pushes me to the side and a little behind him, which is not where I want to go because Candi is approaching from the other direction.

I know why a second later when I hear an unfamiliar voice talking, or should I say *slurring* in a New Jersey accent. "Salvatore, buddy. They-ah you ah."

The man who was at his table at Amuni the first night I met Salvatore comes up and lists forward, offering an unsteady hand to Salvatore to shake.

Apparently, those pre-function drinks were strong.

The capo indicates one of the empty spots at the table. "Sit down, Juniper. Your chair has a great view of the stage."

"My date's not he-ah," Juniper slurs. "She fell asleep." He looks like a child deprived of his favorite toy and not understanding how it happened.

"Don't worry. We've got you covered," Nerissa says, like she's trying to sound accommodating, but there's an underlying current of disgust in her voice.

An actor she is not.

"Bianca!" Candi calls my name and tries to step around Juniper to get to me.

I point to my right, indicating I'll meet her the next table over.

But before either of us can move, Juniper turns fast and leers at Candi. "Are you my date for tonight?"

Ugo leaps from his chair like it caught on fire and inserts himself between Candi and Juniper. "No, sir. If you'll have a seat, one of our dancers will be over to give you a lap dance in a moment."

"I want that one." He points toward Candi.

Ugo blanches and shoots a worried glance toward the other side of the club where a few of the tables are deliberately situated in the shadows. They're reserved for Pitiful Princess's version of VIPs.

"No," Ugo says. "She's on break. Let me just help you to your chair."

Ugo grabs Juniper and guides him with a white knuckled grip on his arm toward the other side of the table.

Salvatore obviously has plans for Juniper tonight and doesn't want him latching on to the wrong dancer. Not that Candi would give Juniper the kind of companionship he's looking for. Her lap dances are strictly noncontact.

Knowing I'm here for a purpose, and determined to play my part in a way that will make Salvatore squirm, I lean down and place a lingering kiss on Salvatore's cheek.

"Back in a bit, daddy," I purr loudly enough for the tables around us to hear.

Not to mention the server who has returned with our drinks. Giving me a sour look, she places the drinks around the table. But when she tries to pass Nerissa's chair to hand Salvatore his, the second snatches the glass from the tray and sets in front of her capo herself.

So, I'm not the only one Nerissa doesn't want near her brother. Pretending not to notice the byplay, I scoot around Juniper and grab Candi's hand.

I immediately start tugging her toward the back.

"Candi's taking a little extra breaktime, Ugo. You don't mind, do you?" I call toward the GM. "I'm sure daddy would be appropriately grateful for making me so happy," I sing song.

Ugo stares at me like I've grown a second head, and Nerissa looks like she's going to hurl.

Oooh, added bonus. Grossing out the overprotective sister.

CHAPTER 45

BIANCA

Candi leans forward as we head toward the back. "You call him *daddy*?"

I turn my head so I can speak close to her ear, though the two inches she has on me in height and the additional six inches of her heels means my mouth is closer to her chest. Oops.

Standing on my tiptoes, I cup my free hand near her ear. "Not my kink, but he wants to play my sugar daddy tonight so I'm letting him. It's a one night only pass though."

"That sounds more like you," she says with a laughs and then she sobers. "Not that actually having a boyfriend sounds like you."

The worry is clear in her tone.

"Who knew? I was just waiting for the right bossy billionaire to come along," I tease.

Candi yanks me to a stop, not laughing. "Did you hit your head during the attack?"

"You know I did," I try humor again. "I told you everything about that morning.

Well not everything. I didn't tell Candi that Salvatore killed three men to protect me, or that he slept with me in my hospital bed to keep the nightmares away.

She shakes her head but nudges me to start walking again. We pass through the velvet curtain into the hallway leading to the rooms for private lap dances (and other things) and the dressing room, which is where I'm headed.

But Candi stops again as soon as we're behind the curtain and pulls me around to face her. "Are you alright? I can't believe I haven't seen you since you got attacked."

Her eyes scan over me like she's taking inventory.

"I'm fine. I texted you pictures."

"That weren't as reassuring as you think they were. You were stabbed!"

"He didn't hit anything vital."

Candi glares. "Don't joke."

"I'm not."

"Your whole body is vital, Bianca." Her voice wobbles. "You could have been killed."

"I'm okay. More than okay. I'm living the high life in a billionaire's penthouse."

"Like you care if he's rich," she scoffs. "The only thing that matters to you with people is how they treat others."

"He's taking very good care of me."

"I just bet he is."

"Not like that." Though the sexual satisfaction is very welcome from my side. "I mean, like making sure I eat and rest."

"That's good." She doesn't sound convinced though.

"My roommates tried to kill Vee and he's trying to nurse it back to health." Because he knows the plant is important to me.

"That's something real, I suppose. And he's making sure you rest, like actual sleep?" Candi knows how hard it is for me to sleep, if not why.

"He's big into me taking naps." His new way of getting me to sleep isn't something I'm going to share, even with my best friend, though.

She nods grudgingly. "He got you out of that awful apartment where you slept on the dang floor, so he can't be all bad. Even if he is rich."

"Most people would not see that as the detriment you do."

"Is he trying to force you to do anything?" she asks as she tugs me toward an unoccupied private room. "If you need to get away, I can smuggle you out the backdoor and you can go to my apartment. Mom knows you might come, so she'll let you up."

"You already talked to her?" Unexpected tears prickle at my eyes.

What is with me and this surfeit of emotion lately?

"Of course, I did. You can live with us as long as you need to. And I'll check your wounds every day," she says wryly, clearly remembering the excuse Salvatore made for me staying at his place.

I told her in one of my texts with laughing emojis. Apparently, my friend didn't take my agreement to stay at face value.

"I want to be there," I tell her. "When he touches me, I don't freak out."

Candi is the only person I've ever told that I don't like being touched by men. I didn't give her the details, or tell her about my past, but she didn't need me to. She accepts my limitations for what they are and doesn't judge me for them.

She's the only dancer who never gave me crap for not working the floor at least.

"You sure you don't want to run?" she asks. "I know rich guys think they can have whatever they want."

"Positive. He's not like that." My defense is vehement.

When the truth is? Salvatore does think he can have whatever he wants. Not because he's rich, but because he's a capo. Only, he would *never* force me to have sex with him.

Keep me trapped in his apartment until I saw reason? Yes.

Hurt me physically? No.

With a final measuring look, Candi flips the sign to occupied and goes into the room. The smell of sex mixes with citrus and mint based disinfectant is strong, reminding me what these rooms are used for.

"Are you sure we should be using one of these rooms?"

"It's not that busy tonight and we won't be here very long." Candi shrugs. "We've got thirty minutes max before Ugo comes knocking. He's figured out how much I make in tips and he wants the house's split."

There are two seating options: a sofa, upholstered in easy to clean microfiber and two armchairs. They look like expensive armchairs with tufted backs like the sofa, but the vinyl upholstery means that there are no lingering body fluids caught in the fibers after being wiped down with disinfectant.

"Are you two doing the dirty?" With no concern for what the microfiber might be hiding, Candi kicks off her heels and plops down sideways on the sofa, putting her feet up.

I gingerly lower myself into one of the chairs, keeping my arms close to my sides. "That's on a need to know, and you, my friend do not need to know."

"Well, everyone out there sure thinks you are. Sitting on his lap like that sold it." Candi jerks her thumb in the direction of the club.

"Sitting on his lap was Salvatore's idea."

"You didn't scream bloody murder or throat punch him, so we all figured you wanted to be there." Now that I've allayed her worries, Candi is in full on nosy friend mode.

"You all?" I ask.

"Girl, if you don't think your warning caused a buzz of gossip then you don't remember this place very well."

Fair point. "Our server didn't get the memo."

"Oh, she got it alright, but she's new and thinks she's irresistible because of all the new girl attention she's getting."

"I was ready to punch her in the vagina," I admit.

Candi laughs. "Yeah, well if she moves on one of Piper's regulars like she tried to move on Salvatore, she's going to get a six-inch stiletto up her ass."

Piper is one of the dancers who has been at Pitiful Princess the longest. "Yeah, well you don't mess with a fellow dancer's income."

"Not if you don't want that stiletto heel in your back."

We smile at each other in understanding.

"So, Salvatore..." Candi says leadingly.

"He's mine." I shrug. "For now."

"We all definitely got the *he's mine* impression."

And Candi still checked in to make sure I wasn't putting on an act. I love her for that.

"No one in the club has seen you so much as touch a guy. Then you walk in on the billionaire's arm and sit on his lap?" She fans herself. "Girl, he would give a lot of women daddy fantasies. Now that I know he's not a typical rich douche, I don't blame you for playing."

They'd better keep their kinks to themselves around Salvatore.

Dio mio.

You are getting very possessive for a temporary bedmate, aren't you, Bian-ca?

Temporary is right. I can't forget that. But I can't deny that my snarky inner voice is right either. Again.

"Like I said, it's just for tonight." After what my dad put me through, daddy play is a big fat *no*.

"The possessive way he looks at you doesn't seem like it's only for the night. He didn't glance at the stage once."

"You were watching?"

"Weren't you?"

I shrug again. "He promised no lap dances."

"That's not the same as looking and he didn't."

We both know how rare that is. Men come to the Pitiful Princess to look.

Even when they're here with business associates. This time my inner voice sounds thoughtful, not sarcastic and that's dangerous. That means my subconscious is considering things we've got no business thinking about.

"Do you have a daddy kink I don't know about?" I tease Candi, not wanting to dwell on my thoughts, or the inner voice that is right more than she's wrong.

Someone else might call it my intuition manifesting in self-talk. I read that in a self-help book. I call it annoying.

Candi bursts out laughing. "I think you have to have experience with sex to have a kink."

My friend, the virgin stripper.

"How are things now?" I ask seriously. "You okay?"

"Ugo has taken over management of the dancers personally and he's making sure no one is being pressured to offer extra curriculars they don't want to."

"Good. He's still a tool."

"Pretty much." Candi grabs some paper towels from the handy access dispenser on the wall behind the couch and starts dabbing at the sweat on her face, careful not to ruin her makeup. "Piper told me she'd fix the problem if he didn't. I'm glad he came through though."

More like Salvatore did, but I can't say that and give away his connection to the Pitiful Princess.

Candi tosses her paper towels into a discreet trashcan. "Now, tell me everything."

"You already know it all." Well not the details about the sex stuff, but no way am I sharing that.

"Texts are not the same as talking. I've missed you." Sadness washes over Candi's face. "It's not the same here without you. No one else even remembers my real name."

"It's Kathleen."

"I prefer Kath."

I know that. And I never use it because calling her by her stage name is how I keep my friend at a distance.

Since Mr. Ruhnke died, I haven't let anybody in. But living in Salvatore's penthouse has made me remember what being part of a family feels like. What having people around me who care feels like.

I stand and take my chances with the couch to sit down beside Candi's stretched out legs.

Pulling my friend in for a hug, I say, "I miss you too, Kath."

Candi grills me some more and reiterates that I'll always have a place to live with her at least three times before Ugo sends someone looking for her.

SALVATORE

Nerissa shifts over to sit beside me and Ugo rises to leave. Then the two women we hired to keep Juniper company arrive at the table, one sitting on either side of him.

Neither woman is aware of my plans for Juniper, but they don't need to be. They only need to be willing to keep him occupied while his lower dose of Special K takes full effect, making him malleable enough to sign the paperwork.

Ugo has one of our lawyers and notaries waiting in his office to oversee the proceedings.

How long is a little extra break time?

"Staring at the curtain to the backrooms isn't going to make her magically appear, Salvatore," my second informs me wryly.

"How long is a little extra? Five or ten minutes? More?" It had better not be more.

Candi's break is supposed to last fifteen to begin with.

"Chill out, Salvatore. She's only been gone a few minutes."

It feels longer. I don't like her being out of my sight. "This is not a safe place for her to be hanging around the back room."

"We make sure it is a safe place for all our girls."

I whip my head around so my sister can see my pissed off expression. "She's not one of the working girls."

"Never said she was."

It's too close to the conversation I had with Bianca before she left. I don't think she's going to fuck another man, but that doesn't mean I want any other men close enough to touch her.

"I should go check on her."

"Would you relax, capo? Pietro followed them. Per your orders, he's always got his eyes on your *baby girl*." Nerissa snickers.

I know he's with her. I don't know why I'm so antsy.

"What the fuck was that daddy shit?" I ask to change the subject.

"You're asking *me*? If I had to guess, I'd say Bianca's not thrilled about being your cover and decided to get a little of her own back."

"Probably. She's no pushover." And why that should make me proud, I have no idea.

She's my temporary girlfriend.

Right?

"You seem different." Nerissa cocks her head and studies me. "Not so broody. Are you happy Salvatore?"

"You ask that like it would be a miracle if I was."

"Ever since you became made I would have said it was."

"What the hell are you talking about? I'm happy." I'm fucking glad the music and angle of the tables around us mean no one else can hear our conversation.

Not even the security teams taking up the tables on either side of us.

"No, really. This is different." She waves at me. "I was too busy worrying she was another Monica yesterday to notice, but when she's around, you're relaxed. At peace."

"Are you getting soft on me, second?"

"No, capo, but if she makes you feel good like this, keep her around a while."

"Even if she's an outsider?"

"I'm not saying marry the woman, but..." Nerissa shrugs. "She makes you happy."

"That wasn't your attitude yesterday."

"I was in protective sister mode then."

"What are you in now because you are not sounding like my second-in-command. We don't talk feelings and shit."

"Because you don't have them."

"Are you saying you do?"

She shrugs. "None that I'm willing to share."

"What the hell does that mean? Are you dating?"

Nerissa's laugh is too spontaneous not to be genuine. "Salvatore, I've been dating the same guy for a year. He's met mamma and papà and been vetted by dad."

"That guy you brought to Thanksgiving?"

"Yes."

"You didn't bring him to Christmas. I figured you broke up."

"And you didn't ask."

Unlike the rest of my family, I don't feel the need to force my way into personal business. If her relationship impacted her job as my second-in-command, that would be different. But Ernesto is part of Domenico's crew. The only other crew I trust as much as my own.

Besides Severu's crew, but that is to be expected. They work directly for our don. If they aren't trustworthy, they are dead. No demotion from any of his personal teams.

"You weren't sad," I explain. "I didn't have to kill him."

"No killing my boyfriends."

"He is your boyfriend now?"

"He wants to be more."

"What do you want?" Is my sister going to get married?

She shrugs. "I'm not sure. Ernesto understands the life because he's in it. He doesn't treat me like I'm too fragile to be your second."

"Smart man." The whole time we're talking, I'm watching that damn curtain leading to the back rooms.

It doesn't move. No one goes in. No one comes out.

"You sure Pietro went with her?" I ask over whatever Nerissa is saying now.

"Yes, capo, I'm sure." My second sounds exasperated. "I also think it's time to take Juniper into Ugo's office."

She indicates the man now leaning sideways, the woman beside him the only thing stopping him from face planting on the floor.

CHAPTER 46

SALVATORE

"Watch for Bianca. Make sure she stays at the table while I'm gone." I don't want her roaming around the strip club on her own.

Some *stronzo* would try to touch her and I would have to cut off his hands.

"You do remember she used to work here, don't you?"

"She doesn't anymore. And never will again."

"Ugo already said he'd have her back any time," Nerissa taunts.

"If Ugo wants to keep breathing, he'll rescind that offer." I grab Juniper by the shoulders and yank him up. "Let's go."

"Huh? Whe-ah ah we going? Ah the ladies coming?"

I jerk my head toward the one he was leaning on and she jumps up, sliding her arm around Juniper from the other side.

Once we reach the office, I dismiss her with gesture of my hand.

"What ah we doing he-ah?" Juniper looks around the office hazily. "Whe-ah's my date?"

"You just need to sign some paperwork and you can get back to her."

"Paperwork?"

"I've got the deed transfer on the properties ready for you to sign."

"You're going to pay me a lot, right?"

"Yes." My original offer was more than fair.

I wanted to finish the deal quickly, so I initially offered the high end of fair market. Juniper was salivating for that deal before Stellar Holdings stepped in.

Too bad for them and Henry fucking Caruso, I fight dirty, and I fight to win.

After reminding Juniper that his dates are waiting, he signs every single document, including the permission to transfer the funds directly into his bank account.

Proof of that transfer and the signed sales agreement is all my people need to expedite the sale of three out of five of the bar properties. We have people on our payroll in the Manhattan County Clerk's Office already and the transfer of ownership will be finalized first thing tomorrow morning.

We were able to bribe clerks in two of the other offices to bypass what could be as much as a ninety-day wait and record the deed changes within twenty-four hours.

The other two aren't in the City. In counties with smaller Clerk's Offices, it's not worth the risk of trying to bribe someone when taking ownership of them is not critical.

"Any sign of Gino?" I ask Ugo while one of my guys leads Juniper out to the club to a different table, where he can party as long as he wants with his dates on my dime.

Don't say I'm not generous in victory.

"About that." Ugo tugs at his collar. "I think he's in the soup."

The way he says *soup* lets me know he's not using a euphemism for in trouble. He's talking about the chemical bath we use to dispose of bodies in the subbasement of the Oscuro building.

"Che cosa?"

Ugo swallows. "One of the dancers mentioned to Angelo that Gino had been pressuring Candi to work the backrooms."

"When?"

"Before I got a chance to talk to him."

"Because you weren't doing your job, she told our don's top enforcer so he'd do something about fucking Gino stealing her money."

Ugo nods, misery in his expression. I was already pissed at him, but this makes our crew look bad and me look like I don't have control of my people.

I point at the GM and then to the chair Juniper vacated. "Sit."

Ugo sits.

Going to the door, I instruct one of my men to get Bianca and Nerissa. He doesn't have to tell Pietro to come. My top bodyguard goes where Bianca goes.

A couple of minutes later Nerissa brings Bianca into the office.

She walks across the room, her hips swaying with exaggerated motion, her pretty lips pursed. "Daddy! I missed you."

She's mocking me and about as sincere as the guy selling "Rolex" watches on the sidewalk. Those fucking words still hit me center mass.

"Knock that shit off," I tell her even though what I really want is for her to say it again. This time without the sarcasm

Refusing to examine why, I pull her into my body and hold her tight to me. My cock wakes up and my hands itch to caress every luscious curve her dress clings so sensually to. I knew I'd love this on her.

Bianca looks up at me through her lashes, her eyes glimmering with disdain. "But I thought you wanted me to play your girlfriend."

I don't like that disdain, or the implication that she's only playing the role of my girlfriend.

"You *are* mine." I lean down and speak softly directly into her ear. "You are my good girl. If you want to be my baby girl, I can be persuaded."

She shivers against me and sighs. "I'll pass."

"You sure?"

"The whole daddy thing does not carry good memories for me," she says with more candor and less rancor than I expect.

I want to ask her why but not in front of everyone else. So, I let her move to the side of me.

"Make Ugo's demotion to Gino's position permanent," I say to Nerissa, informing Ugo of his change in status at the same time.

The former GM doesn't look happy but he's smart enough not to protest.

Bianca goes stiff beside me. What is that about?

Finding out will have to wait. Her being here for this meeting is not the norm, but I don't want her out of my sight for one more minute in a club full of horny customers.

"Put someone in the GM position who will pay better attention to what is happening under their watch."

Giving Ugo a look of frustration, my second tells me, "I've got some candidates. The assistant manager at the Red Room is ready for more responsibility."

"I want to interview her before you offer her the position." I'm not risking this happening again.

"Is that really necessary? Having you participate in the interview will further undermine the confidence our crew has in me as second-in-command."

She's right. Under other circumstances, it wouldn't cause much comment. But coming on the heels of her punishment for disloyalty, it will be another blow to her reputation among our people.

Maybe they should question her fitness to lead. Maybe I should.

Nerissa should have noticed how much leeway Ugo was giving Gino. I may not know every employee at Amuni and Festa, but I sure as hell know the bar, kitchen and staff managers at both clubs. And how they perform.

My second should know the same for the strip clubs. "Yes. It is necessary. And I want you spending more time here and at the other clubs under your purview."

She can oversee our business

"This was a one-time thing, Salvatore," she says in protest. "Ugo delegated to the wrong guy."

"Ugo delegated too much and so did you. If you don't think the strip clubs are worth your time, I'll give them to someone who sees differently," I tell her.

The strip clubs are the second's responsibility. If I give them to someone else, I'm giving them her job too.

Nerissa's jaw clenches, but she nods without saying a word.

"Well?" I say, wanting the acknowledgment made out loud.

"I know I fucked up, okay? It won't happen again. The strip clubs are worth my time," she grits out, showing she knows exactly what I want from her. She flicks a glance to Bianca and sighs. "I will apologize to the dancers personally for letting them down."

Bianca's tension eases a little. "I think that's a good idea. They need to know they can come to you, or the GM, if there's a problem."

"I am sorry, Bianca," Nerissa says sincerely. "It is my job to oversee the strip clubs and I let you all down. I'll be checking in with the dancers at the other clubs too."

"Thank you," Bianca says.

I'm not sure if she's thanking my sister for the apology or the promise to check the other clubs.

"We aren't going to have any more problems with management, are we Ugo?" I ask the other man in a tone that lets him know there is only one right answer.

"No, no, of course not."

I turn to Bianca. "Happy now?"

"Not particularly, no."

She's still pissed about me using her as cover tonight. I need to take her on a real date and show her that temporary, or not, she *is* my girlfriend. And yes, I fucking want everyone to know it.

"Are you ready to leave?" I ask her, done with this place.

But she might have more friends she wants to catch up with. And for some reason, I'm channeling a guy who cares.

She steps away from me and turns toward the door. "Yes."

Bianca moves fast when she wants to and if Pietro wasn't blocking her way in the hall she would be outside before I caught up with her.

I grab her hand and incline my head toward my lead bodyguard. "Let's go."

When we get to the car, instead of sitting beside me like she has been all night, Bianca sits as far away from me as she can on the bench seat.

"I told you it wasn't a date," I remind her.

"You didn't tell me you were using me." Her look could incinerate a high-rise to a pile of ash. "You didn't tell me dinner was just so we were seen together to support the girlfriend pretense."

"For the fucking last time, it is not a fucking pretense. You are my girlfriend. And yes, I wanted you fucking seen with me. I want everyone to fucking know you are mine and to stay the fuck away."

"That's a lot of *fucks*."

"Not as many or the kind I really want," I tell her with frustrated honesty.

"You're not funny."

"Good, because I'm not joking."

Pointedly looking away from me, she stares out the window. "Why was I there for that?"

"I already told you." And she wasn't happy to hear it, so am I going to repeat it? Fuck, no.

"I meant for your meeting with Nerissa and Ugo."

"Did you want to hang out in the main area watching the dancers?"

"It's always fun to see what new moves or techniques other dancers are trying."

"But you don't work the pole any longer."

"It's still great exercise. Whether, I dance to make a living, or not, I'm not giving it up."

My cock likes the sound of that way too much. My inner caveman? Not so much.

"Where would you dance?"

"At a studio." She shrugs. "Does it matter?"

"I could have a pole installed in my gym."

She gives me a look that's a lot less angry, but a lot more questioning my intelligence. "I won't be able to use it until the cut on my back is completely healed. It would put too much strain on the recently repaired tissues."

"You sound like a doctor."

"I can Google like everybody else."

"I apologize that using you as cover tonight hurt your feelings." If my second can express regret, so can I.

No matter how little experience I have doing it.

"I wish you'd told me instead of just saying it wasn't a date."

If I told her, she wouldn't have acted naturally, making people wonder why we were together. Okay, so I used her and knew I was doing it.

I sigh. "I am sorry for that too."

"Don't do it again."

"I won't."

She turns her head and our gazes meet. "Promise."

"I give you my word as a capo." Does she know how serious that is?

Something flares in her bright blue gaze that says she does. "Okay."

She opens her mouth and then closes it again, looking uncertain.

"Che cosa?"

"Nerissa sounds like she really wants to do better overseeing the strip clubs."

"Yes." She'd better if she wants to remain my second-in-command.

"But Ugo..." Bianca's voice trails off.

"What about him?"

"I get that demoting him to assistant manager works to punish him, but is that what's best for the dancers?"

"He wouldn't dare pull the shit Gino did." Especially knowing that Gino died for his misdeeds.

And that if Angelo hadn't killed him, I would have. Nobody steals from the mafia and lives.

"That doesn't mean he'll be a good manager over the talent. If he doesn't respect them..." Her voice trails off.

"Why would you say he doesn't respect them?"

"Because he never once checked to see how Gino was managing us. He checked in with the bar manager every night to see if there was enough liquor stocked, but when it came to managing people who earn as much, or maybe more, for the mafia as the fricken liquor license, he left it entirely to Gino."

"That doesn't mean he won't do his job."

"Really? Is it worth the risk? Most of the dancers are sex workers, all of them are in the sex industry. That puts them at risk in a way other employees are not. Half of their job is illegal and there are no OSHA guidelines for how many johns a dancer takes into the backrooms in a single shift."

"We provide healthcare and they're routinely screened for STDs."

"To protect the customers. What protections do they have?"

"The mafia protects them from overzealous customers and getting picked up by the cops. And the women get to choose whether to take on a customer," I remind her.

"Really? Once a dancer starts offering extra services, she has to pay a base rate per night for protection."

"That's normal and it's less than our average 50% take." They don't pay protection on top of their 50%, but Bianca is right.

There is a minimum amount every dancer is expected to pay for the use of the back rooms and the security we provide. Some nights their 50% doesn't cover it, but most nights it does.

"Do you know why their 50% take covers that base rate so many nights?"

"Because it's not hard to make enough to cover it." I'm sure about that. It's a policy I instituted when I was in charge of the strip clubs before my father moved me to the nightclubs.

He wanted me working the legit businesses in public to distance me from the illegal aspects of our business on paper in preparation for me taking over as capo one day. We thought that was a lot farther into the future than it turned out being.

"You make money offering hand jobs, your mouth and your ass for one night and tell me how easy it is."

"The sex workers never complained to me when I was in charge."

"And no one complained to Ugo or Nerissa when Gino started his shit either."

"Are you saying I wasn't paying attention? Because I was. I checked in with Ugo when he was assistant manager."

"Yeah? Did you talk to the dancers?"

"I didn't have time to talk to every employee then any more than I do now."

"Your employees at the nightclubs aren't facing the same kind of risks the dancers and cocktail waitresses who turn tricks are. When a dancer is too sick to dance, she still has to cover her backroom fee for every night she's on the schedule, whether she works or not."

"That's business."

"That's shitty."

"Look, I pay taxes, rent and utilities whether we are open or not."

"You mean your shell company."

"The shell company is me." Effectively.

"More like the mafia," she mutters, but then her jaw sets at a stubborn angle. "Whoever. That shell company makes tens of millions of dollars in profit."

"At least," I say proudly.

"So if you have to eat overhead costs the impact on your bottom line is minimal. If one of your hourly workers has to, the difference could be between making rent that month and not. Or between groceries and paying the heating bill."

"It's too hot to run heat right now."

"Don't. This isn't funny."

"You never did back room work. Why do you care so much?"

"You've never been don, but that doesn't stop you from caring about Severu De Luca's wellbeing."

"I owe him my allegiance."

"If you expect loyalty from your employees, whether they manage the bar or make the mafia extra money with their bodies, and I know you do..." She pauses, daring me to contradict her.

I don't. I do expect loyalty.

"Then you have to give it to them too."

"Write up your concerns and send it to Nerissa. I'll give you her email address."

"What stops her from dropping it straight into the trash folder?"

"Do you think she would do that?" I'm genuinely curious what Bianca's take on my sister is.

I know Nerissa will consider Bianca's concerns and if she finds them valid, look for a way to mitigate them. Despite overstepping out of concern for me, she's a good second and there's a reason our soldiers are loyal to her which has nothing to do with being my sister.

Bianca takes a minute to consider my question. "No, I don't think she would. Especially if you tell her to expect my email."

No one pushes me like this woman. "Done."

CHAPTER 47

SALVATORE

B ianca stares up in awe at the Art Deco building through the car window. "Your don owns this building and the top two floors are his home?"

I don't like how impressed she sounds. "I own the building my penthouse is in too."

Her head turns so our eyes meet. I have no interest in the view out the window. I have seen it many times before, but I will never tire of looking at Bianca.

"How?" she asks, her brows furrowed. "No wonder the only access to the rooftop garden is from your penthouse."

"My father signed it over to me when I became capo." I'd been managing the building as part of my duties as his second-in-command for nearly a decade at that point.

I still manage it and assign other responsibilities to Nerissa.

"You know that's ridiculous right? To be given an entire Manhattan high-rise as a gift for a job promotion."

I shrug. "My grandfather gave it to my father when he was named capo. My father gave it to me when I was."

"How does that work? One son became don, and the other was a capo."

"When the capo in my father's position had to be removed from his position. My grandfather needed someone to take over he could trust. Since his underboss, Uncle Enzu would become don after him, he chose his younger son."

"Your father."

"Yes."

"How did your grandfather become don?"

"He was a behind the scenes money guy without an arrest record. After RICO, the leadership had to be squeaky clean to keep us off law enforcement's radar."

"Makes sense, I guess." She bites her bottom lip and gives me a worried look. "Have you been to prison?"

"No." All my illegal deeds are buried along with any evidence they ever happened. "We're a lot more careful not to get caught for even petty crimes now."

Once they get you in the system for anything you fall under more scrutiny and are more vulnerable to search warrants and being held for questioning.

Not that either would do law enforcement any good. We are too fucking careful. And a modern Genovese doesn't talk. They know it's a death sentence with a side of grisly.

"I'm glad."

"You don't think I should pay for my crimes?"

"No. There's too much corruption and greed that's legal for me to think you deserve jailtime for protecting your family." She smiles softly. "You might have been bossy about it, but you watched out for me. You're even trying to save my poor Vee."

I still find it hard to believe she named her African violet. I should set Bianca straight and tell her that I am more monster than man. But I won't.

I like the look of admiration in her beautiful blue eyes too much.

My driver pulls into the parking space set aside for me in the underground parking garage.

Bianca doesn't unbuckle her seatbelt right away. "Why am I here?"

"Because you are my guest and I was invited."

"But *why* am I your guest?" she persists.

I realize where this is coming from. "It's not like last night. There are no ulterior motives."

Not now anyway.

"This is dinner with your *family*, Salvatore. You had a reason for asking me to come."

She sounds completely convinced of that fact. And she's right, damn it. "I thought bringing you would stop my cousin's wife matchmaking without getting my mom's hopes up about marriage and grandchildren."

"Because I'm not a mafia princess." The way she says it bothers me.

Like she's somehow less than.

It bothers me even more that she's not wrong. "My mother is usually a stickler for people knowing and staying in their place. She doesn't even let Pietro call her Ilaria and she's known him since birth."

"But she was really nice to me when I met her and she was pretty adamant I call her Ilaria."

"I am aware."

"That doesn't mean she'll start imaging wedding bells in our future. If she didn't know before, I'm sure Nerissa has informed your mom by now that I am a pole dancer turned cocktail waitress."

"She knew that you were a server at Amuni."

"Did you tell her?"

"No, but I'm sure Rosa did." What Rosa knows, my mother knows, which is why I need to find a new housekeeper.

"But I'm still an outsider." She sighs. "Your mom was just being nice."

My mother is unfailingly polite. She can be kind. She is loyal. She loves her family fiercely, but she is not *nice*. I don't burst Bianca's bubble about that either.

I tell her the one thing that should not be true. "You don't feel like an outsider."

Maybe my sister is right to be concerned about my judgment when it comes to Bianca. I've been patting myself on the back because the skittish woman so obviously trusts me, all the while being blind to how much I am growing to trust her.

A temporary lover and an outsider, like she just reminded me.

But she doesn't feel like an outsider. She feels like mine. Like my crew is mine. Like my family is mine.

Fuck.

Bianca opens her mouth and closes it without saying anything.

"Are you angry?" I ask after several long seconds.

"No."

"But I was going to use you again."

"Yeah, you're kind of mercenary like that." She doesn't *sound* angry. Only thoughtful.

"Your presence will still stop Catalina from throwing her sister at me all night long."

"Good."

Good? What the hell does that mean.

A tap on the window reminds us it's time to go.

Bianca jumps like it was a gunshot and the click of her undoing her seatbelt is loud in the back of the car.

We're in the elevator with Pietro, the rest of my men in the freight elevator per protocol, when she speaks again. "Tell me about the don's wife trying to play matchmaker."

Pietro covers a bark of laughter with a cough.

I scowl at him. He won't think it's so funny if I put him forward for the position of Madonna Carlotta Jilani's husband. Lottie has grown up a lot in the last year and done her best to be a good sister to our don's wife. She's still a self-involved princess, used to getting her own way though.

"Catalina invited her younger sister to dinner too."

"She'd be a good match though for you, right?"

I shake my head in firm negation. "Lottie is too young, impetuous and selfish."

"A dangerous combination for the sister of the don's wife."

Surprised she gets it so easily, I nod. "I'm lucky Severu doesn't consider me the answer to his sister-in-law headache."

"She wouldn't be any less problematic as a capo's wife," Bianca says.

"Got that right," Pietro mutters.

They're both right. And Severu is savvy enough to know it.

"If I wasn't here, your mom might get in on the matchmaking too," Bianca guesses. "That woman wants grandchildren. "But she's too polite to trip another woman and watch you land on top of her when you have a date."

Neither Pietro, nor I stifle our laughter at this assessment. That is my mother in a nutshell.

"You got to know mamma very well in a single afternoon."

"She's pretty open about what she wants, and that's you married."

My mother is in fact *not* open around people outside the family. That she was so open with Bianca surprises me.

That Bianca figured mamma out from whatever she did share doesn't. "You're good at reading people."

"Sometimes," Bianca says, like she has memories of bad judgment calls about people in the past.

"Who hurt you?" I ask.

"Too many people."

"Do not fall for me," I warn her, though the words taste like ash on my tongue. "I don't want to be one of them."

"You're driving into conceited territory there, capo."

"I like it better when you call me your capo."

"Both you and your sister have a hard time sticking to a lane. Is it a family trait, or something? You don't want me to fall for you, but you want me to claim you. That's fine for sex talk, but bordering on delulu outside the bedroom."

She's absolutely right. It still pisses me off.

"While you are living in my home, you are mine and I am your capo."

"Dream on, caveman."

Pietro cough-laughs again, reminding me he's there. How the fuck did I forget, for even a second, that her bodyguard was in the elevator with us?

There's no time to answer her sass before the elevator dings and the doors slide open to Severu and Catalina's foyer. Stepping in front of Bianca so she can't exit, I shove my friend out of the elevator and push the button to close the doors.

Pietro's guffaws of laughter echo off the doors as they close.

I pull the button that stops the elevator from moving and then press my thumb against the print scanner beside it, effectively creating a locked room for privacy.

Spinning to face Bianca, I am determined to get her to admit she is mine.

She's got a point, genius. You are crossing lanes like a racecar driver making for the outside track.

And like that driver, I am fucking determined to cross the finish line as the winner.

Bianca's arms are crossed, lifting her beautiful tits framed by a sweetheart neckline in mouthwatering display. She's wearing the black dress tonight. More modest than the blue one I convinced her to wear last night with its lowcut neckline and spaghetti straps, this one is still sexy as hell.

Too sexy. A trash bag would be too sexy on this woman.

"Staying on the elevator defeats the purpose of us actually going to dinner at your don's home," she drolly points out.

"You are not stepping off this elevator while you are pretending to believe you are not mine."

"Uh...this thing..." She waives her hand between the two of us. "It's temporary, dude. You said so yourself."

"As long as it lasts, no other man touches you."

"That's not the problem you seem to think it is." Her eyeroll questions my intelligence. "I don't like being touched."

"You like my hands on you." But I notice how she avoids close proximity with others.

"You're the exception." She gives a disgruntled sigh. "I don't know why, but you are."

"Don't sound so happy about it."

"You're a freaking capo in the Cosa Nostra. Of course, I'm not happy about it. There's no future for us, no place our lives meet and stay connected."

"What if there was?" What the fuck am I saying?

She doesn't latch onto my words like a lot of women would though.

Sadness flashes briefly in her pretty eyes before she dispels it. "There isn't. We both know it. In eighteen months, I finally get my degree and I'm leaving New York. In two months, or sooner, you forget about me altogether."

"Are you saying you are going to forget me?"

"I'm not saying anything."

"Which means you won't." It had better mean that.

"Don't get a big head. It's not every day a woman ends up in the bed of a mobster. It's pretty unforgettable."

"Fuck that. I'm not just any made man. I am *your fucking capo*."

"We've only known each other thirteen days." She's still arguing.

And I won't fucking have it.

I step forward until I am a hair's breadth from her banging body. "Say it. Or I will fuck you against the wall of this elevator until you're screaming it."

"Can't do that yet. The plastic surgeon would yell at you for messing up his work."

"That supercilious fucker has too much instinct for self-preservation to yell at me about anything." But she's right. I'm not fucking her against a wall. Yet. "And you are too damn smart not to know that I'll have you yelling *capo mio* loud enough for them to hear in the penthouse if you don't say it."

"Stop it! *Ho detto basta*." She pounds the side of her fist against my sternum. "Are you trying to break my heart?"

I have no answer for that. Not two minutes ago, I told this woman not to fall for me, so I don't hurt her. But there is nothing I want more than for her to go head over heels for me.

No woman has touched my heart since Monica and now I want to own Bianca's. No matter what is best for her. Or my mafia.

Cazzo.

Grabbing her curled up hand, I gently unfurl her fingers and press her now flattened hand over my heart. "What if we don't put an expiration date on it? What if we just see where this goes?"

"Can a capo do that? See where it goes? I thought you had to marry for the good of the family. For heirs and other medieval crap like that." She's glaring at me like I'm the one who made the rules.

But I'm not that man. I'm the man, who for the second time in my life, is considering breaking them. For her.

"I'm not talking about marriage." Yet.

But I'm not letting her go. Not today. Not a week from now. Not two months from now when she's fully healed and can go back to work.

And you can fuck her into the wall.

Maybe not ever.

"Marriage should be the furthest thing from my mind." Bianca's nose squishes in disgust. "We were complete strangers two weeks ago. This is ridiculous."

"Pretending there's nothing real between us, no matter how quickly it developed, is more ridiculous." I know what I feel, and I know that I'm not alone.

"I'm not."

"You are. I have too, but that ends now." I'm not falling alone.

"Salvatore," she sighs my name like a prayer.

I cup her nape and squeeze. "Admit that I am yours."

She keeps her lips together, silently refusing.

Leaning down, I kiss her. At first her lips are immobile, but as I flirt at the seam of her mouth with my tongue, she makes a soft little sound and lets me in.

I devour her mouth until we are both panting and then I lift my head just enough to speak against her lips. "Say it, *brava ragazza mia.*"

Her breath hitches.

"*Io sono tua.* You know it."

"You're *my capo,*" she says with a gusty sigh, trying to sound fed up with me, but the words hold weight and she knows it.

"And you are mine. "

"Yes." She kisses me like she can't stop herself and then ruins it with her next words. "For now."

"For as long as we want it to last," I promise her.

She shakes her head, but she doesn't argue with me again.

"Are you two coming out?" Severu's voice comes over the elevator speakers. "Or are you staying in there all night? We have guestrooms if that's what you need."

Stronzo.

Bianca groans and her forehead lands against my sternum. "I can't believe this."

"Be careful," I admonish her. "You've got a healing wound there."

"I know." She looks up at the ceiling where the speaker is. Does she see the camera as well? "Can he hear us? Has he been listening this whole time?"

"I can hear you now, Miss Gemelli," Severu says. "But no one has been listening in on your *conversation.*"

"He thinks we've been in here having sex," Bianca whispers to me, horrified.

"We haven't been fucking," I inform my cousin, trying to make her feel better.

Severu makes a sound that might be amusement. "Noted."

He jokes more since he married Catalina. By more, I mean at all.

My statement and Severu's agreement should make Bianca happy but now she's scowling at me while she tries to push away from me, her cheeks bright red.

I'm not going anywhere just yet.

I squeeze the back of her neck again. "Remember who your man is when you meet Miceli."

Women fall all over themselves to be with him. God knows why. His charm is a thin veneer over a stone-cold killer every bit as ruthless as any other man in our family.

Bianca's gaze softens and she whispers, *"Il mio lui,"* before pushing my suit jacket aside to press a kiss over my heart.

The word *sempre* is heavy on the tip of my tongue but I hold it back. Barely. I cannot claim her forever.

Yet.

CHAPTER 48

BIANCA

My thoughts are spinning while I am introduced to the rest of the De Luca family.

Salvatore wants to be *my capo* which is not the same thing as merely being a Cosa Nostra capo. He wants, no *insists* on me laying claim to him.

He wants to see where this thing goes.

He said he wasn't talking about marriage. He didn't say *yet*, but I heard it whispered between us, a silent word that we both refused to voice.

This is so messed up.

"Pleased to meet you," I say by rote to Don De Luca when we are introduced.

Incredibly handsome, he gives off an aura of menace that would terrify me if it weren't for the way he looks at his wife, Catalina. Like she is the sun, the moon and the stars all in one beautiful package.

He does not invite me to call him Severu and studies me like a bug under the microscope. I would probably fidget under his intense scrutiny if my mind wasn't so occupied with my conversation with Salvatore in the elevator.

Still, I'm relieved when he, his brother, Miceli, Salvatore, and his dad leave to talk in private. Big Sal De Luca seems about as impressed with me as his daughter.

Speaking of, where is Nerissa? Isn't she joining this family dinner?

The don's mother, Aria De Luca is good friends with Ilaria and those two are chatting on the far side of the luxurious Art Deco living room.

Pietro stands aloof near the entrance to the room, his eyes scanning back and forth like there could be a credible threat in the don's home. He's not alone in his diligence though. No less than two other mafia soldiers have similar stances around the room.

The don is just a little over-protective of his wife.

She and her sister seem happy to include me in their conversation. Though it's pretty much the Lottie show, with her talking about her adventures at culinary school while Catalina (who did insist I call her by her first name) and I listen.

I don't mind because I'm still playing that elevator conversation over in my head. Word by confusing and heart wrenching word.

Salvatore went from telling me not to fall for him to demanding I admit that he is *my* capo. And the most messed up thing about it is how much I wanted to say the words, how good it felt to tell him I am his.

Che palle.

"Excuse me," I interrupt Lottie's lecture about a new cooking technique she learned this week . "Where is the bathroom?"

"I'll show you," Catalina says before her sister can answer.

Even though Catalina is only a smidge shorter than my five-feet-four-inches, she's wearing ballet flats. I'm in three-inch heels, so I'm half a head taller, but her curves are a little more pronounced. Not that I'm slender by any stretch, but dancing keeps my muscles more toned than an average woman of my size.

She also has one of the kindest dispositions I have ever encountered, which shows itself in her words on the way to the guest bathroom.

"I'm sorry," she says for the second time after I told her not to worry in response to the first. "I didn't know Salvatore was in a relationship. If I had,

I wouldn't have invited Car— I mean Lottie. She doesn't like being called Carlotta anymore."

"He said you were hoping to get them together."

Catalina winces. "I just worry about her. My sister is not exactly my husband's favorite person."

"Why?" I ask. "She seems nice."

"She can be, but she's also the woman who left him standing at the altar."

I feel my eyes grow wide, my own spinning thoughts forgotten for a second. "He was supposed to marry her? But she's younger than me."

I slap my hand over my mouth. I should not have said that.

Catalina's laugh is like tinkling bells and it makes me want to laugh too. "He's the Genovese don. She's the most beautiful mafia princess of our generation. Our father was his consigliere. It all made sense at the time."

"Nope. Still not getting it. Your sister is no more beautiful than you are. And I mean it's pretty obvious he's so into you, other women don't exist for him."

Catalina blushes, but smiles. "The feeling is mutual."

I can't help the little squiggle of envy that slithers through my brain. If my father had been a different man, a loyal mafioso, Salvatore and I could have something like Catalina and the don.

Maybe. Probably. Oh, I don't know.

She leaves me to it outside the surprisingly small bathroom for such a spacious home. I suppose with all the bathrooms attached to bedrooms; the guest toilet doesn't need to be that big.

I close the door before plopping down to sit on the closed toilet lid. I need a minute. Maybe ten.

I look up and realize this is one of those bathrooms where you can see your face and shoulders in the vanity mirror while sitting on the commode.

Like yesterday morning, I find myself looking intently at my reflection, but there is no Salvatore behind me now. No sexy view of us together.

It's just me.

Bianca Gemelli. *Bianca Russo.*

My red hair may be the exact same shade as my sister's, our features identical and our bodies so similar, it would be hard for our mom to tell us apart at first glance, but my life is nothing like Bea's.

She's the acknowledged daughter of a wealthy socialite married to a minor politician. I am the hidden daughter, left behind when our mom decided I was too much like her mafia husband to take me with her.

Bea might be my twin, but as far as the rest of the world knows, she's an only child.

The only other people, besides my mom and sister, who knew she was a twin are dead.

If Salvatore and I stay together, I have to tell him though. About Bea. About what I did to protect her. About what happened to me later?

Is this the real source of my refusal to even consider a future with the capo?

My stomach twists. What happens when he finds out my secrets?

There's so much about me he does not know.

How angry will he be when he learns that I've been lying to him about being part of the mafia? If he can get past that, will he be able to stomach it when he finds out that my father was a rat?

Even if he can get past all that, will he reject me like my mother did when he learns I killed a man when I was thirteen?

Unlike my society mom, Salvatore has killed plenty of men and at least one woman. Maybe he can deal with that part of my past. I can't apologize for it because nine years later, I still feel no remorse for killing the man trying to assault my sister.

Telling him about what happened when I was sixteen is worse though. The shame is not mine. Didn't Mr. Ruhnke say that over and over again? And all the books I read trying to get a handle on the dark shadow inside me said the same. To reject the shame. To refuse to own it.

And still, this ball of humiliation and pain is always there, deep down inside me.

No matter how much I don't want to, I have to tell him about it. Isn't that what you do when you love someone? Tell them everything.

I look into my own troubled gaze.

Girl, you can't fall in love in a couple of weeks. That's not the way it works. No matter what you think you're feeling, it's not love.

For once my inner voice is talking sense and I don't want to listen. It *feels* like love. All consuming. Terrifying. Impossible to ignore.

If he loves me, he'll accept my past like I accept his present. Right?

Only, wanting to possess me is not the same thing as love, is it? Hard enough to believe I have feelings this deep after such a short time, how can I even begin to think the brutal capo shares them?

A brisk knock sounds at the door.

SALVATORE

Severu's office has subtle changes since he married Catalina a year ago.

A stack of Catalina's composition notebooks sits on a small table kitty-corner to Severu's desk. To Domencico's crew's dismay, she still insists on keeping her records analog. She has her own office, but these two are sickeningly inseparable.

There is even an armchair behind the desk beside where my don sits. It's for his wife whenever she is in the room and *not* in his lap. Which when it is just family, is pretty damn rare.

For the first time, I get it.

"Everything still going smoothly with the bar properties?" Severu asks leaning on his giant desk facing the rest of us.

The rest of us make up a semicircle around him.

Since I'm the one giving a report, I'm in the center facing my cousin. "The transfer of ownership for the three New York city properties have gone through. The other two have been filed with their respective county clerks and are awaiting approval."

"No interference from Stellar Holdings?"

"Juniper didn't wake up until after all the papers had been filed. He did so with three women in his bed and hasn't tried to use his phone yet or leave the house."

We've had his cell phone jammed since my people picked him up yesterday. The jammer drains the phone's battery, so it looks like it's dead because he forgot to charge it. A side effect of his pre-function cocktail is Juniper's memory will be too fuzzy to know the truth.

"What about the escort Lombard sent with him?"

"Nerissa dumped her phone in a full margarita pitcher once she passed out last night." That phone is toast.

"Good thinking," my father praises my sister.

I agree with a nod. Nerissa is hella smart.

"And the jammer on Juniper's phone?"

"Now that the paperwork is filed it is set to self-delete once he sets his device to charge."

"I'm surprised Matthew Lombard hasn't sent people to check on him."

"No reason to. The GPS on the woman's phone still registers at the house and the false GPS signal Domenico's people set up for Juniper's phone does too."

Miceli frowns. "It's still sloppy."

I agree.

"Lorenzo called me." Severu looks at me expectantly.

The little bitch went running to the don and tattled on me like the rat he is.

I cross my arms, meet my cousin's gaze and say nothing. If he's looking for an apology for my actions, it's not happening.

"He says you were very disrespectful when he came to Amuni," my father drops into the silence between me and Severu.

I flick a glance toward my father. "I'm sure Nerissa already told you, but he followed one of my people into the ladies' room and accosted her."

Papà doesn't even flinch when he nods his acquiescence to my accusation. "Still, your reaction was not respectful."

"I should respect that pile of shit?" Everyone in this room is aware that Severu has Lorenzo under investigation for skimming the drug profits. "He's lucky I did not kill him. If he tries to touch her again, I will slit his throat."

Miceli barks a laugh. "It's Severu all over again. No woman is going to turn me into a Neanderthal like you two."

Severu frowns at his brother. "Good luck with that. You share my DNA."

"But not your obsession for your wife."

"If you did, I would have to kill you."

Another joke from my serious cousin? Something has put him into a good mood tonight.

"You know what I mean, brother. I will never obsess over a woman like you do Catalina."

"Never is a dangerous word you could end up eating," Severu warns.

Miceli just shakes his head.

But my father is looking at me with both anger and concern. It has been more than a decade, but I remember that look.

I put my hand up. "Do not tell me you would do any differently if he tried to maul mamma."

"Oh how the mighty have fallen," Miceli says pityingly.

My father stares at me in blatant disbelief. "Are you saying this nobody, this outsider you have known less than two weeks, is your woman? Monica worked you for six months before you were serious enough about her to ask Enzu's permission to tell her the truth about your role in *la famiglia*."

The way my father says *worked you* would have made me check myself in the past. Not now. Yes, I was a fool when I was twenty. I'm not one now.

Bianca is not Monica.

Severu doesn't speak, there's a question in his silence though.

I have a choice to make. I can back down, or I go with my gut. Backing down has never been my strong suit. It's not even in my deck of cards.

My gut it is. "She is mine."

"Are you saying you are not open to being the husband in the alliance deal with Shaughnessy?" Severu studies me intently.

Miceli is supposed to marry the Irishman's niece. I do not know what Severu wants me to say right now. But for the first time in my life as a made man, what my don wants is not my top priority.

I am not giving Bianca up.

Miceli glares at his brother. "I'm the sacrificial lamb in that scenario. The deal is done."

"You two fight like cats and dogs," Severu tells his brother. "Maybe Salvatore won't piss her off so easily."

"She is my fiancée," Miceli grinds out between clenched teeth, his hands fisted at his sides with white knuckle intensity.

"I am not marrying her," I insert before the argument between the don and underboss comes to blows.

Both men stare at me in surprise. My father's mouth gapes like a fish.

I just refused my don. Point blank.

Instead of jumping down my throat, Severu nods and then turns a glare on his brother. "Figure your shit out with Róise then. This marriage is supposed to cement an alliance, not start a war."

CHAPTER 49

BIANCA

"Bianca? Let me in." Salvatore's deep tones are muffled by the thick wooden door, but I have no trouble understanding him.

"I am using the bathroom, Salvatore. Go away."

"You have been in there a long time."

"What are you? The bathroom police? I'll be out in a minute."

Now that I need to rush, I have to pee. Of course I do. It only takes a minute and then I wash my hands.

When I open the door, I'm not even a little bit surprised to find Salvatore leaning against the wall opposite, waiting for me.

I roll my eyes. "Seriously? You're going from cheesy pickup lines to stalking? You have zero game, Salvatore De Luca."

"I have all the game you need, *bella mia*." His expression intent, he pushes away from the wall.

I shake my head and sidestep, knowing if I back up into the bathroom it is game over. "No way. You are not getting me all wound up before we have to sit down to dinner with your family."

"I'll make sure you are sated when we join them."

My ladybits are shouting *hell, yeah* while my brain is yelling *don't you do it.*

"There you two are. Everyone else has gone up to dinner," Ilaria says. "Your father was wondering where you were, Salvatore."

"Was he?" My lover sounds less than impressed.

A minute later, I find out what Ilaria meant by *gone up*. Two rooftop gardens in one week? How freaking wealthy is the De Luca family?

"Where is Nerissa?" I ask Salvatore as he pulls a chair out for me at the table between his mother and Miceli.

"She's working tonight," Ilaria answers while Salvatore taps his cousin's shoulder.

With his fist. "Move, Miceli, this is my seat."

"Catalina didn't assign seats tonight," the other man says, reaching for his glass of wine.

Salvatore snatches it up first, walks around the table and trades it with an empty glass at the only other unoccupied spot. "I'm assigning them. Move your ass."

"Salvatore, you cannot speak to the don's underboss that way," Ilaria admonishes her son.

"That's rich coming from you," Salvatore retorts with some bite while glaring at his cousin.

"Miceli, come and sit by me." The unoccupied spot is beside Catalina. "I want you here when me and Severu make our announcement."

Announcement? The don's wife glows with happiness and I'm pretty sure the whole table knows what's coming next.

Miceli jumps from his chair though and circles the table to sit down beside Catalina. "Have you got a bun in the oven, *cara?*"

"Don't call my wife endearments," Severu orders. Then he smiles at Catalina before turning to look at the rest of his family at the table. "We're expecting the next little De Luca around Christmas."

I do some quick calculations in my head. That would make the don's wife about two months pregnant.

What would it be like to have so much confidence in the future, you were willing to announce your pregnancy before passing the three-month mark when the chances for miscarriage drop significantly?

I'd probably wait until I was showing and couldn't hide it anymore.

Everyone congratulates the couple, including me. We drink sparking grape juice because Severu won't have everyone drinking champagne while his wife abstains. A surprisingly sweet move from the scary don.

It's surreal to be here for this important family moment. The De Lucas are all welcoming though. Well, except Iliaria's husband, Big Sal. He watches me like he's expecting me to start taking notes for the FEDs.

Salvatore keeps one hand on my thigh while he eats with the other and whether I belong with his family, or not, I feel like I belong with him.

Dessert has just been served when one of the don's security people comes up and says something in his ear.

A mask drops over Don De Luca's face, taking away every speck of humanity from his expression. "Don Caruso had another stroke." He fixes me with a deadly stare. "That information will not go beyond those at this table."

I nod in instant agreement, unable to speak under the weight of his look.

Ilaria and Aria gasp, giving Severu identical looks of concern. Is he close to the other don. Wait, isn't Don Caruso the godfather?

If he dies, it's not just the New York Five Families that lose their godfather. It's the entire freaking United States Cosa Nostra.

Che palle. The city of New York, the whole fucking country, has no idea how fragile peace between the Families will be in the days ahead. Does Salvatore know who is likely to take Don Caruso's place?

I don't ask.

He's too busy to talk to me, constantly on his phone. But he insists on taking me back to the penthouse. He doubles the security team both around the building and in the apartment.

Once we are in the penthouse, he grasps my shoulder, meeting my eyes. "Do not leave the penthouse for any reason."

A snarky reply about how that's no different than the past two weeks is on the tip of my tongue, but I swallow it back. Now is not the time for snark.

"I won't," I promise.

"Brava regazza mia." He kisses me. "Go upstairs and stay there for the rest of the night."

I nod.

"You do not go outside."

He is seriously concerned about my safety.

"No going outside," I promise.

He kisses me again and then he's gone.

I'm surprised when Pietro doesn't leave with him.

"I thought you were head of his security," I say to Pietro, who is busy texting on his phone.

He looks up. "I am."

"Shouldn't you be with him then?"

"He wants me here."

Protecting me?

"Yes." Pietro smiles at my surprised look. "You asked it out loud. In Italian by the way."

I nod, too flummoxed by how important Salvatore is making me feel with his choices.

The feelings of love I've been fighting shatter the last defenses around my heart.

It doesn't make sense, but I love him.

SALVATORE

Two days after the dinner at Severu's, Pietro texts me to say he'll be waiting in my office when I get back to the penthouse. So, instead of going directly to my bed and Bianca like I want to, I head to my office first.

Pietro is sitting in one of the chairs facing my desk, doing something on his phone.

Veering to the drink's cabinet, I ask, "What do you have for me?"

He didn't tell me why he wanted to meet, but I assume it is because he finished Bianca's background check.

"Everything has been quiet. No problems at the clubs and no attempts to gain access to your penthouse."

"And Bianca?" I pour myself two fingers of my favorite whiskey and take a sip.

It slides down my throat with a smooth burn.

"She doesn't have any social media accounts. Her high school records only list Daryl Ruhnke as her guardian and his contact information. No parents are listed."

It's a little odd, but not completely unexpected, since both are dead. Ruhnke must have gotten himself assigned as her guardian. "What else?"

"Her work history includes a bar, Pitiful Princess and Amuni. No one had anything bad to say about her at the bar or strip club."

"You didn't talk to Nerissa then." My lips twist wryly.

Pietro shakes his head. "Yeah, no. I did talk to Ugo and some dancer named, Piper. He said she's worked there the longest and knows the other dancers the best."

"What about Bianca's friend Candi?"

"She told me to go fuck myself and then went straight to Ugo to tell him that some creep, as in me, was asking personal questions about the dancers and wanted me thrown out."

Amusement alleviates some of my exhaustion. "She's a firecracker, just like Bianca."

"That's one way to put it." He blows out a breath. "Before she went ballistic on me, she confirmed Bianca doesn't use social media."

Pietro's dry tone suggests that the words Candi used to tell him that weren't friendly. "She wasn't impressed with your charm?"

"She told me that Bianca doesn't do social media to keep creeps like me at bay, but I think it's your charms she's the least impressed with. Candi didn't tell me to fuck off until I explained I'm in charge of your security and doing a background check on your girlfriend is part of my job."

"She's offended on Bianca's behalf. They're tight." I bet there are some less than flattering texts about me on Bianca's phone right now.

"Queens college is out for the summer," Pietro continues. "I can have men track down students and professors from the business school, but it will take time."

"It's not a priority." His crew is stretched thin between guarding me and keeping the penthouse secure right now.

While the godfather lingers on the edge of death, I'll be doing a lot of traveling to meet with other capos to solidify Severu's support for godfather with other Cosa Nostra syndicates.

Being both capo and my don's cousin gives me a unique position we are taking advantage of.

"Did you follow up with Ruhnke's family?"

"Both sons and the daughter-in-law refused to talk to me."

That gives me pause. "One of his sons was happy to air their grievances with Nerissa."

"He stonewalled me completely."

"Check into the will through the probate office. That was Nerissa's next step."

"Okay, but why does it matter if the old man left Bianca money?" Pietro asks.

"Any red flags?" I ask.

"None. But I'll feel better when I can identify her parents. That information will be in the registrar's office at QC."

"Now is not the time to break into a university." The city is on edge with the godfather's imminent demise and we need to keep a low profile.

"Do you want me to ask Domenico's guys to use their facial recognition software to dig deeper?"

"No. We'll keep this inhouse. She's my girlfriend, not my fiancée." As soon as we bring in Severu's people, he and my father get access to their discoveries.

I've had enough of papà's interference in my personal life to last me a lifetime.

CHAPTER 50

BIANCA

My heart leaps into my throat when I read Candi's text.

Candi: *Your asshole rich boyfriend sent his security guy around to ask questions about you. Are you sure you like this guy?*

My stomach twists. This is not what I wanted to wake up to this morning. It doesn't help that Salvatore isn't beside me in bed.

Did he find out who I really am? Is he going to kick me out of his apartment and life because my father was a rat?

"I assume by the expression on your face, your friend texted to tell you Pietro is running a background check on you," Salvatore's voice cuts through my spiraling panic.

Jerking my head up, our eyes meet. His are not filled with loathing or anything like that. They gleam with heated desire sending a spear of want directly to my core.

He stands there completely naked, his hair still wet from the shower, his penis already semi-erect. He does not look like a man who just found out secrets about his lover that disturb him.

"Why? Is it because of what your sister told you?"

"It's because you are living in my home."

"So why not run the background check before you had Pietro kidnap me and bring me here?"

"The kidnapping was all Pietro's idea."

That's not an answer, but then maybe Salvatore doesn't have one he wants to share. He *should* have had me investigated before bringing me to his home. The fact he didn't is more proof that whatever this thing is between us, it's more than sex.

And his judgment is just as affected as mine.

"So you say," I tease.

"You can tell Candi that Pietro didn't find any skeletons in your closet."

"You assume there are some to find?"

"We all have secrets."

I nod. Because, truth. "If things get serious between us, I'll share mine. Will you share yours?"

"Yes."

"Okay then." That's crisis averted. For now.

But why should I tell him about my parents or the most painful moments in my past if we aren't serious? As long as this thing between us is temporary, my lips are sealed.

So are his, apparently, because Salvatore is done talking. He wants to do something else instead.

If our relationship doesn't last, I am going to miss the pleasure he gives me.

Almost as much as I will miss him.

~ ~ ~

A few days later, I acknowledge it's not just Salvatore I will miss when I leave here. But Rosa and Ilaria as well. Maybe even Nerissa.

"Stop daydreaming, *dolce ragazza*, or that plate is going to end up as thin as paper on one side and swollen like it has the mumps on the other," Rosa's voice scolds me, bringing me back to the present.

I grimace at the misshapen mess of clay on my wheel.

"Do not look like that," Ilaria admonishes me. "No one throws the perfect plate their first time."

Remembering her pot in Salvatore's conservatory, it's hard to believe the same hands that created it make the beautiful pieces she does now.

So, she must be right.

"Okay, no giving up. But I do think I have to restart," I say ruefully.

We are working in Ilaria's ceramics studio. She and Big Sal have a large apartment one floor down in Salvatore's building, coincidentally on the same floor as Nerissa's place.

While they only use the apartment when they are staying in the city for something, Nerissa lives in hers full time. Ilaria and Big Sal have a mansion on Long Island, where they raised their children and still live.

Since the night of the dinner at the don's, Ilaria and her husband have been staying in their city apartment for safety reasons.

Rosa is thrilled because she gets to spend more time with her friend. They're both trying to teach me how to cast ceramics.

"Are you sure I can't just learn how to paint the pieces?" I ask for the umpteenth time.

But this is really not my skill set.

"You will learn by doing," Rosa encourages me.

The sound of Big Sal's voice booming from the other room makes me flinch.

Ilaria pats my arm. "Do not be afraid of my husband."

"That's easy for you to say. Every time I see him, he looks like he wants to squash me like a bug." And he shares enough features with Salvatore that the older man's disapproving looks are really unnerving.

"Sal has always struggled with the balance between duty and love for family," Ilaria says with a sigh. "He wants our son to marry..."

She doesn't finish her thought, but she doesn't have to.

I blow out a breath and start pounding my clay back into a ball. "Someone who doesn't have pole dancer on her resume."

Ilaria shrugs.

That's one of the things I like about her. She's diplomatic, but honest. With family almost brutally so. That she feels comfortable being this honest with me is a compliment.

I think it's time I returned the favor.

I've been trying to think how to approach this since the first time we met, but it never seems to be the right moment. The reminder that Salvatore and I don't have a future, *can't* have a future, allows me to say what needs saying.

And maybe piss off two of the nicest women I have ever known, but who sport a severe blind spot where Salvatore is concerned.

"You're not as proud of your son being capo as Mr. De Luca is?" I ask Ilaria. "There's someone you think would be better? Or maybe you think he's too young?" This I direct at Rosa.

"Why would you ask such a thing?" Rosa demands, her tone severe, her expression filled with shock.

"No one could fill his father's shoes better than Salvatore," Ilaria says, throwing her hands out in a gesture of vehemence and sending drops of clay colored water flying.

I wipe the water from my cheek, smearing more clay on and roll my eyes at myself.

"Oh, that's it then." I start spinning my plate again, guiding the clay to spread slowly. "You expect him to continue to be a mouthpiece for Big Sal?"

"Of course not. I am proud of my son. He is his own man."

I shrug one shoulder. "If you say so."

"I do say so. Why would you imply otherwise?"

"You undermine him. That first day, you doubted him when he told you I wasn't in the penthouse under duress."

"My son can be brutal."

"So can your husband," I say, certain Salvatore learned how to be a mafia capo from the father who raised him.

"Yes, but..." Ilaria shakes her head. "Never mind."

"Is this about the lover he killed?" I ask.

"Dio mio," Rosa breathes.

"Salvatore told you about Monica?" Ilaria asks, sounding shaken.

Shoot, I shouldn't have brought that up. I'm pretty sure Ilaria would be furious with Nerissa, just like Salvatore was if she finds out her daughter almost spilled the beans.

"I didn't know her name," I say, to put the older women on the defensive. "You know there are rumors about the most brutal capo in the city."

I'm taking a shot in the dark, but the expression on both women's faces confirms my guess.

"If you have heard the rumors and that awful title," Ilaria says sadly. "Then you know that my son's sense of morality is skewed."

"Huh." I stop my wheel, giving up on the lumpy clay. "Who exactly ordered Salvatore to kill her?"

Ilaria looks uncomfortable. "You know I cannot answer that."

"Let me take a guess. His don. Or maybe it was his father. But you think *Salvatore* is the one with a skewed moral compass?"

"I..." Ilaria's voice fades.

Rosa stops her wheel and studies me. "Why are you bringing this up?"

"Because I care about Salvatore, and it hurts him the way two of the most important women in his life doubt him. You are forcing him to either distance himself from you or..." This time it is my voice that trails off.

"Be seen as weak," Nerissa says from the doorway.

I acknowledge her words with a nod.

"Maybe that's what you want." I decide to drive the point home. "You're still training your son to be the emotionless, ruthless man you believe he should be."

Ilaria's protests are drowned out by Big Sal's voice. "You don't know what you're talking about."

I meet his furious gaze. "Yes, I do. My nonna used to tell me I couldn't blame my father for his weakness. That in trying to train it out of him, my grandfather destroyed the good parts of my dad that would have been strong enough to compensate for the pride and the greed."

They don't know my father was mafia, but it's a concept that plays out in other families outside the life too.

"Do you want to destroy your son's ability to love? I get you don't want him to fall in love with me, a nobody in your world, but would you condemn him to a life without the love you and your wife share?" I can't believe I'm asking this.

That I'm challenging the Genovese consigliere.

"You have to stop judging him for killing her, mamma," Nerissa says. "That doesn't make Salvatore a monster. It makes him loyal. To the man you love."

Big Sal makes a sound of grief.

Does he regret pushing his son to do what he did?

I don't know the details, but I guessed that killing the woman he was in a relationship with wasn't Salvatore's idea. He *can* be brutal, I have no doubt. But that was something he learned. He wasn't born with it.

There's too much caring in him for that to be the case.

"I think you might be very good for my son." The words are startling, but who says them makes me breathless with shock.

It's Big Sal. Ilaria is nodding in agreement, her eyes shiny with tears.

If only I could believe they might feel the same later, when emotions aren't running high.

"That's enough drama. You've given us something to think about, Bianca. But now it is time to get back to making that plate. You aren't leaving this studio until you've cast at least two of the same size."

I stare at her in horror and everyone else laughs, breaking the tension.

CHAPTER 51

SALVATORE

Three Weeks Later

It has been a busy and rough few weeks, but when Don Caruso breathes his last, Severu will have the support he needs to step into the old man's role. Part of that certainty is the result of gifting the bar property in Gamino territory to their don.

Henry Caruso hasn't made a peep about throwing his hat into the ring. If he did, it wouldn't do him any good. Not after we informed the other Families he was working with another Cosa Nostra syndicate outside of New York to buy property in our territories.

Breaking longstanding treaties comes with heavy consequences. The Lucchese capos will not allow him to become don upon his uncle's death either. Jockeying for the position is already beginning among them.

The Cosa Nostras outside New York have all agreed to count Don Caruso's endorsement of Severu as that family's vote for the next godfather.

The Boston don has already offered reparations for Matthew Lombard's attempt to buy property in another syndicate's territory. Severu demanded a guarantee from the family that Matthew will never be made capo, much less don to maintain peace between our two syndicates.

The don and his capos all swore on their oaths as made men.

Matthew Lombard's power and reputation within his own syndicate is gone because of his failed attempt to help his cousin become the next godfather.

Try to fuck with a De Luca and you get fucked. Right up the ass without lube.

Which Lorenzo Ricci is going to find out soon enough. Severu's investigation into the capo is done and Lorenzo's death is a matter of when, not if.

When the corrupt capo's name comes up on my phone's display, I narrow my eyes at the timing.

I swipe to answer. "Lorenzo, to what do I owe this interruption?"

"Always the smart ass, aren't you Little Sal?"

"The next time you call me that, I will cut out your tongue," I tell him conversationally.

He gasps and then coughs. "I didn't call to trade insults," he says finally.

It wasn't an insult. It wasn't even a threat. It was a promise and if he knew me at all, he would be aware of that.

"Why did you call?" I ask, what little patience I have for the man already used up.

"Is it true you moved that little whore into your penthouse?"

I clamp my jaw so tight, my teeth grind. The only woman living in my home is Bianca. "Call her that again and I will let you choke on your own blood after I cut out your tongue."

"It's true then? You moved her in? When my mistress told me last night that you took up with a stripper from Pitiful Princess, I didn't believe her. What are you thinking?" he practically whines. "You don't date strippers. You don't even go to your own clubs."

I did with Bianca. Not that I was interested in what was happening on the stage. Why would I be when I had her in my bed?

"I am thinking that who I have in my home is none of your fucking business." And if it took him this long to figure out Bianca is staying here, he's dangerously out of touch with what is happening in *la famiglia*.

"I'm sorry to have to be the one to tell you this." He sounds nervous, but not even remotely sorry. "But when I found out you had her living with you, I didn't have any choice."

I'm not listening to some bullshit story he's concocted to try to get me to kick her out so he can make his play for her. "Give it up, Lorenzo. Bianca is out of your league."

Pathetic loser. He thinks he's going to convince me to throw Bianca out so he can pursue her? Not happening.

"It's not like that," Lorenzo squawks. "I don't want to fuck her, but she's not who you think she is."

"I might believe you if I hadn't caught you trying to corner her in the women's bathroom at my own club."

"Her father was one of my most trusted soldiers," Lorenzo rushes on like I didn't say anything. "Until I found out he was a rat."

That's rich coming from the greedy piece of shit who has been embezzling mafia money for years.

Severu is beyond pissed it took us this long to figure it out. But between paying his soldiers way too little and moving more product than he reported, Lorenzo flew under the radar until last year.

"Her father is dead."

"I know. I killed him."

"I have no doubt you have executed your own soldiers." Probably to cover his tracks when they started asking questions. "But that's got nothing to do with Bianca's dad."

She would have told me if he had been murdered.

"I'm not lying." When someone has to tell you they aren't lying, they probably are. "Alberto Russo was part of my crew."

"Her name is Gemelli."

"She was born a Russo."

"Bullshit."

"I'm sending you proof."

How desperate is this guy to get his hands on my woman? For that alone, I will kill him. My cousin will have to deal with me being the one to mete out Lorenzo's punishment and death.

My phone dings. There are three texts from Lorenzo. All images.

The first is a screenshot of an employment record for Alberto Russo. According to the record, he was Lorenzo's bookkeeper until six years ago. His single dependent listed is Bianca Russo, daughter.

His ex-wife's name is not given, which would not happen in my files. Even though we don't keep centralized files on our people...that would be a FEDs wet dream come true...my records include all important family members. Including ex wives and husbands.

The only files we keep are legitimate employment records linking a capo's crew to his businesses. All of my people work for me, or one of my clubs, in an official capacity. Except Pietro and his team. Pietro owns a security company, and I am his only client. His team are on his payroll.

The next picture is of an urn holding cremated ashes on a dais at a funeral. The framed photo next to the urn is of a dark-haired man in a suit who looks vaguely familiar. A placard in front says, Alberto Russo with the year of his birth and death.

It's not uncommon to give a funeral for a rat, either as a way to spare the family grief, or to keep his death from looking suspicious. But more likely, the funeral was Lorenzo's way of not drawing attention to his supposed rat.

So, why draw that attention now?

Is he trying to set the dead bookkeeper up to be the fall guy in his organization? Does he realize Severu is on to him? There's no question that as his bookkeeper, Alberto Russo would have had to be complicit in the embezzlement or dead because he refused to be.

Six years in his job makes the former more likely.

But how does Lorenzo plan to explain the missing money and product from the past six years? Another conveniently dead patsy the capo will try to convince Severu was Russo's accomplice?

The last image is of a short memorial obituary that says Alberto Russo is survived by his daughter Bianca. The memorial obituary could be faked because it's not from a newspaper and I can't confirm its origin.

For that matter, all of this so-called proof could be faked. Although checking the death record for Alberto Russo wouldn't be difficult. Which means that the man really did die because even Lorenzo Ricci isn't stupid enough to lie to me about something I can check that easily.

Even if Roberto Russo had a daughter named Bianca, that doesn't mean it's my Bianca.

The dates fit and she speaks Italian fluently. You know she's way too accepting of our world for an outsider.

She said she wasn't part of the mafia.

No, you said that, and she didn't disagree.

Cazzo.

"All any of this proves is that you had a bookkeeper who died six years ago." His funeral doesn't prove he was a rat, or that Lorenzo killed him.

"It's Bianca. I'm telling you. When I saw her in Amuni that night, I recognized her right away."

"And then you accosted her?" I ask, letting the skepticism I feel coat my voice.

He called her *new meat*. I'm definitely cutting out his tongue.

"You got that all wrong. I was warning her off. I kicked her out of the family when I passed judgment on her father."

"How old was she?"

"A teenager. Couldn't make myself kill a kid even if that's what she deserved."

"Like fuck."

"I'm old school, Salvatore. We don't kill kids."

"You'd kill your own mother to get what you want."

He gasps, sounding genuinely shocked. "I would never, God rest her soul!"

So, his mother is a trigger for him. Good to know considering my plans for him later.

"Just ask her, Salvatore," Lorenzo stresses my full name. "Ask her what her father's name was."

"Get me a copy of her birth certificate and I might believe you." If he really was her father's capo, that shouldn't be any problem for him.

"You know Domenico's crew is busy with Severu's attempt at godfather right now."

It's not an attempt. Severu will be the next godfather. "It doesn't take a tech genius to order a birth certificate."

"I'm not your secretary. You get it yourself." Lorenzo disconnects the call.

Another thing to punish him for.

Dismissing him and his accusations about Bianca, I get back to work, but the conversation itches at the back of my brain. Has my lover been lying to me from the beginning? Hiding who she really is?

Why would she?

Maybe she thinks I would be *old school* like Lorenzo and blame her for her father's sins. But I judge people on their own merits. She should know that.

She should know me like I know her.

Do you really know her though?

I know she has secrets. Which she says she will tell me if our relationship becomes permanent. Reasonable. There are things I don't tell her now, that I would tell her if she was my wife.

My wife. I shake my head.

Am I ready to take that leap? Yes, everyone expects me to marry a woman who will bring benefit to the mafia, including me. But I am capo and no one, not even my don can force me to let Bianca go if I don't want to.

Every time we have sex, I give her a piece of my soul, something I thought had been destroyed long ago by Monica's betrayal. I would swear on my oath as a made man Bianca gives me a piece of hers too.

My feelings for her are so fucking powerful, they push everything else out. I haven't told her I love her, but I can't think of another label for the way I feel.

However, the last time I told a woman I loved her, I had to kill her hours later. That cured me of any desire to *fall in love* again. Love's a game for suckers.

What if I'm the biggest sucker of them all?

Because damn if I'm not in love with the enigmatic redhead. I need to know if Bianca is who I believe she is, or someone else. A liar.

My gut churning, I text Pietro.

"Get me a copy of Bianca's birth certificate," I say without any preamble when he answers.

CHAPTER 52

BIANCA

The feelings I grudgingly acknowledged the night the godfather had his stroke are stronger than ever. I'm pretty sure Salvatore is feeling them too. Even if neither of us has said the words.

I'm planning to. Tonight. Salvatore said he'd be home for dinner and I have plans for after.

Dr. Anders-Powell says my back is healed enough for the strenuous movements of participatory penetrative sex. That's how he put it, *participatory penetrative sex*. Apparently, there is a nonparticipatory kind where one partner does all the work and the other one lays there and counts the dust motes on the ceiling.

In the penthouse cleaned by maids overseen by the exacting Rosa, that number would be zero. But I have no intention of playing possum in bed. I love what Salvatore and I do together and I'm ready for more.

Salvatore is out of town more often than he's here lately, but we talk on the phone every day. And when he does manage to sleep in our bed, we pleasure each other with hands and mouths. And it is glorious.

I've taken his sex into my mouth and down my throat many times. He's eaten me out and pistoned his fingers in and out of me until I'm screaming his name. I'm confident I'm ready for the one act we haven't performed.

Because every fiber of my being craves his body's connection to mine.

I know Salvatore is waiting for the all-clear from the doctor to fuck me through the bed. Those are *his* words.

I want the final act those monsters stole from me. Consensual sex. Those are *my* words for it.

Tonight is the night.

SALVATORE

I am bone tired. If Bianca were not waiting for me at the penthouse, I would skip dinner and crash in one of Severu's guestrooms.

Ever since Lorenzo's call earlier, I've had a sense of dread, like time is running down on the clock of me and Bianca being together.

Even if I sleep like the dead tonight, I want her in my arms while I do it. Bianca's wounds have healed to the point I can spoon her at night, my front pressed right up against her back.

She sleeps more deeply when we're like that. So do I.

My beautiful houseguest still has nightmares sometimes, but it's not like it was at the hospital. Should I suggest she go to therapy? Find a therapist for her that I trust?

If it's what she needs, I don't care that it's not the mafia way.

When I get home, Bianca is waiting in the living room for me. Her eyes light up, like they do every time she sees me. She presses the button that turns off the TV and recesses it back into the ceiling before dropping the remote and jumping up from the couch.

"Salvatore!" She rushes toward me, eager and sweet.

Exhaustion forgotten, my cock fills with blood.

She's fucking sexy, wearing one of the dresses I bought her. I picked it out because the off the shoulder plunging neckline and short skirt looked like it would make for easy access to her luscious curves. What I didn't anticipate was how much of the curve of her inner breast would be on display.

The deep purple stretchy velvet barely covers her areolas and does nothing to disguise the way her nipples pop at the sight of me.

"You are never wearing that dress outside our home," I say, my voice guttural from the desire coursing through me.

She hooks her forefinger on the bottom of the V and tugs just a little. "Why not? Don't you like it?"

The sound that comes out of my throat is more animal than man and I do not fucking care.

Reaching out, I yank her to me and slam my lips down on hers. She opens for me immediately, allowing my tongue to spear inside like my cock is straining to do to her pussy.

We kiss until we're both breathing heavily.

I lift my head just enough to speak, our eyes locked. "You look beautiful and too damn tempting for anyone else to see you like this."

"You're the only one I want to tempt."

Alberto Russo's daughter, or not, this is my woman. I kiss her again until she squirms, trying to put space between us. While I allow it, I keep my arms around her.

"I helped Rosa make dinner," she says, her lips rosy and swollen from our kisses.

"Did you?"

Bianca nods. "It's one of my nonna's recipes. Rosa's is almost identical."

"Did you have fun comparing?" I ask, loathe to let her out of my arms, even to walk into the dining room.

So, I don't. Leaning down, I slide one arm under her legs and pick her up bridal style.

Her hands come up to cling around my neck and more lust surges through me at her immediate trust and acquiescence.

"Yes. She reminds me a lot of my nonna, though she's a lot younger."

"You miss her, don't you?"

Bianca never talks about anyone else in her family, but whenever she brings up her grandmother, it is with a smile.

"I do. When she died, I lost the only adult I could rely on."

"Were your parents already gone?"

"No." Bianca kisses the underside of my jaw. "I don't want to talk about people who aren't in my life anymore."

It's not the first time she's avoided discussing her parents, but it is the first time I wonder why. Not enough to push it right now. Instinct even deeper than what drives my inner thoughts tells me that if I do, I will regret finding out what I do not know.

Shoving aside thoughts triggered by a corrupt capo's words, I ask, "What do you want to do?"

Bianca has the formal dining room set up as an intimate oasis for us. Candlelight illuminates the single place setting at one end of the table.

"You've already eaten?" I tease, though I'm pretty sure I know her plan here.

"Nope."

She wants to eat off the same plate while sitting on my lap. We've done it a couple of times before, but always at my insistence. Because I crave her closeness. Now, that she's instigating the intimacy, I'm so turned on I will probably come from her squirming in my lap while we eat together from the same plate.

"You know, I'm not really hungry," I tell her. "For food."

Bianca's expression turns serious, all flirting gone. "I want you, Salvatore."

I spin on my heel to head out of the dining room.

She laughs and tugs the short hair at my nape. "Stop, caveman. Eat first, then sex. Nerissa told me you skipped lunch."

My sister and Bianca are slowly thawing toward each other. They aren't friends, but they aren't enemies either. Nerissa has admitted to me that Bianca's ideas for managing the dancers and sex workers are smart and well thought out.

They've been discussing the best way to implement changes since the first email.

"We can eat after." Do I carry Bianca upstairs or is tonight the night we christen the couch?

Bianca's breath speeds up, the scent of her arousal reaching my olfactory senses and increasing my own lust tenfold.

"No. Please, Salvatore. Let me take care of you."

"You are going to take care of me, *brava ragazza mia*."

"You promise to eat after?" she demands a hitch in her breathing.

"Prometto."

Leaning forward she buries her face in my neck and sucks on a spot with a direct connection to my dick.

The couch it is.

CHAPTER 53

BIANCA

S alvatore sits down and maneuvers me around to straddle his lap.

Panting with desire, I lean forward to kiss him, my lips already slightly parted. His mouth is open when our lips meet and our tongues clash, sliding against each other and sending zings of desire straight to my core.

Dio mio. I want this so bad.

He tugs me forward, spreading my legs wider. The hem of my dress slides up my thighs, bunching at my hips. My clitoris presses against the hard column of flesh trying to bust through his slacks.

I moan and rock my hips.

His hand slides over the curve of my ass and into the crease, encountering my naked flesh.

I'm not wearing my pretty La Perla underwear. I'm not wearing any panties at all.

Salvatore's groan mixes with mine as his finger slides unimpeded into the slick folds of my sex. I've had his fingers inside me. Many times.

Tonight, I want more.

Yanking me against him even harder, he thrusts his hips up, abraiding my clit. It's too much. And not enough.

My knees jam into something and I freeze.

The back of the sofa.

Memories flicker behind my eyelids, warring with the need storming my body with gale force.

Going still, my eyes fly open and I take in the scene around me. Salvatore's penthouse. His living room. His sofa. Not the couch in my family home. Not the site of my most painful memories.

Pulling his mouth from mine, he immediately asks, "What is it?"

I stare into stormy gray eyes filled with concern. Yes, there is lust there too, but it's banked. He knows something is wrong because he cares.

Because he is tuned into my tiniest reaction and that's more important to him than the desire making his dick feel like a steel shaft against my ladybits.

I shake my head. "Nothing."

He doesn't go back to kissing me, but searches my expression.

And I know...I know this is exactly what I need to vanquish the ghosts of the past. Us together on a couch. Him still dressed. But I want to be naked and I want to be the one to take off my clothes, not have them torn from me while I am helpless to protect myself.

I am replacing the awful memory with the glorious present.

"I want to take off my dress," I tell him in a husky voice I barely recognize as mine.

He nods and reaches down to help me. This is right. This is better. Together we pull the stretchy purple fabric up over my unfettered breasts and over my head. I throw it over my shoulder.

His hands are already cupping my heavy breasts and playing with my nipples.

I unbutton his shirt and spread it open, so his tattooed chest is on display.

When he goes to shrug the shirt off, I stop him. "No. Like this."

"If that's what you want *carissima*."

"Mmm..." I hum agreement. It's what I want.

Reaching down between us, I manage to get his belt undone. I pull it through the loops on his slacks and toss it in the direction of my dress.

Then I squeeze his hard shaft, marveling at the size, like I do every time we are intimate. He's big and I can't wait to feel stretched by him. Good memories replacing the old.

Unwilling to wait any longer, I open his slacks and push the waistband of his boxers down so his sex springs free. Unable to resist, I swipe my finger through the viscous fluid beaded at the tip and then suck it into my mouth.

His taste bursts on my tongue, turning me on even more.

Lifting up so I can position his head at my entrance, my heart is beating a mile a minute.

Thump. Thump. Thump

His hands drop from my breasts to grab my hips so I cannot move. "Wait," he orders. "What about your back?"

"It's good."

He doesn't release his hold on me.

"I called the surgeon's office."

"And?"

"And he said I'm cleared for participatory penetrative sex."

Salvatore barks out a laugh, then he sobers. "How can he tell? He wasn't here to examine you."

"Rosa sent him a picture of the scar and then he guided her through a physical exam and asked very pointed questions. We're good."

Something wild and dangerous flares to life in Salvatore's eyes.

"Take me into your pussy," he demands in a guttural tone that sends shivers of delight through me.

I press down with my hips, the head of his large erection stretching my sensitive, intimate flesh more than his fingers ever have.

"*Dio mio.* You are huge."

"Do not make me laugh right now, *carissima*. I'm trying not to shove my cock into your wet pussy."

That's the second time he's called me his *very* dear one and it does something to my insides.

"I'm not joking," I breathe, my voice rising at the end as his bulbous head pops into my vaginal channel.

He groans, his hold on my hips tightening. "You are so fucking tight. You feel like a virgin."

I do feel like a virgin. Like he is my first. My one. My only. I am not prepared for the emotion that washes over me and have to blink back tears.

Pushing down, I take more of him inside and release my grip on his dick. Moving my hands to his shoulders, I squirm, trying to get more of him in me.

My breasts swing side to side with my movement, rubbing my nipples against the silky hair on his chest. It feels so good, I do it again on purpose.

"You're killing me."

"Not trying to."

He laughs, the sound filled with unexpected joy. "No, you are trying to bring my heart back to life and it's fucking working."

I have no words to respond, my own heart too full. And then something shifts and my body allows his shaft to surge up inside me.

I cry out.

He yells my name.

And then we are moving together, his hips thrusting, my body meeting his in delicious union.

If he's hitting the infamous G-spot, I don't know, there's so much sensation inside me. Every drag of his thick erection against my tight walls feels like a thousand electric sparks are igniting.

He grabs one of my wrists and guides my hand back to where we join. "Touch yourself, *bella mia.*"

My middle finger slips down over my clitoris and the sparks of sensation turn into fireworks of ecstasy.

My juices are dripping around his hardon, making my passage slick and our movements more and more pleasurable. The sound of our bodies slapping together mixes with our labored breathing.

My forefinger slides alongside my middle finger and I try pressing them together like he does when he's touching me.

Everything inside me contracts as bliss washes over me in a cataclysm of endorphins and pleasure.

"Capo mio," I scream as I come so hard, my vaginal walls clamp around his sex so tight it almost hurts.

He grabs the back of my neck and tilts my head back before slamming his mouth down on mine. His tongue demands entrance and I open for him, letting him conquer both my mouth and my most intimate flesh at the same time.

Moments later, he breaks the kiss and shouts. *"Amore mio."*

The words land on the unprotected expanse of my heart and carve his name into it with indelible marks.

~ ~ ~

For the first time in over a week, Salvatore is beside me in bed when I wake up. He's sleeping so deeply, he does not stir when I turn over to face him.

There is no innocence in his face in repose. He still looks like the hardened mafia capo he is. He also looks like mine.

Amore mio. He called me his love last night.

I didn't ask him if he meant it because I'm not ready to know if it was just sex talk.

We ate dinner together like I'd planned.

Unlike I planned, we were both naked and he licked the rich caramel sauce I made to pour over the homemade gelato off my breasts. Then he laid me back on the table and ate his gelato off my ladybits.

I screamed myself hoarse with my orgasm.

He didn't want me to return the favor, but wanted back inside me.

"I am already addicted to the feel of your tight pussy around my cock."

"Don't exaggerate," I teased before getting lost in the sensation of our joined bodies, coming again before he filled me with his seed.

After he woke me to make love twice more in the night, I no longer think he was exaggerating.

If I hadn't asked the doctor to get me birth control pills, I have no doubt I'd be pregnant after last night. The thought of carrying Salvatore's baby is unexpectedly sweet.

What isn't sweet are the naughty thoughts I'm having about waking up Salvatore the same way he has woken me so many times. With my mouth on his sex.

He becomes alert way faster than I usually do. I barely get my mouth on him before he's groaning and making demands for how he likes it.

Afterward, we cuddle in the center of his bed while I work up the nerve to tell him about my past.

"What we have isn't transactional," is what comes out of my mouth.

He lays me on my back and looms over me, a slashing smile on his handsome face. "The only currency between us is orgasms."

I can think of a currency I would like more. But I'm no more ready to bring up love when I'm not sure of his feelings, than I am my messed up history. Without love on both sides, I'm not sure I'll ever feel comfortable revealing my past to Salvatore.

So, I settle for another orgasm. Or three.

CHAPTER 54

SALVATORE

A few days later, Pietro texts me while I'm working in my office at the penthouse that there is no birth record for Bianca Gemelli in New York on the date of her birth.

In addition to telling him to search vital records in the surrounding states, I tell him to search for Bianca Russo.

My gut clenches at the thought of him finding something under the Bianca Russo name and what that could mean.

I've been in Manhattan for four out of the last six nights, even when I'm out of the state during the day. Because I cannot get enough of Bianca's pussy. Not her taste and not the way it feels strangling my cock when she comes.

The way she fusses at me to eat and drink my water does weird things in my chest too.

I crave everything about her when I am away from her and if things weren't on such a razor's edge with the godfather's impending death, I wouldn't be in my office right now. I would be with her.

My head of security texts again an hour later.

Pietro: *Bianca Russo born on that date in Manhattan.*

Salvatore: *Anything else?*

Pietro: *Father is A. Russo from East Rutherford, NJ.*

I recognize the name of the town immediately. That's where Bianca said she lived with her dad before he died.

Or his capo killed him.

Fuck.

Salvatore: *What did you find out about the will?*

Pietro: *Bianca Gemelli is listed as a beneficiary.*

Salvatore: *How much?*

Pietro: *Fifty K but there's something off.*

There sure as hell is. Bianca lied to me about inheriting money from the old man she lived with. She lied about everything.

She's not an outsider, alone in the world. She has family from here to Detroit.

Dread twists my stomach into a gordian knot while my brain plays back every conversation between us. Every fucking lie that fell from her beautiful lips.

Eleven years ago, Monica lied about everything and I killed her.

An image of Bianca with a gunshot wound in the center of her forehead and her eyes drained of life flashes in my brain. I retch uncontrollably, sprinting to the bathroom attached to my office.

I barely make it to the toilet where I throw up the contents of my stomach and then dry heave.

"Salvatore!" My sister's voice sounds from my office.

Cazzo.

I force my heaving stomach to settle. She cannot see me like this. Splashing my face with cold water from the sink, I refuse to look at myself in the mirror.

I don't want to see the face of a man who has managed to fall in love twice in his fucking life to women who turned out to be con artists.

My hand trembles as I open the door after I dry off. I force it into stillness by sheer will alone and my face into an emotionless mask before I step into my office to face my sister.

Nerissa looks almost as bad as I feel. She sits in one of the chairs facing my desk, but instead of looking at me she stares at the floor.

"What the hell is going on, Nerissa?" What more can this day bring?

She lifts her head, her eyes filled with both rage and pity.

Ice forms in my twisted gut. Nerissa knows.

I sit down and keep my features schooled. "Talk."

"I didn't want it to be true. You were happy, like I haven't seen you in years. I was even starting to like her. But they're genuine. Ernesto analyzed the photos in secret. They're not fakes," Nerissa rambles.

My sister never rambles.

"What photos?" I ask in a voice devoid of emotion.

If I let the smallest crack form in my façade, the tsunami of rage and grief swirling through me will crash through and lay waste to everything and everyone in its wake.

She sets a large manilla envelope on the desk. "There's a copy of the will in there too. She lied about it. Ruhnke left her fifty-thousand dollars just like his son claimed he did."

It's not as bad as it could be. Nerissa makes no mention of Bianca being Alberto Russo's daughter. And the will is no longer a surprise, so it's not hard to maintain control of my features.

But she says there are pictures too. Of what?

Bianca in a risqué position with the old man, Ruhnke?

Foreboding making my hands clammy, I pick up the envelop and upend it to spread it's contents on my desk. At first, I can't make sense of what I am seeing.

It's Bianca dressed like a socialite in a long designer gown and wearing diamonds worth at least a million. I would have adorned her in jewelry worth ten times that.

But she's with another man.

That man is Matthew Lombard.

Son of a fucking bitch.

Cold fear washes over me. It should be fury, but there's no room for that when I see the proof of her betrayal in front of me.

It is one thing for her to lie to me about her past. It is another to sell out the mafia.

Severu will order me to kill her.

I won't. And I won't let him kill her either. Even if it means burning down the city and the mafia I've spent my life serving.

"No one is killing her," Nerissa says, her dark gaze filled with sisterly worry.

I stare at her, nothing in my brain but white noise and the constant refrain. *I will not kill her.*

Not this time. Not this woman.

Somehow, Nerissa is standing beside me, her hand on my shoulder. "Calm down, brother."

I don't know how many times she has said those three words, but they finally penetrate. I don't have time to lose my shit.

I force my brain to look at this situation through the strategic eyes of a capo. "Where did you get the pictures?"

How many people know about Bianca's betrayal?

"They came in as texts from an anonymous number."

Relief sends more synapses firing in my brain.

That's one person. My guess is Lorenzo. Since I don't see him following Bianca around like the paparazzi to get her picture with Matthew Lombard, he probably sent one of his guys to do it.

That's two men I have to neutralize.

"We burn the printouts and delete the files."

If Severu sees those pictures, Bianca is dead.

There's a slim chance he will let her live if he continues to believe she's an outsider. None if he discovers she's a Genovese.

Nerissa nods without hesitation. "But Salvatore, someone took those pictures."

"Probably fucking Lorenzo."

Nerissa's brows draw together in confusion. "Why? What does he get out of this?"

The reality of why Lorenzo called me and told me about Bianca's past suddenly hits. I would have seen it sooner, but I wasn't thinking straight.

She fucking does this to me.

"Turmoil," I say. "If it gets out, it will undermine the confidence of the other capos and their dons. I'm not just Severu's capo. I'm family and his top campaigner."

I've spent the past three weeks talking to other capos and dons all over the country, encouraging them to support Severu as the next godfather.

If I'm shown up for a chump, everything I've said to them comes into question. Image is everything in the mafia.

For some fucking unfathomable reason, Lorenzo doesn't want Severu to be the next godfather.

"Lorenzo has to die," my sister and I say at the same time.

"And we have to get Bianca out of New York." Even if I wanted to keep the manipulative liar, I couldn't.

I can't kill her, but I'll never trust her again.

Nerissa nods.

"Why are you going along with this?" I question my second's easy acquiescence.

"You love her, Salvatore. Killing Monica changed something in you. You lost part of your humanity. If Bianca is killed, you'll lose what's left of it."

"Some would say that's what a good capo needs to be."

"No." Nerissa shakes her head firmly. "Even if he is harsh and even brutal at times, a good capo has to care about his people. If you lose that last link to your heart, you stop caring about everyone."

I don't know if my sister's perception is right, but I do believe she believes what she's saying. I either trust her, or I kill her.

"Bianca's father was a Genovese soldier," I tell my sister, choosing trust. "Lorenzo claims he executed him for being a rat."

Nerissa's face contorts in shock and fear.

She knows what this means.

"Bianca is not an outsider," she breathes.

"No one else can know about any of this, not our family, not anyone."

I'll have to swear Pietro to secrecy about the research he's done on Bianca's birth. He's not stupid. He'll have guessed that she was born Bianca Russo. But without the pieces that I have, his puzzle won't show a Genovese mafia princess in the picture.

I won't tell him she was a Lombardi plant.

Nerissa nods. "I know. I made Ernesto give me his word he wouldn't tell anyone about the pictures. Right now, he has no idea who is in them. You've kept Bianca out of sight the whole time she's been here except that one night you took her out to Per Se and Pitiful Princess."

There are no pictures of us at either place. Standard security protocols I am grateful for now. It's all word of mouth about my gorgeous redhead girlfriend.

No one will be surprised when they see me next week with a blonde on my arm. I don't do girlfriends.

Pain spears through my chest. I ignore it. "Do you trust him?"

More importantly, do I trust him? Can I afford to let him live? Can I risk killing another capo's soldier?

Fuck.

"As much as I trust anyone besides you." She frowns. "I deleted the files from his computer and cloud storage myself."

"He knows what she looks like."

"So do a lot of people. But can he link her to the bar deal? Would he even think to? The reports on the Lombards list his girlfriend as a Boston socialite, with no connection to the mafia. Bianca must be his side piece."

One they didn't come across when they researched the Lombards for connections with the Five Families. Once we uncovered the familial connection between the Lombards and Henry Caruso, that's where we put our focus. Not on Matthew Lombard's girlfriend.

Rage overrides my fear for Bianca's life and I roar out my frustration.

She is *not* his girlfriend.

She is my woman.

That I have to let go. That I should want to let go.

CHAPTER 55

BIANCA

The sound of Salvatore yelling has me jumping up from the couch where I've been pretending to read.

Nerissa came in about twenty minutes ago and rushed past me without even saying, "Hi." She glared at me though.

I've been trying to figure out why the renewed hostility. Ever since she walked in on me talking to her mother and Rosa about how they treat Salvatore, she's thawed toward me. I consider her a friend.

She listens to my ideas for the women working in the strip clubs. We talk about other stuff too.

She even confided in me about her brother's harsh punishment for what he considers her disloyalty. Nerissa thinks she deserves having to earn the respect of their men again. I disagree, but I don't get a vote.

The sound of Salvatore's harsh shout tapers off. Did the godfather die? That shout sounded filled with pain. Even if he's not close to the godfather, the loyalty he feels toward the man has to be deep.

Or maybe something has gone wrong in his cousin's bid to be the next godfather. I know that's important to my lover. Salvatore hasn't told me about it, but he doesn't make me leave the room when he takes phone calls and I've heard plenty.

Because he trusts me.

It's time to prove I trust him with more than my body. I'm not sure how much of my past I want to reveal to him, but at the very least, I need to tell him that I used to be part of the Cosa Nostra.

Unsure how he's going to react to learning who and what my dad was, I'm so nervous I'm sweating. Salvatore despises disloyalty. He even told me he is planning to replace Rosa with a housekeeper who has more loyalty to him than to his mother.

Rosa's cooking and pottery lessons are the only reason I'm not climbing up the walls with boredom. Salvatore won't even consider me going back to work while things are so volatile in his world. When he played *the you could be kidnapped or hurt to get to me card*, I gave in.

Since I'm not paying rent and don't even have to buy my own groceries right now, it's not a hardship.

If this godfather thing isn't resolved yet, things are going to get dicey when classes resume at QC though. There's one I can take online, but most required for my degree are in person this semester.

Climbing the stairs to the second floor, I smile tentatively when I see Nerissa walking toward me. "Hey!"

I wait for her to notice today's t-shirt. She says if she wasn't second-in-command, she'd wear the shit out of shirts like mine. I don't tell her that Salvatore bought them for me, but I do plan to get her the perfect one for her birthday.

The black t-shirt I'm wearing with jeans today says: *My dark little heart skips a beat when I see KARMA catch up to somebody who deserves it.*

Nerissa's eyes widen when she sees me. Her gaze drops to my t-shirt but instead of smiling, she looks like somebody kicked her in the stomach.

Her tone grim, she says, "The capo wants to talk to you."

The capo? She never refers to him like that to me anymore. It's always Salvatore, or when he's not around, *my lovesick brother*.

If only.

"I need to talk to Salvatore too." Saying it out loud makes it real.

It's a promise to Nerissa to come clean to her brother, even if she doesn't know it.

"But will you say the things he needs to hear?" Her words should be a joke, but Nerissa's dark eyes reflect disappointment.

I put my hand on her arm. "Are you okay?"

Is Salvatore okay? I don't ask because that's not a question for Nerissa to answer. I'm careful never to ask her things that Salvatore should tell me himself.

He'll never consider her disloyal on my behalf again.

She jerks her head up and down. "Don't keep him waiting."

Okay, whatever this is, it's serious.

But not an excuse to put off telling him about your dad.

My inner voice can be such a judgy bitch sometimes.

I knock on the partially open door when I reach it.

"Enter." It's Salvatore's capo voice.

Is he on a call? I'm quiet as I go inside just in case, closing the door behind me. What I have to tell Salvatore is for his ears only. We'll decide together if we need to tell the rest of his family about who my dad was.

His phone is silent and he's sitting rigid behind his desk, staring down at some papers on his desk.

"Nerissa said you wanted to talk to me about something?"

He looks up, no expression on his handsome face. "Want to talk to you? No. However, it is necessary."

"That doesn't sound good." I grip my hands together in front of me.

Is the A/C turned down in here? It feels as cold as a walk-in cooler.

He stands and comes around his desk, his movements deliberate, an aura of menace settled around him like a dark cloud. "It's not."

Not good? "What's not good?"

"Tell me about your father, Bianca."

He hasn't called me by name in weeks. It's always *my beauty*, or *my good girl*, or *dearest darling* and always in Italian. My favorite is *my love*. But he only says that during sex.

Why am I zoning out on endearments when he just asked me about my dad?

"Funny you should ask that. Timing wise, I mean." I cut the babble short before it can get out of control and swallow. "His name was Alberto Russo. He worked for Lorenzo Ricci as a bookkeeper."

Not a flicker of surprise shows in Salvatore's expression. No emotion leaks into his gray eyes at all. Why do I feel like I'm not telling Salvatore anything he doesn't already know?

"You fucking lied to me."

I glance at the papers behind him on the desk. What are they? My birth certificate, or something?

"I withheld the truth from you."

"Don't play fucking semantics with me. You lied. You are part of the Genovese mafia."

"No, I'm not. When Lorenzo executed my dad, he kicked me out." Out of my home. Out of the mafia.

The murderous capo ripped every mooring from my life.

"Is that why you did it? To get back at him?"

Did what? "I don't know what you are talking about."

"You were raised in the life." He says it like an accusation.

"Yes." I am not ashamed of that, or of the life I have built for myself since. Both are me.

"My father cut Marco's tongue out on *your* word. Did you get off knowing your lies cost a good man so much?"

"Good man? Are we talking about the same Marco? Because not only is he a big-mouthed Soprano wannabe, he beat my roommate so bad she was in the hospital for three days."

"You didn't get your inside knowledge into the Genovese mafia from him."

Like hell I didn't.

"Everything I told you I know because of him is true. When I got kicked out six years ago Enzo De Luca was still alive and he was still the don. You weren't a capo. How would a sixteen-year-old girl know that stuff anyway?" I'm talking fast, but it's like my words are sliding right past him.

When he says nothing, I add, "I only figured out that the Genovese control Pitiful Princess after going to work there. I didn't know about your connection to it until *you* told me."

"Fuck that!" He looms over me, for once his nearness not making me feel safe. "I stood up for you with my father. I vouched for you to Severu. I told my sister to fuck off. *For you.* And you've been lying to me about everything since the beginning."

"What beginning?" I ask snidely, getting angry too. "The one where you propositioned me for five thousand dollars to have sex, knowing it would cost me my job?"

"No wonder you didn't take the money. You already had a sugar daddy for your whoring ass."

I shake my head, my ears ringing. "Did you just call me a whore?"

"If the title fits. Or is he your *boyfriend?* Newsflash: fucking me to get information for him still makes you a whore."

"Is who my boyfriend? Do you think I'm dating Lorenzo?" I ask, confusion interrupting my anger. "First, eww. Second, did you miss the part where he threw me out on the street?"

"Stop with the innocent act. I know the truth."

"That my dad was a rat who stole from the mafia? So what? Newsflash," I throw back at Salvatore, my anger back in full force. *"I'm not him."*

My father's sins cost me more than anyone but him. And for a long time I wondered if dying wouldn't have been better than what happened to me.

Salvatore grabs some papers from the desk behind him and shoves them at me. "Go ahead. Lie some more and tell me that's not you."

I take a small stack of photos and flip through them. Stifling a gasp of shock, pain pierces my heart.

They're pictures taken without the knowledge of the people in them. If Bea knew her picture was being taken, she would have changed her expression. I don't do social media. Neither did Bea before she and mom left. But they both set up on the different platforms after.

I created a catfish account for a glamourous model living in the UK to stalk them. It's not tied to anything related to me and I only sign in the web at Internet cafes. My dad's insistence we keep a low profile is drilled into the depths of my consciousness. Besides, I didn't want to come to Lorenzo's attention.

Bea's social media shows my sister is very good at curating her image.

In these pictures, she's dressed like the socialite she is, her hair pulled up in an elegant French twist. The guy she's with looks just like her type.

White. Preppy. Rich.

I like the candidness of the photos though. Until I notice a detail that sends shards of more pain slicing through my heart.

Bea is wearing an engagement ring. A classic, tasteful diamond solitaire. Not too showy, but I bet the clarity and cut are perfection.

She's engaged.

And I didn't know. Our dreams of being each other's maids of honor are ashes. I'll never even meet her fiancé. And if she has children? I won't be allowed to meet them either.

Because I'm tainted with my father's blood.

Which somehow Salvatore seems to realize even though he doesn't know about the most shameful moments in my past.

The ones that draw the dividing line between me and Bea with permanent marker.

So, why is he so convinced I'm the one in the pictures?

Even though the style hides the fact her hair is about eight inches shorter than mine, the differences between the two of us are obvious. Bea might be my identical twin, but she is at least two sizes smaller than me. Diet, exercise or surgery?

Or maybe just really good shapewear.

It doesn't matter. Her cleavage is still impressive and that's probably all Salvatore notices.

"This is not me."

"Stop with the fucking lies."

"You know who my father is, so you have to know that could be my sister." Why is he acting like this? "Why would you even assume it was me?"

"You are a good actress, I'll give you that." He sounds disgusted, not impressed. "You don't have a sister."

The words hurt in a way nothing has in a long time.

Because in their own way, they are true.

"No matter what she and my mom like to pretend, I do. Bea is my twin." But he has to know that.

Derisive laughter flays my already lacerated heart. "Alberto's employment file lists one daughter. *One*," he emphasizes.

"Well, our birth records prove he has two!"

He grabs more papers from his desk and waves them in front of me. "Did you fucking sleep with that old man to get him to leave you the money, Bianca? How low will you go?"

Sickened by his question, I snatch the papers from him and skip to the highlighted parts. Mr. Ruhnke really did leave me $50,000? And his greedy sons hid it from me? Doing a quick scan of the unhighlighted first paragraphs, I see that Mr. Ruhnke made his oldest son executor of the will.

Well, that explains how they got away with not informing me of my inheritance.

Is that why his wife texted me? Maybe slipping my existence by the probate court isn't as easy as they thought it would be.

My eyes prickle with tears. This is too much.

The reminder that my sister is no longer my family. Apparently, she and my mom weren't even listed in my dad's employment file.

The knowledge that Mr. Ruhnke left me something in his will. The reminder that he considered me family, the daughter of his heart, hurts too. Because he's dead. And his children withheld his final act of love from me.

I am alone.

The man I've fallen in love with thinks I'm a whore. If he loved me, this conversation would have been questions, not accusations. He would be glad to hear I'm not the one in the picture, not flat out refusing to believe it.

No wonder he never calls me his love outside of sex.

He does not fucking love me.

CHAPTER 56

BIANCA

Turning, I stumble toward the door.

"Where the fuck do you think you are going?"

"Away from you." I need time to process all of this.

I reach for the doorknob but a heavy hand on my shoulder spins me around. The cold mask is gone. Hot rage is in its place. It radiates from Salvatore, filling the air between us.

"You are not leaving without telling me the truth." He grabs my throat with his big hand, shoving me up against the door.

My heart races. Panic flares for the first time from his touch. I thrash, trying to pull away.

"Please," I gasp out. "I can't breathe."

"You're talking. You're breathing," he says pitilessly, his eyes chips of granite under the lights.

For a second, there's more than fury in his expression. There's pain too. Then it's gone. Was it ever really there? More likely my wishful thinking, wanting him to be affected by this like I am.

"You're fucking lucky your plan didn't work," he grits out. "You whored yourself out for nothing, didn't you?"

"Not a whore."

"Call it what you want." His face set in a rictus of disgust, he lets me go and shoves me away from him. "You're lucky I don't kill you, but you're not worth it."

Scored by a thousand tiny cuts from his disbelief, I don't feel lucky.

"Get out!" he shouts, the muscles in his neck cording with strain.

Without turning my back to the angry predator, I feel for the door handle. When my hand latches onto it, I twist my wrist and pull the door open before sidling around it and slipping through the opening.

Something heavy lands against the door as I yank it closed. The words he shouts are muffled, but the rage in them bleeds through even the heavy wooden door.

Intent on getting my birth certificate and the small photo album I brought with me when I left my family home, I turn away from Salvatore's office and rush down the hall. If he can take pictures as proof of my guilt, he can accept the ones of me and my sister together as children as proof of my innocence.

I don't know if we can come back from this, but I'm not leaving here with him believing I'm a liar.

The whore part I can't change.

I have no proof I never had sex with Mr. Ruhnke. That I had no clue about the $50,000 he left me in his will. The wording of it should be proof enough though. Only a sicko would call a woman he's used sexually *the daughter of his heart.*

Bile rises in my throat at the thought of someone thinking Mr. Ruhnke was that kind of man when he had been all that was decent and good.

I force it down and shove open the guestroom door.

Nerissa is near the dresser, putting clothes into a Louis Vuitton duffel bag I've never seen before.

"You're packing my things?" I ask, my voice accusing.

She doesn't bother to look at me when she says, "Yes."

"Why?"

"He wants you out."

My newly vulnerable heart cracks in my chest.

Salvatore is throwing me out. Just like Lorenzo. Just like Daryl Ruhnke's family. Once again, I am losing my home through no fault of my own.

And Nerissa is helping?

"I thought you were my friend." Why am I so stupid?

She spins, a pile of underwear in her hand, her beautiful face twisted with contempt. "Friends? Well, you know the old saying, keep your friends close and your enemies closer. Who do you think gave the capo those pictures? I ordered that copy of the will from the courthouse."

Who doctored my father's information to list only one daughter? It could have been Nerissa, or their father. As consigliere, Big Sal has access to all the capo records.

Neither one of them wants me in Salvatore's life, but I stupidly believed that both had changed their minds.

Nerissa drops the underwear in the duffel. "Now that you are here, you can pack your own shit. You have fifteen minutes."

She leaves. Numbness starts in my feet and moves up my body until the pain inside me smothers under it too.

Even though Salvatore and I have shared a bed every night since the first one I spent here, all my stuff is still here in the guest room. What does that say about what has really been going on?

I told Salvatore I wouldn't sleep with him for money, so he figured out my currency. Orgasms. Affection. Feeling like I belonged.

Now that he's done with me, he's ripping it all away.

The last two months have been a lie. Every touch, every moment of protectiveness was a pretense. His demands I call him *capo mio* part of the Off-Broadway production he was directing to keep me in his bed.

My need to prove my innocence to him disappears in the face of this painful truth.

Knowing my time is limited, I quickly repack the duffle with practical clothes. The first thing I will do when I get a chance, is hock the pretentious designer luggage and get something that will make me less of a target for predators.

After taking a quick picture of my birth certificate, I transfer my important papers and money stash into a pouch meant for travel I got at the secondhand store. It attaches to my belt and flips over my waistband to tuck inside my jeans.

Shoving a smaller stash of money into my backpack, I also put a change of clothes and my essentials in there along with the photo album I refuse to leave behind.

I don't know what I'll do about Vee. I don't even know if Salvatore managed to bring my African violet back from death's door. I've been too afraid to ask, not wanting the grief that would come from a negative answer.

Alive, or not, I can't take the plant with me when I don't know where I'm going.

The beat up looking backpack looks wrong with the designer duffle. Just like I look wrong in a billionaire's penthouse.

I'm still packing the rest of my things into the set of matching luggage I find in the closet when Nerissa comes stomping into the room. "Time's up."

Ignoring her, I finish packing.

When I'm done, I stack the luggage and boxes against the wall of the walk-in closet.

"What are you doing?" she demands.

"I can't take it all with me now." I don't even know where I'm going. "I will text you an address to ship my things later."

"Fine," she agrees, surprising me.

No threat to burn them or throw the stuff away like Salvatore is doing to me.

After slipping my arms through the straps of the backpack, I pull the handle up from the back of the rolling duffle. "Let's go."

Without a word, Nerissa spins and stomps back out of the room.

I follow. Hating myself for it, I turn to look back over my shoulder to see if Salvatore has come out of his office to watch me leave.

The hall is empty.

SALVATORE

My chest tight, some kind of weird burning at the back of my eyes, I slam back a double shot of eighty-year-old whiskey.

This is not fucking happening again.

Compared to Bianca, Monica was an amateur.

With a rich boyfriend in Boston, no way Bianca is a student at Queens College like she claims. I keep calling Matthew Lombard her boyfriend, but that damn ring on her left hand says he's more.

How did we miss it?

Or is the piece of jewelry a shut-up-ring for a *goomah?*

Just like Monica, Bianca Russo has been playing me for a fool while committed to another man. And I let her do it.

A master manipulator, she wove a complete backstory that made her look like the plucky heroine who never gives up. And she played the part so damn well.

Right up until I saw the pictures of her with Matthew Lombard, I was looking for excuses for the lies about the will and who she is.

I never would have gone with the twin farce though.

How did Bianca think she was going to convince me of that bullshit?

I pour myself another shot, but I don't pick it up.

I am not weak.

You're so strong, you arranged to get Bianca out of New York before anyone else finds out about her lies and you can be ordered to kill her.

I slam my fist down on the desk. I fucking despise her, but I am not killing her.

BIANCA

Nerissa drives and I don't ask where we are going.

Right now, I can't make myself care. My heart hurts and my brain insists on playing over every minute in Salvatore's office. My throat constricts as if his hand is still around it, squeezing.

"Why did you stay after the attempt to buy the bars out from under us failed?" Nerissa asks in the heavy silence of the car.

Her words burn through the fog of memories playing like a loop in my brain.

Why is she still pretending to think I'm some kind of spy? She knows about Bea. She has to. She's the one that gave the pictures to Salvatore.

Does she want to be able to tell Salvatore she grilled me and I refused to answer? Why not just tell him that anyway? What is one more lie on top of all of the others?

Or is she rubbing in her success at getting rid of me? Pushing home how easily and quickly Salvatore believed the ugly pretense she created.

"Answer me, damn it!" Nerissa pounds on the steering wheel. "Do you even realize how much Salvatore is risking by letting you leave?"

I press my lips together, refusing to answer the crazy.

"My brother put his position as capo and his own fucking life at risk for you," she says passionately.

I almost believe her.

"If my dad or Severu figure out you ratted on Salvatore to Matthew Lombard about the bar properties, they'll want you dead. And maybe him too."

The only two things I take from that are the name of my sister's fiancée and the threat against Salvatore's life.

"Why would they kill him?" I ask.

"You don't rat out the mafia and live. If Severu orders Salvatore to kill you like his dad ordered him to kill Monica, he will not only refuse, but he will protect you to his last dying breath." She sounds disgusted and angered by that fact.

Can I believe her? Is it possible she doesn't know about Bea? Does Nerissa believe the story the pictures tell too?

"Where did you get the pictures?" I ask.

At first, I think she's not going to answer.

But finally, she says, "They were sent to me via an anonymous email address."

"You didn't trace it?"

"We don't have tech guys on our crew that can do that. Once Ernesto confirmed they are genuine, I didn't want him tracing them back to their source either."

"Why?"

"To protect Salvatore."

Cold dread slithers through the numbness enveloping me. Because I believe her. I hate him, but I don't want Salvatore to die.

"Tell them the truth then."

"You *want* him to die?" she demands with disbelief.

"Those pictures aren't of me. They are my twin," I tell her.

"Right," she scoffs. "Even if that were true, and trust me, I don't believe a single word out of your lying mouth, then it just means you fed her information and not directly to Matthew Lombard. You're still a rat and Severu will still want you killed."

I know I can prove the lack of connection between me and Bea no matter how much it hurts, but I don't mention that. I want answers to other questions because if she's telling me the truth, things aren't adding up.

"Why not just let them kill me then?"

"Salvatore won't and I'm not letting him die because he insists on protecting you."

He killed Monica, but he won't kill me? That doesn't make any sense. Not if I'm right and he doesn't love me.

I can't even think about that right now. Letting hope blossom in my heart after everything would be beyond stupid. It would be suicidal.

"What happens to you if someone finds out you hid this too?" I ask. "Your loyalty to the don will be put in question just like his."

"You think I care? My first loyalty is to my brother. My first priority is protecting Salvatore."

"So, you're not going to tell your dad or your don?" I press, to make sure.

"No. But you have to stay out of New York. If this comes out, I'll make sure you die slowly. A day of torture for every hour they put Salvatore through."

Severu De Luca would torture and kill his own cousin? Big Sal De Luca would stand by and let him do it? What am I asking? Of course, they would. It's the mafia way. Loyalty above all else.

My father forgot that and that's why he's dead.

I won't let the same thing happen to Salvatore. Or Bea. She might not recognize me as her sister anymore, but no way am I going to risk her being tortured and killed because of mistaken identity and a misunderstanding I can put right.

The sound of a jet overhead answers the question I did not ask. We are headed to the airport.

"I texted you the details of your flight while you were packing."

I haven't checked my messages since Salvatore blew my world up with his cruel words and accusations. I check now and see the text Nerissa is talking about.

The flight isn't for three hours. Way more time than I need to get through security screening, but not enough time to leave and come back.

I'm not doing either.

The only way to protect both Bea and Salvatore is with the truth. The whole sordid story that started when I was thirteen. I have to spin it though. It doesn't protect Salvatore if his don thinks he hid things from him.

Unfortunately, the only way to sell it, I have to make Nerissa the heroic messenger.

Instead of the deceptive manipulator she really is.

Keep your enemies closer.

Stop pretending like you could live with yourself if she was killed as punishment for hiding information.

Once again, my inner voice is right. Nerissa might not be my friend, like I believed, but my feelings toward her are genuine.

I was *her* friend.

As soon as I get inside the airport, I call Catalina De Luca and ask if we can meet.

"Will you come here? I'm not allowed out of the building right now without a security team bigger than the president's."

I would rather meet at a restaurant where I have at least a slim chance of getting away if things go wrong, but I agree to come to her home. I don't have a choice if I want to make her my ally.

Without that happening, we're all screwed.

I spend an hour and a half drinking overpriced coffee on the main level of The Atrium Business & Conference Center at LaGuardia while I compile the evidence I need to prove the truth of my story to Severu De Luca. After putting together the digital file, I make a print copy too.

My ready cash in my backpack seriously depleted, I head toward the rideshare pickup location.

Remembering the rideshare Pietro made me miss by kidnapping me from the hospital makes me ridiculously nostalgic. What do he and Rosa think of my abrupt departure?

Or have they been expecting it all along?

Their boss, *Captain Playboy*, has a different beautiful woman on his arm every time he attends a notable event. He isn't known for having serious relationships either.

Yeah, I found that nickname while compiling the things I need. Searching my name connected to Salvatore De Luca didn't bring up anything about us. However, it brought up a ton of articles about *Captain Playboy* and his many women.

There aren't even any pictures of us together at Per Se. Other than the selfie I took, which I'm not deleting.

It's a reminder that he was using me all along.

Just like his orchids remind him not to trust women. I should have taken that for the stadium sized red flag it is.

I didn't and here I am. About to step into a rideshare to take me to Don De Luca's building and maybe my own death.

CHAPTER 57

SALVATORE

I hang up my phone after arranging with Lorenzo Ricci to meet at Amuni. Tonight, that miserable cretin's time is up.

A perfunctory knock sounds on my office door before Nerissa steps inside. Her expression is grim.

"What?"

"She hasn't checked in for her flight yet."

She's not leaving New York. Why not? Lombard is in Boston. Is he sending his plane for her, or maybe a car?

I pull up the tracker app I put on her phone. The little dot is moving back toward the city.

Managgia la miseria. Where the fuck is she going? To Henry Lucchese? But why would she go to him?

What is there for her here in New York?

A tiny kernel of hope sparks in my battered soul.

Not you, genius. You threw her away like trash.

A first-class ticket to Boston is not the garbage heap.

A ticket she's not using.

"Lorenzo is meeting me at Amuni in two hours," I inform my second. "I want you and your team to take him."

"Done."

"Put him on ice until I decide how I want to spin killing another capo without my don's approval," I spell out for her.

Nerissa is putting her life on the line for me, for my need to keep Bianca alive. She has to go into this with her eyes wide open.

"We're in this together, brother. Lorenzo is a rat. He betrayed *la famiglia*. We're just taking out the trash for Severu."

It's too close to what I thought about throwing Bianca out. *Cazzo.*

I pound my chest to dislodge the weight that settles there.

A loud knock sounds.

I nod to Nerissa. She opens the door and Pietro steps inside, his mom hot on his heels.

Sweat is beaded on my top bodyguard's forehead. "Boss, did you give Bianca permission to leave the penthouse without an escort?"

"She's gone, Salvatore. I looked everywhere, even the roof." Rosa rings her hands. "How did she get out? I thought she wanted to be here."

"We broke up." The words cause a cavern to open up inside my chest.

"But why? She's so good for you." Rosa's eyes fill with tears. "I thought you were finally over what happened when you were young."

Do you ever get over killing a woman you believe you love? It changed me permanently. But not so much I am capable of killing Bianca.

"It is what it is."

Pietro is looking at his phone. "Is she going to stay with the don while you work things out?"

"She'll be safe there, I suppose, but you two need to make up quickly. This is where she belongs," Rosa says. "I don't understand why she didn't go to your parents' apartment though. That is just an elevator ride away."

"What are you talking about?" Nerissa demands. "Bianca is not going to Severu's place."

Pietro shows his phone screen to my second. Of course, he's tracking her. He's the one I asked to install the app on her phone, and her safety has become his number one assignment.

I should have relieved him of those duties before I kicked her out. I wasn't thinking.

When am I ever not thinking?

Right now, apparently. Because it is only registering now what the tracking information means. Bianca is headed to talk to Severu.

She's going to get herself killed.

Without another word to anyone else, I sprint out of my office. Pietro's big feet pound behind me.

I don't close the door behind me when I hurtle out of the penthouse. Jabbing the button over and over, I will the elevator doors to open.

I have to get to Bianca before she gets herself killed.

BIANCA

My hands are clammy as Severu's security checks my identification and then scans my bags and tests them for who knows what all. Explosives? Drugs?

It's definitely more thorough than anything I would have gone through at the airport if I'd taken that flight to Boston. Finally, I'm back in the elevator headed to the top floor of the building.

I try to block out the memory of my last ride up to the De Luca's home, but little bits keep flashing in my brain like one of those best of your life highlights videos.

Che palle. My time with Salvatore was not the best of my life.

Wasn't it?

I want to throat punch my inner voice, but then I wouldn't be able to talk to Catalina and tell her the things I need to. Because that inner voice is me calling me on my own bullshit.

The don's wife is waiting for me when the elevator doors slide open.

Her hazel eyes widen when she sees the duffle beside me.

"Um..." She gives me a questioning look.

I step out of the elevator, pulling the Louis Vuitton bag behind me. "Salvatore and I broke up."

"I'm sorry to hear that. I thought you two were good together."

Did she? Then he fooled her too.

"It was never going to last. A capo doesn't marry a pole dancer turned cocktail waitress." I hate the sound of self-derision in my voice.

I am not ashamed of who and what I am. Salvatore has killed how many people? He's not too good for me. If anything, it's the other way around.

"He's not exactly royalty." Catalina leads the way into the living room.

"Pretty sure his dad would disagree with you."

"Big Sal? Is he the reason you two broke up? Maybe Severu can talk to him."

I shake my head. "No point."

She sits down on the end of one of the sofas without replying. Putting my duffle out of the way behind it, I take the closest chair to her. This is not a conversation I want overheard. Not even by her ever present security.

One bodyguard stands near the entrance and the other is closer, probably so he can leap on top of her in case of an invasion.

Like anyone is getting up that elevator without approval.

I keep my backpack in my lap.

"Do you need a place to stay for a few days?"

I'm tempted to say yes because Salvatore would blow a gasket over me staying here.

"No but thank you for the offer." Her kindness makes my throat tight with emotion.

"I have some things to tell you that I'm hoping you will be willing to share with your husband." On the way here, I decided that Catalina telling him would give the truth a better chance of being heard.

"Things about Salvatore?" she asks warily.

"No. Things about me. Things Salvatore doesn't know." I tell my first lie. "Things that Nerissa has shown me could be misconstrued without the whole story."

"Why aren't you telling these things to Salvatore?"

"Our breakup wasn't pretty. We're not speaking to each other." Not a lie. "But I have to tell someone in your um...family." I don't know how much Salvatore has told the don that I know about the mafia. "Or my sister could be in danger."

"What do you mean?"

"My sister is engaged to Matthew Lombard. I guess he's one of Salvatore's enemies, or something." My lack of knowledge is not feigned.

I still have no idea what the property developer has to do with the New York Cosa Nostra.

"A rival maybe," Catalina muses. "Do you mind if I take notes?"

I shake my head.

I'm surprised when the don's wife jumps to her feet and leaves the room, one of the security team hot on her heels. Is her phone not with her? I keep mine with me all the time, even at home.

And I barely have anyone contacting me on it.

That number decreased by all but one as of a few hours ago. Of course, my phone rings right then, making a liar out of me. I jump in shock.

I can't talk to Candi right now. I look down to ignore the call and see it is Salvatore. Did he check to see if I took my flight and find out I didn't? Is he wondering what I'm doing?

Well, he can keep wondering. I decline the call.

A text dings second later.

Salvatore: *Do not speak to Severu. Get out of there.*

I don't know how he knows I'm here and I don't care. I power down my phone. The bossy capo abdicated all rights to try to tell me what to do when he dumped me.

Catalina returns carrying a composition notebook and a pen.

"Wow. Old school."

She laughs. "I prefer pen and paper. It helps me keep my thoughts in order."

To each their own. I take notes on my phone. I don't remember the last time I carried a pen, much less a pad to write on.

I'm glad I printed out the documents I compiled though. I get the feeling, Catalina will find them more compelling than an image on a screen.

She opens her notebook and looks at me expectantly. "Okay, start at the beginning."

I do. Sort of. I tell her about meeting Salvatore for the first time.

"You told him he has no game?" Catalina asks with a grin.

"Yep. Honestly, I find it difficult to believe he's called Captain Playboy. Not that he hasn't had a bazillion lovers, but being a playboy implies a certain level of smoothness. And smooth, he is not."

Catalina laughs, her whole face lighting up with her amusement. "I hope you two can patch things up. The De Luca men tend toward bossy arrogance. Salvatore needs you in his life."

I wish I could agree.

Once I tell her the rest of the story, she'll change her mind too.

"My dad was Alberto Russo. My mom is, was, Elizabeth Butler. For a while she was a Russo and now she's a Harrington."

"Your father died?"

"He was executed by his capo for stealing from *la famiglia*."

"The mafia has no mercy for traitors." Catalina's eyes reflect deep grief.

I don't know why, or how, but she gets it.

"My dad was my mom's big rebellion against her society parents. Their marriage wasn't a happy one."

Catalina scribbles away as I talk, but her pen stills when I tell her about that night when I was thirteen.

"She left you there?" Catalina asks, horrified. "Alone?"

"I had my dad."

"Who was stealing from the Family." Catalina grabs her phone and sends a text. "Severu is in his home office. He'll be here as soon as he can break away."

"Why?" I ask, terrified.

I don't want to talk to the don.

"Because my husband will insist on hearing your story directly from you to judge your honesty."

"Doesn't he trust you?"

"The question is, do you? You must have at least a little to come here to talk to me. Trust me when I tell you, talking directly to Severu is the best thing you can do right now. This situation is complicated in ways I'm not sure you know about."

"Honestly, I don't. All I know is that Nerissa said the don might think I'm a rat like my father." Not a lie, but not the strict truth either.

"The best way to convince him otherwise is for you to be completely honest with him."

I'm scared and it must show on my face because Catalina pats my hand. "Don't worry. My husband has a soft spot for courageous women who try to protect their sisters."

Catalina offers to play the piano for me while we wait. Not wanting to engage in meaningless chatter, I accept.

Surprisingly the beautiful, sometimes haunting music she plays helps my nerves to settle.

Until the elevator dings and the sound of footsteps approaching from different directions jerks me back to my terrifying present.

CHAPTER 58

BIANCA

Forcing myself to turn and face the don, shock holds me immobile. It is not Don De Luca heading toward us, but Salvatore.

And he is running across the marble floor like the hounds of hell are nipping at his heels, not Pietro.

"Do not say a word, *bella mia*," he orders.

That breaks my paralysis alright. Glaring at my ex-lover, I jump to my feet. "You are not the boss of me, Salvatore De Luca. This isn't about you."

Another lie. It is about protecting him as much as it is about protecting Bea.

He skids to a stop in front of me, his eyes narrowed, his jaw set in that stubborn way he gets. "You are not talking to my don."

"I most definitely am." There is so much I want to say right now, but if I say it, my implication that he doesn't know about my sister and Matthew Lombard goes out the window.

From the top of a high-rise like this one, that's a pretty big fall.

"What is this about?" Severu De Luca looms behind Salvatore, his expression forbidding, proving his are one of the sets of footsteps I heard.

"Bianca is trying to protect her sister from mafia reprisal. Does that sound familiar?" Catalina smiles at her husband like she can't help doing so.

The don's stern face softens when he looks at his wife. "Yes."

"For fuck's sake, Bianca, stop this." Salvatore yanks me to his side, like that's where I belong.

When we both know it isn't. Not anymore.

"Something you want to tell me, cousin?" Don De Luca asks as the room fills with his men.

Okay, there are only four, but with Catalina's bodyguards, that's six. They block the only avenues of escape, to the foyer and the hallways on either side of the living room. Two of them come to stand near the don and his wife, the menace in their postures making goosebumps of terror break out on my skin.

Salvatore meets his cousin's gaze unflinchingly, like there are no men with guns glaring at us. "Bianca is mine. She's not talking to you."

There is so much wrong with that statement. I start with the most important bit. "I am *not* yours. You threw me out."

"I don't want you talking to her. Whatever she may have done was done in ignorance," Salvatore says to his cousin, ignoring me. "She is not part of our world."

What is he trying to do? If Salvatore doesn't knock it off, there's no way I convince his don that the capo didn't know about the Bea situation.

All the softness that came into Don De Luca's face when he looks at his wife is gone. He is tense, like he's ready to strike and it's scaring the crap out of me.

Salvatore's insistence on opening his big mouth is not helping.

"That's not strictly true, is it?" Catalina asks before I can tell Salvatore to shut up. "She was born into the Genovese family."

"You were?" The don looks at me, both question and demand for an answer in his expression. "And you have done something my capo believes I will punish you for."

"Like hell you will," Salvatore grits out.

The two guards nearest him draw their weapons, but for now, they don't point them at anybody.

"Stay where you are!" Don De Luca barks. "If you pull that gun from its holster, my men will kill you."

I look where his glaring gaze is pointed, because it's not directed at me and Salvatore right now, and my terror ratchets up several notches. Pietro is standing in the foyer, his hand on his weapon.

"He is Bianca's bodyguard. Her safety is his top priority."

"I am his don." Don De Luca's glacial tone freezes my insides.

"Stop it," I cry. "Pietro, don't you dare touch your gun, or I'll shoot you myself."

When he doesn't move, I spin to face the don. "Will you please tell your men to put their guns away?"

"No."

Catalina makes a sound of disapproval, but this time the don does not spare his wife a glance.

Dio mio.

Neither Pietro, nor Salvatore are getting out of this alive, much less me. I will not wet myself.

Two weeks after I was assaulted to pay his debts, I watched my father's execution. I killed a man to protect my sister when I was thirteen. I might be afraid, but I am not weak. I can handle this. Even if it feels like there's enough tension in the room to squeeze the life out of me like a hungry boa constrictor.

There is only one way to get through this situation. With the truth. And that's not a guarantee for amnesty.

I can only hope it will be enough.

There has been no betrayal here, no matter what Salvatore believes.

"My father was Alberto Russo," I say. "He was Lorenzo Ricci's book-keeper until his capo killed him."

Don De Luca looks at Salvatore, his expression grim. "Did you know?"

"Not until today."

Che palle. Does the man have no sense of self-preservation? He couldn't tell one tiny lie?

Severu opens his mouth to speak, and I'm pretty sure it's to tell his men to take us into custody.

Catalina stands up quickly from the piano bench. "Let's move this discussion somewhere more comfortable. I don't know about Bianca, but this pregnant lady doesn't need a bunch of trigger happy made men looming over her."

The change in Don De Luca is instantaneous.

His attention goes from Salvatore to his wife, his gaze showing deep concern he does nothing to hide. "Are you alright *mi dolce bellezza*?"

She nods. "Yes, but I would prefer not to risk my piano if you and Salvatore start trading blows."

By blows she means gunfire. I shiver.

Don De Luca sweeps his wife into his arms. "As you wish."

"You don't have to do this anymore." She loops her arms around his neck, showing her protest is an empty one.

"I enjoy it, as you know." He leads the way down to the sunken living room, carrying his wife.

The bodyguards follow them, moving their bodies between us and the married couple. Catalina's attempt at diffusing the situation is clearly a temporary stay of execution.

I swallow on a dry throat, terror for Salvatore and now Pietro mixing with the storm of emotions inside me.

Taking a breath for courage, I try to follow King and Queen of New York, but Salvatore's hold keeps me from moving.

He spins me to face him and leans down so our faces are almost touching. "What the hell are you trying to do? Get yourself killed?"

"I am trying to clear up a misunderstanding that could get more than one person offed," I hiss back angrily.

"Stop this. I will protect you. Trust me."

My laugh is harsh. "If you had trusted me, none of this would be necessary." I glare up at him. "You didn't and it is. But maybe stop trying so hard to get yourself in trouble with your don."

"I'm going to admit to knowing all along and wanting you anyway. I'll remind him that Lorenzo kicked you out of *la famiglia* and offer to take whatever punishment Severu wants to mete out in your place. You just need to stay quiet."

For a second, I am completely speechless. Believing what he does about my supposed betrayal, Salvatore knows if he does that, Don De Luca will order his death.

"Why would you do that?" I demand.

"Because I will not let you die, *amore mio*."

It is the first time he has called me his love outside of the bedroom.

What should be a profound moment of joy is soured by the circumstances in which he uses the endearment. In one breath accusing me of whoring myself out for the business interests of another man and the next saying he will as good as die in my place.

"You're a very confusing man, capo."

"Your capo."

"Now is not the time," I say harshly. "Focus, Salvatore."

"I am focused." And all of it is on me.

No, that's not true. His body is held taut, like he's aware of where everyone else is in the room. Particularly in relation to me as he shifts us around so he's between me and the others.

Like *he's* my bodyguard, not Pietro. "And could you please tell Pietro to stand down?"

"No."

I'm going to be sick. "You and your cousin have a lot in common and that's not a compliment for either of you."

Salvatore doesn't bother to reply.

I sigh. "I have done nothing wrong, Salvatore. But according to Nerissa, you trying to smuggle me out of town could get you killed."

"Stop this. *Per favore*. I know you think your story is a good one, but the fantasy of a twin sister isn't going to convince my cousin of your innocence. And even if he believes you have a sister, he'll assume you were feeding her information for her fiancé."

"You really don't trust me." What am I supposed to do with that?

He is begging me to let him handle this. The man is willing to take any punishment for me, up to and including death, but he doesn't believe a word I say in my own defense.

I don't understand what's driving him, but it can't be love. If he loved me, he'd trust me. He wouldn't have thrown me out like yesterday's garbage.

"I am not going to shut up and if you don't, you could get us both killed." I shove away from him and this time he lets me go, his gorgeous face filled with uncertainty for once. "Don't think I've forgotten that you accused me of having sex with the only decent father I ever knew either."

With that, I turn my back on him and head to the don and his wife, my anger overriding my fear.

The don is standing near the sofa, his wife still in his arms. They are kissing. I'm pretty sure that's Catalina's attempt to give me and Salvatore time to talk with a hint of privacy.

As if he senses the moment we come close, Don De Luca lifts his head and kisses Catalina's forehead before settling her in the center of the sofa and taking the seat beside her closest to the chair I was in earlier.

Two bodyguards are now stationed at either end of the couch though, preventing me or Salvatore from getting too close.

I grab my backpack and sit down before pulling the papers out and laying them face down on the coffee table.

Salvatore is hovering beside me.

I look up at him. "I need you to send me an email with the don copied on it."

I don't explain why. This is his chance to show he trusts me at least a little.

After jerking his head in acknowledgment Salvatore pulls out his phone and taps on the screen. A few seconds later, I get a notification for a new email.

Clicking into it, I see that Salvatore hasn't sent a blank email, but written something.

No matter what happens, I will protect you.

Same here, caveman, same here.

Instead of copying his cousin, he has included Don De Luca's email address in the body of this message.

After copying and pasting the don's email address after Salvatore's in the *To* field, I send the email I prepared with the attachments. Then I flip over the papers I printed off at the airport business center and push them toward Catalina.

The page on top is a screenshot from my sister's social media. It is dated the first night I started work at Amuni. It's a selfie of her and Matthew, along with a picture of both their dinners. They are eating out at one of Boston's most exclusive restaurants.

They're both smiling and looking happy.

More screenshots follow. Some are like the first one, my sister chronicling her dates with her fiancé. Others are pictures of them at social events from sites like TMZ.

All are with dates and times that Salvatore and the don can easily verify as ones I was either working, or living with Salvatore at his penthouse.

Today is the first time I have left the penthouse without Pietro as my bodyguard and Salvatore knows it.

CHAPTER 59

SALVATORE

Seeing more proof of an ongoing relationship between Matthew Lombard and my woman fills me with jealous rage. I want to bellow my anger and break things, but most of all I want to kill that fucker after at least a week of torture.

"Look at the dates," Severu says.

All I can see are that *bastardo's* hands on her, their faces next to each other selfies I want to fucking obliterate from existence. I growl, my fingers tightening on my phone until I can feel the case crack.

My cousin barks, "Calm the fuck down and look at the damn dates."

Instead of doing what my don orders, I lift my gaze to Bianca. She is watching me, no sign of guilt on her beautiful face. Her brows lift in challenge. *Are you going to look at the dates?*

I finally look and pain rips through me as one thing becomes inescapably clear. There is no way that these pictures are of Bianca. One was taken last night for fuck's sake, while she was wrapped tightly in my arms. In *my* fucking bed.

Then other details start to register. The woman in the pictures wears her makeup differently than Bianca. She prefers more muted colors of clothing. Instead of blue the color of their eyes, she chooses sky blue and sage green instead of bright emerald.

Lavender instead of violet. The only color they wear in common is black.

"She looks just like you, Bianca," Catalina remarks.

But I disagree.

"Her hair is shorter than yours," I say hoarsely. "And she's too fucking skinny."

"She's a socialite like our mom. Keep looking." The expression of vulnerability on Bianca's face tells me I'm not going to like what comes next.

She's right.

The next attachment is a picture of two birth certificates side by side. Dated the same, one is for Bianca Butler Russo and the other is for Beatrice Butler Russo.

What I thought impossible is the truth. Why was I so quick to dismiss her claim to have a twin? Maybe because she said she had no family.

Any way I look at it, Bianca still lied to me. But now I'm wondering if the reason is because of something other than betrayal.

The next attachment is another screenshot. This one is from Elizabeth Butler's social media made on Bianca's fourteenth birthday. She wishes her beloved daughter *Bea* a happy birthday with gushing affection.

There are pictures of a baby, a toddler, a little girl and then a young teenager. With red hair the exact same shade as hers and heart shaped face so like what I imagine my lover looked like as a child, they could all be Bianca. They aren't though.

They are her sister, with nothing to indicate that Bea has a sibling, much less a twin. Their mother makes no mention of Bianca at all.

I go hot and then cold. I thought her mom was dead too, but Bianca never said that. My vulnerable lover said her mom was *gone*. And from these pictures, it's clear Bianca has no place in the socialite's life.

"What happened?" I ask, a leaden feeling in my gut.

Severu asks, "Why does your mother only mention one daughter?"

Did Bianca's parents each take one of the girls in the divorce? That would explain Alberto's employment record, for a sloppy capo like Lorenzo anyway. Why didn't Bianca go to her mother after her father died?

Bianca takes a deep breath and then starts talking, her voice like it is coming from someone else's body.

"Things were rocky between my parents for as long as I can remember. Mom came from Boston high society. Marrying my father was her act of rebellion, but it didn't turn out the way she expected."

"In what way?" Severu asks.

"She didn't like not having money. I guess my dad flashed a lot of cash around when they were dating, saying what a big man he was in the family. He was only 19 and not the son of anyone important, just another soldier. He didn't get promoted to bookkeeper until a couple of years later when he finished his associate degree."

It's no surprise Lorenzo made such a young, inexperienced man with only a two-year degree his bookkeeper. The corrupt and soon-to-be-dead capo was hiding his own thieving and would have wanted someone malleable in the position.

"My dad played up being related to the Detroit don, but that connection is a distant one. I don't think Don Russo ever even knew my dad's name. But my mom didn't know any better. She expected the same pampered life with people to cook and clean for her that she'd had back in Boston."

"As the bookkeeper for Lorenzo's crew he made more money than some of them, but that cheap *stronzo* doesn't have *any* rich soldiers," I say with disgust.

"How did you learn all this?" Severu asks.

"My parents fought constantly. I knew every lie Alberto had told and every way he fell short of her expectation by the time I was five."

Catalina scrunches her nose. "Your mother sounds like a piece of work."

Bianca smiles wryly. "If she hadn't gotten pregnant, the marriage probably wouldn't have lasted past the first year, but she did and they stayed acrimoniously married for almost 14 years."

"What happened then?" I am compelled to ask.

I need to know everything about this woman.

"When we were 13, my mom was at a luncheon with some of the other wives." Bianca shudders and stops for several long seconds. "A man came to the house. When we didn't answer the door, he forced his way inside."

Unable to stay away when she sounds so vulnerable, I drop to my knees beside Bianca's chair and put my arm around her shoulder. "You don't have to say any more."

"I do though, don't I?" She looks at me with unfocused blue eyes. "If you and Don De Luca are going to believe me when I tell you that there's no way I'm feeding information to my sister and her fiancée."

"I believe you, *amore mio*."

She sighs. "Good." Then she looks at Severu, clearly determined to finish her story. "We didn't call the cops because we were more scared of what the capo would do to us if we did than the man."

Catalina makes a wounded sound.

Bianca nods. "We should have called 911."

How did I ever think this woman was an outsider? She thinks like mafia.

"He said my dad owed him money. We told him our dad wasn't there, but he searched the house anyway. He couldn't find any money though. He said..." Bianca swallows. "He said..."

"I can tell them what you told me if that's easier," Catalina offers.

But Bianca shakes her head and squares her shoulders and keeps talking. "He said that he was going to take payment on account and leave a message for my dad."

Fury erupts inside me with volcanic force and somehow I keep it from exploding outward. Whoever this man is, I will find him and I will kill him. Slowly.

I press a kiss to Bianca's temple. "We get the idea. You don't have to say anything more."

"We didn't know what he meant, but then he grabbed Bea and he threw her onto the couch," Bianca continues, her voice devoid of emotion. "At first I didn't understand what was happening, but Bea screamed, and I saw he was tearing at her underwear."

CHAPTER 60

BIANCA

9 Years Before

I try to pull him off of Bea, but he's too big. He shoves me back and I land hard against the coffee table. His jacket rides up and I see a gun in a holster at his waist. I grab it.

He doesn't notice. Bea is kicking and screaming.

I point the gun at his head and pull the trigger. It just clicks.

He looks up and laughs. "Put that down before you hurt yourself."

I pull again and again, but the gun just clicks and clicks.

"I can see you're a feisty one," he says with a disgusting leer. "You'll get your turn soon enough."

I can't make the gun work and he's not afraid I'll figure it out. The gun must be empty. What *stronzo* wears an empty gun?

He thinks I'm funny. That what he's doing is funny.

My sister screams again. I grab one of my mom's crystal lamps we aren't allowed to touch. She can punish me as much as she wants, but I have to get this man off of Bea.

I swing for his head, but he shifts at the last second and it hits him on the shoulder.

"Fuck. You little bitch!" He yanks it from me fast and throws it against the wall, where it shatters into tiny sharp bits.

Except one big piece still attached to the base. It looks like a knife and it gives me an idea. I run into the kitchen and grab the knife my nonna used to use to filet fish from the market.

A memory of my dad talking to one of his friends, his voice thick with admiration, plays through my mind. "That's how you use a knife. You don't stab the fucker. You cut his throat so he can't scream."

I approach the man again, being as quiet as I can, trying to tune out my sister's screams. If I mess up, there's no one else to save Bea.

He's unbuckling his belt and I know it's now or never. I jump on his back and slash the knife across his throat with all my strength. Blood sprays everywhere, covering Bea, the sofa and the carpet around them.

He throws himself back, landing on top of me, knocking all the air out of me. He rolls off me and tries to crawl to where I'd dropped his gun.

If he wants it, then the gun must work. I didn't do it right. My lungs burning, I crawl faster and shove the gun out of his reach. The man tries to crawl toward me, but he's getting slower. Eventually he stops.

Bea is still screaming and trying to wipe the blood off of her. I want to help, but she won't let me touch her.

Suddenly, mom is there and she's yelling while she checks Bea for injuries.

"It's not her blood," I say, hoping to calm my mom down. "It's his."

Mom looks from me to the dead man on the floor, horror etched in every line of her face. "What happened to him? Where is your father?"

"I killed him." I drop the knife.

SALVATORE

Present

"That night, she and my sister left," Bianca's voice is hollow as she finishes her account of what must have been the worst day of her life.

"She didn't take you?" I ask in the hushed silence that falls after Bianca stops speaking.

My precious love shakes her head. "Mom said I had my dad's bad blood, that I was a violent criminal just like him."

Severu looks as furious as I feel. "That bitch."

"I sickened her, and Beatrice couldn't even look at me," Bianca says like anything could explain her mother's actions. "Maybe my mom was right. I still don't feel any remorse for killing that creep. They split custody in the divorce. Bea went with mom, and I stayed with our dad."

Catalina's brows furrow. "There's no divorce in the mafia."

That's the rule, but there are exceptions. Divorces happen. More often made men abandon their wives and children to live with their lovers, without the formality of divorce. As long as they provide financially for their family the don and his capos don't get involved.

"There are annulments," Bianca says on a sigh.

"How can you get an annulment when there are children involved?" Catalina asks.

"The state grounds for annulment and in the Catholic church are broader than you'd think, love," Severu says. "But don't go getting any ideas."

Catalina rolls her eyes and then looks at Bianca expectantly.

"My dad felt guilty about what almost happened." Bianca's head tips infinitesimally toward mine, seeking comfort.

Or at least that is what I tell myself.

"He didn't dispute what mom claimed when she filed for the annulment in New York and with the Church."

"That would have made you and your sister illegitimate." Catalina sounds shocked.

As well she should. No made man with any honor would deny the parentage of his children. To allow his daughters to become legally born out of wedlock goes against centuries of tradition and belief, stretching back to our Sicilian roots.

"I'm pretty sure my mom's parents preferred their daughter and granddaughter to carry their name rather than Russo. They're kind of waspy, if you didn't figure that out from the types of events my sister attends."

"When your father died, Lorenzo didn't send you to live with your mother?"

She laughs, the sound harsh. "He threw me out into the street and told me I was lucky he didn't kill me too."

Lorenzo is a cruel man. He'd known that a sixteen-year-old girl had no chance of surviving on the street on her own. He would have expected her to end up dead or turning tricks.

After I kill Lorenzo, his son will be ten times the capo that old bastard is.

"How did you survive?" Catalina asks.

Bianca told me and Nerissa the gist of this that day on the roof, and says pretty much the same thing now, adding that she had been terrified Lorenzo would change his mind about killing her.

"What about Elizabeth?" I ask, planning the woman's slow demise in my head.

"She gave me ten thousand dollars and told me to stay away. There was no place in her life for my father's daughter."

"You and Bea share the same fucking DNA," I say, incensed on her behalf.

Identical DNA.

Bianca shrugs. "Mom was right. If I suddenly showed up, it would have hurt her reputation and Bea's too. That's important in the world they live in."

"You should have been important," I growl.

She shrugs me away. "People find it easy to throw me away."

I have no excuse. I fucked up and the look she's giving me says fixing it isn't going to be easy.

But it starts with the words I owe her. "I'm sorry I didn't believe you when you told me the pictures were of your sister."

"I told you my family was gone." She shrugs again and I'm learning to dislike that particular action from her. "We were never going to last anyway. You're destined for a mafia princess and I've got a whole world outside of the New York *famiglia* to explore."

She is not leaving New York, but I'm smart enough not to say that out loud right now. I've got ground to recover with her.

"You're going to reconnect with your mother?" Catalina asks, sounding worried about that possibility.

Bianca shakes her head. "As far as she and Bea are concerned, I don't exist. I'm okay with that as long as my sister doesn't have to pay a price for looking like me."

She looks expectantly at Severu.

He's looking at me though and his expression isn't friendly. "You didn't just know about Bianca's connection to the Genovese mafia, you knew about her connection to Matthew Lombard."

"She doesn't have a connection with that *stronzo*," I say forcefully.

"But you thought she did, and you were going to hide it from me." Severu silently signals to his men.

I use a quick hand gesture to tell Pietro to stand down. Bianca is no longer at risk from our don, and I will not allow Pietro to stand against our don on my behalf.

The four guards not standing beside the couch all draw their guns. I release a silent breath of relief when Pietro makes no move to follow suit.

"I wasn't going to let anyone hurt her," I tell my cousin.

"Even if she was a rat?"

"Even if she fucking sent Matthew Lombard the information on a silver platter," I affirm.

Now that I know Bianca is safe from my cousin's wrath, I will not stoop to hiding anything from him.

Severu gives another silent signal and the four men close in on me. My cousin's reaction is no surprise. I betrayed him and Severu isn't going to settle for monetary reprisal to punish my disloyalty.

Unaware of what the movement of my don's men means, Bianca stares at me in disbelief. "What is wrong with you? Do you think I came here and laid my soul bare to your don for shits and giggles? I'm trying to save your stupid life."

"I don't lie to my don."

"Unless it's to protect the woman you love," Severu says with an edge.

I shrug. I'm sure as hell not going to admit to my cousin that I love Bianca before I tell her. Would it make any difference if I did?

Catalina worriedly chews her bottom lip. She's worried. Unlike Bianca, she notices the movement of her husband's men and knows what it means.

She, more than anyone else, knows that Severu will not spare family for the sake of sentiment. I don't regret my actions though. I would do it again with the same information.

The only thing I regret is not believing *mi amore* when she told me the truth about her sister and being stupid enough to throw her away.

CHAPTER 61

BIANCA

I cannot believe the big dope kneeling on the hard marble floor beside my chair. He's been there since I started talking.

His knees have to be killing him.

"Get up. Sit on a chair like a normal person," I tell him.

"Stay there," Severu barks, once again scaring the crap out of me.

The look he's giving Salvatore is 100% merciless don without a trace of caring cousin in there.

Salvatore doesn't move, but there's no fear emanating off of him either.

Stupidity or courage?

The don stands and draws his gun before pointing it right at Salvatore's forehead. "You broke your vow to me."

"He didn't," I disagree, trying to stand up so I can put myself between the gun and Salvatore.

These two predators needed a cool down moment.

But Salvatore's arm over my shoulder turns into concrete. I'm not going anywhere.

"Do not move, Bianca," Salvatore bosses, his gaze never leaving Don De Luca's face. "If I survive the discussion to come, Severu, you and I will have words about you pointing a gun so close to her."

"What is wrong with you?" I demand, pretty sure it's not the first time I've asked today.

If he survives? Like that's in doubt and he's okay with it. He probably is. Severu isn't the only one who considers Salvatore's actions disloyal.

Both men have an overdeveloped sense of what constitutes loyalty and apparently Salvatore is willing to judge himself as harshly as he would anyone else.

"Let me go!" I struggle to get out from under that heavy arm.

"I don't like you so close to a gun," Salvatore explains. "But if I let you go, you're going to try to get between me and Severu."

I can't deny the truth. So, I say nothing.

"You are safer where you are." He squeezes my shoulders like he's comforting me.

I want to scream, but I'm not risking tipping the scales of this dangerous situation with my very understandable frustration with the capo and his don.

I'm not going to stay entirely silent though. "He only found out today," I tell Don De Luca. "Telling you he knew all along was a lie." The one lie he was willing to utter, the *scemo*.

"Severu knows that because there was no betrayal on your part," Catalina says pointedly.

The fear in her eyes is not giving me any comfort. She's worried her husband is going to kill my capo.

Che palle.

"But there was on his," Don De Luca says, his gun unwavering.

"He didn't want you to kill me."

"If he had trusted you, the issue would be moot."

"I know," I grumble, but I don't mention my other grievances against Salvatore.

The don has enough of his own.

"Correct me if I am wrong, but I assume the breakup today happened *because* my cousin believed you to be a rat."

Not sure I would correct him even if he was wrong, not with a gun pointed at Salvatore's head. But in this case, he's not wrong, so I just nod.

"After taking advantage of you sexually, he threw you away."

Pain spears through my fear. "I am aware."

"I did not take sexual advantage of her," Salvatore says, emotion bleeding through this voice for the first time.

And I remember that day with his mom and Rosa.

"Of course not. Severu didn't mean it that way," I say, with a frown for the don.

Doesn't he realize his opinion matters to Salvatore?

"But you did throw me away," I can't help adding to Salvatore.

His chest rumbles, but he doesn't agree verbally. What the heck is that supposed to mean?

"Salvatore, you have two choices. Both require you to give up your life."

"No," I shout. "What kind of man are you that you could kill your own flesh and blood?"

How do I get out of this nightmare? Equally important, how do I get Salvatore out of it?

"I am not a man. I am a don," Severu De Luca says with a shrug.

"Hate to break it to you, but a don is still a man."

He does not deign to answer me but stares at Salvatore, like he's waiting for something.

"I willingly offer my life," Salvatore says solemnly.

Don De Luca intones, "I accept your sacrifice."

Tears burn the back of my eyes and I blink rapidly, but they don't go away. Hot moisture spills down my cheeks. I shouldn't have come here.

My attempt to save Salvatore is what is going to get him killed.

The don re-holsters his gun and then makes a hand motion and the sound of other guns sliding back into their holsters penetrates the pounding in my ears. The soft glide of shoe leather on marble tells me the men I didn't realize were so close are moving away.

The don is so confident in Salvatore's promise, he doesn't feel the need to keep his men on alert. Even the bodyguards at either end of the sofa melt into the background.

Salvatore releases my shoulder and stands. I look up at him, but there is no grief on his handsome face to match the feeling in my heart. Why would there be?

He's a made man and death is part of his life.

But not his death, my heart cries.

I wait for him to move away so I can breathe.

But instead of moving back to his seat, he picks me up and a second later, he's sitting where I was and I'm on his lap. "That's better."

Catalina's laugh startles me, especially under the present circumstances. "That's definitely a De Luca trait."

"Well, I'm not a De Luca wife," I mutter.

Salvatore takes my left hand into his right, and laces our fingers so our arms create a band across my body. "Yet."

My confusion and grief morph into horror as his exchange with his cousin plays back through my head.

I willingly offer my life.

I accept your sacrifice.

It cannot mean what I think it does. I shake my head in denial, but a rock settles in my stomach.

I accept your sacrifice.

That rock starts to play with some friends, making me queasy.

"If your father or even your capo had done right by you, they would have arranged a marriage for you." Severu looks intently at me, like he's expecting me to agree.

"Maybe in a medieval mafia fairytale." But we're living in the real world. "I am the daughter of a thief. I don't belong in *la famiglia* anymore."

"The New York Cosa Nostra does not make the child pay for the sins of the father."

Personal experience tells me this is not true. However, I know what he is trying to say. Don De Luca does not believe that I am responsible for my father's betrayal. He doesn't see me as dirt because of what my dad did.

I would appreciate that more if Salvatore's life had not just been offered and accepted as payment for his disloyalty to the don.

"Your capo betrayed you." The look on the don's face would send those rocks in my stomach knocking against each other if it was aimed at me, but it's not. His next words prove it. "It was his job to make sure you were taken care of in the absence of your father."

Like that was ever going to happen. According to him, I was lucky Lorenzo Ricci didn't sell me to make back the money my father stole.

"What is done is done," I say now. "My past cannot be changed. I am no longer part of *la famiglia*."

"That is not true. You were lost but now you have been found and we will do right by you." Why does that resonate with as much threat as promise?

"That sounds almost biblical." I say it like a joke but no one else laughs.

"One of my capos put you on the street when you were still a child. Another took you as his mistress." The look he gives Salvatore sends a chill of dread through me. "You should have been protected."

"Everything that happened between me and Salvatore was consensual." Other than Pietro kidnapping me. "And I am nobody's mistress. Again, not the Middle Ages here."

"And that is why I will not kill him," Don De Luca says.

Relief pours through me. He is not going to kill the man holding onto me like he will never let me go.

"If we can make this right," the don adds, sending that relief on a long trip without a return ticket.

He cannot be saying what I think he's saying. Salvatore is destined for a mafia princess, someone who brings benefit to the mafia. A woman with the upbringing and pedigree to match his.

Offer my life. Accept your sacrifice.

The word *sacrifice* resounds through my brain over and over.

I look at Catalina and say, "Please tell me your husband is not talking about what I think he is."

"If you think he's talking about marriage then I cannot do that." She gives me a sympathetic, almost hopeful smile.

"No, no, no." Panic courses through me. This is not happening. "My life is not getting derailed by mafia don guilt."

What else could this be? He believes two of his capos screwed up in their treatment of me, so now, he's determined to make it right. With Salvatore's sacrifice.

And mine.

Wait, what if he's not talking about making his valuable capo marry me, but someone else? What if the sacrifice is letting me go before Salvatore is ready to?

Does that even make any sense?

My brain is spinning and I'm pretty sure that if I try to stand up right now, my knees will not hold me. Panic courses through me, sending the rocks in my stomach tumbling and every nerve synapse firing with stress.

"I'm pretty sure mafia don guilt is not a thing," Severu De Luca says, sounding amused.

Gone is the grim reaper.

The man I met at dinner that night we were all here is back, but now I know who lurks under the calm façade. An emotionless killer who would sacrifice his cousin for the sake of mafia loyalty.

Catalina gives him a look. "It so is a thing."

Oh, God. What am I going to do? I can't let Don De Luca choose a husband for me.

"If my father had done right by me, I wouldn't get nauseated when a man touches me." I speak the only truth that might change the don's mind.

Salvatore makes a pleased sound. The jerk. "You don't mind when I touch you."

"You're the only exception I've found so far. Go figure," I say with no attempt to blunt my sarcasm. "But that doesn't mean I can get married and have a normal sex life with some stranger."

Despite my lofty hopes when this thing between us started, the thought of another man touching me sends horror crawling along my skin.

"I know I am not your favorite person right now, Bianca, but I am no stranger," Salvatore whispers in my ear.

My first conclusion was the right one. Why doesn't that make me feel better?

"This is ridiculous," I nearly shout. "I have been living on my own since I was 16. No one can tell me who I have to marry."

Instead of getting angry at my outburst, the don gives me an appraising look. "Are you willing to allow Salvatore to die? He promised his life in exchange for his insult against his don."

I look to Catalina, hoping for a sign that her husband doesn't mean what he says. He cannot kill Salvatore. But the grief in her hazel gaze says her husband is capable of doing just that if I don't marry the capo.

"There has to be another way," I say desperately. "Salvatore, tell the don you are sorry and promise never to do it again."

"I am not sorry and I would do it again in a heartbeat to protect you," he says instead.

Whatever happens, I will always protect you.

CHAPTER 62

SALVATORE

P oor Bianca is on the verge of hyperventilating.

It's not an ego boosting response to hearing that Severu wants her to marry me, but after my fuckup earlier, it is an understandable one.

I let go of her hand to dig in my pocket for the item I've been carrying around for the last week. My grandmother's engagement ring. There is nothing understated about the ten-carat emerald cut diamond my grandfather got her after being made don.

Five years later, he had a three-carat yellow diamond added on either side of the main stone. I replaced them with dark purple amethysts two weeks ago.

I place the ring in her hand and curl her fingers over it. "I'm going to ask you the way you deserve, but I want you to hold onto that until then and remember that I've been carrying it with me since I got it back from the jeweler."

"Is that nonna's ring?" Severu asks.

I nod. Most of our nonna's jewelry was passed down to Aunt Aria, but she left this ring to my mother. Mamma had her own engagement ring and wedding set, so she never wore it.

She was over the moon when I asked her for it.

"It's your grandmother's ring?" Bianca asks. "You've been carrying it around in your pocket?"

"Yes. And yes. Now, please save my cousin from having to execute one of his favorite capos and tell him you will marry me. You can wait and give *me* your yes until I've asked you properly."

"You're so sure I want to save you?" she asks.

After the risk she took coming here to save me from my cousin's wrath? "Yes."

I'm under no illusions Bianca loves me after today. That feeling is on another continent when it comes to her heart. How can I expect anything else after how badly I fucked up?

But I can be a patient man when I need to, and my cousin's decree is giving me a lifetime to woo my beloved's heart.

"I killed a man and I'm not sorry," she reminds me.

"He deserved death. Do I?"

She huffs out a breath and makes me wait almost a full minute until she shakes her head. But she doesn't look happy about it.

"Is that a yes?" Severu asks.

Bianca glares at him. "It is a you-twisted-my-arm-and-I'm-not-go-ing-to-forget-it yes."

"Welcome to the club," Catalina says with more humor than I think Bianca is ready for.

"The De Luca wives club?" The wry twist to Bianca's mouth indicates she remembers what she said earlier.

Does she remember my response?

"The forced to marry an arrogant De Luca who turns out to be a pretty great husband club." Catalina grins up cheekily at Severu.

"Less of the *pretty great* and more of the *supremely awesome* wife."

"I'll think about it."

"I see that you have luggage with you. You'll be staying here until the wedding then?" Severu asks Bianca.

She goes rigid, like she's remembering why she has the duffle with her.

My arms tighten around her reflexively. "Please don't. Come home with me." I am not ashamed to plead with this woman.

"It's not my home though, is it?" She pushes for me to let her off my lap. I don't want to, but I do anyway.

She stands and takes a step away from me and I hate it.

I fucked up when I let my past superimpose itself over my present. I should have trusted her. At the very least, I should have heard her out. Asked questions and not made accusations. We both know it.

My only hope is that Bianca is even more furious with Severu for forcing her into the marriage than she is with me.

"Rosa is really worried about you." Yes, it's a blatant attempt at playing on her emotions.

No, I don't regret it.

"She noticed I was gone?" Bianca asks, flicking a glance to Pietro.

My head of security is now standing sentinel at the entrance to the living room. He backed off on my signal, but not so far away he couldn't intervene if she got in trouble. He's protective over her.

Since he looks at her like she's a sister, or something, I don't have to kill him.

"Mamma went gonzo when we couldn't find you in the apartment," Pietro says with a critical look for me, his capo. "I was not told you would be going anywhere."

Bianca opens her mouth, probably to say something about Nerissa taking her to the airport, glances at Severu and snaps her lips together.

How did I ever believe this woman was anything like Monica? She's protecting my second, even now.

"Rosa can come here and assure herself of Bianca's wellbeing." Severu indicates the hall that leads to his office. "Salvatore, we have business to discuss. Catalina can help Bianca plan the wedding."

"I can?" Catalina asks, her tone unimpressed.

"You did an excellent job planning ours."

"With your mother and sister's help."

"Now you will have both my mother and my aunt's help."

"I don't want a big wedding," Bianca inserts.

"You are marrying a capo, Bianca. That's not going to happen at the courthouse with two witnesses." My cousin smiles, like he's trying to be conciliatory. He looks like a shark going in for the kill. "With only thirty days to plan, it will be less of a spectacle than it would be otherwise."

"Thirty days?" Bianca shouts. "I'm not getting married in thirty days."

Severu looks at her stoicly. "That is your choice, of course."

Bianca doesn't look even a little relieved. Because she's learning how my cousin operates.

"If you are not married to my cousin in thirty days, I will order his execution. My patience only extends so far. Salvatore believed he was risking undermining my bid to replace Don Caruso as godfather. The only reason I am giving him an out is because up to this point, he has been one of my strongest and most loyal capos."

"Not to mention your cousin," Bianca says snidely.

"Who put the woman in his bed above family." My don's voice is arctic and uncompromising.

Severu is doing me a solid, demanding the marriage as a way to redeem my disloyalty.

If Bianca had been the rat I believed her to be, there would be no chance to redeem myself though. And he will follow through on his threat to kill me if the wedding doesn't take place.

That's why he'll make a good godfather. My cousin is utterly ruthless when it comes to protecting *la famiglia*.

"I'm not staying here with you," Bianca seethes. "Or are you going to threaten to kill *me* if I don't?"

"Where you live prior to the wedding is entirely your choice. As you said, this is not the Middle Ages."

Catalina's snort of derisive laughter causes the first crack in my don's expressionless demeanor. A flicker of worry enters his familiar gaze before he scowls at me as if his wife's unhappiness is my fault.

Which ultimately, it is, I suppose. Just like Bianca's anger and mistrust. I have a lot to make up for.

"Since you *understandably* won't be staying," Catalina says to Bianca with a challenging side-eye to her husband. "Will you keep me company for lunch while the don and his capo conduct their business? We can eat on the rooftop."

Every word is a barb directed at Severu. Unless she has other commitments, Catalina would usually join us and put off eating until she could share the meal with her husband. I doubt he's thrilled she's decided to eat in their rooftop garden either.

Severu has the entire rooftop surrounded by a clear shield with a Level 8 bullet resistance rating and the latest anti-drone technology in place. He still doesn't like Catalina going up there when security is on high alert like it has been since Don Caruso's stroke.

"You can eat in the dining room," he says.

"Oh, I don't think so," Catalina replies. "After all, we have all sorts of modern technology, this *not* being the Middle Ages and all."

When we reach his office, Severu rounds on me. "You are welcome."

"Don't start calling yourself the mafia matchmaker just yet, but I owe you."

"Indeed, you do." Severu crosses his arms and gives me the stare that has made grown men piss themselves. "Lorenzo."

"He's on ice at Amuni."

"You had him picked up."

"I did."

"I didn't give the order," Severu observes.

"He was a risk to Bianca and he's a rat."

"Nevertheless, I was going to wait until things calmed down to take him out."

"Every day you let him live is a risk someone else finds out he's stealing from the Family," I say with force. "That will make you look weak."

Severu rubs his chin in thought. "That's what Micelli said and I agreed. Which is why I gave my brother the order to pick him up. But strangely enough Miceli and his team can't find Lorenzo."

I pound Severu's desk with my fist. "No one is killing that *stronzo* before I get a chance to ask him some questions."

"Do you want Miceli or Angelo there for the interrogation?" Severu asks without hesitation.

It's an easier concession than I expected. "Miceli."

I'm still pissed at Angelo for killing Gino before I got a chance to mete out his punishment.

My don nods. "Tell Bianca to call me Severu. We're family now."

CHAPTER 63

SALVATORE

Pietro is driving my Audi RS7 and the privacy screen is up between us, but Bianca gives me the silent treatment.

She keeps her lips pressed tightly together when I tell her what Severu said about using his first name, and when I bring up the wedding. She does not reply when I ask about her lunch with Catalina.

"We need to tell my parents you are a Russo."

"I am *not* a Russo," she claims.

"Whatever your last name is now, you are still part of the Genovese Family."

"Not according to Lorenzo."

"Lorenzo's opinion doesn't count for shit," I tell the side of her face.

She refuses to look at me, her gaze toward the view out the tinted car windows.

When she doesn't answer, I add. "Your don and *your* capo claim you. That is all that matters."

She flinches when I say *your capo*, but remains silent.

"Your mother is a selfish bitch and your father was a fool, but you are Genovese Family." And soon to be my wife. "Your new last name does not change that, but when you are a De Luca, no one will question your place."

"I prefer Gemelli."

"Did you take that name because it means Gemini?" The constellation that represents the twins, Castor and Pollox.

Greek heroes, not Italian, but the symbolism would matter to her more than their origin.

She shrugs, which I take for a yes.

"Have you tried to talk to Beatrice since you became adults?" Do I need to punish the sister as well as the mother?

"There is no place for me in her life." Sadness laces Bianca's voice.

I will bring her sister back into Bianca's life, kicking and screaming if I have to.

"She didn't run as far from the mafia as you think. Her fiancé is part of the Lombardi Cosa Nostra in Boston." Not that Matthew Lombard has any power in his syndicate any longer.

He has risen as high in the ranks as he ever will because of the peace agreement Miceli brokered on Severu's behalf.

Bianca's head turns quickly and she finally looks at me. "I thought he was a property developer."

"He is. Stellar Holdings is a front for the Lombardi Family. The Lombards are heavily involved in regional politics too."

"That must be how he and Bea met. The Butlers have been part of local politics for generations. The guest list for their wedding probably includes a senator or two." Pain dulls her blue eyes.

"If you want senators at our wedding, we'll have them."

"It's not politicians I want at my wedding." She looks away again, her shoulders slumped.

She wants her sister there. Her twin.

"If Matthew Lombard is Cosa Nostra, why would me talking to him be a betrayal?" Bianca asks without turning back to me.

The thought of Bianca being with the other man even though I know the pictures are of her sister, sends killing rage through me. "You *didn't* talk to him."

She doesn't reply.

I grind my teeth. "He tried to outbid me for some strategic properties."

"That's what you thought I told him about?"

"I didn't think you told him anything before this morning." And this morning, I was too consumed with fury and hurt to consider what exactly she had told me.

"But you did think I told him about the properties?" she presses.

"If you want an answer, look at me."

She shrugs without changing the angle of her gaze, her answer as clear as if she'd spoken out loud.

Fuck off, capo.

I take another tack to get her to talk to me. "I think you should get therapy for the nightmares. A professional can help you work through what happened when you were thirteen."

It works.

She sucks in a breath and then says, "That's not the mafia way. Besides, my nightmares aren't about that day."

"What are they about then?"

I expect renewed silence.

But I'm wrong.

"What happened when I was sixteen." Her voice is hollow, like earlier.

I should have guessed that. Watching her father's execution had to have been horrifying for her. "Lorenzo killing your father."

"No."

What does she mean, *no*? What else happened to her that year? "Did something happen during your time on the streets?"

"No."

You're batting a thousand, genius.

"What then?"

She just shakes her head.

I lay my hand on her arm. "Please tell me, Bianca."

"I don't have nightmares about being there to protect my sister," she says. "My nightmares are about the day no one was there to protect me."

Regardless of what I say or ask, she remains silent for the rest of the ride.

Fuck.

No one was there to protect her. From what Bianca saved her sister from? From being kicked out onto the street not once, but twice?

All of the above?

I ask, but she just shakes her head.

Something scarred her psyche more than killing a man at thirteen, or watching her father get executed three years later. She'll tell me when she's ready. Maybe after I tell her my secrets.

We are in the elevator headed up to the penthouse when Bianca finally speaks again. "Will Don De Luca punish Pietro?"

My head of security frowns. "You don't need to worry about me, Bianca."

"You don't," I agree. "I convinced Severu to let me handle it."

My cousin understands loyalty. If Don Caruso had threatened Catalina back when he still had the strength to carry through on that threat, Severu would have killed our godfather before he let him touch her.

"What are you going to do?" Bianca demands as the elevator doors slide open.

We all step out and then I nod to Pietro. "Thank you."

His lips tilt at the corners. "My pleasure."

"That's it?" Bianca asks suspiciously.

"That's it."

She turns and heads to the door, waiting for me to open it.

But I guide her through putting her biometrics in the system so she can open it at will. "That gives you access to the elevator as well."

Her shoulders relax a little. Is that because she thinks she can run now? No matter where she goes, I will follow her.

This woman is mine.

When we get inside, she hugs Rosa and then goes straight upstairs. I follow her and watch as she makes a beeline for the guestroom.

I don't miss the snick of the lock after she closes it either.

BIANCA

A sharp rap sounds against the door, too firm to be Rosa.

Besides, she already came in an hour ago. Fussing over me, she insisted on unpacking my things. All of them. As if having my clothes back in the dresser and closet would make everything okay.

Like it never happened.

Salvatore must have told her about the upcoming wedding as soon as we walked in the door, because she was full of ideas for that too.

So many ideas.

"Go away!" I yell now.

"It's me, Bianca. Please let me in," Nerissa's voice calls through the doorway.

Accidenti!

"Fuck off!" Not wanting her to be killed does not equal wanting to be her friend anymore.

"I'm sorry. I should have talked to you before I took the pictures and will to Salvatore," she says through the door.

Pretty sure that was *never* going to happen.

"I'm not listening," I yell back.

Oh, that was mature.

Shut up. But I can't silence my own conscience.

"I have already resigned as Salvatore's second-in-command, but I don't want to lose you as a friend. Please talk to me, Bianca."

She did what?

I go to the door, but don't open it. "Why did you do it?"

"The pictures were delivered to me. I thought they were you with a mafia rival."

I have questions about Matthew Lombard I didn't want to ask Salvatore, the man who offered to *sacrifice* himself by marrying me to make up for his sin against his don.

I throw the door open. "Tell me everything you know about my sister's fiancé."

Nerissa drops her hand, clearly intending to knock again.

Her perfect brows draw together. "Didn't Salvatore tell you?"

Crossing my arms, I move aside so she can come into the room.

She does before I shut the door, relocking it. Then I wait in expectant silence for her to answer.

Finally, she says, "Matthew Lombard is part of the Boston Cosa Nostra. Your mom being from Boston, you probably know as much about them as I do."

"Are you serious? I didn't even know Boston had a Cosa Nostra syndicate before today."

Contrary to what Salvatore seems to think, my knowledge of the mafia is limited to the Genovese Family. And I didn't know the De Lucas owned so much real estate in New York either.

They're the kind of mafia family my mom thought she was marrying into.

"They do."

"I got that," I say dryly. "So, Matthew Lombard?"

"He's the nephew of the don."

"How close are his ties to the criminal enterprises of the Lombardi Family?"

Nerissa opens her mouth but I put my hand up. "Don't try telling me you don't know either."

"I wasn't going to." She hops up on the top of the dresser, planning to stay a while. "Up until he tried to outbid Salvatore for the bar properties, Matthew Lombard wasn't involved in mafia business. He's an aspiring politician. I guess he thought he would try his hand at mafia politics too."

"Explain."

When Nerissa is done telling me about his attempt to buy the bar properties and how it all plays into Severu De Luca's bid to be the next godfather, I'm sitting cross-legged on the bed, my back against the headboard.

Two things are clear. One, Nerissa's not the one who doctored my dad's file. Two, she acted as she did in the hope of protecting both me and her brother. She could have taken the pictures to her father, but she brought them to Salvatore, believing he would try to protect me.

"You're the one who told me he killed a woman he was fucking before. Why would you think he was going to protect me?" I ask skeptically.

"Because I know my brother. I saw how he was with Monica eleven years ago and I see how he is with you now. If my brother still has a heart in there somewhere, you own it."

I scoff at that.

But Nerissa's expression says she's dead serious.

"Why let me go if you thought I could take Matthew information. Why not just kill me?" I push.

"I couldn't. We'd become friends. I don't have friends. Mafia colleagues? Yes. Family? Yes. Friends?" She shakes her head.

That shouldn't matter. The mafia comes first.

"That's not what you said on the way to the airport," I remind her.

She sighs. "I was being a bitch because I thought you broke my brother's heart."

"He doesn't have a heart."

"Before you came along, I would have agreed with you. Now, not so much."

He was willing to *die* for me, to protect me even when it meant betraying his own family. Why else would he do that if he didn't feel something for me? But then why not *ask* me about the pictures instead of accusing me?

Those are questions only Salvatore can answer and I'm not ready to talk to him right now.

"He was willing to die for you," she says echoing my thoughts. "I think he's in love with you, Bianca."

I wave my hand, dismissing her words. I'm not accepting proxy declarations of love from my capo's sister.

"Why did you resign?" I ask.

Her face twists in grief. "Salvatore deserves a better second."

"Pretty sure there isn't one." Nerissa is fiercely loyal, smart and strong. And yes, a Grade A bitch when she needs to be.

"How can you say that?" she demands.

"Everything you've done to hurt me has been in an attempt to protect your brother and capo. I killed a man to protect my sister."

"What?"

"Ask your brother." I'm not reliving that day again. "Tell him I said he could tell you. Or Pietro. He was listening in too."

"Pietro isn't speaking to me."

That's got to hurt. From what I have seen those two are as close as brother and sister.

"I can't believe Salvatore still is." She looks at me intently. "But he doesn't blame anyone else for his fuckups."

"You didn't look for an alternate explanation because I told you that all my family is gone," I give her the out because it's true.

"I didn't think you had *any* siblings, so the whole twin thing wasn't even on my radar. I'm sorry she's not part of your life anymore. I know how much it hurts to lose family."

She told me about her parents dying and ending up in such a bad foster care situation that the streets were a better alternative. That's when Big Sal De Luca found her and instead of walking on by, he took her home to Ilaria and suddenly they had a daughter.

A teenage daughter with a big mouth and even bigger attitude, according to Nerissa.

"I should have told you about my family when you told me about your past." If I had, she would have known the pictures weren't me.

But the will still made it look like I'd lied about Mr. Ruhnke.

"You got used to pushing people away," Nerissa excuses me. "I lived with the De Lucas for three years before I told them what happened to me in foster care."

"What did Big Sal do?"

"He told Salvatore. It was a couple of months after my brother was made. He went after the man who hurt me and made sure he never got the chance to hurt anyone else."

"Do you sleep better knowing he's dead?"

Would you sleep better if you knew the men who hurt you were dead?

I don't know.

"If I'd told the De Lucas right away, he would have been stopped sooner."

That's not an answer. Or maybe it is. Maybe she stopped dreaming about what happened to her and started having nightmares about what happened after she left.

"It's not your guilt to carry, Nerissa."

She shrugs. Then she sighs. "I know you won't forgive me right away, but I hope someday we can be friends again."

"Tell Salvatore you want your job back and you keep working on improving conditions for the dancers and sex workers in your club and we'll talk."

"Whoever he puts in my place can do that."

"Maybe they will. Maybe they won't. But you'll listen to me and that means something." She's made changes based on my suggestions already, and it's not only because I was Salvatore's girlfriend.

It was because underneath her gruff exterior, Nerissa cares about the people that rely on her. Now that she sees the employees in the club in that light, they are the recipients of her fierce loyalty and protection.

"I'll ask Salvatore if I can still manage the clubs, but I don't think he trusts me right now."

I grab my phone and unblock Salvatore's number so I can dial it.

He answers on the first ring.

"Make Nerissa your second-in-command again."

"Okay."

A small thrill runs through me at his easy agreement, but I hang up and block his number again. "You're still his second. Use your powers for good."

"You do realize what a second-in-command to a capo does, don't you?" But there's a light in her eyes that has been missing since she walked into the guestroom.

"If you didn't mess with my dad's file, who did?" I ask her.

"If anyone messed with it, it would be Lorenzo."

"What do you mean if. He only had one child listed."

"Lorenzo doesn't keep records as meticulously as my brother. He doesn't care about the families of his men either."

"But my dad became his bookkeeper before my parents got their marriage annulled and my sister went with my mom to Boston."

Nerissa frowns. "Then he probably *did* doctor the file. We'll ask him."

The way she says it makes me think by ask she means interrogate. "Where is Salvatore right now?"

"Having a talk with Lorenzo."

And he answered his phone on the first ring. Huh. "What kind of talk?"

"The kind that doesn't have Lorenzo walking out of the room alive."

"Please tell me he got the don's approval for this talk. I didn't agree to marry him to save him just to have him throw his life away a few hours later."

"He has Severu's approval now."

"But he didn't before?"

Nerissa shrugs.

"That silence right there. That doesn't work for me."

"Salvatore had me pick up Lorenzo and put him on ice while he went running after you. And I do mean running. He sprinted out of the office faster than I've ever seen him move."

Another huh.

"Why have you got Lorenzo if you believed the pictures were real."

"Lorenzo was a risk to you."

"And you picked him up on Salvatore's orders without the don's approval?" Salvatore made those orders.

Just how far had he been willing to go to keep me alive?

You know the answer to that. He was willing to die.

He was willing to die.

CHAPTER 64

SALVATORE

Lorenzo's eyes are wild, darting between me and Miceli. Sweat runs down his forehead into his eyes and drool runs down his chin from the corners of his mouth stretched around a ball gag.

Too bad for him, he can't wipe it away. The traitor's hands are cuffed above his head, hanging from a chain attached to the ceiling.

The temperature in The Box is chilly and despite his sweat, goosebumps cover his bare flesh.

"While I appreciate not having to listen to the traitor lie and beg, we can't get the answers with that in his mouth." Miceli leans against the wall by the door, his arms crossed over his chest.

"After that Lucchese asshole bit through his own tongue to avoid interrogation, my crew don't take any more chances."

"You'd think we had a reputation for brutality, or something." Miceli's mouth twists sardonically. "We're not that bad, are we?"

Lorenzo tries to shout something, clearly disagreeing with the underboss's assessment.

I swing the specially designed cattle prod I'm known for using up from my side and slap it into my other palm to gain his attention. When his gaze finds me, his eyes widen in alarm.

I smile the smile I give before meting out punishment. There's nothing friendly about it.

Tears mix with the sweat on Lorenzo's face.

"I haven't touched you yet. You might want to save your tears for when it really hurts." I flick the on switch on the prod.

It buzzes and crackles just like it is designed to do.

Psychological triggers are as useful as pain in getting information, but no way is this asshole getting away without the pain.

Taking one slow step at a time toward him, I smack the non-electrified length of the cattle prod against my palm over and over. "You know how this goes, Lorenzo. Answer my questions and you spend less time with me and my toy."

I say nothing about the time he will spend with Miceli after. Or the denouncement in front of the other capos and their seconds he will have to endure before death.

Stopping two feet away, I press the prod against his inner thigh. Even the ball gag can't silence his screams completely.

"Miceli is going to undo your gag and you are going to answer my questions." I don't ask. This is not a negotiation.

The pain in his thigh and cramping muscles will last as long as twenty minutes. A continuous reminder of how much he doesn't want me shifting the prod a couple of inches to the left and pressing against his junk.

Miceli pushes away from the wall and removes the ball gag in silence and tosses it toward the wall of implements and metal bench under them.

He pats Lorenzo's cheek forcefully. "Start singing cuckoo before I feel the need to get involved because I'll cut your balls out of your nut sac and feed them to you."

"Her dad was my bookkeeper. He stole from me. I didn't want her around *la famiglia*."

"Wrong answer." This time, I press the prod against his other thigh so the pain radiates around but doesn't quite reach his cock and balls.

He screams and begs me to stop.

I do when his screams devolve to whimpers and his face is covered in tears and snot.

"Try again." I press him with the prod, but don't press the button to release the electric current.

He jolts anyway, trying to get away from it. "I thought he had told her stuff about me."

"Stuff like you've been stealing from the Cosa Nostra?" Miceli asks, his voice colder than the room.

"Drugs are *my* business," Lorenzo sniffles.

"Run with money from the mafia. You get to keep half of the profit and you're supposed to pay your soldiers 40% of that."

"No way is that happening," I add. "Not with how poor most them are. Hell, your bookkeeper couldn't even afford to live in our territory. You had him fucking living in New Jersey."

"He was stealing from me," Lorenzo squawks, like that's supposed to justify his stinginess.

Miceli makes a sound of disgust. "You stole from *la famiglia*. From your don and the men in your crew."

"It was my money," Lorenzo wheezes.

And then grunts in pain when Miceli kidney punches him.

"What were Lucchese hit men doing in Manhattan and why did they attack Bianca?" I've had time to reassess our meeting with Henry and the godfather.

Now that I know how desperate Lorenzo was to get rid of Bianca, I no longer believe the Lucchese capo that the attack was random.

When he doesn't answer immediately, I bring the cattle prod up and slide it along his thigh toward his low hanging balls.

"It was a hit," he sputters trying to kick his body backward.

Dark rage tightens my grip on the prod and I send a jolt of painful electric current into the crease between his thigh and scrotum. He shouts hoarsely and then starts to sob.

I wait until he's got his blubbering under control and then ask, "Did you tell Caruso you had our don's approval for the hit?"

"Yes. He wouldn't send his men otherwise."

"He would have checked," Miceli says.

He's right. Even Henry Caruso wasn't stupid enough to take the word of a *stronzo* like Lorenzo without confirming with Severu the hit on another Family's territory was sanctioned.

"He wanted to be godfather. I gave him a way."

"You knew about the bars." And he tried to frame Bianca as the rat.

I went to zap him again, but Miceli grabbed my wrist. "Information first then retribution."

"How did you know about the property purchase?" the underboss asks.

"I have my sources."

If he's trying to sound important, the effect is getting lost in his sniveling.

"What sources?" I demand.

It takes a prod directly to his nut sac before the cuckoo is singing like a canary. Two of my father's men are feeding him information.

One now. Marco isn't telling anyone anything with his tongue gone and working as a grunt without access to anything important. But one of the men my father transferred to his crew from Francesco Gilani's is Lorenzo's half-brother.

Cazzo. That explains a lot.

No one would expect the pompous capo to be friends with a lowly soldier, but blood tells.

"I actually liked that asshole," Miceli gripes. "Now I have to torture and kill him."

"You did not like that blabbermouth."

Miceli shrugs. "Okay, like is too strong a word, but I didn't object when Uncle Sal brought him onto his crew when he became consigliere."

"None of us did." There were no red flags, not like with Marco.

And even though my dad didn't take Marco onto his crew, the man still caused problems blabbing his mouth.

There's a theme here.

"You sold out your don and tried to have an innocent woman killed for what, you traitorous prick?" Miceli snarls. "Our don had you under investigation already."

"No." Lorenzo's denial is like a little kid thinking he can lie about eating the chocolate cake with brown frosting all around his mouth.

"His guy found your duplicate books and your hidden accounts," I say.

"All of them," Miceli adds with relish.

Lorenzo moans, the words hurting him as much as my cattle prod to his balls.

"You'll be happy to hear that money is already being disbursed to Genovese Family accounts."

Once we have the names of the soldiers who knew about what Lorenzo was doing, Severu will give the ones who weren't complicit a lump sum to make up for what their capo withheld from them during their years of service.

It takes another ninety minutes of interrogation and *persuasion* before we are sure we have all the names in the right column.

Lorenzo's son is one of the innocent. He spent his teen years living with his mother in Detroit when she left Lorenzo's cheating ass and returned to her family there. When it came time for college, she asked Severu to arrange for Dario Ricci to train with the don in Vegas.

He's an asshole, but his commitment to the Cosa Nostra is unfailing. By the time Dario came back to New York, he was everything his father wasn't. Lorenzo never promoted him to second-in-command and that's what is going to keep Dario alive during the coming culling.

Once we have all the information we need, I leave Lorenzo to Miceli. If I don't, I will kill him. But I have been ordered not to do that. Severu wants Lorenzo to die in front of his fellow capos and their seconds.

Like the last traitor who betrayed his don and the vows he spoke as a made man.

I'll return for the execution.

Right now though, I have things I have to take care of. Beginning in my conservatory.

CHAPTER 65

BIANCA

The marble floor is hard under my knees and cold seeps up my legs.

Salvatore and I kneel in front of Severu, the don's eyes cast judgment on us both. Catalina hands her husband a gun. A huge pistol, the end of the muzzle a gaping dark maw.

He walks around us and points the gun at the back of Salvatore's head, the muzzle pressing into my lover's dark hair.

My heart races and my stomach roils.

"Will you marry him?" Severu's voice reverberates around the room, hitting me from every direction.

Terror makes my throat tight. I try to open my mouth to say yes, but my jaw is locked. I desperately try to nod, but my shoulders and neck are frozen.

"It is your choice," Severu says. "This isn't the Middle Ages."

Catalina looks pityingly at Salvatore and accusingly at me. "It looks like your sacrifice was for nothing."

Then the don pulls the trigger.

Blood and brain matter spray, landing on my face and body.

Finally, my mouth opens and I scream.

And scream. And scream.

I try to wipe the gruesome bits of my lover off of me, but they cling.

Severu throws a chair and it bangs against the floor. He grabs my arms, and I thrash, yelling for him to let me go.

"Bianca, *brava ragazza mia*, you must wake up." Salvatore's voice infiltrates my mind, pulling me from the scene in the De Luca living room.

Gasping for air, my eyes snap open. The room is dark, but light filters in from the hall through the open door. A door I locked before going to bed earlier.

It's hanging at a weird angle.

"Did you kick the door in?" My throat is raw and the words hurt.

Salvatore lifts me into a sitting position and rubs my arms. "Shh... You are alright."

Only as his words penetrate do I realize I'm whimpering.

He jostles me and I hear the sound of water splashing into the glass from the carafe on the bedside table. Even though I don't need pain pills anymore at night, Rosa always leaves a fresh carafe of water on the table beside Salvatore's bed just in case.

Tonight, she left it in here.

Salvatore holds me like he has so many times after waking me to take my analgesics and tips the water to my lips. "Drink, *amore*."

I obey, first sipping and then gulping the water until the glass is empty. My throat is still a little raw, but it feels better.

"More?" he asks.

I shake my head.

There's a small click of glass against wood as he puts it down and then both of his arms are around me, holding me close. The dream is too fresh for me to push him away.

"Do you want to tell me about it?" he asks as my breaths become less labored.

"It was us in the living room at your cousin's house. Only I was kneeling beside you. Catalina handed him the gun. It was huge." I let out a halting breath.

"Your nightmare was about earlier?"

"Mostly. But Severu walked behind you and put the gun against the back of your head, like Lorenzo did to my dad. I couldn't get the words out to tell him I would marry you." I shudder. "He shot you and your blood and brain matter sprayed on me."

It doesn't take a genius to figure out that what happened at the don's triggered memories of my father's execution. My brain mixed them up with recent events to destroy my sleep.

I'm still tired, but have zero desire to go back to sleep and relive that nightmare.

"Sleep, Bianca." Salvatore, settles me so I'm resting more comfortably against his chest. "I'll keep your nightmares at bay."

"You won't sleep sitting up like this," I say softly.

"I won't sleep regardless. The door's lock is no longer operational."

"But your people are here, protecting the penthouse." Like they always are.

The number of guards on duty has doubled since the godfather's stroke.

Salvatore muscular chest rises and falls under my cheek as he shrugs. "And I am here, protecting you."

"You don't have to hold me in my sleep. I'll be fine." A lie, but not one meant to hurt.

"You think I am here for your sake?" he asks. "I have discovered I do not sleep well without my *woobie blanket* either."

Laughter bubbles up dispelling the lingering horror from the dream. "Are you trying to say that I am your protection from bad dreams?"

"You are my protection from loneliness."

Dio mio. This man.

"I already agreed to go through with the wedding. You don't have to convince me." Severu's threat to kill his cousin did that just fine.

"I have thirty days to court you and I am going to use every one of them, but that is not what this is. This is my truth. I sleep better with you in my arms."

And I sleep better surrounded by his warmth and scent.

"But you're not going to sleep at all like this."

There are no words accompanying the shrug this time. Just silence that says everything his mouth doesn't.

He's not going anywhere and he's not going to sleep in a room with the door hanging off its hinges. Because he thinks it's his job to protect not only my dreams, but my body too.

"When I was twenty, I fell in love," he says into the silence that has stretched between us. "Her name was Monica and she was everything I wanted in a woman."

My heart twinges at hearing him confess his love for another woman. But it doesn't bleed.

No, he hasn't said those words to me, but he has called me *amore* twice today.

His beloved.

"Is she the woman you..." I let my voice trail off, not wanting to say the words.

"You know our world. It is brutal and I was raised to embrace that brutality."

"Yes."

"She took me in completely. Everything about Monica was an act put on to reel in the big fish."

"You."

"Me."

"She wanted to marry you?"

"No. I thought she did and I wanted to marry her. I wanted to tell her everything, that I was part of the mafia and would one day be capo like my father. I wanted to share everything in my life with her."

"My father always said made men didn't share business with their wives."

"No, but most wives know what business we are in."

"I'm not okay with being kept in the dark." He needs to know that.

I'm not my mother, willing to pretend my life is something other than what it is. I'm not Salvatore's mother either. I won't pretend not to see the brutality in his life, but I won't judge him for it either.

"There are things I won't tell you to protect you, but what I can share, I will."

It's more than I expect without an argument. "Okay. What happened to Monica?"

"Uncle Enzo ordered a deep dive background check on her when my father told him I wanted to bring an outsider into the family. And he instructed my father to do it."

"That makes sense. She could have been a FED planted undercover with you." It's why I didn't go ballistic when Salvatore searched through my phone.

Vetting anyone who gets close enough to learn their secrets is standard protocol for the mafia. A future wife would definitely fit that criteria.

"Was she a FED?" I ask when Salvatore doesn't continue.

"No. It was worse. At least to me. I was her mark. She and her real boyfriend were scam artists and they'd set me up for a quarter of a million dollar payout."

"How?"

"She pretended to be a botany student at NYU. She played me for six months, softening me up. All so that when she came to me sobbing and desperate because she'd accidentally killed a rare orchid she'd been studying but wasn't supposed to touch, I would insist on saving her."

"I don't understand." How had he saved her?

"I bought a replacement orchid. One so rare it cost a quarter of a million dollars and she would have been able to sell it on the black market for even more."

"You didn't buy it on the black market?"

"No. It was so rare, and took so many years to grow and flower, there weren't any available anywhere but through the company that had developed and nurtured the plant. I *convinced* them to sell me a plant intended for someone else."

He might not have bought it on the black market, but he'd used mafia tactics to persuade the growers to sell him the plant. All for a woman who was scamming him. That would have been a blow to his pride and his heart.

I scoot up Salvatore's chest until my head rests against his shoulder and I hug him.

His arm tightens around me too.

"Nerissa said your conservatory is a reminder not to trust women, especially outsiders."

"It used to be."

"It's not anymore?" What does he feel when he looks at his orchids now?

"No." He pulls me so my body is fully on top of his.

I think he wants to me try to sleep like this, which is seriously not going to happen.

But then he starts talking again. "I told Monica I loved her and less than twenty-four hours later, I was ordered to kill her and her boyfriend for trying to steal from the mafia."

"You didn't use mafia funds to buy the orchid." Salvatore would never have done that.

"No, but that didn't matter to my uncle. It was my test of loyalty and strength."

"That's awful." I'm not sure Severu would be any less merciless, but it sounds like his father was completely void of compassion. "Your father didn't stick up for you?"

"My father gave me the order. He and my uncle witnessed the kill together." Salvatore's tone is flat, like what he's saying didn't devastate him.

But he's not the unfeeling guy so many people seem to think he is.

"I don't think I like your dad. That was a cruel thing to do to you."

"It changed me. Molded me to be the man who could and would take over as capo one day."

Nerissa said something like that on the drive to the airport. "You refused to kill me though."

A thirty-one year old man might not be willing to do what a twenty-year-old would. Or is it something else? Something more personal.

Amore.

"Yes." His tone resonates with absolute conviction.

"Instead, it ended up being your life on the chopping block."

His laugh surprises me. "An unexpected outcome, but then that's how things seem to go with you."

I push against his chest and sit up, trying to read his expression through the gloom. "You offered to sacrifice your life for mine."

"Yes."

"And your cousin accepted your *sacrifice*." I still don't like thinking of us getting married as Salvatore's lifetime sacrifice.

"Marriage to you is not a sacrifice. Losing you would have been that."

"Are you reading my mind?" I ask, only half teasing.

How does he know me so well after such a short time?

"You didn't look happy when Severu accepted my vow."

"I'm pretty sure I didn't look happy during any of that."

"No, but when he said those words, you looked hurt."

It's my turn to shrug.

"It is my life to promise. My sacrifice to make. My loyalty to pledge."

"Uh...I'm not sure what that is supposed to mean. If those are your wedding vows, they need work."

"Those are the vows I spoke when becoming a Genovese made man."

Chills wash over me. "You were renewing your promise to your don."

"Reminding him of my promise."

"And it worked. He gave you the option of marrying me instead of dying."

"Yes."

"That was your plan all along. Well at least once you realized the only one who had betrayed anybody was you with your don."

He doesn't wince, or look even a little repentant. "I am coming to realize there are different layers of loyalty. Some commitments supersede even my vows to the mafia."

"Your mom, sister and Rosa will be happy to hear that."

A smile ghosts over his lips. "I am sure you are right."

A jaw cracking yawn takes me by surprise.

"You need to sleep, *amore mio*. You must take better care of yourself."

There it is again. *Amore mio*. My beloved.

"You're going to have to say the words at some point," I warn him. "Pretty sure that's part of courting."

Did he really mean it when he said he has thirty days to court me? Of course he did. Salvatore doesn't say things he doesn't mean. Which is why I want those three little words.

"When the time is right," he promises. "Now lie down."

I shake my head. "We *both* need our sleep."

"Are you trying to kick me out again?"

"Nope. I can compromise."

"Really?" He sounds skeptical.

Which...fair.

"If it means both of us getting the rest we need, I'm willing to sleep in your bed." It's not like I was getting quality sleep in here. "I can't believe you broke down my door because I was having a nightmare."

Salvatore stands and lifts me before I have a chance to change my mind. "I did not break down *your* door." He carries me into the hall. "I broke down the guestroom's door."

Stopping at the threshold to his bedroom, he says, "This is our door." He steps inside, shuts and locks the door behind us. "This is our room." He carries me into the walk-in closet that now stands completely empty on one side. "This is our closet."

"I get it. You know how to share."

"Only with you."

Warmth unfurls in my chest. I believe him.

He carries me to the bed and lays me onto the mattress before climbing over me to spoon against my back.

"You could have gotten into bed on the other side," I grouse without heat.

"Not as much fun."

We're snug in our cocoon of blankets, when I say, "When I was sixteen, my dad got in debt to some bad guys again."

CHAPTER 66

SALVATORE

My entire body goes rigid at Bianca's words.

She presses more tightly into my arms. "He was home when they showed up to collect, but he didn't have the money they wanted."

Rage burns through me, but I keep my arms gentle around her. She doesn't need my fury right now. She needs me to listen.

And I will, no matter how hard her words are to hear.

"They told him they would take something on payment."

The tension in her body. The way she shies away from touch. The little clues that while she was up for trying anything, she hadn't done very much before me. It's all there.

And it adds up to one word. An ugly, selfish act.

"They took you," I say.

She nods. "My virginity. It hurt so much Salvatore. I didn't know being touched there could feel so good until you."

"And your dad just watched?" I ask, unable to stop some of my fury from leaking into my voice.

"That was his punishment. To watch. They said if he didn't get them the money, they would come back and this time, they wouldn't settle for a fuck."

"They threatened to sell you?" I killed a made man who made a similar threat to someone who owed him money.

My crew knows that family doesn't pay the debts of others. Torture and kill the fucker who stole from you, but leave his, or her, fucking family out of it.

"Yes. But Lorenzo showed up first. Part of me was relieved when he killed my dad and kicked me out."

"You had to be afraid they would come after you though."

"I was, but they didn't know where I went to school and for the first year, I never left the building. Not once."

Fuck. What she went through. "I am sorry, *amore mio.*"

She turns and presses her face into my neck. I'm starting to get that is her go-to when she needs comfort.

I pull her tight. "I will never let another man touch you."

"No one ever has, not since then. Until you."

My heart beats a staccato in my chest. "I was your first."

"No...they..."

"What those sick bastards did wasn't sex. It was rape. I was your first."

She nods, but her tears wet my neck. Bianca doesn't cry. But she trusts me. Even when I proved my own trust is shaky.

"Do you know their names?"

"Only one of them. He was on Lorenzo's crew with my dad. I never saw the other two before."

"Tell me."

She whispers the name, like it's a secret.

It won't be a secret when I cut off his cock and balls and shove them down his throat. But that will only come after I get the names of the two other men I have to kill out of him.

My wedding present for Bianca will be a world without her abusers in it.

~ ~ ~

"Uh, I don't think that's going to be the great gift you think it is, capo." Nerissa frowns at me after I tell her my plans.

I am going to find the men who assaulted my beloved. Then I am going to torture and kill them.

"She'll be glad they are dead," I argue.

"Probably, but the whole give her a picture of their faces twisted in pain just before death? No woman wants that as a wedding gift."

"You would."

"If that had happened to me, I would kill the men myself."

"You think Bianca wants that?" She killed the man who tried to rape her sister and doesn't regret it.

"Maybe. Ask her."

The more I think about it though, the more I think Nerissa is right. And if Bianca doesn't want to mete out the justice they deserve, she can at least see them reduced to nothing.

"I mean it, Salvatore. *Ask her.* Maybe she doesn't want to add images of mutilated rapists to the slide show in her head."

I think those are just the images she needs to counterbalance the memories of when she was helpless against their violence and cruelty.

"I'll ask." After I show her the changes I've made in the conservatory.

BIANCA

Warm sunlight across my face wakes me up and I smile at the sensation, snuggling against my pillow and inhaling Salvatore's scent. The lack of a warm body against my back tells me he's already gone from his...no, *our* bed.

Relief that I have time to process our middle of the night confessions before I see him again overrides my disappointment at his absence.

Last night was the first time since Ilaria caught us kissing in here that we slept in the same bed without touching sexually. After the rollercoaster of a day and our middle of the night revelations, I was emotionally and physically exhausted.

Somehow, Salvatore knew I craved the safety of his arms and gave me exactly what I needed, holding me tightly throughout what was left of the night.

A sound near the window catches my attention and my eyes flash open.

Rosa puts a tray with breakfast on the table by the window, the open drapes the reason for the sunlight that woke me.

When she sees that I'm awake, she smiles. "Good morning, *dolce ragazza.*"

"Morning." I yawn and stretch before sliding out of the warm cocoon of covers.

The air conditioning keeps the penthouse apartment at a moderate temperature, but the air feels cool against my skin and I grab the silk robe someone thoughtfully left at the end of the bed. Probably Rosa.

She thinks of everything.

Tying the belt, the sudden urge to pee has me hurrying toward the bathroom.

I'm surprised to find Rosa still in the room when I come out a few minutes later. She's staring out the window, her hands clasped in front of her.

When I sit down, she joins me at the table and pours steaming coffee into two mugs. She came up prepared to have a chat.

"Thank you." I take my coffee from her, inhaling the rich aroma and faint scent of cinnamon.

"It is my pleasure."

We both sip our coffee, but then Rosa puts her mug down and clasps her hands again. "Pietro told me what he discovered about your birth yesterday."

I thought Lorenzo told Salvatore about my father and I say so. She explains Pietro's search for my birth records and what he found when he searched under Bianca Russo.

"Last night, he told me that your father was Alberto Russo."

"Yes."

"My aunt married a Russo from Detroit."

Chills run down my arms. "What are you saying?"

"Your grandfather moved from Detroit to marry my aunt, but my uncle and my father never got along. After nonno died they had a big fight and never spoke again." Rosa dabs at the moisture pooling in her eyes. "I was only six at the time. From that point on, the name Russo was never allowed to be spoken in our home. I knew that I had a cousin, but I never met him."

She can't be saying what I think she is saying. "I don't understand."

"Alberto Russo was my cousin."

"But I never met you." I'd never met any of my nonna's family.

"My papa tried to reconcile with your grandmother after your grandfather died, but she rebuffed him."

I am not surprised. "My dad told my nonna that if she tried to reconcile with the family that had treated his father so badly, he would cut nonna out of our lives."

Nonna chose me and Bea over her own brother. It couldn't have been easy for her, but she never showed any resentment toward us. Not even to my dad.

"He sounds like he took after your grandfather."

I can only nod. Both nonno and my dad only adhered to mafia traditions that suited them.

"So many things make sense now. From the very first, you reminded me of my grandmother."

"Your grandmother's recipes are so similar to those I got from my nonna because she got them from the same woman."

"Her mom." My *bisnonna* was Rosa's grandmother.

"Even the pattern on our family dishes are the same." Because they came from the same place.

Although my nonna's dishes were lost along with my home.

Rosa laughs. "No wonder you and Pietro get along like siblings."

That's one way to describe our relationship.

"He's very good at playing the annoying older brother." And protective.

I will never forget his willingness to stand by Salvatore in protecting me, even in the face of the don's wrath.

"It's a new role for him, but he's taken to it very well." Rosa smiles, but the expression seems forced.

"What's wrong? If you don't want to acknowledge our family connection, I won't tell anyone." But saying the words hurts.

I want this woman to be my family.

"Do not even think that, *dolce ragazza*!" Rosa throws her hands into the air for emphasis. "You are my family."

"Okay, but you don't seem happy about it."

"If you do not want to marry the capo, we will get you out of New York," she says in a rush.

Che palle.

I throw my hand up in a stopping gesture. "Don't say another word. If Salvatore hears you, he'll be livid. I'm already engaged to one man to save him from the don. There's no one I can marry to save you from the capo."

"Our family let you down in the worst way possible. You should never have been thrown into the street." Rosa's nurturing nature is appalled by my past. "We won't let you down now."

"Pietro told you everything," I say with dawning understanding.

No wonder Rosa is ready to launch a mafia rebellion to save me.

Rosa shrugs. "I may have listened in on a conversation between him and Salvatore and then pressed my son for more details."

"None of what happened to me is your fault," I assure her.

Rosa's mouth sets stubbornly. "You will not marry anyone you do not wish to."

"Even your bossy tone is like my nonna's," I grumble. "This marriage thing is a done deal."

Even if I didn't love Salvatore, I wouldn't allow him to die for trying to save my life. But marrying him is not the big sacrifice Rosa is making it out to be either.

"It does not have to be," Rosa stubbornly insists.

"Your don would disagree. Pietro dodged a bullet yesterday. Let's not create another one with his name on it."

Rosa's face blanches. "What do you mean?"

After I'm done telling the older woman the stuff her son left out about yesterday, she's ready to give him an earful. "He went against his don? Has my son lost his sense?"

"Uh...what do you think hiding me from Salvatore and his cousin is doing?"

"That is different. A woman should not be forced to marry a man she does not want to."

"It happens in the mafia all the time."

"Arranged marriages. Not forced ones," she argues.

When the bride and groom have no choice in the matter, how are the two things different? I don't ask because that's not what is important right now.

"I am doing this willingly."

"I saw the guestroom door this morning."

Oh, no. No. No. We are not back to that. "You didn't tell Ilaria?"

Rosa's mouth sets in a mulish line. "And why should I not tell his mother about her son's deplorable behavior?"

"Maybe because it wasn't deplorable. I was having a nightmare and Salvatore wanted to comfort me. The locked door was in the way."

Rosa's mouth opens and then closes three times but no words emerge.

"You and Ilaria *have* to stop thinking the worst of him. I know you both love him, but you don't trust him and that's not okay."

"You do trust him," Rosa says wonderingly.

"I do."

"Even after yesterday?"

"Especially after yesterday. His lack of trust in me hurt a lot. I won't deny it, but Rosa, he was willing to *die* to protect me. In the mafia, every made man is willing to kill to protect *la famiglia*, but to die for someone else?" I shake my head. "That's rare."

Rosa's eyes fill with tears. "I owe Salvatore an apology."

"You do, but how about you keep it to your previous distrust of him and not mention today's misunderstanding?" That would hurt him.

Rosa nods. "I need to talk to Ilaria before she chastises her son for breaking a door."

As funny as that sight might be, it also has the potential to hurt Salvatore if Ilaria lets him see her concern for my wellbeing because of the broken door.

"What you said that day in the ceramics studio is true. It is time we stopped thinking the worst of him because he obeyed the orders of his capo and his don."

"I would take it as a personal favor if you did that. I would hate to lose the family I just found and have nothing but a chilly, distant relationship with my mother-in-law after my marriage."

I let the words and their meaning hang in the air between us. Salvatore might forgive them for the way they judge him, but I will not.

I killed a man for my sister. I will cut two women I have grown to love from my life for the man who owns my heart.

Rosa jumps up, as if galvanized by the underlying threat in my words. "My father will want to meet you."

"I would love that."

With a hug and an extracted promise from me to meet her for a cooking lesson later, Rosa leaves.

CHAPTER 67

BIANCA

I grab my phone to check messages while I finish my breakfast. There's a text from Candi. And before I read it, I change her name in my contacts to KathB.

My friend. She has never called me by my stage name, not even once. I'm lucky she's been so patient with my standoffishness and still worked at being my friend.

KathB: *Hey, girlfriend. What's up.*

Bianca: *I'm getting married. Want to be my maid-of-honor?*

KathB: *WTF?!!*

My phone rings the second the text comes through. I answer and somehow explain my whirlwind wedding without telling my best friend about the mafia or the don's threats.

"I knew you had it bad for him, but this is next level. Are you sure you want to marry him? I mean he's giving you the milk. Why buy the cow before you're sure you want to keep it?"

"I am sure."

"Okay, but you do realize the other dancers are going to want to come to your bachelorette party. I know you don't think anyone else is your friend, but you're wrong."

"Okay. As long as they don't mind partying with the boss lady."

"You want me to invite Nerissa James? That woman is scary."

"She's going to be my sister-in-law *and* she's the one implementing the changes to protect the dancers and backroom workers at the clubs."

"She listens to you so she can't be all bad, but you do remember that until a few weeks ago, she'd never spoken to a single dancer?"

"Attitude adjustment." And Nerissa had taken it without bitching.

"Okay. Gotta go. I've got a bachelorette party to plan and a bunch of dancers to tell about the wedding of the century. Oh..." Her voice trails off.

"What?"

"Um, I assumed you'd want to invite them to the wedding, but maybe not. Mr. Billionaire's friends probably don't mix with strippers in public."

"He's marrying a pole dancer, I think he can deal."

"Ex pole dancer."

"If our friends can't mix at our wedding, how are we going to mesh our lives after?"

It's a question I'm still thinking about when I meet Salvatore up on the roof later.

He's standing at the conservatory's doors, his gray gaze devouring me as I walk toward him. "You look beautiful."

"Um...thanks." I'm wearing my usual snarky t-shirt, capri yoga pants and tennis shoes.

He reaches for my hand. "You are always beautiful."

"You don't have to butter me up with compliments to tell me you couldn't save Vee."

"Who said I couldn't?"

Excitement surges through me. "You did? It's okay?"

"More than okay." He leads me into the humid warmth of the cli-mate-controlled conservatory.

I blink and then blink again, trying to take in what I'm seeing. "Where are all the orchids?"

The super expensive, ridiculously rare orchids?

"Gone."

"I can see that."

"They reminded me of my past. These remind me of my future."

All the shelves are filled with African violets amidst the shade ferns. Purple ones, pink ones, white ones and variegated petals, but by far the highest number are the plants with blue flowers. All of them are planted in pots made by his mother and aunt.

In pride of place, where his Shenzhen Nongke Orchid is Vee in the pot I picked out. Thrown and painted by my own newly discovered second-cousin.

It's vibrant with life again, the leaves dark green and a plethora of furled buds in the center that will flower soon.

"How did you do this so fast?" I ask. "What did you do with the orchids?"

"I donated them to an arboretum."

"Even the Shenzhen Nongke Orchid?"

"Yes."

"But it was worth so much money."

"Not as much as the violets are to me."

"Um, I don't know much about rare African violets," I admit. "My botanical knowledge is pretty limited to how to take care of Vee."

"I don't either. These aren't rare, they are hardy. And the blue ones remind me of your eyes."

"You found all these this morning?" Yes, I know the man is rich, but I'm still impressed.

"Not this morning. I only wanted blue that exact shade and didn't want any others the same purple as Vee. Your friend should stand out."

Okay, that's really sappy. And so incredibly sweet. "What do you mean *not this morning*?" I ask. "Did you order all these last night?"

"I've been working on the transition from orchids to violets for the past few weeks."

"But why?"

"I already told you."

"But you didn't know I was your future."

"Didn't I?" His hand drops from mine.

Unable to believe the message in his words, I turn around to face him. He's kneeling on one knee, the expression on his face making my heart beat too fast.

"I should never have doubted you about your sister. My only excuse is that I was terrified."

"You aren't afraid of anything." My voice comes out just above a whisper.

"Before I met you, that was true. I did not fear death. I did not fear pain. Or killing. But once I met you I had something to fear."

"What?" But I think I know. The same thing I learned to fear.

"Losing you."

"Is that why you kept me locked in your lair like Beauty and the Beast?"

"It's not a lair. It's a home. Our home."

I notice he doesn't deny keeping me locked up, because even though he said I could go once I was better, I think we both know that's not true. This man is obsessed with me.

Another woman might hate that, but for me, who has been discarded too many times in my life, knowing this man will *never* let me go heals old wounds I never thought would stop hurting.

"You were going to let me go." I frown. "You sent me away."

"If you had gotten on that plane, I would have been right behind you."

"How?"

"Private jet." He shrugs. "It was waiting on standby at the airfield."

"Then why send me in the first place?"

"I was in panic mode. There was no way I would ever kill you, but I didn't want to have to kill my cousin either."

The true depths of the quandary he'd put himself in fills me with terror. He would have killed his don to protect me. And died, horribly, as a result.

"You threw me away. You hurt me."

"I will regret that for the rest of my life." He grabs my hand and presses it to the side of his face. "You are the very air that I breathe *anima gemelli mia.*"

My soul mate. Literally the twin to his essence.

I will never stop missing Bea, but Salvatore's soul is twined with mine now, filling in the lonely hollows of my heart. And unlike my sister, he will never be horrified by who I really am.

"Anima gemelli mia," I repeat. Because I accept and love the very essence of this man too.

His gaze traps mine. *"Ti amo."*

"I love you too," I breathe.

"Will you save me from a life of empty loneliness, *amore mio* and marry me? Become my wife for this life with our souls joined for eternity?"

"Yes."

A grin splits his face as he surges to his feet and picks me up to kiss me senseless. Only when my butt lands on the empty potting bench do I realize we were moving.

We tear each other's clothes off, our hands greedy for bare skin. My hands press on his chest and I feel plastic against my hand.

Breaking the kiss, I look down, panting.

Where there once had been a monochromatic black tattoo of a coiled viper over his heart, there is one so new, it is still red around the edges and covered with a transparent bandage.

A cluster of vibrantly colored blue violets, it has the words *anima gemella mia* in a stylized curve under it.

That is what he was busy doing this morning, putting my claim to his heart on his skin and erasing any trace of Monica. Just like he did in here.

"It's beautiful." I trace around the clear bandage. "You put me on your skin."

"You are carved into my soul."

"And you are twined with mine."

"For eternity."

"Now and forever," I agree.

This time when he kisses me, his lips are reverent, sealing our vows with more power than any clerical blessing.

The frenzied passion of seconds before turns into something profound. We touch and kiss, making promises with our mouths and hands until he slides his big hardon into my swollen and ready vagina.

Leaning back on the bench, my legs splayed wide and my knees hooked over his arms, I eagerly accept him inside me. He stretches me like he always does and it is perfect.

Salvatore fills my empty places. And I am his sanctuary.

Ecstasy dances along every nerve ending in my body until I come with a crescendo of pleasure as I scream Salvatore's name.

"Bianca, *amore mio*!" He shoves himself forward and hot jets pulse inside me. "You are mine, now and forever."

CHAPTER 68

BIANCA

For the next month, Salvatore courts me just like he promised.

He wakes me with orgasms. When he learns of my family connection to Rosa, he invites my great-uncle to dinner for us to meet and hovers protectively until he's sure the man who insists I call him nonno isn't going to say anything to hurt my feelings.

One day Daryl Ruhnke's sons arrive with a check for fifty-thousand dollars and obsequious, if not sincere, apologies for how they treated me. When they go to leave, the oldest begs me to call off the dogs and I know giving me what Mr. Ruhnke left me in the will isn't enough for Salvatore.

He's probably bankrupting the Ruhnke sons. That night I tell him to stop. That it is enough. Mr. Ruhnke would not want his sons to suffer complete annihilation. Salvatore isn't thrilled but he agrees to back off.

"I should have waited to have them come until they were both jobless and on the verge of losing their homes."

"Yeah, no. What they did was petty and cruel." But it doesn't rank with the other trauma in my past.

And we leave it at that.

Salvatore and I tend the violets together in the conservatory, adding a new plant for the first pot I make that doesn't crack in the firing. We have dinner with his parents and Big Sal is positively friendly, making jokes about grandbabies and beautiful daughters-in-law.

It's weird, but I'll take it.

When Salvatore's mother is concerned about me inviting several exotic dancers to our wedding, both my fiancé and Rosa set her straight. Catalina casts the deciding vote, decreeing my friends *will* be invited.

As the don's wife, she has seniority, even over her mother-in-law, and the not-so-subtle attempts to expunge them from the guest list end.

Rosa, Ilaria and Aria are forces to be reckoned with when it comes to planning a wedding though. It is Catalina who makes sure everything is what *I* want it to be on my wedding day. Having her as an ally is every bit as powerful as I suspected it would be.

The night before Kath and I are supposed to go for our dress fitting, we are having dinner at Catalina and Severu's again.

I haven't seen the don since the day he threatened to kill my soulmate.

But it's not his voice that jerks me to a grinding halt as soon as I step off the elevator. It is a voice almost identical to my own. Only now that voice speaks with a distinctly Bostonian accent.

Bea is here?

Salvatore's hand rubs my back. "She can't wait to see you."

"Why didn't you warn me?" I ask.

"I wanted to surprise you." He comes around to face me, his craggy face drawn in lines of concern. "Was that bad?"

"I..." I shake my head. "I don't know. You said she wants to see me?"

He nods. "Very much."

"Bia." My sister's voice is low and uncertain.

I haven't heard that nickname in almost ten years. My father always called me Bianca or Bibi. Beatrice is the only one who called me Bia.

Salvatore looks down at me in question and I nod.

He steps to the side, but maneuvers us so he has his arm around my back when my sister steps forward.

She is dressed like the socialite she is, but her eyes are filled with tears. "Is that really you?"

Suddenly, I can't stand the distance between us and I lurch forward to hug her. She does the same, and we collide in a bone-crushing hug.

"I'm so glad you were willing to see me," she says into my ear. "I've missed you so much, Bia, like a piece of my soul was gone and I couldn't get it back."

I pull back and stare, unable to comprehend what she's saying. "Mom said you didn't want to see me, that you were ashamed of me."

"Mom told me you didn't want to ever see me again after you had to..." She doesn't go on, unsure if I've told my fiancé and his family about my past.

I can still read my sister like she is myself.

"But that night, you wouldn't talk to me."

"I was in shock. I've never been as strong as you, Bia. I don't think I could have done what you did to protect you and I knew it. I felt so guilty."

"But it wasn't your fault."

"That's not how it felt."

Catalina steps forward. "Come on you two, you can use my office to catch up without an audience. I can have dinner brought to you."

Bea looks horrified. "We couldn't possibly miss dinner. That would be rude."

"Not at all," Catalina says smoothly.

But Bea is shaking her head. "We'll talk in your office if that's alright, but we'll join the rest of you for dinner."

The difference in our lifestyles in the last near decade couldn't be more apparent. I don't care about societal expectations, but Bea is bound by them.

"Could you send someone to tell us when everyone is sitting down for dinner?" I ask Catalina.

"Of course." She leads the way down the hall to the right of the living room.

Salvatore sticks right by my side the whole way, but once we reach Catalina's office, I put my hand on his chest to stop him. "That's as far as you go. I'll see you in a little bit for dinner."

"I don't want to leave you alone with her."

"You wouldn't have invited her if you didn't think I was safe in her company," I tell him.

"She might say something that hurts you."

"Probably. And I'll probably say something that hurts her, but we'll get through it. Please, Salvatore, I need to do this alone."

He glares at Bea, but nods. "I will be—"

"In the living room with the others," I instruct, with zero give in my voice.

Catalina tugs his sleeve. "Come on, Salvatore. Give them some privacy."

Once we are alone, Bea looks at me with wide eyes. "He's pretty intense."

I nod. No point in denying the truth. "I like it."

"Better you than me."

That makes me laugh. "Are you saying Matthew Lombard is a pussycat?"

"He's nothing like your Salvatore, that's for sure."

I wonder if she knows if he's in the mafia, but as we catch up on the past decade it becomes pretty obvious that Bea has no clue that Matthew Lombard is part of the Lombardi Family.

Salvatore told me that Matthew Lombard won't ever advance within his Cosa Nostra, so she'll probably never find out either. Ten years ago, hiding a big part of my life from my sister would have been unthinkable.

Now, sharing anything important with her is harder to imagine.

"I tried to see you, after I graduated high school. I wanted us to go to the same college, but I couldn't find you. I didn't even know dad was dead until then and Mr. Ricci said you had left New York."

"Mom paid me five-thousand dollars to change my name. Since I thought you never wanted to see me again, I agreed."

"I don't understand why she did that. You're her daughter too."

"Not since that night."

"But you saved me."

"That's not how mom sees it. She thinks I lost my soul." I know she's wrong. I have a soul and it is connected permanently to Salvatore De Luca's.

"I want you to be a bridesmaid in my wedding," Bea blurts out. "It will make mom mad, but I don't care. You're my sister and I'm done pretending like you don't exist."

"Are you sure? We don't have to go public with our family connection to have a friendship."

Bea chews on her lip. "Even if I was willing to do that, I don't think your fiance would stand for it."

"What do you mean?"

"He won't allow me in your life unless I'm willing to publicly acknowledge you." She shakes her head when I open my mouth to protest. "The warning wasn't necessary, Bia. You are my twin and I want you in my life. Mom is going to have a conniption though."

"Conniption? Who says that?"

"What would you call it?" Bea teases back.

"Temper tantrum. Heart attack. Aneurism."

Bea laughs. "All of those too." Then she sobers. "She's going to be humiliated when everyone finds out she has another daughter she's never mentioned."

"Knowing her, she'll play it off as if she was too heartbroken by dad keeping me away from her to talk about me." Not that I'll play along, but even I am not going to make a big scene at my sister's wedding.

Which is the only time I plan to see my mother in the near future. I'm sure as hell not inviting her to mine.

I learn that Bea is here now because Salvatore thought I might want her in my wedding and we're dress shopping tomorrow.

CHAPTER 69

SALVATORE

Bianca is very happy I brought Beatrice back into her life. Making her happy is my priority.

Not because I'm courting her but because seeing her happy is so damn satisfying.

I don't tell my beloved that I investigated Beatrice before I would consider approaching her. When I decided she could be a positive addition to Bianca's life had a necessary conversation with Matthew Lombard. I made it clear that if his fiancée hurt my beloved in any way, I would relieve the earth of both their presence.

"Bea thinks mom is going to play the poor, brokenhearted mother, when news gets out in Boston society of my existence." Bianca cuddles against my side, her body lax from lovemaking.

"Not going to happen." I have plans in place.

Not only will the fact that Elizabeth abandoned Bianca come to light, but everyone is going to know that when Alberto died, the socialite left her daughter to fend for herself at the age of sixteen.

My fiancée pushes me onto my back and drapes herself over me, in what has become both our favorite position after sex. Propping her chin on her fists, she's careful to rest her biceps against me and not her elbows. As if I might be bothered by the small pain.

"I feel like you have plans for my mom." Her beautiful blue eyes sparkle at me.

"Because you know me well."

"Care to share?" Beautiful blue eyes reflect a soul the perfect match to mine.

"She will be humiliated."

"I figured with you being adamant that Bea and me not keep our family connection under wraps."

"There will be no opportunity for her to play injured anything," I say with pleasure. "Everyone in Boston society will know what a horrible mother she has been to you."

The Boston Cosa Nostra has an effective disinformation machine developed over decades playing in the political arena.

"If Beatrice and Matthew don't distance themselves from her, his political chances will die the same death as his future in the Cosa Nostra."

"You are ruthless."

I shrug. My soulmate already knows that and she loves me anyway.

"She deserves to pay for what she's done to you, but if you want me to dial it back, I will." Only for this woman would I dampen my natural inclination to go for the jugular.

Bianca's grin is the sun coming out after weeks of gray skies. "She kept me and my sister apart for almost ten years. She deserves what she gets."

"You are so perfect for me *amore mio*."

"We're kind of perfect for each other." She frowns. "I'm worried that Bea will want to stand by mom and Matthew will dump her though."

"He's an opportunist. It's possible."

"I think he loves her." Bianca's lips twist in uncertainty.

"Maybe, but not as much as he loves her political connections. If she becomes a liability..." I don't finish my thought.

My sweet fiancée knows.

"If he's that shallow, Bea is better off knowing now than later," Bianca says with certainty.

"True."

She sighs. "We're so different now."

"You and Bea?"

"Yes. She thinks I'm stronger than she is, and she might be right, but I think I'm harder too."

"You were born twins, but your lives diverged that night nine years ago. She was a victim. You were a savior. She went to live among the Boston elite and you stayed in the mafia world."

"And then I was a victim."

"You survived and learned to thrive. You made the last years of Daryl Ruhnke's life better and fought hard for the life you wanted. The fact you danced at Pitiful Princess for two years after what happened to you awes me." Beatrice is right.

My woman is stronger than her twin. She's stronger than most of the people I know.

"It was my way of reclaiming my power. If I hadn't done it, I don't know if I would have been able to let you touch me, no matter how over the top our attraction is."

"You would." It is my turn to be certain. Because anything else is unthinkable. This woman was meant to be mine. "You have more courage and tenacity than anyone I know."

"I'm not perfect."

Running my hand up her back, I revel in the feel of her body so relaxed against mine. "You are perfect for me. You accept me as even my own mother struggles to do. You do not shy away from the darkness in me."

"It is part of who you are, but it is also part of who I am."

"No." I brush her face.

She turns and kisses my palm. "Yes. If I were Bea, that might hurt me to accept, but I'm not. I'm not even Bia anymore. I'm your soulmate."

"My heart."

"Your darling."

"My good girl."

"Maybe not so good."

"Very, very good, *amore mio*." Then I once again show her just how good she can be.

BIANCA

The news of my mother's abandonment breaks a week later.

She calls, crying and trying to spin the story she wants to feed to the press.

"You're forgetting that I was there when you called me a monster and left me with dad," I say dispassionately. "I was there when you gave me a measly $10,000 to go away when I was sixteen and five more to change my name two years later."

"You can't tell anyone about that. Think of what it will do to your sister. Her reputation will be ruined right along mine."

She can't see my eyeroll at her attempt to manipulate me. "Not if she publicly denounces your actions."

"Bea would never do that. She's not like you."

"I think you'll be surprised at what my twin is capable of when it comes to protecting herself." We're all capable of things we don't expect when we're backed into a corner.

I've stared my darkness in the face and come out stronger for it. Bea has to decide how she wants to live her life. I can't do it for her, but I won't try to protect her by protecting my narcissistic mother either.

"I'll fight fire with fire," my mother threatens. "Get your fiancée to back off or I will go to the authorities with what I know about the mafia."

"I'm going to do you a favor and not pass that on to Salvatore because the result would devastate Bea."

"Are you threatening me?" My mom demands shrilly.

"No." It's not a threat and I'm not implicating myself.

My mother was married to a made man for over a decade. She knows what happens to snitches.

"I'm your mother!"

"You'll have to get better at defending yourself than that," I warn her. "Even Boston society isn't going to forgive a mother who abandons her child to the streets."

"I left you with your father."

"But then he died." And she'd refused to help me.

"I couldn't do anything then. Ronald would have been appalled to find out I had another child."

She's talking about Ronald William Harrington III, the man she married three months after my parents' marriage was annulled.

"I'm sure he would have been," I agree. I doubt he's thrilled about it now.

"My parents would have sent me and you girls away someplace without any real society to mitigate the scandal."

And that would have been hell for my mother.

"So, you sacrificed me for your own comfort."

"You wouldn't have done well here. You're too much like your father."

"You think so? I think I'm more like nonna and *bisnonna*. I do what I need to in order to survive and protect the people I love."

"You aren't doing anything to protect me," she accuses in a voice bordering on hysterical.

Elizabeth Harrington is seconds away from a full-on temper tantrum.

Not something I'm willing to listen to. "You aren't one of the people I love."

"How can you say that? I gave birth to you."

The words reverberate in my head long after I disconnect the call with my mom.

"What is wrong?" Rosa asks as I pound my clay back into a single lump for the third time.

"I don't love my mom."

Rosa's gentle face takes on a look of distaste. "I don't love her either."

"She didn't give birth to you."

"Giving birth to someone does not make you a mother." Rosa looks to Ilaria for confirmation and my soon-to-be mother-in-law nods her agreement. "Caring for your child. Protecting them. Raising them. That is what makes you a mother."

"She raised me until I was thirteen." Why doesn't that carry more weight with me?

Shouldn't I feel something for her?

"And then cruelly abandoned you."

"But shouldn't I feel something for her? I mean I hate that she manipulated me and Bea to keep us apart for so long, but I don't even despise Elizabeth." Calling her by her first name feels more natural that calling her mom.

Huh. Good to know.

"How did you survive her rejection?" Ilaria asks, eyeing her own beautifully thrown plate for imperfections. "You had to cut your heart off from her or wallow in never ending grief."

"How poetic you are today, Ilaria," Rosa teases. Then she looks at me with understanding eyes. "But my friend is right. You had no choice but to put away feelings of affection that only caused you grief. If your mother had returned sooner, or at all, you might have been able to resurrect those feelings."

She's right. Even now Elizabeth isn't returning to me with apologies and words of love. She only called me because she was desperate.

"It is not healthy to love someone whose every action toward you is selfish and harmful." Ilaria sprinkles water on her clay and smooths away an imperfection I cannot see.

"You don't think something inside me is broken because I don't love her?" I ask both women.

Bea still loves our mom.

"No, *dolce ragazza*, there is nothing lacking in you. Your love runs deep and strong, but you don't love indiscriminately."

"You love Salvatore and have forgiven him for hurting you," Ilaria adds. "That is not the action of a woman with a heart of stone."

Rosa nods firmly. "That you even worry about not loving that viper shows how tender your heart truly is."

"Salvatore told me that if I wanted him to leave her alone, he would," I admit to them. I leave unsaid the obvious truth. That I didn't.

"He might." Rosa shrugs. "But Pietro would not."

"Sal wouldn't either. Though my husband wants to kill her and be done with it," Ilaria says as she places the wet clay plate on the rack to dry.

"Big Sal wants to kill my mom?" I squeak. "I mean he's been nicer lately, but I thought that was because you and Salvatore read him the riot act."

"Nerissa did too, but that's not why."

My almost sister-by-marriage hired me as the talent manager for all three De Luca owned strip clubs.

My position is the same level as a general manager and my decisions supersedes all the other managers when it comes to the dancers and women who offer services in the back rooms.

The job is challenging, but I love it.

Determined to keep them as safe as possible and to provide good work conditions, I have met with each of the dancers and club sex workers one-on-one.

Those meetings have been enlightening and I have at least two more issues I plan to bring up with Nerissa at our next meeting.

Ilaria smiles at me. "Once Sal learned how you ran to Severu to try to protect our son at great risk to yourself, he became your fan for life."

"He asked me to call him papà," I admit.

"And?"

I shrug. I never called my dad papà per my mother's insistence, and Mr. Ruhnke became the name that meant dad to me with him.

But Big Sal De Luca is something else. "I have a feeling if I call him papà, he'll become as insufferable as his son about my wellbeing."

The consigliere supports his daughter in her position as a soldier in the Cosa Nostra, but he gives Nerissa a lot more grief than Salvatore about putting herself at risk.

"He won't be offended if you choose to call him Sal," Ilaria says. "But I'm hoping you will call me mamma."

Tears prickle at my eyes and I turn away from my wheel. That lump of clay is not turning into anything worth firing today.

"You deserved better than you got growing up, but you have a family that loves you now, Bianca," Ilaria adds.

Rosa smiles. "Two families."

Two families that don't think I'm a monster. Two families that don't judge me for not loving the woman who left me to suffer a fate I'll never tell her about. Two families who don't look down on me for being an exotic dancer when my mother did nothing but judge that choice earlier in our conversation.

Two families that I love deeply.

I am not broken.

I am a survivor.

CHAPTER 70

BIANCA

S alvatore and I are married in the same cathedral where Catalina married Severu De Luca, but our wedding has to take place in the middle of the day on a Wednesday because of the short notice.

I don't even try to guess what Salvatore is paying to have the sanctuary decorated and undecorated within the space of three hours.

My dress and veil are the same one worn by my *bisnonna* on her wedding day to the man she had never met. Rosa brought it to me after dress shopping netted gowns for Kath and Bea but nothing I liked.

"Your nonna would be so proud," my 78-year-old great-uncle says as he offers his arm to walk me down the aisle.

Pietro wanted to give me away. So did Big Sal.

But Umberto Abati told me he wanted to do it for my nonna and I couldn't say no. He lost his sister to my grandfather's intransigence.

I know what it's like to lose a sister and how grateful I am to have Bea standing at the front of the church, waiting for me along with Kath.

"Thank you," I tell him.

"Thank you for giving me back a part of my sister. I do not regret I never got to know my nephew, may God rest his soul." Uncle Umberto crosses himself. "He took too much after his father, but you are the greatest gift an old man could receive in his final years."

"Enough with the final years. You'll outlive us all. And Bea is happy to have gotten to know you too," I remind him.

Bea hasn't taken to our Italian family in New York like me, but she's cordial with them all.

He shrugs. "She is sweet, but you are so much like my sister, it is as if she is here again."

The compliment wraps around me like the perfect woobie blanket and I walk down the aisle in a cloud of bliss, my nonna's presence all around me.

Salvatore is waiting for me with Pietro and a man named Angelo, who is as beautiful as his namesake, but also scary. He's not the best man, but he walked Kath down the aisle. When I asked Pietro about it after the last minute substitution at the rehearsal, he said he liked his hands attached to his arms.

Salvatore's gaze locks on mine and the message in his molten eyes is one of absolute adoration. The most brutal capo in New York loves me to the depths of his stained soul. And I love him to mine.

I was born a twin, but now my twin soul resides in a man who will kill for me and willingly die to keep me safe too.

When he says he will follow me into the afterlife I believe him. That man will never let me go.

And I will hold on to him just as hard.

EPILOGUE: PUNISHMENT

SALVATORE

Henry Caruso thinks he is safe when my cousin does not take out a hit on him. The fool does not realize that if Severu wants him dead, no contract is needed.

Miceli and I fucking rock, paper, scissors for the right to kill him. Miceli wins with scissors to my paper.

I'm still pissed about it, but as long as Henry dies painfully, I can accept it.

BIANCA

Two weeks after our wedding, Salvatore brings me to the Oscuro Building, but we don't go in the main entrance. We take an elevator from the parking garage down to a sub-basement and he leads me to a room called The Box.

The sound of low voices and bodies shuffling reaches me before I see the men filling one side of a large room. An impression midway down the wall on both sides looks like it houses another wall that can be used to divide the space in two.

All the capos and their seconds are here. Salvatore leads me through the group of mostly men so we stand in the front. Nerissa takes a position on my other side. Pietro stands behind me.

He's not a capo or a second-in-command, but he's here like me to witness justice being served.

"You are here today to witness the punishment of a traitor," Severu intones. "Lorenzo Ricci has stolen money from *la famiglia* both in tithe and what he owes his own men from the profits of their enterprises."

"It looks like he's already been punished," someone behind me says.

Severu shrugs. "One session of torture is not enough for such an offense."

"Damn right," a handsome man to my right says. His second is sending surreptitious looks to Nerissa.

Oh, this must be her boyfriend and his capo, Domenico.

"Because his offense was against the entire family, you are all here not only as witnesses but to participate in his punishment as well."

What follows is a brutal display of violence. After each of the capos and their seconds have taken a turn, Lorenzo hangs limply in his bindings. The capo that terrorized me and murdered my father is reduced to a whimpering mess.

"Put him on his knees," Severu says.

Miceli and Angelo step forward to do as the don ordered. When Lorenzo is kneeling on the floor like my father on that long ago day, Severu steps behind him, but he doesn't have a gun.

He grabs Lorenzo's head, lifts and twists. A sickening crack sounds and Lorenzo topples to his side. Dead.

"Lorenzo Ricci will have no funeral and no gravestone to mark his burial. He will return to the nothing he chose to become by breaking his oath to the Cosa Nostra." The floor opens silently and Severu kicks the dead capo over the edge.

A small splash sounds and the floor closes again.

Severu warns his people about disloyalty and each capo and second renews their vows to their don.

I am stricken to the depths of my soul how much Salvatore was willing to sacrifice for me. He squeezes my hand as if he knows what I'm thinking and he's telling me silently it was worth it.

I squeeze back telling him risking my life for him was worth it too.

The others file out, but Salvatore keeps me back.

After everyone is gone, Pietro and Nerissa drag three men into The Box, one by one.

All three men are naked and all their genitals are black and shrunken. The telltale string dangling down one of their thighs tells me why. They have something tied around them cutting off blood flow. For them to be in this condition, it must have been there quite a while.

The pain would be ferocious.

When Salvatore notices where I am looking, he says grimly, "I wanted to castrate them and make them choke on their own cock and balls, but that's not how they need to die."

"Oh." It's all I can think to say.

Then my gaze slides to one of the men's faces. Recognition hits instantly. I look quickly at the faces of the other two men and despite the bruises on one of them, I know exactly who they are. The men who raped me when I was sixteen.

"You found all three of them."

"He helped me find the other two." Salvatore indicates the man from Lorenzo's crew with his chin. "I am going to kill them, but you do not have to watch. Or..." He looks at his sister and then back at me. "If you want to kill them, that is your prerogative."

"I don't want to kill them." I'm sure of that.

I can kill to protect someone I love, but not in retribution. That doesn't mean I want them to live though.

As if he knows exactly what I'm thinking Salvatore nods. "I will kill them, then. Do you want to stay?"

"You know me as well as my own inner voice. You tell me."

For a second, Salvatore's lips twitch. "Now that I am with you, my inner voice doesn't get nearly as loud."

"Mine either."

Because we have become that to each other.

"Alright you two love birds. Rhapsodize over how your inner voices are as perfectly matched as you are later. We have things to do here," Pietro grouses.

"I want to stay," I say, in case Salvatore has any doubts.

Nodding, Salvatore picks up a knife that looks like the one my nonna used to filet fish and I suddenly know what he is going to do.

I am not wrong. He goes behind the first man, grabs him by the hair and lifts his head. Then he slices across his throat. As blood sprays onto the metal floor, it begins to wash the pain and terror of a sixteen-year-old from my soul.

When all three men are dead, Pietro pushes a button on the wall and the floor opens again. Pietro, Nerissa and Salvatore dump the now dead men over the edge of the floor.

There are splashes for each body.

I don't know what is under the floor. Maybe an underground river. I don't care.

My tormentors are gone. They can never hurt me again.

Salvatore turns me gently and holds me tightly to him. "I was not there to protect you six years ago, but I will never leave you unprotected now. I will always stop the monsters from hurting you."

I believe him.

THE END

AFTERWORD

If you enjoyed BRUTAL CAPO, please consider leaving a review, or rating. Thank you!

Want to read bonus content for this book and the others in the Syndicate Rules series and to be kept up to date on her books? Sign up for Lucy Monroe's newsletter: https://www.lucymonroe.com/newsletter

ACKNOWLEDGEMENTS

A huge hug and heartfelt thank you to everyone who has helped me make this book what it is:

My husband, Tom, who listens to endless ideas, scene snippets and character revelations as I write and *still* reads the complete book from start to finish when it is done.

Andie, my amazing editor at Beyond the Proof who excels at catching dangling threads and inconsistencies. Her insights make my books better. Full stop.

Two very special ARC readers who take the time to proofread after the copyedits are done before writing their reviews, Dee Dee & Haley.

And with special thanks to fellow authors Josephine Caporetto for her invaluable help on Italian phrases and Monica Burns who always wanted to be a villain and leant her name to Salvatore's scheming ex.

Any remaining typos, mistakes, or translation errors are my fault and mine alone.

ITALIAN GLOSSARY

Note: certain words are not italicized in the book because of their common use in American English. Also, these translations are not literal. They are the more common vernacular. Italian as it is used in Northern or Southern Italy (and Sicily) as the case may be.

accidenti – (positive) wow, gosh, my goodness (negative) darn, drat

amore mio – my love

anima gemella – soul mate (no masculine form/same for either)

basta – stop, that's enough

bastardo – bastard

bella mia – you are my beautiful one, or listen to me i.e. in an argument to get the person's attention (alternate uses from Southern Italy)

bella ragazza – beautiful girl

bellissima - gorgeous

bisnonna – great grandmother

bisnonno – great grandfather

brava ragazza – good girl

cara/o – darling

carissimo/a – very dear

cazzate – bullshit

cazzo – dick/fuck equivalent

caspita – yikes/wow

che palle – oh balls/fuck it equivalent

Dio mio – my god

dolce ragazza – sweet girl

dolcezza – sweetheart, honey (literally sweetness)

mamma – mom or mother

fottuto stronzo – fucking asshole (see also *stronzo del cazzo*)

goomah – mistress or side piece

il mia lei – my her (possessive endearment for a woman)

il mio lui – my him (possessive endearment for a man)

managgia – damn

managgia la miseria – damn it (literally misery or poverty)

manaja – damn (variant from Southern Italy)

meno male – thank goodness

nonna – grandma/grandmother

nonno – grandpa/grandfather

oh merda – oh crap/shit

per favore – please

porca miseria – damn it (not literal)

puttana – bitch

stronzo/a – asshole (also another way to say bitch)

stronzo del cazzo – fucking asshole (see also *fottuto stronzo*)

tesoro mio – my treasure

vaffanculo - fuck

Phrases:

A accidenti. – (teasing or serious) darn him/her/you

Ho detto basta - that's enough, I said enough

Io sono tua. – I am yours.

Prometto. – I promise.

Tu sei mia! –You are mine. (jealous: another man or woman involved)

Sei la mia anima gemelli. – You are my soul mate. (no masculine form – same for either)

Sei mio. – You are mine.

Zitto. - Shut up.

ABOUT THE AUTHOR

With more than 10 million copies of her books in print worldwide, award winning and internationally bestselling author, Lucy Monroe, has published over 85 books and had her stories translated for sale all over the world. While her latest series is mafia romance, written as an indie author, all of Lucy's books are passionate, deeply emotional and adhere to the concept that love wins. Even if that victory isn't an easy one.

Want to talk about the characters, read snippets of Lucy's WIPs before anyone else, and chat with other readers who love Lucy's books? Join her FB Group Lucy's Book Nook.
https://www.facebook.com/groups/lucysbooknook

FOLLOW LUCY ON SOCIAL MEDIA
BookBub: Lucy Monroe
goodreads: Lucy Monroe
Facebook: LucyMonroe.Romance
TikTok: lucymonroeauthor
Instagram: lucymonroeromance
Pinterest: lucymonroebooks
YouTube: @LucyMonroeBooks
Threads: lucymonroeromance
Lucy's website: https://lucymonroe.com

Printed in Great Britain
by Amazon

51469623R00288